Unbeara[ble]

The body on the mattress was [...] and a pale, inhuman yellow. It lay at an awkward angle, the eyes closed and so sunken they appeared to be missing.

The smell was almost unbearable.

Madison wrinkled her nose. "Stinks like hell, doesn't it?"

"Dead people are supposed to do that, aren't they?" Aidan replied.

Parker laughed and shook his head. "I know dead people. I work with dead people. Dead people are not supposed to stink like *that*." With that, he crouched down right next to the body, as if challenging the odor to overcome him.

"Check this out," he murmured. The right shoulder had a shallow square depression. A divot of flesh was missing altogether, revealing pale pink muscle tissue. "No blood."

Madison pulled on gloves and crouched down next to him, wincing at the smell.

"The flesh is still supple," she said. "It looks all shriveled and dried, but it's still soft."

"I know. Press it a little harder," Parker told her.

As Madison pressed, the wound began to ooze a yellowish, oily liquid. The intensity of the smell in the room immediately kicked up a notch.

"Probably some kind of embalming fluid," Aidan said.

Parker started to stand, but Madison stopped him.

"Wait a second. What's that?" She indicated a thick black wire that was protruding about an inch from the base of the skull.

Parker grunted and eased the body further onto its front. An identical second wire was sticking out from the other side of the head. He snorted. "So, what've we got now? Alien fucking autopsy?"

Praise for the C.S.U. Investigation series . . .

"[A] fascinating look at how C.S.U. works . . . takes off at Mach speed and accelerates into light speed."
—*Midwest Book Review*

"[The] detailed approach and lively characters make an immersive read; anyone waiting for a *CSI: Philadelphia* spin-off should be pleased."
—*Publishers Weekly*

Freezer Burn

A C.S.U. INVESTIGATION

D. H. Dublin

BERKLEY BOOKS, NEW YORK

THE BERKLEY PUBLISHING GROUP
Published by the Penguin Group
Penguin Group (USA) Inc.
375 Hudson Street, New York, New York 10014, USA
Penguin Group (Canada), 90 Eglinton Avenue East, Suite 700, Toronto, Ontario M4P 2Y3, Canada
(a division of Pearson Penguin Canada Inc.)
Penguin Books Ltd., 80 Strand, London WC2R 0RL, England
Penguin Group Ireland, 25 St. Stephen's Green, Dublin 2, Ireland (a division of Penguin Books Ltd.)
Penguin Group (Australia), 250 Camberwell Road, Camberwell, Victoria 3124, Australia
(a division of Pearson Australia Group Pty. Ltd.)
Penguin Books India Pvt. Ltd., 11 Community Centre, Panchsheel Park, New Delhi—110 017, India
Penguin Group (NZ), 67 Apollo Drive, Rosedale, North Shore 0632, New Zealand
(a division of Pearson New Zealand Ltd.)
Penguin Books (South Africa) (Pty.) Ltd., 24 Sturdee Avenue, Rosebank, Johannesburg 2196,
South Africa

Penguin Books Ltd., Registered Offices: 80 Strand, London WC2R 0RL, England

This is a work of fiction. Names, characters, places, and incidents either are the product of the author's imagination or are used fictitiously, and any resemblance to actual persons, living or dead, business establishments, events, or locales is entirely coincidental.

FREEZER BURN

A Berkley Book / published by arrangement with the author

PRINTING HISTORY
Berkley edition / June 2008

ISBN: 978-0-425-22194-5

IT WAS supposed to be springtime.

There was supposed to be at least a day or two of fresh breezes and warm sunshine between the aching cold of winter and the reeking heat of summer. But even with the last dark, dirty nuggets of plowed snow still melting in shady corners of parking lots across the city, an early hot spell had the morning pushing eighty degrees.

Fucking April.

Riding on the back of a City of Philadelphia sanitation truck, Tillman Underwood was bundled up for the previous week's weather and he was heating up quickly.

Up in the cab, Raphael Ortega was in get-it-over-with mode, keeping the truck moving at a brisk, steady pace. They were back on schedule after Good Friday, and with Memorial Day still more than a month away, there was no reason to go slowly. Neither of them wanted the workday to last any longer than necessary, but Tillman was already working up a heavy sweat.

The truck hardly slowed as it turned the tight corner from Snyder Avenue onto Bucknell Street. It was a typical South Philly block: parking on one side, illegal parking on the other side. Uninterrupted walls of redbrick on either side of the narrow street were punctuated every few feet by alternating doors and windows. The truck barely squeezed between the cars parked on either side.

Swinging off the back of the still-moving truck, Tillman grabbed a green plastic trash can and hoisted it up into the compactor in one fluid motion. Crossing the street, he grabbed two more, one in each hand, dumping one, then the other.

He caught up with the truck twenty feet down the street and frowned at a single trash can piled high with trash bags. No lid.

An open invitation, Tillman thought, shaking his head. People put their trash out any old way, then when the dogs or squirrels or rats make a mess, everyone blames the trashman.

With a sigh, he grabbed the bag on top. It was one of those thick, heavy-duty black plastic ones, the kind contractors use. The top was tied in a loose knot.

He grunted with the effort, surprised by the weight of it, and brought his other hand around to get a better grip. He could lift some heavy shit, but this had to be close to seventy pounds.

Probably chunks of plaster or cinder block, he thought. But the way it swayed as he held it, the contents seemed to be sloshing around.

A big, dark droplet welled up at the corner of the bag. As he watched, the drop grew swollen and fell heavily onto the street. He stared at it for a moment, then looked back at the trash can. There was a second black trash bag on top, but underneath it were white kitchen bags, streaked with a vivid red that seemed to glow in the morning sunlight.

Tillman's eyes moved back to the bag swinging in his straining grip. A big part of him wanted to just chuck it into the back of the truck and be done with it. But as much as he didn't want to look inside, he knew he was going to.

The door of the truck opened and Raphael slid out, continuing a barrage of obscenity that had probably started when Tillman first paused by the can.

Tillman ignored him, tugging at the knotted plastic without taking off his gloves. When he opened the bag, he was relieved at first. He didn't know exactly what he expected to find, but inside it didn't look like much.

"Come on, goddammit," Raphael was barking at him. "Shit, we ain't getting no fucking overtime. What the fuck you doing?"

Tillman smiled with relief. "Sorry, Rafe." He laughed. "It's just . . . I just thought . . ." Tillman realized he didn't know what he thought. "Nothing, man. It's nothing."

As he said it, though, something in the bag caught his eye. He paused.

Raphael tilted his head as he watched. "What is it, man? You all right?" He walked up behind him, craning his neck to see over Tillman's shoulder.

Holding the bag open now, Tillman raised one side and lowered the other, rolling the contents of the bag until his brain pieced together what his eyes were looking at. He yelped and jumped back, dropping the bag like it had bitten him.

The bag hit the ground with a heavy splat, and as its contents sloshed out across the asphalt, the contents of Tillman Underwood's stomach splashed across Raphael Ortega's boots.

Cresting the bloody wave that slid out of the bag was the top two-thirds of a human head, sheared off at the jawline. The head tumbled, making an audible click as it paused for a moment right side up, the front teeth resting on the street as if it were taking a bite. It teetered for an instant, then fell over onto its left ear.

Under a layer of partially congealed blood, the eyes were open. The face was intact above the upper lip. Behind the exposed upper teeth and palate was a mass of spongy tissue and bone, cleanly sliced through.

Next to it was a foot.

It took Raphael a moment to look up from the mess on his feet. When he saw the cause of Tillman's reaction, he took an involuntary step backward. His feet slipped in the vomit as he turned and ran stumbling back to the truck.

CHAPTER 1

FROM A distance, the red smudges that scuffed the median divider and the inside lane formed a sixty-foot-long dotted line along the Schuylkill Expressway. The beginning of the line was just inside the border of the City of Philadelphia. Lying at the end of it, slumped against the concrete divider, was the crumpled figure of the morning's first murder victim.

"Fucking typical," muttered Tommy Parker, sipping his coffee and looking over the railing at the masses of cars inching their way on the road below him, detoured there because of the body behind them.

Madison Cross was crouching next to the body, taking pictures from every angle. She had already documented the red scuff marks, evidence of the high rate of speed at which the victim had been ejected from his car. She paused and looked up at him, distracted. "What're you saying?"

Parker drained his coffee and leaned on the railing. "Just that if this dumb shit here could have got hisself thrown out of the car a hundred yards *earlier*, it would have been Narberth's problem, not ours."

He waved at the two Narberth uniforms manning the roadblock sixty yards away. One of them waved back.

Detective Ted Johnson, chewing on a toothpick and observing them at work, laughed and shook his head. "You a trip, Parker."

Even in the unseasonable heat, Johnson looked as put together as always. His suit was flawless. His shoes were shined. His hair was cut close to his head, with a small part etched on one side. When he laughed, his teeth were white and perfectly straight.

Madison winced at Parker's callous reference to the body.

The kid was young, barely twenty, Latino. His clothes were in tatters and so was the rest of him. He was covered with trapezoidal patches of exposed flesh, bright pink separated by a lattice of skin. They combined to form a pattern that looked vaguely like a giraffe's hide. He had a shaved head, gold chains, and the skin he had left was covered with gang tattoos.

Madison knew Parker had little sympathy for gang bangers.

She stood up and walked over to him. He smelled strongly of smoke from the arson fire over on Oxford Street in North Philly. Most of the crime scene unit was still there. Their senior chemical analyst, Aidan Veste, had been there since early the previous evening and so had Melissa Rourke, one of the other crime scene investigators.

Madison had been there as well, and the whiff of smoke made her shudder at the memory of what she had witnessed. The scene was ghastly, six bodies so far, two of them children. She bristled as she thought about how she had been forced to leave the scene.

She and Rourke had been quietly working together when the news crews had shown up. Neither of them had said a word, but even in her short tenure with the C.S.U., Madison's dealings with the press had been problematic. Someone in the brass had spotted her in the background on the eleven o'clock news. By eleven thirty she was on her way back to the lab.

They told her it was because they needed the DNA analysis on the bodies ASAP, but the lieutenant confided that the real reason was that the brass was still nervous about her and the media.

The wind shifted, bringing another smoky whiff from Parker.

He looked tired. No doubt staying awake twenty-six hours wasn't helping his attitude toward the dead kid.

Up the road, the sun was still low, shining almost horizontally from the east, like it was rolling toward them down the highway.

It was the middle of the Monday morning rush hour and the Schuylkill Expressway—the main east-west artery into the city—was closed. The body had ended up on a stretch between the Roosevelt Expressway and City Avenue, a location that gave the diverted traffic a number of options. But even combined, the detours couldn't handle all those cars.

It felt strange walking across the expressway, empty except for the handful of official vehicles parked haphazardly in the fast lane. A hundred yards in one direction, the Narberth police were diverting traffic off the highway. A hundred yards in the other direction, Philly's finest were doing the same on the other side of the median. Between them, Madison felt like she was standing in the middle of the parted Red Sea, with a mass of cars in either direction wanting desperately to come roaring over the spot where she was standing.

Parker turned and looked at her, raising one eyebrow, waiting to hear what she had to say.

"I'm sure if he'd known it would have made your life that much easier, he would have jumped out earlier," she said sarcastically. "That is, if he hadn't been shot through the chest."

Johnson took the toothpick out of his mouth and straightened up. "GSW?"

Madison nodded. "Looks like he was already dead when he hit the ground."

"I was wondering about that," Johnson said. "'Cause there was so little blood."

"Blood's getting pretty dry, but not dry yet," Parker observed. "He ain't been here too long." He smiled. "I wonder how many cars passed him by before someone thought to call us."

"Anyway, Parker," Madison continued, "if it makes you feel any better, if your buddy over there got tossed out fifty yards earlier, we'd be *sharing* jurisdiction with Narberth. Wouldn't that be fun?"

She waved to the two uniforms at the roadblock just outside the city. This time they both waved back.

"Good point," he conceded. "That does make me feel better." He looked back at the body. "Gee, you think I was being too hard on the kid?"

The wagon from the ME's office came through the roadblock and started toward them diagonally across the empty highway. They watched for a second as it approached. Then Parker abruptly clapped his hands, rubbing them together.

"Right," he said. "Well, let's wrap this up so these guys can get him out of here. Let those poor bastards down there get on their way to the jobs they hate so much." He looked up, squinting in the low sunlight. "Tell you what, how 'bout I buy you guys some breakfast. Then I'm going home to get some fucking shut-eye."

Johnson shook his head. "Going to have to take a pass on breakfast. I'm on my way over to Oxford. You guys were there before this, right?"

Madison stayed quiet.

Parker nodded grimly. "Yeah, all fucking night. Rourke and Veste are still there. Place went up like kindling. Six dead, two of 'em kids. At least one gunshot wound to the head." He sighed. "Looks like someone got in the bastards' way. The rest of them, they just happened to be there when the fucking animals torched the place to hide their tracks."

Johnson shook his head. "Yeah, a lot of guys from homicide are working the scene, too. Calling in another shift. Anyway, sounds like you guys had a long night. Why don't you get on out of here. I'll wait until they load this guy up, then head over to Oxford."

PARKER DROVE, leaning on the accelerator, speeding across the empty expanse of highway until they passed the next on-ramp and were joined by a steady stream of detoured traffic making its way back onto the expressway.

"Where should we eat?" Parker asked.

Before Madison could answer, his cell phone chimed, playing a tinny version of "Sweet Home Alabama." She gave him a dubious look.

He shrugged as he pulled it out of his denim jacket. "Hey, this way I always know when it's my phone."

To her relief, he answered the phone before the singing started. He listened for a few seconds, grunting a couple of times and pressing even harder on the accelerator as he did. "Okay," he said, and he put his phone away.

"What's up?" she asked.

"Looks like I'll be buying you lunch, instead."

CHAPTER 2

PARKER PULLED the car onto the sidewalk of the two thousand block of Bucknell Street. Madison paused before she got out.

"What a fucking mess," Parker said.

She nodded but didn't reply.

Much of the blood had already drained into the gutter, trickling into the storm drain twenty feet away. Left behind, spilling out of a black trash bag and partly drying in the bright sun, was a jumbled jigsaw puzzle that had once been a human being.

A few feet away was a splattering of vomit, footprints of the stuff trailing away from it.

As they approached the pile on the street, they could see the top half of a head, a foot, and a chunk of meat that could have been part of a thigh. It was all covered with a thin coating of the same red that was puddled around it. It looked like there was a lot more still inside the black trash bag, but it was impossible to tell if all the pieces were there.

As they crouched down beside it, Parker pulled on a pair of gloves and lifted the lip of the bag. Inside it, they could make out a hand, an elbow, and some other pieces wrapped in clothing.

"So, you think he's dead?" Parker asked.

Madison shot him a wry smile and put on gloves as well.

"You been working at the C.S.U., what, almost a year?" he asked.

"Nine months," she replied, surprised to hear herself say it. When she had accepted the Crime Scene Unit job offer from her uncle—Lt. David Cross—she never expected she would stay more than a month.

"You work any psycho cases yet?"

She'd seen a lot of crazy stuff working with the C.S.U., but nothing quite like this. "No," she replied.

They both stood up.

"Well, best get used to it, Newbie," he told her. "Looks like we might have one here."

Parker's southern drawl always seemed to thicken when he was dispensing wisdom. It was an unfortunate tendency, but what he said in that accent was usually right.

"So," he said, standing up. "What do you notice about it?"

It bugged her how he constantly quizzed her, tested her. But she had learned a hell of a lot from him.

"Looks fairly fresh . . . the pieces are small, or at least smaller than you'd need to fit it into a trash bag . . . There doesn't seem to be a complete body here, not enough mass . . ." She stood up and walked over to the trash can. "This is where it was, right?"

Parker nodded. "I think so, yeah."

She gently tugged at the loose knot on the other black bag sitting on top of the can, peeking inside before quickly closing it. "I think the rest of it's in here," she said quietly.

He came over and had a look, squinting into the bag. "You think that's the same person?"

She shrugged. "Could be two people . . . Hell, could be parts of fifteen people, right?"

Parker shrugged and closed the bag. "Anything else?"

"I'm sure there's plenty," she said, turning back to the body parts lying on the asphalt. "But one thing stands out. The cuts are incredibly clean." She held a finger over the edge where the skull had been sheared off. "What do you think could have done that?"

Parker crouched down next to her again and grunted. "Yeah, look at that. Had to be sharp as shit. I don't know, maybe . . ." He stopped in midsentence and lowered his voice. "Aw, shit, here comes another fucking mess."

"What's that?" Madison asked, but she had already followed his gaze to see a pale, gangly figure approaching them in a failed imitation of a purposeful stride. "Is that Vince Fenton?" she asked out of the side of her mouth.

"Might as well call this a cold case right now," he muttered, looking down again, pretending he hadn't seen the guy. ". . . 'Cause if that asshole's involved, this case is going nowhere."

Detective Vince Fenton was the cousin of Deputy Commissioner Harold Fenton, a familial relationship that seemed to be Vince's only qualification for the job. He was universally despised and disparaged, but nevertheless seemed to be on the department's fast track.

As the sound of footsteps came closer and then stopped, they both looked up again.

"So, what do we have here?" Fenton asked in a voice that was trying to sound casually chummy, but came out nervous and whiny. His face looked shaken and pale, his eyes avoiding the mess on the street.

"Fucking mess." Parker laughed. "That's what you got."

"Well, no shit, I already know that," Fenton snapped, failing to see the humor. "You're supposed to be the crime scene investigator; so tell me, what else do we have?"

Parker turned to Madison. "What do you think he's got here, Cross?"

Madison opened her mouth to answer, but Fenton cut her off. "Sorry," he said, holding up a hand. "I asked *you*, Parker, not your little helper. I want to know what the investigator thinks, not a technician."

Madison's mouth stayed open for a second. Even as she saw the muscles in Parker's jaw clench, she could feel her cheeks grow warm.

Parker shook his head. "You don't want to know what I think, Fenton, 'cause I think you're a dick with ears—big, flappy fucking ears—and it's a good thing you got 'em, too, 'cause otherwise you'd just be a dick."

He smiled as Fenton's face turned red. Madison was still in shock, wondering whose face was redder, hers or Fenton's.

"Cross probably would have said something nicer," Parker continued. "She probably would have said something about how it looks like a psycho went a little crazy, using a very sharp instrument. How the other half of the body is probably in that other bag right over there and how it appeared to have been dead less than three or four hours, most likely dumped here, so there wouldn't be much in the way of physical evidence in the area. Hell, she probably wouldn't even have mentioned how much of a dick you are, or how big those fucking ears are." He shrugged. "But there you go; you asked me instead, right?"

"Fuck you, Parker," Fenton hissed. "Now, knock off the—"

"Oops," Parker interrupted him. "You know what, I'm sorry, I got to go take care of something right now. But my assistant here will be happy to help you."

Then he was gone, disappearing down the street, pretending to look at the trash truck.

As was often the case when Parker made an exit, he left an uncomfortable silence in his wake. Fenton was fuming.

"Okay, Miss Cross." He sighed, not looking at her. "Tell me what you've found."

Madison scratched the back of her neck under her long, black hair. Keeping her eyes straight ahead, she exhaled loudly and plunged ahead. "Well . . . like Parker said, the bags were probably just dumped here. I doubt we'll find any clues in the surrounding area. I'm looking at the way that head is sheared through . . . I don't think that would be easy to do. It's not at the neck, it's through the base of the skull. It doesn't look like someone just trying to dispose of a body, you know?" She shrugged. "Seems like a lot of trouble when you could just lop off the head."

"Hmm," he grunted when she was done, judging her words rather than considering them. "Well, tell your friend Parker that I'll expect his report ASAP."

As Madison watched him walk away, a voice behind her laughed. "A dick with ears? Is that what Parker called him?"

Eddie Amato was watching Fenton walk away. Madison hoped she was doing a better job of concealing her contempt than Amato was.

Eddie had been one of the uniforms on the scene of Madison's first case, her first day on the job. Since that time she had worked with him a number of times. He could be a pain in the ass, but he did his job well and for the most part they got along.

"What are you thinking there, Cross?" Eddie asked.

Madison shrugged. "I don't know, Eddie. I'd like to see what else is in those bags. What about you guys, you found out anything?"

Eddie flipped open his notebook. "Homeowner's name is Ida Parella, or the trash can–owner's name, I should say . . . Old lady. Widow. Lives alone." He gestured with his head toward the row house behind them.

In the darkened front window, Madison could see the outline of an old lady in a housecoat, watching the scene taking place in front of her house.

"She said the bag wasn't there when she put the trash out the night before. She didn't notice one way or the other in the morning. Says she knows nothing about it, and I believe her. Doubt she could lift one of those pieces, much less a whole fucking bag." He laughed. "Of course, Fenton'll probably have her in lockup by morning."

Parker walked up behind them, looking over Madison's shoulder as he approached. "Is that asshole gone yet?"

Eddie laughed again, a little too much. One of Eddie's least endearing qualities was the way he seemed to idolize Tommy Parker.

"I was just filling Cross in on what we know so far," Eddie reported, looking back at his notes. "Anyway, we got guys canvassing the block, but so far no one has seen anything."

He turned and motioned for them to follow. "The trash collector was the one who found it," he said, leading them across the street. "That's who lost his lunch there, all over his partner's boots." He lowered his voice as they approached a big guy in coveralls sitting on a neighbor's steps. "His name's Tillman Underwood."

Underwood was maybe six-four, but sitting on the steps, he looked small and scared. He seemed pale, too, even under his dark skin, a pallor that seemed to spread out from behind his haunted eyes.

He started to cringe when he saw them walking up to him, but when he saw Madison, he flashed her a smile.

She gave him a nice smile in response. The poor guy had been through a lot.

"How you doing, Tillman?" she asked softly. "You okay?"

He nodded but looked away.

"I know you already told me, Mr. Underwood," Eddie said, "but can you tell it again, what happened?"

Underwood sighed and shivered slightly despite the heat. "We came around the corner, I grabbed the bag and it was heavy as shit. It kind of wrenched my wrist, 'cause I wasn't expecting it, you know? I saw something dripping, but I couldn't see what it was, then I looked back, saw the other bags was all red . . . I knew it was blood, soon as I seen it," he said, adding, "I was in Desert Storm . . ." His voice trailed off to a whisper. ". . . Then I looked inside."

His face tightened, clenching down on itself as he snuck a glance in the direction of the black bag on the street. "I dropped it and ran."

"Did you take off your gloves at any time?" Madison asked.

Underwood thought for a moment, then shook his head.

They thanked him for his help and returned to the body.

Parker handed Madison the camera and while she circled the carnage with rapid-fire flashes, he circled wider, canvassing the area, looking for anything that could be evidence.

When she was finished with the camera, she got out the fingerprint kit. She dipped the small brush into the flat container of powder and gently but briskly dusted a thin layer of powder onto the outside of the trash can and inside the rim.

Close to a dozen clusters of prints revealed themselves. She dutifully lifted each print with a piece of tape, but she was pretty sure they would all turn out to be unrelated to the crime. They might have more luck with the bag itself, but that would have to wait until they got back to the lab.

The guys from the ME's office, Freddy Velasquez and Alvin Tate, were standing behind her, trying to look respectful as they quietly muttered back and forth, occasionally trying to suppress a snicker.

Parker walked up to her, stifling a yawn. "There's nothing around here."

She nodded. "Yeah, I figured."

"You get any prints?"

"There's plenty on the can, but I doubt any of them matter.

Probably all from the old lady. I figure we'll wait on the bag until after we get the remains to the ME."

He nodded and turned to look at Velasquez and Tate, who were shifting their weight from one foot to the other as they waited to take the body away. "All right, boys. You can go ahead and take this away now. Try to be discreet, okay?"

He turned back to Madison. "I'm gonna stop back at the C.S.U., start writing up that knucklehead from the expressway. Then I'm going home to get some sleep. You coming back, or you want to ride with those guys, see if Spoons has any first impressions?"

"I could do that."

He turned to go, then turned back. "Tell you what, though, before you go, make sure you get some prints from the old lady over there so we can rule them out. Matter of fact, if you're going to the ME, get this guy's prints and get some off that knucklehead from the Expressway while you're at it."

"What about lunch?" she called after him as he walked away.

"Rain check," he replied without turning around.

Madison got the ink pad and fingerprint cards out of the forensics kit. "Hey, Tate," she called out.

He looked up. "Can I get a ride with you guys, back to the ME?"

"Fine with me," he called back. "But we ain't waiting around for you. Busy fucking day already."

As Madison turned toward Ida Parella's front stoop, the figure in the window backed away, dissolving into the darkness.

Madison gave the door a knock that was firm but not too hard, then stepped back.

After a few minutes she tried again, harder. Tate and Velasquez had already removed the trash bags and were gingerly picking up the remaining pieces.

Madison was starting to wonder if the old lady was going to ignore her completely when the door opened the two or three inches allowed by the chain.

"Who the fuck are you?" Ida Parella demanded, her sunken eyes narrowed in suspicion.

She was barely five feet tall, a bony gray wisp in a house-coat and slippers, but her lips quivered with rage.

"Hi, Mrs. Parella." Madison reassured her with her "nice young woman" smile. "I'm with the police Crime Scene Unit."

"I don't know nothing," Parella rasped defensively. "I told them everything already, so what the hell do you want?"

Madison smiled again. "I actually just need to take your fingerprints, just so we know which ones we don't have to look at."

"Fingerprints!" she exclaimed. "Jesus, you think I did that? You people are crazy. I couldn't do nothing like that!"

Madison glanced over and saw that Velasquez was already inside the van. Tate was leaning against it, making a show of looking at his watch.

"Mrs. Parella, I—"

"You people need to be out locking up criminals, not going around scaring old ladies."

They went back and forth a few times, Madison politely and patiently trying to explain why they needed Mrs. Parella's fingerprints, but when Tate started tapping his horn, Madison blurted out that if they didn't get her fingerprints, they couldn't finish cleaning up the mess outside her house.

The old lady looked over Madison's shoulder one last time before she finally relented.

CHAPTER 3

"PIZZA'S HERE!" Velasquez announced as he and Tate wheeled the gurney through the swinging doors and into the autopsy room. Madison came in behind them.

Frank Sponholz turned around in his bloodstained apron, motioning with his hands where they should position the gurney. A ring of unruly hair circled the bald head that topped the medical examiner's oddly pyramid-shaped body. He was wide around the middle and sharply tapered toward the top. The apron tied around his belly somehow accentuated the effect, causing his head to look even smaller than it was. He breathed noisily.

"Pizza, huh?" he said, stripping off his gloves. "What I hear, it's more like marinara."

He looked at Madison. "How ya doin', kid?"

"Hey, Spoons." He looked tired. She knew he'd probably been working most of the night on all those bodies from the Oxford fire. "How you holding up?"

"Hell of a way to start the week."

She could tell at a glance that the body he had been working on when they arrived was not from the fire. He was young and skinny, with a childlike face and a dark bullet hole in the ribs. A sheet partially covered him and it took her a moment to recognize the tattoos and abrasions—it was the dead gangbanger they had found on the highway that morning.

Spoons followed her gaze. "Someone you know?"

She shook her head. "That's the kid from the expressway this morning, right? I worked the crime scene with Parker."

Spoons nodded.

"So I guess that's probably gang related, huh?" she asked. "With all the tattoos?"

"Him?" Spoons said disdainfully. "Those tats are bullshit. Kid was a wannabe. Probably what got him killed. The real gangsters don't take kindly to tattoos that aren't earned the old-fashioned way."

"So he wasn't a gangbanger?"

Spoons shrugged as he slid the kid's body back into the cooler. "He wasn't a Crip or a Blood or anything like that. Maybe some bullshit street-corner gang."

Tate and Velasquez opened the body bag and hefted the two trash bags of remains off the gurney and onto the stainless-steel autopsy table. The four of them paused for a moment, watching the bags slowly spread out as the contents settled.

Tate took a step back. "Alrighty then," he said with a grin. "You guys have fun." He and Velasquez chuckled as they turned and pushed their way out the door.

Sponholz pulled on a fresh pair of gloves and looked up at Madison as he tugged open one of the bags. "So, what do you think?"

"Only first impressions so far, Spoons. I think it's probably one body in two bags. Pieces are smaller than they need to be for disposal's sake, you know?"

He pursed his lips and nodded, then opened the bag and looked inside. "Yikes."

She smiled grimly. "Tell me about it."

"All right," he wheezed, tugging one corner of the bag. "Let's see what we got here."

He sloshed the contents out onto the autopsy table. The body parts formed a pile in the middle of the table. Some were meaty chunks of flesh with bones sticking out here and there. Other parts were organs, some whole, some sliced into pieces. The segments of the trunk may have started out larger than the limb pieces, but the organs had slid out, and in some places detached entirely.

A mixture of blood and other fluids immediately started seeping out, meandering toward the drains at the end of the table.

With a loud sigh, he emptied the second bag onto a separate table.

For a moment, they surveyed the scene.

"Same shoes," Madison observed, wagging her finger between the two identically clad feet lying on separate tables.

Spoons scratched under his chin. "You're gonna do DNA on 'em, right?"

She nodded.

"All right, well, why don't you get a few samples from pieces on each side, make sure they all match up. We'll get some film on the pieces and then lay 'em out, see what it looks like."

Spoons leaned over and grabbed the piece of the head that had been lying on the street and placed it at one end of one table. He sorted through the other pile with his gloved hands, producing a sound that made Madison think of stirring potato salad. When he found a foot, he placed it at the opposite end of the other table.

"You any good at puzzles?" he asked, looking up at her.

She grimaced, but she pulled on a gown and a pair of exam gloves and started separating the pieces, examining each one and carefully putting it in place.

The hands and feet were the easiest parts, followed by the lower part of the head. After that it got tricky.

It reminded her of an anatomy midterm she once took: all the body parts out of order, and she had to reassemble them. She had aced that exam, and once she started thinking on those terms, she picked up her pace. A sucker for any challenge, she was soon drawn into the process, reassembling the body, piece by piece.

As she finished one table and turned to the other, pulling on a fresh pair of gloves, she looked up to see Spoons standing and watching her, absentmindedly holding a section of pelvis.

"Ooh, I need that," she exclaimed, plucking it out of his hands and laying it at the top of the reassembled left leg.

Spoons looked at her with a disturbed expression on his face.

"What?" she asked defensively, her hands selecting pieces off the pile and laying them in place on the table.

"You seem to have this under control," he said slowly. "Why don't I leave you to it, and you can give me a yell when you're done."

She nodded without slowing down. "Sure. I'll be done in a minute."

The truth was, she loved puzzles.

Ten minutes later, standing back and admiring her work, she called him back in.

One table held primarily pieces from the top half and the left side of the body; the other table mostly held the lower half and the right side. Each table was an approximate inverse of the other. It was obvious that the two bags together contained a single person. The effect of the reassembled bodies was unsettling, like some sort of macabre collage. But Spoons seemed almost more affected by the sight of Madison, grinning proudly at the job she had done putting it all together.

Spoons grunted. "Great."

"What?"

"Nothing." He shook his head. "Good work."

The two tables seemed to hold a slightly built, young male, maybe a couple of years younger than the dead gangbanger from the expressway. He had dark hair and, where the blood had been wiped off his face, pale skin, although it was hard to tell how much of the pallor was due to death and dismemberment.

Madison's smile soon faded into a queasy feeling in the pit of her stomach. Without the distraction of the intellectual challenge, she now confronted a gruesome scene of unimaginable violence.

Watching her face, Spoons seemed to sense the change. "Tell you what," he said, confused but concerned. "Why don't you get some prints off your buddy from the expressway there."

"Sure thing," she replied quickly, retrieving her fingerprint kit from her bag and pulling the other body from the cooler. Lifting one skinny, tattooed arm, she rolled each finger with the ink roller and pressed it gently but firmly onto the fingerprint card.

As she moved to the other arm, Spoons took out his camera and set a tiny digital recorder on the counter between the other tables. He recited the basics as he began taking pictures of the tableau of body parts: time, date, where the body was found, etc. His narrative slowed as he exhausted his meager supply of facts.

". . . It's going to be tricky determining the time of death . . . It's already quite cold to the touch, but pieces like this wouldn't hold much heat . . . no way really to check for rigor mortis . . . no signs of putrefaction . . . hmph . . ."

Madison finished with the fingerprints and came back over. "What about the edges, here . . ." she said, holding her finger over the gap between the upper and lower portions of the head. "Look how clean the cut is. What kind of instrument could have done that?"

Spoons leaned in close, then turned away and came back a moment later with a large magnifying glass. Studying the edges closely, he grunted again. "Hmph. You're right. It must have been sharp as shit . . . There's no trauma on the adjoining tissue . . . Weird."

He took a close-up shot of the area Madison had pointed out.

"Another thing I noticed," she said, gently poking the exposed skin on one of the chunks of thigh. "The flesh seems spongy. I know it's been through tremendous trauma, but it seems almost . . . mushy."

Spoons pinched the skin around the place Madison had been poking.

"Yeah, maybe." He shrugged, squeezing it between his fingers. "We'll send some samples to the lab, see if there's any chemical residue there. Meanwhile, how 'bout you print him for me, run a DNA profile, see if we can at least find out who the fuck he is."

While Spoons took blood and tissue samples for toxicology and chemical analysis, Madison picked up one of the disembodied hands and rolled the fingers with the ink roller. She pressed each finger onto a print card like she had with the other body moments before.

By this point, the fact that the body was dismembered was no shock. But being able to manipulate the hands independently in any direction, without any resistance, without even the scant weight of the other kid's bony arm, it bothered her. It made the task of washing the hands and taking the finger-prints much easier, but it was also extremely unsettling.

She tried to keep the severed ends out of her field of vision. Knowing what she was doing was bad enough; she didn't need any visual reminders.

When she was finished with the fingerprints and had put each hand back in place on the table, she took the two trash bags to another table and dusted them for prints. One was clean, but the other gave up what looked like a single, complete set, five fingers splayed out, eighteen inches from the edge of the bag. As she lifted the prints with tape, she noticed that the trash bag showed no signs of stress around the prints; the plastic was not stretched, as you would expect if someone had grabbed it there to pick it up. She did find stretching else-where on the bag, but no prints there. Presumably that was from Underwood's gloved hand. She made a mental note to include that in her report.

Once she had lifted the prints and packed them away, she returned to the dismembered body and set about taking samples for DNA. She took samples from each table—two blood, two hair, two bone—just in case there was more than one body.

The longer she stayed there between the tables, surrounded by pieces of what she was increasingly sure was a single person, the more her vague desire to leave coalesced into an urgent need. She slid the fingerprint cards into a small envelope and packed away the samples and fingerprinting equipment.

"Okay, Spoons," she said. "I gotta get going."

"Whoa, whoa, whoa," he said, looking up. "Where you going in such a hurry?"

"I just . . . I just got to go, okay?"

His laugh didn't quite disguise his annoyance. "Well, can you at least wait a minute, so I can give you these samples for chem analysis?"

"You know what, Frank? I don't know." She could hear her voice getting sharp despite her efforts to keep it under control. "I got to get going, okay?"

He looked in her eyes and smiled slightly, his face showing

sympathy and a little relief. "Yeah, I get it," he said gently. "Hey, I'll have these done in a second. Why don't you go wash up and I'll bring 'em out to you, okay?"

Out in the scrub room, Madison washed her hands and splashed water on her face. She dried off with a paper towel, and as she threw it in the wastebasket, Spoons came out holding a plastic bag containing a handful of little vials and stoppered tubes.

"You okay?" he said, trying to read her face.

"Yeah, yeah. I'm fine." She smiled to prove it.

"Some fucked-up shit in there. It can get to you. Gets to me sometimes and I see it every day."

"It was weird . . . It didn't bother me so much at first. But for some reason, taking the prints . . . holding those hands."

"Goddamn right it's weird." He smiled. "That shit stops seeming weird, *that's* when you got a problem. Now, you sure you're okay?"

"Fine. I swear it."

"Good. Give me a yell when you find out anything. I'll do the same from over here."

CHAPTER 4

MADISON GOT a ride back to headquarters with Tate. He must have sensed something was bothering her; he nattered away the entire two miles back.

She let him.

By the time they pulled up in front of the Roundhouse, the police department's sinuous concrete headquarters, the distress she had felt at fingerprinting the disembodied hands had been replaced by embarrassment and annoyance at herself for having lost her cool. The lab was pretty quiet when she walked in, but she was still relieved to be headed to the DNA lab, where she could get back to work—alone—for a while.

She unpacked the samples she had taken at the ME and began preparing them for analysis, calmly losing herself in the task.

Using a pipette, she covered each sample with an enzyme solution that would extract the DNA. Afterward, she applied different enzymes to digest the DNA and separate it into smaller segments. A little while later, she put the tubes into the thermocycler and turned it on, beginning the cycles of heat and cold that would split each double helix into separate strands before reassembling them into two new twisted pairs, doubling the number of DNA molecules over and over again until a few hours later the tiny tubes were packed with hundreds of thousands of exact copies of the original DNA, easily enough to create a profile that could be checked for a match against the FBI's Combined DNA Index System, or CODIS, the national DNA database.

With the thermocycler humming away, Madison took out

the envelope with the fingerprint cards. She opened the door to leave, but jumped back with a startled squeal.

"Jesus! Uncle Dave, don't sneak up on me like that!"

She usually called him Lieutenant Cross at work, but he had startled her out of her decorum.

At six foot four, his frame filled the doorway. He looked down at her, shaking his head and trying to suppress a grin.

"I'm sorry, Maddy girl," he said. He had always gotten a kick out of her exaggerated startle reflex. "I didn't mean to sneak up on you . . . I hear you got yourself a good one."

"You mean the Bucknell Street guy?"

"The one in the trash, yeah."

She smiled flatly. "Yeah, it was a good one, all right."

"I called Frank Sponholz to see what it looked like from his end." He lowered his voice, tilting his head in a familiar way and looking her right in the eye. "He said you were a little shook up. You okay, Maddy?"

She couldn't help but smile.

There were times when it was great having her uncle as a boss and times when it was awkward, but most days, working with him was just part of working. Other times, just a word or a glance or a mannerism immediately evoked a feeling from her childhood.

Even when she was little, Uncle Dave had always been straight with her, and he always expected the same.

He never spoke to her like she was a little girl who didn't understand what was going on. He spoke to her like he knew what she had been going through, and he knew that she understood more about it than anyone else. When he would give her that look, tilting his head, focusing on her eyes and quietly asking if she was okay, it wasn't with the patronizing sympathy of the school counselors or the social workers. He said it like he knew the answer wasn't always going to be yes.

That's how he was looking at her now, leaning in through the door to the DNA lab. All those feelings came back to her.

"I'm fine, Uncle Dave," she said quietly.

"Alright," he murmured, like he didn't believe her. "What are you up to now?"

"I just put the samples from Bucknell Street into the thermocycler." She held up the envelope with the fingerprint card. "While they're running, I'll be scanning these fingerprints, see if we get a hit on AFIS."

He nodded slowly, staring at her. Thinking. Still giving her that look. She knew he was assessing the situation, deciding for himself if she was fine or not. "Right then, I'll let you get on with it."

He gave the doorjamb a couple of brisk pats and then he was gone. But as she went about her work, in the back of her mind, she continued to think about her childhood.

She couldn't remember exactly when she had officially started living with Uncle Dave and Aunt Ellie. She had stayed with them a few times when she was six years old, just after she lost her mom. There were a few stretches of what seemed like weeks at a time.

A couple of years later, when her dad's drinking started getting bad, she began to stay with them again.

Some days her dad would drop her off, maybe because he was working undercover or on a stakeout or something. More often it was with no explanation other than a wordless, guilt-ridden acknowledgment that he just wasn't up to the task.

Some days Uncle Dave showed up at school to get her. She later learned there were calls from her school, calls about hygiene or lateness or attendance. The feeling of security with Uncle Dave and Aunt Ellie was palpable, a sense of stability that she almost didn't recognize after years of constant upheaval.

As time went on, she stayed with them more and more. One day, when she was about ten years old, it occurred to her that she had been living with them a long time.

Her dad was in rough shape by then. He was off the force, barely able to take care of himself. Drinking constantly. It was out of the question that he could take care of her at that point. Or as it turned out, ever again.

Madison sighed and turned back to the fingerprint workstation. She laid out her stack of fingerprint cards and scanned in the first one—the prints from the dismembered body. The image of the card appeared on the screen and she tapped a few keys and moved the mouse, isolating each print.

One by one, she clicked on each print, waiting a couple of seconds as the computer plotted a series of points on each image, translating each picture into a quantifiable digital map, numerically describing the landmarks of each fingerprint.

When she had completed the first card, she opened a window in the Automated Fingerprint Identification System. She tapped a few more keys to start the search through the massive AFIS database of fingerprint records. While waiting for the search results, she scanned in the card from the kid they'd found on the expressway, then she started on the others.

As she was just finishing up with the prints from Ida Parella's trash can, she got a match on the prints from the dismembered body. All ten prints. She called up the images and visually confirmed the match, then saved the comparison so that Parker or Rourke could double-check it later.

She was relieved to see that both hands were from the same person. James "Jimmy" Dawber. Twenty-three years old. Arrested on a DUI two years ago. Last known address: 237 Forest Road, Bartlett, Pennsylvania.

As the report was printing, she set the computer searching for matches to the prints from the other body, the dead gangbanger from the expressway. Then she Googled Jimmy Dawber's address and found it in rural Bucks County, seventy miles away, halfway to New York state.

"Welcome to the big city, Jimmy Dawber," she whispered to herself. "What the hell did you get yourself into?"

When the printer finished, she took the report into the lieutenant's office. He was sitting behind his desk concentrating on some paperwork. His reading glasses were sliding down his nose, the arms nestled in his closely cropped, salt-and-pepper hair.

"Got an ID on the dismemberment case." She handed him the printed report. "Jimmy Dawber, Bartlett, Pennsylvania. Had a DUI a couple years back."

Cross took the report and held it with his arms almost straight, far enough so he could read it. "Bartlett? Jesus, that's out the other side of Bucks County, isn't it? Wonder what he was doing down here?"

He stared at it for a second, then shrugged and handed the

paper back to her. "Okay. Why don't you take this downstairs, give it to Fenton. Let him know his vic's got a name."

"BARTLETT, PENNSYLVANIA?" Fenton said, his intonation identical to the lieutenant's, but his voice an octave higher. "That's got to be fifty miles from here."

Madison read him the rest of the report.

"All right." He sighed, as if it still didn't make sense. "Thank you, Madison," he said insincerely. "I'll give a call out there, see if they can tell us anything more about Mr. Dawber."

"You're not going up there?"

He laughed, shaking his head and leaning back so he could look down his nose at her. "How about I let you know if I need any advice, okay?"

Several cutting replies crossed her mind, but she didn't want to spend any more time than necessary in Fenton's presence. She let the paper drop onto his desk and walked away, shaking her head.

Back at the fingerprint station, she saw that the computer had found a match on the prints from the expressway body.

Luis Castillo. Twenty-two years old. His rap sheet included robbery, assault, possession with intent to deliver, and resisting arrest.

Last known address was on Third Street, just off Girard. Castillo was local. His list of known associates was mostly from the same block of Third Street, all with roughly the same kind of rap sheets.

While the report on Castillo was printing, she started processing the prints from the trash can. There were a bunch of them, but she put them through the database together, figuring they could run while she printed out the report and brought it back to the lieutenant's office.

This time, Ted Johnson was in there, too. He looked up and nodded as Madison walked in.

The lieutenant was hunched over, awkwardly motionless behind his desk. Madison wondered what had preceded the uncomfortable silence in the room, but as she opened her mouth to break it, a disembodied voice spoke up and the lieutenant quieted her with an upraised finger.

"Sorry about that, Lieutenant," the voice said with a laugh. "That was one of our older residents, down the road. Honest to God, calling about her cat, stuck in the attic."

Johnson smiled and his shoulders shook, but he remained silent.

"No problem, Chief," Lieutenant Cross replied. "Frankly, I wouldn't mind a few more cases like that around here."

"Anyway," the voice continued. "It's a bit of a mess out here. I figured since it was one of your citizens, and such an illustrious one at that, and since the car was reported stolen in your fine city, I should probably give you a call, give you a heads up about it."

"Well, I appreciate the courtesy, Chief Boone," he replied to the speakerphone. "You let us know if there's anything we can do to help you."

"Well, that's mighty kind of you, Lieutenant Cross." The voice laughed awkwardly. "Actually, um, I could use a little help processing the crime scene."

The lieutenant frowned. "I'm afraid you caught us at a bad time here, Chief. We have a bit of a situation here, too. Shooting and an arson fire at a drug house in North Philly. Six bodies so far. Got pretty much all of my investigators working it."

"Yeah, I understand. I saw that on TV. Looks like a lot of work."

"I'll see what I can do for you, okay? Maybe you could try the state police."

The voice laughed again. "Yeah, I probably will. They're usually pretty good about sending in help. It's getting them to leave that's the problem."

"I hear you, buddy." The lieutenant laughed again.

"Anyway, I'll fax over the ID on the vic and the info on the car."

"Thanks, Chief. Sorry I couldn't help you out more."

"No problem, Lieutenant. Thanks. See you around, Detective."

"Yeah, you take care of yourself," Johnson replied. "Watch out for them cats."

The fax machine whirred and started printing just as the phone line clicked dead, cutting off the chuckling from the other end.

The lieutenant sighed.

"What's the matter?" Madison asked.

"Ah, nothing. I just feel bad. Boone's one of the good ones. I feel bad turning him down when he's asking for help, especially when it involves a miscreant we exported. But I just can't, not right now."

"He'll figure it out," Johnson said, dismissively, pulling the pages out of the fax machine and looking them over one by one.

"Anyway," the lieutenant said, his tone changing with the subject. He turned to Madison. "Did you need something?"

"Wanted to show you this." She held out the report on Luis Castillo. "This is the guy from the expressway," she elaborated, turning her head to include Johnson.

"Thanks," Cross said, scanning the file on Luis Castillo as Johnson scanned the fax.

They finished at the same time.

"Hernan Alvarez," Johnson murmured as they exchanged reports.

Madison turned to leave, but as she did, they both reached out and snatched back the pages they had just exchanged.

She stopped and turned back. "What?"

Johnson and the lieutenant looked at each other for a moment before looking back at her.

"What?" Madison asked again.

"Probably nothing," Cross said with a shrug.

"Known associates," Johnson muttered.

"What about them?"

Johnson gently pulled the Castillo report out of the lieutenant's fingers and held them both out for Madison to see.

"Hernan Alvarez and Luis Castillo. Apparently, these guys are buddies," he told her. "A lot of friends in common. Most living on Third Street. Cases could be related."

Each list had about eight names; half of them were on both lists.

"You going to head on out there?" the lieutenant asked.

Johnson shrugged. "I don't know. Hell of a coincidence."

The lieutenant nodded. "I see at least one other name on each of those lists that got referred to Spoons in the last three months. Wouldn't be that much of a coincidence."

Johnson shrugged. "Still."

"So, you are going out there?"

"Probably. Why?"

"I don't know. I feel bad. Guy's asking for crime scene help. But I can't spare an investigator. Not with this mess on Oxford Street." He rubbed his cheek, thinking for a moment. "Maybe you could take Ms. Cross with you, see if she can't help out with the crime scene investigation?"

It bugged Madison when they talked about her as if she wasn't there. She had a pretty firm suspicion that was why they did it.

The lieutenant paused before turning to her. He seemed to be suppressing a grin.

"Okay, Ms. Cross. You've been on the job for a while now. One of our colleagues out in the hinterlands needs some help with a crime scene. What say you go lend him some of that expertise you've been gaining?"

"What, you want me to do the crime scene investigation?"

He shrugged noncommittally. "Let's just say, you'd go out there and walk him through it. Take some pictures, see if there's any physical evidence. Basically, see what you can see."

"Whatever you'd like me to do, sir."

He turned to Johnson. "Hell, Ted, you leave now, you could be back by six."

CHAPTER 5

LIEUTENANT CROSS had called ahead to let Chief Boone know who was coming. He told Boone about the overlapping lists of known associates, and the names that appeared on both lists.

Before they left, Madison checked the prints from the trash can against the prints she had taken from Ida Parella. She could tell from looking at them that they all matched, and when she digitized them, the computer agreed. She had also started the database search on the prints from the trash bag. The results should be waiting when they got back.

Johnson drove, maintaining a rock-steady seventy-five miles an hour, out the Pennsylvania Turnpike and up the Northeast Extension.

Madison was apprehensive. This would be her first time working a crime scene on her own, although for the past several months, she'd been unofficially doing pretty much that. Occasionally she worked with Melissa Rourke, and Rourke was the kind of CSI who liked to do things herself. But most times, she worked with Parker, and after the first couple of months, he pretty much let her take the lead.

She had a tricky relationship with Parker. He was an inveterate womanizer, a fact she discovered her first day on the job; he started hitting on her in the lobby before she had even signed in. He was pretty persistent and not without his strange version of charm, but eventually he got the hint and backed off.

Since then, he had become sort of a mentor.

At crime scenes, he usually stood off to the side, cracking wise and imparting the occasional morsel of advice.

But although he might look like he was drinking coffee and letting her do all the work, and she razzed him for it, she knew he was watching her intently. Often, he would say something hours later, a suggestion or an observation, just to let her know how closely he'd been paying attention. And at the crime scene, if she came remotely close to missing something or screwing something up, he would be right there, immediately. That happened less and less frequently, but still, at the thought of doing it all on her own, she could feel her stomach tighten.

She had learned a lot from him in the nine months she'd been on the job, and they'd become friends.

Of course, she had no delusions that he wouldn't try to get into her pants at the slightest sign of weakness.

She smiled, looking out the window and thinking again about Parker's strange appeal. But her smile faded as another wave of anxiety swept over her.

The fact that it was another jurisdiction didn't help with the anxiety, although in a way, it could make things easier; since she was just there to help out and not in any official capacity, if she botched things up really bad, she could just head back to Philly.

She smiled mischievously as she thought about the other reason for her apprehension.

Bartlett was in Bucks County and Lawson was in Northampton, both big counties. But as it turned out, the towns themselves were less than five miles away from each other.

Madison had looked it up and grabbed a copy of the printout on Jimmy Dawber before they had left. Maybe it was too much trouble for Fenton to drive all the way there, but Madison figured if she was going to be that close, she owed it to Jimmy Dawber to find out what she could. It wasn't his fault he got cut up in a hundred pieces.

The way she figured it, the worst that would happen was that Fenton would act like even more of a prick next time he saw her. That was a price she was willing to pay, she thought with a smirk.

"What are you looking all sly about?" Johnson asked, looking over at her from behind the wheel.

"What's that?" Madison asked, her face warming at having

been caught. "It's nothing. How much farther do you think?" she asked hurriedly, realizing she didn't actually want him to repeat himself.

He laughed, aware that his question was being dodged. "We'll be there in about twenty minutes, I guess."

They had picked up a couple of turkey wraps before they left, and the beginning of the trip was occupied by small talk and eating. The quiet that set in after that had been relaxed and casual until that moment, when Johnson called her out. Now, each moment of silence hung in the car, repeating his unanswered question.

"So how's it been, working for you uncle?" Johnson finally asked.

Madison shrugged. She knew Johnson was pretty tight with her uncle. "It's been fine. I mean, it's strange sometimes, wondering what other people think, if they think you're getting special treatment or something."

She gave him a sidelong glance to see how her answer went over. She had worked with Johnson a bunch of times, and they got along pretty well. She had a lot of respect for him, but she wasn't about to open up to him.

Johnson was smiling to himself. "You mean like Fenton? Don't worry, Cross, I know you ain't getting any special treatment. At least not in any good way." He laughed. "I seen enough fucked-up shit flowing your way."

She laughed. "Yeah, there's been no shortage in that department."

"Besides, I've known the lieutenant for a long time." He laughed. "I don't think he'd cut his own mother any slack."

THE POLICE station in Lawson was a squat building with storefront windows and pale blue siding. There were three parking spots out front with the word "visitor" stenciled across them and a Lawson Police Department SUV parked in the fourth.

When they got out of the car, the air was noticeably colder than it had been in the city; spring was a few weeks later up here.

At the front of the office, behind a low partition, a woman in her early sixties sat at a desk. She was wearing a headset and typing effortlessly on a computer keyboard. The nameplate on her desk said Gloria Hunt.

"Hello. Can I help you?" she said, looking up with a smile. Her fingers didn't slow down.

Johnson held up his ID. "Detective Johnson, Philly PD. Chief Boone's expecting us."

Before she could reply, a door opened in the back and Chief Boone stepped out.

"Philly PD, huh?" He made a show of how unimpressed he was. "Nice of you to come all the way out here to our quaint little town."

The voice was the same as the guy on the lieutenant's speakerphone, but the tone was completely different. He was younger than Madison had expected, and much better looking, except for the unpleasant smirk on his face.

Boone and Johnson eyed each other for a moment, but neither said anything. Madison was about to speak up, but Johnson beat her to it.

"Well, it's our pleasure," Johnson said sarcastically. "It's a real treat coming out here. It's like stepping back in time. Like fucking Mayberry."

Madison was taken aback at the level of animosity they had reached, so quickly and without provocation. She was looking back and forth from one to the other when Boone stepped up closer.

"Like stepping back to a time when people knew their place," he said, looking Johnson up and down, contemptuously. For a moment, Madison thought she heard a trace of a southern twang creeping into Boone's voice.

As the tension skyrocketed, Madison couldn't get her brain to spit out a recommended reaction. Instead she stood there, stunned.

The woman behind the desk looked bored and Madison wondered what bizarre alternate universe she had stepped into.

"You like what you see?" Johnson hissed at Boone, not backing away as the police chief stepped even closer.

"You're a good-looking black man, that's for sure," Boone said, leaning in even closer.

"Then why don't you kiss me," Johnson replied.

Madison's mouth dropped open as Chief Boone puckered his lips and came in closer, like he was about to plant one somewhere on Johnson's face.

Johnson cracked first, pulling away, laughing uncontrollably.

Boone started laughing, too, but not as hard. "What?" he said through the remnants of a straight face. "C'mon, kiss me, detective."

"You're a sick bastard, Boone," Johnson said, unable to stop laughing. Now, Boone had lost control, too, and they were both incapacitated with laughter.

Madison shook her head. She could see the humor in the situation, but not quite as much as they apparently did. Gloria caught her eye and slowly shook her head.

"Does this happen a lot?" Madison asked.

"He doesn't get out all that much." Gloria stopped typing as she replied, then her fingers resumed their flurry across the keyboard.

When Boone and Johnson were done laughing, they exchanged a quick handshake and slapped each other on the back. After an exchange of mumbled "how ya doin's" and "same-olds," they both turned to Madison.

"Madison, this is Matt Boone," Johnson said. "We went to the academy together."

Boone held out his hand.

Without the smirk on his face, he was even more striking. His dark hair was curly but cropped short, and he had sideburns that were not quite long enough to be ironic. His high, sculpted cheekbones seemed to have come from the same place he got the square chin with the little cleft in it. His eyes were complex, dark, and intelligent, almost piercing, but surrounded by enough lines that you could tell he liked to laugh.

"Hi, Madison. Pleased to meet you," he said with a slightly embarrassed smile. The trace of a southern twang had disappeared. "Sorry you had to witness that."

Madison smiled sweetly. "Me, too."

"Madison's a technician with the C.S.U.," said Johnson.

"Oh, that's great," Boone said politely. His eyes wandered over their shoulders, through the plate-glass window and into the parking lot. "Is there someone else?"

Johnson cocked his head. "Someone else?"

"Yeah, an investigator? I asked for a crime scene investigator. When Cross said he was going to send someone out from the C.S.U., I assumed he meant an investigator."

Madison breathed deeply and focused her energy on keeping her color down.

"Sorry, dude." Johnson shook his head. "It's a mess over in North Philly, got half the damn department working on it. And *all* the C.S.I.'s. You lucked out man, Madison here is at least as good as most of them, and better than a lot."

Johnson's praise did not counteract Boone's disparaging remarks, at least not as far as the capillaries in Madison's cheeks were concerned. Instead, they exacerbated each other, combining to bring forth a warm rosy glow that Madison struggled mightily to conceal.

She clenched her jaw, as if that would help.

Boone was quiet for a second. "Right," he said. "Well, sorry if I don't seem grateful. I am. I'm just surprised is all. I appreciate the help."

Madison nodded but didn't say anything. The jaw clenching actually seemed to be helping and she didn't want to let up just yet.

Johnson didn't say anything, either. He just looked on with a bemused smile.

"All right," Boone said, clapping his hands together. "I guess we should go to the scene, then. You guys want to take my car?"

"We'll follow you," Madison said, before Johnson could agree.

Boone shrugged. "Suit yourself. It's about a mile."

Madison got in the car first. "What an asshole!" she exclaimed, as soon as Johnson's door slammed shut.

"Who, Boone?" He laughed, starting the car. "Naw, Boone's okay. Boone's my man."

"He's an asshole."

"No, he's not." He laughed again. They backed out and followed the patrol car down the road. "He was expecting an investigator, and you ain't one." He grinned broadly. "Just wait 'til he sees how good you are; he'll see the error of his ways."

Johnson laughed some more and Madison frowned.

"So you guys went to the academy together?" she asked. "In Philly?"

"Yup. Getting to be a long time ago, too."

"How'd he end up out here?"

"He ended up *back* here. Couldn't wait to get out of here, you know? Gets through college, through the academy, boom, ends up back here." He laughed. "Sound familiar?"

"A little bit, yeah."

Less than a year earlier, Madison had been finishing med school, living in Seattle with her boyfriend, Doug. She had worked her ass off to get out of Philly. She had graduated first in her class from the University of Washington School of Medicine, completed a string of prestigious internships, and was headed for a great residency at Stanford. Then one day she woke up and realized it was all wrong, all of it. She bailed on the residency, the whole thing. Even the boyfriend.

Uncle Dave had offered her an entry-level job on the Crime Scene Unit and she took it. She didn't know who was more surprised about it, Uncle Dave or her. But after all that hard work to get the hell away from home, she had suddenly found herself back.

"Boone's dad was the police chief out here," Johnson continued. "A one-man department. Just after Boone finished at the academy, his dad got sick. Boone came back to help out." He shrugged. "The old man died, Boone took the job. Or the job took him."

As they followed Boone's patrol car, the winding, wooded road opened out into an intersection with a small cluster of storefronts on each corner. Among them was a drugstore, a bank, a bar, and completely encircled in yellow police tape, a small gas station with a single garage bay.

Boone parked on the narrow stretch of pavement between the police tape and the road. Johnson pulled in behind him.

"The body's on ice," Boone told them as he got out of the

patrol car. "But I've been able to keep the scene roped off." He laughed. "Usually the proprietor would be hot as shit to get the place open, howling about all the business he's losing."

"Not this guy?" Johnson asked.

"I think he's spooked. Apparently he got a good, close look at what happened. Folks say it scared the shit out of him, and he took off. Dale Hibbert. He's pretty skittish at the best of times."

Madison stepped under a length of police tape. "Okay, so what do we have?" she asked.

"Well, we got a war zone is what we've got," Boone replied, stepping over the police tape. "Witnesses at Fred's Bar over there said there was bullets flying all over. Two of them hit the wall over Fred's window. Seems there were two carloads shooting at each other. Two or three guys in one car and maybe four in the other. One of the cars was shot up pretty bad. That's this one here. They left it." He pointed at a silver Maxima parked at an angle next to the gas pumps.

Half a dozen bullet holes perforated the body of the car, two of the tires were flat, and there was a wet stain of antifreeze and motor oil that had spread out from underneath it. The doors were all open and the windows were broken.

"It was reported stolen in Philly, from outside a house in Manayunk. Anyway, they came here, ditched this one, pulled a lady out of her Ford pickup, and took that instead. She was scared shitless and I can't blame her. Lucinda Bailey. On her way back from visiting a cousin near Poughkeepsie. Lucky she didn't get shot, all the bullets flying around."

"She get a look at them?" Johnson asked.

He shrugged. "Not really. I think she was screaming with her eyes closed the whole time."

He led them around to the far side of the Maxima, where there was a chalk outline on the ground between the passenger-side rear tire and the door to the cashier's area at the gas station.

"This is where we found Alvarez," Boone told them. "Lieutenant tells me you guys picked up one of his known associates."

Johnson nodded. "Luis Castillo. Shot and dumped along the expressway."

Without a body lying inside, the chalk outline had a cartoonish quality about it that made the bloodstains emanating from it that much more jarring.

"One in the neck, one in the gut?" Madison asked, crouching down. "Maybe some kind of nick or cut on his hand?"

"Yeah, that's right," Boone replied, surprised but not yet impressed.

Johnson smiled and raised an eyebrow, but Boone ignored him.

Madison nodded, thinking. "Where's the body?"

"County coroner. I can get you the report when it comes in." He stepped over to the cashier's booth. "Dale was right in there, so he probably got a real good look."

"Did you talk to him?" Johnson asked.

"Briefly. He took off just after I got here. Haven't seen him since. He's not at his house." Boone paused. "Dale's got some, uh . . . issues. If he got spooked enough, he could have gone to ground, be living out in the woods somewhere. He's pretty comfortable out there."

"So what the hell were these guys doing out here?" Johnson asked. "I mean, no offense, but this is like the capital of bumblefuck."

"No offense taken, man. Matter of fact, it ain't even the capital anymore; they moved the capital when they built the interstate." Boone laughed. "Seriously, though, we do actually see some drug stuff here and there. There's been some gang activity around Allentown, over in Scranton. Stuff's not as far away as you might think." He looked around at the bullet-riddled car. "Still, though, nothing like this."

CHAPTER 6

"OKAY," MADISON said, "Here's what we're going to do. You said there were a couple of bullets over that window, at Fred's over there. You get them out yet?"

Boone shook his head. "Nope."

"Okay, why don't you guys get on that. Chip out the wood around them, so you don't mess up the actual slugs."

They both seemed a little put out at being told what to do. Madison didn't want to annoy Johnson, but Boone's discomfort more than made up for it.

She ignored them both.

While Boone and Johnson crossed the street and started stacking trash cans they could climb up on to reach the bullets embedded in the window, Madison got busy with her camera.

She took photos of the chalk outline on the ground, the damage to the plastic sign over the gas pump, and the dozen or so spatters and puddles of blood. A can of motor oil on the display rack had a hole through it, spilling what looked like much more than a quart of motor oil down the display and across the concrete.

A paper sign advertising a deal on oil changes was perforated with scores of little tears. The holes were clustered in the shape of a crescent, with no holes in the middle, like a void pattern. Some object had blocked whatever made the holes. She took a picture of that, too.

Moving on to the car, she took a series of shots of the bullet-riddled exterior and then started on the interior.

The inside of the car was covered with broken glass and drenched in blood. It smelled of rot and decay, even though the carnage inside was barely twenty-four hours old.

Madison took two dozen exposures of the inside of the car, trying to isolate the different puddles of blood that intermingled on the leather. Getting good samples was going to be a bitch.

As she put away the camera and got out her crime scene kit, Johnson called over that they had retrieved one of the bullets.

"Very good work, boys!" she shouted patronizingly. "Now see if you can get the other one."

Out of the corner of her eye, she could see them whispering to each other and then laughing as they started working on the second hole.

A couple of old boys in flannel shirts and fly-fishing vests came out of Fred's to watch the proceedings, each holding a heavy glass mug of beer. She couldn't hear what they were saying but they seemed to be directing their questions to Chief Boone.

Opening the crime scene kit, Madison began the laborious task of dusting the car for prints. She found dozens of sets of prints, so many that, as she lifted them, she began to worry that she wouldn't have enough tape. By the time she was finished inside the tight confines of the car, her back was aching, she was nauseous from the smell, and she was starting to resent the fact that she was doing all this work for some hayseed who didn't even want her there in the first place.

After making sure all the prints were properly labeled and put away, she went to work on the bloodstains.

Crouching on the pavement, she poured a small amount of distilled water onto a quarter-inch square of sterile cloth and blotted the stain. When the patch had turned a rusty red, she placed it in a "bloodlift" holder, a vented plastic box not much bigger than the patch itself.

She moved on to the next stain, and then the next one. When she was done, she had ten blood samples, each one in its own little plastic box sealed in its own envelope.

Then she started pulling bullets out of the body of the car.

One of the slugs had spent its energy puncturing the steel and had come to rest on the floor of the car, sitting in plain view amidst the blood and the broken glass.

Of the two that had penetrated the engine, one was lying on the pavement below and the other was in the wiper fluid reservoir.

There was one inside the door, and she pried off the inside paneling to get at it. She found it sitting on a steel lip at the bottom of the door.

Two more had hit between the rear passenger window and the back window. One was lodged in the steel and she gently pried it out with forceps.

The last one was the trickiest. It had punctured the steel, but had not penetrated the interior. She peeled back the fabric on the roof of the car and removed the foam. By the time she found the slug, resting just above the right front passenger window, the interior of the roof was completely stripped.

She backed out of the car and stretched, then conducted a brief but unsuccessful search for the bullet that had pierced the motor oil display. She turned to see Johnson and Boone crossing the street toward her.

Johnson had two small evidence bags in his hand, a flattened slug in each. "Well, that was a pain in the ass," he said

"Yeah? This wasn't," she said. "This was a walk in the park."

"What did you find?" Boone asked.

"We've got a lot of physical evidence." She told him about each of the bullets and where she had found them, then described the fingerprints and the blood samples she had taken. "All these bullets flying around, there's probably even more. The motor oil display got shot up—should be a bullet lying around from that, but I couldn't find it."

"Okay," Boone said, "so what now?"

"So, we run ballistics on what we've got. We get the car owner's prints, take them out of the mix, then put the DNA analysis and prints through the databases, see if we can come up with some IDs. Judging from the rap sheets on Alvarez and Castillo, I bet the rest of their buddies are in the database, too. All this blood around, wouldn't surprise me if one or two of them end up in a hospital somewhere, so I'd keep an ear out for any ERs reporting gunshot victims."

Johnson laughed. "That's a lot of shit you got there. You think the lab's going to do all that?"

Madison shrugged. "It's a big scene, here. And if the lab's not going to do it, why did the lieutenant bother sending me up here?"

He laughed again. "I'm just saying. Especially with all that stuff from the Oxford house coming in. I mean, they're going to be running damn near every scrap of that place through the lab. Veste's going to be up to his eyeballs in it; I don't see him getting to this for weeks . . ." He smiled coyly. "Unless he owes you any . . . favors, that is. Maybe you could use your feminine wiles."

"Oh, fuck off, Johnson," Madison growled.

Boone looked confused, glancing back and forth between them. "What?"

Aidan Veste was the Crime Scene Unit's senior chemical analyst. He and Madison had come close to something at one point, maybe at a couple of points. Madison thought they had been pretty discreet, but apparently Johnson knew about it.

She knew he was just jerking her chain about it, but it was getting to her. For some reason, it bothered her even more that it was in front of Boone.

Johnson mumbled out of the side of his mouth to Boone. "I guess you shouldn't count on getting your results anytime soon."

Madison sighed wearily. "Ted, you're an idiot. I don't even have anything for chemical analysis in here. And I don't know how backed up ballistics is, but I can run the prints myself. And I can do the DNA."

"You can do the DNA?" Boone said, surprised.

"I told you, man." Johnson laughed. "The girl's good."

"Yes. I can do the DNA."

"Wow."

Madison fought the urge to remind him he had almost sent her home.

Johnson might have sensed she was going to say something snotty. "All right, then," he cut in. "Got a lot of stuff; guess we should get it back to the lab and get started on it."

"Actually, there is one more thing," Madison said. She took out the report on Jimmy Dawber and handed it to Boone. "How far are we from Bartlett?"

Johnson's head whipped around. "Bartlett? That ain't even in this county. What's this about?"

Madison shrugged. "Wondering if he knows anything about Jimmy Dawber."

Boone shook his head. "No, Bartlett's not far, just a few miles. Why? Who's Jimmy Dawber?"

"Dawber?!" Johnson exclaimed. "Ain't that Fenton's case?"

"Dawber's a murder victim. Turned up in a couple trash bags in South Philly. He's from Bartlett, so I figured while we were out here, wouldn't hurt to take a look around, see if we could find anything."

Johnson shook his head. "You got questions about Bartlett, you need to talk to Bartlett PD, right, Boonie?"

Boone shrugged. "Actually, they're unincorporated, so there is no Bartlett PD, but . . ."

Johnson cut him off, turning back to Madison. "Does Fenton know you're doing this?"

Boone held the paper tentatively, again looking back and forth between them. "Is there some kind of dispute on this case? I mean, I'm not sure I should really . . ."

"Fenton's a lazy piece of shit," Madison said, cutting him off. "He probably won't even get around to *calling* up here for another week."

Boone looked up at Johnson for confirmation.

"You do have a point there," Johnson said, his expression softening. "Guy's the laziest piece of shit on the force."

Madison turned to Boone, then looked at the crime scene around them. "And frankly, I believe at this point you owe me."

Boone looked back up at Johnson, who shrugged and nodded.

"Okay," Boone said. "You want, I could take you there. No problem."

BOONE SUGGESTED they all take his cruiser. Madison made sure she got in the front. Normally, she wouldn't care, but there was no way she was going to ride in the backseat. She wasn't going to sit on the hump, either, and she stared defiantly at Johnson as she opened the door, letting him know that he would be sitting in the back.

Johnson smiled and shook his head, holding up his hands with the palms out. Don't shoot.

As they drove, Boone asked about the Dawber case. Johnson knew a fair amount about it, but he sat forward, listening closely to the details.

When she was done, they were both shaking their heads.

"And Fenton really said he wasn't going to go out there?" Boone asked.

"Pretty much. He said he was going to make some calls. When I said, 'You're not going out there?' he blew me off. Said he'd let me know if he wanted my input. I got the distinct impression he thought it wouldn't be necessary."

Boone nodded slowly. "So what is it you hope to find?"

Madison shook her head. "I don't know, but somebody killed the kid and chopped him up into little pieces. Seems like having a look around, seeing if anything pops out is the least that should happen."

"Here it is," Boone said, pulling over in front of a large, worn-looking house covered in dark gray cedar shake. Two steps up from the street was a porch with a couple of old rocking chairs and a jelly jar full of cigarette butts.

One half of the double-doored entrance was wide open, but the screen door was shut.

Boone rapped on the screen door, which in turn slapped against the door frame. Madison and Johnson stayed a few steps back.

"Hello?" he said. "Anybody in there?"

He rapped again a few seconds later and an older woman in a faded apron came toward them through the shadows.

"Hello?" she said cheerfully, but when she saw Boone's uniform she said it again, more subdued. "Oh, hello. What can I do for you, officer?"

"I understand there's a Jimmy Dawber lives here?"

"Jimmy Dawber?" she repeated, pausing to do some sort of mental calculation. "I got a John Dennison, but he ain't here."

"I beg your pardon?"

"Are you looking for John Dennison?"

"No, ma'am. We're looking for Jimmy Dawber. Young guy, about twenty-three years old. Dark hair."

"Oh, Jesus, Jimmy Dawber, now I know who you're talking about. Oh, Lord, no, he moved out of here about two or three years ago. I thought maybe you were talking about John Dennison. He lives upstairs."

"Do you know where Jimmy is living now?"

"I don't know. He got into some trouble a while back. That's when he moved out of here. I think his boss took him in."

Boone looked down at the paper Madison had given him. "And his boss, is that . . . George Krulich?"

"It might have been. Guy owned a couple boats, had a fishing guide company. This was about two years ago."

Boone looked at the paper again. "Could that be Upstream Guides? Was that the name of the place?"

"Yeah, I think so. Yeah. I hope Jimmy's not in trouble again. He's a good kid; he just screwed up."

"What kind of trouble was that, ma'am?"

"Getting skunk drunk and driving ninety miles an hour."

"Oh."

"And getting caught."

Boone smiled noncommittally. "Well, thanks for your help, ma'am."

Madison offered a polite smile, but the old woman just turned and disappeared inside.

GEORGE KRULICH'S house was at the bottom of a dip in the road a little over a mile away. It was set back behind a low stone wall and a wraparound porch. The wide driveway curved around the side of the house before sloping steeply down to a large creek in the back.

They pulled into the driveway entrance and as they got out, Madison took a deep breath, filling her lungs with the fresh smell of the creek. It had that cold, raw feel to it; spring was just starting but the ground hadn't finished thawing yet.

Boone looked at her and smiled. "Yeah, don't you just love that smell?"

Madison smiled back.

Johnson looked at the road sloping uphill on either side of them. "Bet it's a bitch down here when it rains, though," he muttered before joining Boone and Madison on the porch.

"He's not here," Boone said.

"You haven't even knocked," Madison said.

Boone gave the door three hard, loud knocks, then immediately repeated, "He's not here. I mean he's away. Probably off guiding his boat somewhere."

"Why do you say that?" Johnson asked.

"Well, there's no car, and his boat's not in the back, either. Which means he's off in it somewhere. Plus there looks like a couple of days' worth of mail on the floor in there. I think he probably took a tour out somewhere."

Boone scribbled a note on the back of a business card and stuffed it in the door. He turned around and shrugged.

"So . . . that's it?" Madison asked.

Boone smiled, shaking his head. "What else do you expect me to do? Unless he's got a boat phone and you got the number, that's about it."

Madison frowned, then frowned even more when she saw Johnson smiling.

"He'll call me when he gets back," Boone assured her.

"And what then?"

"And then I'll call you."

CHAPTER 7

CHUCK GERALD stood quietly in the doorway to the Firearms Identification Unit. It was almost seven, but Madison had a hunch that Gerald would still be there. He was always there.

Gerald listened but he didn't react. He never did.

"Anyway," Madison said, finishing her explanation of the situation, "if you could do this for me, I'd really appreciate it."

Gerald had been in the army a little too long to lose that military demeanor entirely. He'd been out ever since a grenade removed most of the meat of his left thigh in the first Gulf War, but you'd think he just got out yesterday. Or, more to the point, that he was still in.

He took the sheaf of evidence envelopes out of her hand and gave them a shake, listening as the spent bullets rustled around inside.

He frowned. "Lawson, huh?"

She nodded. "But it ties into a case we're working on."

"I'll see what I can do."

"HOLY MACKEREL!" the lieutenant exclaimed, watching Madison unpacking all the prints and samples she had brought back from the Lawson crime scene. They pretty much covered her desk.

"Do you think you have enough evidence, there, Maddy?" It was late and he looked like he'd had a long, rough day, but he still wore a bemused smile.

"Tell me about it," she replied. "And I already dropped off the slugs with ballistics. There might have been only one body, but the crime scene looked like a battlefield. The car was shot to bits, blood everywhere, prints all over the place. I spent most of the day out there, or in transit. Now I have all this to process."

"Well, I appreciate you're helping them, but it's okay to back-burner it, too. If anything else comes in, anything local, you do that first, okay?"

"Don't worry about that."

"Good." He turned to leave, then turned back. "That reminds me, Fenton called while you were gone. He wanted to know if you'd had any luck with the prints from the trash bags."

Her eyes narrowed. She had started the search before she left for Lawson and had not had a chance to check on it in the ten minutes since she got back.

She glanced at her phone. The message light was not blinking. "Did he call me or did he call you?"

The lieutenant paused for a second, chewing the inside of his cheek. "He said he tried to call you. When he called me, I told him you were out in the field."

She frowned.

"Maddy, can you just send it over to him? For me?"

She sighed. "Sure. Whatever."

As the lieutenant walked away, Madison looked at her watch and stifled a yawn. Weighing her exhaustion against how much she wanted to get this big pile of work behind her, she sighed and lined up the blood samples she had collected at the gas station. She got out a rack and filled the slots with microtubes, then used a pipette to inject a small amount from each vial into its own tube. Next, she pipetted a small amount of enzyme solution into each of the microtubes and capped them, swirling each one a few times before she inserted them into the thermocycler.

Once the thermocycler was running, she went to her computer to check on the prints for Fenton. The screen came to life, revealing a match for what she lifted from the trash bag. She did a visual confirmation, then checked the ID.

The prints belonged to Arnold Prager. Served three months for assault seven years earlier. Last known address was on Bucknell Street, five doors down from Ida Parella. *You're a lucky bastard, Fenton,* she thought. She e-mailed him the report, but included a notation that the plastic surrounding the prints showed no signs of the stress you would expect from somebody grabbing or lifting it.

When she checked her watch again it was almost nine and this time, the yawn escaped despite her efforts to stop it. It was going to be a fight to keep going.

She turned on the scanner so she could input the prints from the gas station. As it warmed up, she yawned again, and by the time the light on the scanner changed from red to green to let her know it was ready to go, she felt devoid of energy.

Looking over at the fingerprint cards, she was engulfed by another yawn and decided they would have to wait. She was too tired to get any more work done and she'd be damned if she was going to spend the rest of the night working for Chief Boone.

CHAPTER 8

SHE IS six years old and she is hiding in the closet with the door almost closed, watching Daddy through the gap. He is wearing his police uniform, sitting at the dining room table.

In front of him is a bottle and a glass.

He picks up the bottle and fills the glass with a foul-looking brown liquid. A small sip somehow consumes it all. Instantly, he is drunk, and she gets a bad feeling in her tummy, the sick, hollow, churning feeling she always got when he was drinking.

His eyes are closing, his lips already sloppy and wet. Then his head sags forward, his chin touching his chest. He slumps forward, passed out. As his head hits the table, it knocks over the bottle and the brown liquid gurgles out onto the table, spilling onto the floor, first a trickle, then a torrent.

A candle is on the table. It wasn't there before, but now it is. Suddenly the alcohol ignites, a blue flame that is cool and angry at the same time, flaring orange as it follows the spilled liquid, spreading out, coming across the floor.

The fire knows where she is. It knows she's in the closet, and it is coming toward her. She can't close the door, can't close her eyes; she can only watch as the flames advance across the floor. She is screaming now, screaming and screaming, terrified as the flames come up under the door, around the door, filling the closet, but Daddy's asleep now and Daddy isn't waking up, because she's not screaming for Daddy, she's screaming for Mommy, and as the flames slither across her Winnie the Pooh nightgown, she screams louder and louder. But she knows Mommy can't hear her, either, because she knows, she *knows* Mommy is already dead.

* * *

MADISON COULDN'T tell if her screams were reverberating in her apartment or only in her skull. The clock looked inscrutably back at her, telling her only that it was 5:16 a.m., nothing more. As she looked on, it changed its mind; make that 5:17.

The sheets were sweaty and her stomach was in knots but the pounding in her chest was already slowing down as the nightmare receded. She swung her feet out of bed anyway, if only to put more distance between herself and her dreams.

Stumbling into the bathroom, she splashed cold water on her face, avoiding the mirror so she wouldn't have to see the haunted look that followed her nightmares.

She turned on the shower and muttered to herself, "Hell of a way to start the day."

In the nine or so months that Madison had been working at the C.S.U., she had become less and less of a morning person. Too many nights worked straight through, sleeping from six a.m. to noon. Somehow, after leaving so many crime scenes just in time for the morning rush, passing so many freshly scrubbed nine-to-fivers on their way to work, the idea of getting an early start on the day had lost some of its righteousness.

The occasional viscerally terrifying nightmare didn't help, either.

Still, the relative quiet of the crime lab early in the morning made it easier to get things done. As an added bonus, she got to make an extra strong pot of coffee without hearing any complaints. She even drank most of it herself.

Working without interruption from six to seven thirty, she scanned in all the prints from the gas station in Lawson and ran them through the database. She was rewarded with two hits.

Ramon Perez and Jorge Parga, two petty criminals with vaguely familiar names.

"Son of a bitch," she muttered, fishing through the pile on her desk and coming up with the files on Castillo and Alvarez. She pulled out both lists of known associates. She picked up a pen and searched Castillo's list, ticking off Perez, then Parga. Scanning Alvarez's list, she quickly found the same two names and checked them, too. Ramon Perez and Jorge Parga.

As she was putting down her pen, the computer found another match. Luis Castillo.

"Son of a bitch!"

She called Johnson, reached him in his car.

"Turns out you and your friend Boone have more in common than a sick sense of humor," she told him.

"What are you talking about, Cross?"

"I got IDs on three sets of prints from the car in Lawson. The first two were Ramon Perez and Jorge Parga, two of the names that are on both known associates lists, Castillo's and Alvarez's. The third ID was Castillo himself. He was in that car. These were probably the guys who dumped him on the expressway."

Johnson grunted. "You tell Boone?"

"No, not yet."

"Why don't you give him a call. Neither Castillo or Alvarez have any family around to talk to. Maybe these other guys do. I'll talk to some of the uniforms working around these guys' turf, see if they know anything. Maybe we can find Perez or Parga."

She was leaving a message on Boone's voice mail when Aidan Veste came in and took the last cup of coffee from the pot she'd made.

It was ten past eight.

"Morning, Madison," he said, sipping his brew and looking at it appreciatively. "Mmm, that's good coffee."

Madison looked up from her work, eying his coffee cup and then scowling past him at the now-empty pot. "Morning, Aidan."

He took another sip. "I ran some tests for Spoons on that Bucknell Street case. Heard you were working on it, too."

Their eyes met for a moment that stretched into awkwardness. There was still tension between them, though at times it seemed like they had just skipped ahead to being mostly amicable exes.

"Find anything?" she asked.

He shook his head. "Kid had a couple beers in him, but somehow I doubt that's what did it."

She gave him a quick smile and returned to her work.

He took another sip of coffee. "One of these days you're going to have to tell me how you do it."

"What's that?"

"How you get that piece-of-crap coffeemaker to produce such decent coffee."

She leaned forward and whispered. "Easy on the water."

He turned to leave. "I'll have to try that."

As he left, she caught the slightest trace of his aftershave, a faint scent of cedar and ginger that evoked times she had been close enough to smell it more clearly.

She watched him walking away and wondered if she'd made a mistake declining his advances. He had a swimmer's body, broad shoulders, and a narrow waist. He was smart and he could be funny, and he was definitely hot. There had been an undeniable spark between them from the beginning, and if it hadn't coincided with her first day on the job, things might have gone differently.

Since abruptly breaking up with Doug, her ex-boyfriend in Seattle, she had told others—and herself—that she had been keeping her love life "uncomplicated." But it had been nine months now, and she had the feeling people weren't buying it anymore. To be honest, she wasn't buying it, either.

At the end of the corridor, Aidan turned and caught her watching him, a half smile on his lips. She opened her mouth, as if to explain—explain what, she didn't know—but her phone went off and then Aidan was gone.

She bobbled the phone as she picked it up.

"What?" she said, flustered and a little jittery from the coffee.

"Morning, Newbie!" Parker's voice boomed on the other end.

"Parker?"

"Got another good one for you."

"I thought you had the day off."

He let out a raucous laugh. "Yeah, I thought so, too. Apparently not all of it."

"What've you got there?"

He laughed again. "I don't even fucking know."

"What do you mean?"

"I seriously don't know. Lookit, just get on down here." He gave her an address on Germantown Avenue in North Philly.

"I'm on my way."

"Is Veste there?"

"Aidan? Yeah, he's here."

"Bring him, too."

"Why?"

He laughed again, but it sounded more tired than raucous. "Just bring him down, okay? I'll explain it when you get here."

"SO DID Parker say anything about what we're coming down here for?" Aidan asked, looking out the passenger window as Madison drove.

"He didn't, really. Said it was a 'good one,' but that was about it. He actually seemed a little taken aback."

Aidan gave her a look of mild surprise, then he shrugged.

Madison took Fifth Street north, through Northern Liberties and into North Philly. Some of the blocks didn't look so bad, but some looked postapocalyptic. The images of neglect and decay made it difficult to imagine them ever having been habitable.

As the clean, modern high-rises of Temple University drifted past them a half dozen blocks to the west, it reminded her of the Oxford Street fire. She remembered standing there in the smoking ruins, half a dozen blocks on the other side of those towers, surrounded by death, charred bodies, and murdered children. When she had looked to the east and seen those same high-rises in the distance, she thought it looked like another world.

She knew the Oxford scene was still buzzing with activity, and although part of her was definitely relieved not to be there, she could feel her annoyance level rising as she thought about how unfairly she'd been excluded from it. When her cell phone chimed she was grateful for the distraction.

She could tell from the area code that the call was from Lawson.

"Madison Cross," she said, trying to sound businesslike.

"Hi, Madison. It's Matt Boone, returning your call."

"Hey, Matt. Another cat stuck in an attic?"

Aidan turned and looked at her, making her feel suddenly self-conscious. She realized she had a grin on her face and she immediately toned it down.

Boone forced out a small, embarrassed laugh. "Heard about that, huh? Yeah, it was something like that."

"Well, I just wanted to let you know I got some of the results on the fingerprints from your crime scene. Two more guys who were on both 'known associates' lists were in that car. Ramon Perez and Jorge Parga."

"Interesting."

"It gets better. There was another match, too. Luis Castillo."

"Huh. That's your roadkill case, right?"

"That's the guy. That car was stolen just the day before, so if he was in it since then, I figure these other guys are the ones who dumped him."

"Right. That's great." He paused. "Thanks, Madison. I do appreciate it. And sorry if I didn't seem grateful before."

"Don't worry about it. I understand." She felt Aidan looking over at her again and made an effort not to smile.

"I guess there's nothing on the DNA yet. How about ballistics?" he asked.

"Nothing yet. I'll call you when I get anything."

"Thanks. Oh, hey, I might have a couple leads on the whereabouts of that Krulich guy. I should know something later on today."

"Thanks, Matt. I appreciate it."

As she put her phone away, she could sense that Aidan was still watching her, but she kept her eyes facing front and didn't say a thing. She veered left onto Germantown Avenue and started checking the addresses.

Looking around at the boarded-up storefronts, it was hard to believe this same street continued almost through the entire city, starting practically at the Delaware River, through blighted areas and historic districts, up into the tree-lined, cobblestoned shopping district of Chestnut Hill, where it left the city and extended another fifteen miles into the suburbs as Germantown Pike.

The avenue angled to the left, and they immediately saw the place they were looking for: flashing lights and emergency vehicles surrounding a dense web of police tape.

As they parked and got out, a pair of figures in hazmat suits waddled awkwardly out of a narrow structure that stood alone in the middle of the block. The house had obviously once been in the middle of a row; a ghostly imprint of stairs and wallpaper ran up one of the exterior walls, and it was flanked on either side by vacant lots at least twice its width. The front door appeared to be missing.

The two guys in the hazmat suits pulled off their hoods as they slowly descended the crumbling concrete steps. They were talking to the small crowd of uniforms milling around on the sidewalk. There was a brief back-and-forth, then the two hazmat guys looked at each other and shook their heads, shrugging noncommittally.

The cluster of uniforms quietly parted, giving the hazmat guys a wide berth when they reached the bottom step. Then Tommy Parker emerged from the building behind them, waving his hand in front of his face, as if from a bad smell, and laughing loudly.

Madison smiled.

He was wearing jeans, a denim jacket, and a worn pair of tooled cowboy boots. Same thing he always wore.

Parker said something out of the side of his mouth as he walked past the hazmat guys. One of them replied with his middle finger.

"Fucking nuts," Aidan muttered.

When Parker saw Madison, he motioned her over.

"Hey, Newbie!" he yelled from the bottom of the steps. "Wait'll you see this shit."

Madison walked over without waiting to see if Aidan followed. She pressed through the throng of uniforms, nodding a greeting to the ones she knew, including one of the hazmat crew, who held up a hand to stop her.

"Hey, Larry," she said, stopping just short of his hand. "What've you got in there?"

He shook his head wearily. His face was damp and his hair was sweaty, with little wet spikes sticking out in every direction. "Apart from that crazy asshole Parker? Damned if I know. Can't guarantee it's safe in there." He shrugged again.

Parker came up behind him. "Come on, Newbie, don't listen to that wuss. You gotta see this shit. It's fucking crazy."

She gave him a dubious look, but he just smiled, knowing her curiosity would get the best of her.

With a sharp, barking laugh, he turned and scurried back up the steps.

As she sighed and followed him through the gloomy entrance, she heard Aidan behind her. "Yeah, I know," he was saying to the hazmat team. "You can't guarantee my safety."

With the windows covered up, the gloom inside quickly deepened to darkness. As Madison's eyes adjusted, she could see that the floor was strewn with debris: crumpled paper, fast food containers, bottles, cans, soiled clothes.

The stench was intense, a mixture of raw sewage, body odor, and decay, with a chemical hint of fake citrus, as if someone had tried to cover up the odor with a single spritz of dollar-store room deodorizer.

Parker was halfway up to the second floor by the time Madison found the bottom of the stairs.

She could see Aidan behind her, squinting and looking around as his eyes adjusted.

"Over here," she said.

She waited until he was a few steps away. "Upstairs," she said, and she started up.

The second floor was a little bit brighter, but no less squalid. The steps led to a short, narrow hallway. Straight ahead was a bathroom, missing the toilet and most of the floor. Three other doors led to small bedrooms. Parker was in the second one, standing and looking down at a flattened old mattress.

The glassless windows were partially covered by tattered roll blinds, ribbons of vinyl snapping in a stiff breeze.

As Madison joined Parker, she heard Aidan's hushed voice behind them.

"Holy shit."

"What is it?" Madison asked quietly.

Parker shook his head. "Fuck if I know."

The body on the mattress was naked, slightly curled, lying at an awkward angle with its arms at its sides. The skin was strangely shriveled, almost like it was puckered or wrinkled, but not exactly. The color was a pale, inhuman yellow, and the eyes were closed and so sunken they appeared to be missing. A few wisps of white hair extended from the top of its head.

The smell was almost unbearable.

Madison wrinkled her nose. "Stinks like hell, doesn't it?"

"Dead people are supposed to do that, aren't they?" Aidan replied.

Parker laughed and shook his head. "I know dead people. I work with dead people. Dead people are not supposed to stink like *that.*"

With that, he crouched down right next to it, as if challenging the odor to overcome him.

"Check this out," he murmured, reaching out a gloved hand and gently pushing the body onto its front. The right shoulder had a shallow square depression, four inches across, maybe two inches deep. A divot of flesh was missing altogether, revealing pale pink muscle tissue. "No blood."

Madison pulled on gloves and crouched down next to him, wincing at the smell. "There's another one on the hip," she said, indicating with her finger. Even with the exam gloves, she didn't want to touch the thing. She took out a wooden scraper and pressed it against the skin around the wound.

"The flesh is still supple," she said. "It looks all shriveled and dried, but it's still soft."

"I know. Press it a little harder," he told her, then turned to Aidan, shifting out of the way. "You should see this, too, Veste."

Aidan bent in close, but the smell was visible on his face.

As Madison pressed a little harder, the wound began to ooze a yellowish, oily liquid. The intensity of the smell in the room immediately kicked up a notch.

A snuffling, gurgling sound came from Aidan's throat, but to his credit, he leaned in even closer, squinting. "What the hell is that?" he asked.

"That, my man, is the reason you're here," Parker said with a smile.

Aidan pulled on his gloves and took out a specimen vial. "Probably some kind of embalming fluid."

Using a wooden scraper he scooped a small amount of the yellow substance into the vial. As he tightened the cap, he straightened and stepped back, clearly anxious to get back to the lab.

Parker started to stand up, too, but Madison stopped him. "Wait a second, what's that?"

"What?" Parker asked.

Aidan didn't care what; he stayed where he was, halfway out the door.

"This," Madison said. She turned the head slightly and indicated with her finger. A thick black wire was protruding about an inch from the base of the skull.

Parker grunted and eased the body further onto its front. Aidan took a single step closer to them.

An identical second wire was sticking out from the other side of the head.

Madison touched one of the wires with the scraper; it bent slightly and stayed that way.

Parker snorted. "So, what've we got now? Alien fucking autopsy?"

Aidan cracked a smile despite the distress on his face. "I was thinking *The Mummy's Curse*, but yeah, maybe it's more like *E.T.*"

Madison felt a chill as she took out her magnifying glass and looked even closer. It occurred to her that she really had no idea what was going on here, and all sorts of bizarre explanations scurried about in the shadows at the back of her mind. "There are incisions around those wires. And there doesn't seem to be much healing around them."

"Some sort of medical device?" Aidan suggested.

"Nothing I've ever heard of. Something experimental maybe."

She looked at Parker, but he just looked blankly back at her. He often let her take the lead for training purposes, but this time she suspected he was truly stumped.

She shrugged. "We'll see what Spoons can tell us."

"Oh, yeah." Parker grinned. "Spoons is gonna love this."

"Jesus, what the fuck is that?" exclaimed a breathless voice behind them.

It was Tate, standing with Velasquez in the hallway just outside the door. Velasquez crossed himself.

"Thank God," Aidan said, slapping Tate on the back as he squeezed past them out the door. "He's all yours. I'd better get this back to the lab." He held up the vial as he clambered down the steps.

CHAPTER 9

"WHOA, BOY," Spoons exclaimed when they pulled back the sheet to reveal the figure on the gurney. "That *is* a good one."

He started to cackle, but the laugh died in his throat. He leaned forward, squinting. "Jesus," he said, scratching the wiry gray hair behind his ear. "Is that thing even human?"

"Well, now, I don't know," Parker said dryly. "I was hoping we could find a trained medical professional to render an expert opinion."

Madison and Parker were leaning against the wall, smugly unfazed now that they'd had an hour or so to get used to the appearance of the thing.

Tate and Velasquez had dropped the body off and left quickly, Velasquez crossing himself once more as they left.

"Fuck you, Parker," Spoons said without rancor. "Look at this thing. What am I supposed to make of it?"

"Did you see the antennae?" Parker asked mischievously.

"The what?"

"There are wires," Madison explained. "They're sticking out of the neck, right at the base of the skull. And the right shoulder and the right hip have some very strange wounds. They're oozing a viscous yellow fluid. Probably what's giving the skin that color."

Spoons rolled the body halfway over and briefly examined the wires and the two wounds. He grabbed the flesh around one of the wounds and pinched, squeezing liquid out of the exposed muscle tissue.

"Some sort of embalming fluid?" he asked, partially under his breath.

Madison shook her head. "Not like any embalming fluid I've ever seen."

He stepped back from the body without taking his eyes away from it. A worried look had crept into his face. "And what's up with those fucking wires? What are they, probes or something? I mean, is this like some secret defense department thing?"

"We're thinking you could have an alien autopsy," Parker cracked.

Spoons shot him a serious look. "I hope you didn't say that shit in front of Tate and Velasquez. Tate's probably already told the story a dozen times. Probably added a flying saucer and a death ray to liven it up some."

As Spoons looked back down at the body, the furrow in his brow deepened. "All right, well, before I crack this strange beast open, let's try to figure out a little more about what we're dealing with. Let's send some of this fluid to the lab . . ."

"Aidan's already working on it," Madison cut in.

"Okay, well, I'm going to get this guy into the cooler. I want to know a little more about him before I open him up. Maybe we'll shoot for tomorrow."

He wheeled the gurney off to the side.

"I'll tell you what, though," he said, stepping around it. "There's something on that Dawber kid I want you to see. Come on in here."

He led them down the hallway to one of the microscopy rooms, a small room with a counter running around three sides. In the middle of the counter was a digital microscope; to the left of it, a small video monitor.

On the platform under the lens was Jimmy Dawber's disembodied left hand. It was positioned so that the cut end was pointing up, facing the lens. It was held in place by a rubber band.

"Jesus, Frank, I knew you were shorthanded," Parker said with a snort.

Spoons nodded his head indulgently—maybe he'd thought it was a little bit funny the first time he'd heard it. "Look at this." He sat at the stool and fiddled with the knobs on the microscope. "Madison, remember what you said about how whatever made these cuts must have been sharp?"

The picture on the screen jerked around, then came into sharp focus. It showed the whiteness of the severed ulna surrounded by a mass of spongy red flesh.

"All right," he said, stepping away from the microscope. "What do you see?"

Madison stepped up to the microscope while Parker leaned in toward the monitor.

"Can you tilt the specimen?" Parker asked. "So it's at an angle to the light?"

Madison tilted the platform, careful not to touch the hand strapped to it.

"That bone is almost flush with the soft tissue," Madison observed.

With the light coming across it, there was a tiny sliver of shadow around the bone.

"There's no tearing, no sawing, nothing," Madison said. She looked up and rubbed her eyes. "What could have done that?"

Spoons shook his head and turned to leave the room. "Beats the fuck out of me."

Parker grunted.

"So what are you going to do next?" Madison asked, as they followed him out.

Back in the autopsy room, Spoons stopped next to the mummy on the gurney.

"Sanchez is going to see if she can find any trace residues on the exposed edges. After that, I don't know."

Parker looked at his watch. "All right, I gotta make some calls. I'll meet you outside, Newbie."

He turned and hurried out the door.

"Okay, kid," Spoons said. "I got some things I gotta take care of, too. I'll be back in a minute, but can you take some samples for DNA analysis before you go, see if we can get a profile?"

As Spoons shuffled off, Madison took out a swab and a specimen vial and approached the strange, yellow body.

Since the body was so strange in so many ways, she figured the least damaging, least intrusive sample would be a swab from the inside of the cheek. But as she reached out to open the creature's mouth, she stopped.

Looking down at the creature's bizarre, skeletal face, the hollow cheeks and the sunken eyes, somehow staring up at her through puckered lids, she recoiled. The hairs on her neck stirred once again, just as they had when she'd taken Jimmy Dawber's prints.

Her hand hovered over the creature's face for a moment, over the pursed mouth that looked like it was just about to tell some horrible secret. Then she put away the swab and quickly but carefully plucked a couple of the hairs from its head.

She hated the fact that she was spooked once again, but the one thing she wanted more than anything else at that moment was to get out of that room and away from that body.

Parker was just walking up as she stepped out.

He gave her a quick double take. "Hey, you okay?"

"Fine," she said, trying to compose herself. "You ready to go?"

In the ten minutes it took her to drive back to the Crime Scene Unit, the unreasonable fear she had felt in the autopsy room had been replaced, once again, by a deep sense of embarrassment. She snuck a few glances at Parker as she drove, but he didn't seem to think anything was up.

When she got back to the Crime Scene Unit, she went straight to the DNA lab, relieved to be alone. Once she got the thermocycler started, she went to her computer and saw that the rest of the database results were waiting for her.

She tapped a few keys on the computer and scrolled down. Three of the samples matched Luis Castillo; no surprise. There were two each for Perez and Parga. And there was one other hit . . . Frank McGee?

Who the hell was Frank McGee?

She checked her paperwork and saw that the McGee sample came from the blood spatter on the second gas pump, away from the gas station's cashier area.

She punched up McGee's known associates, then Castillo's, then Perez's and Parga's. No overlap with McGee. None.

McGee was forty-two. His rap sheet read like a duplicate of Castillo's and the others, but the dates on all the crimes, the trials, the incarcerations—they were all roughly twenty years earlier. His file said he worked for a reputed gangster named

Ralph Caprielli; he had been arrested with Caprielli for armed robbery, but apparently McGee had taken the rap. He served three years at Graterford State Prison. His most recent arrest was fifteen years ago, assault. Case dismissed.

Maybe Frank McGee had cleaned up his act, she thought. Or maybe he just got better at being bad.

THE LIEUTENANT was on the phone but he waved her in anyway, holding up a finger as he finished the call.

"What is it, Madison?" he asked, leaning forward over his desk to he put the phone down. "I heard about the mummy or whatever. What's that all about?"

She shook her head. "I don't know. I'm running DNA on him, but there's nothing yet."

"Strange case."

"Tell me about it. I did get something else." She held up the printout on Frank McGee. "Another ID on a bloodstain at that gas station in Lawson."

"Another one of Castillo's friends?"

"Nope. Frank McGee, forty-two. Lots of priors but nothing recent. Used to work for a reputed gangster named Ralph Caprielli." She dropped the file on his desk. "The sample was away from the others, on the other side of the gas station. I think this might ID one of the other guys."

He opened the file, nodding slowly as he read. "Frank McGee," he said under his breath. "Okay," he said abruptly, sliding the file back across the desk. "Did you tell Johnson or Boone?"

"Not yet. I will."

He smiled. "Thanks. You know, Fenton thinks the Bucknell Street lead you found is looking promising. This Prager guy has a history of violent crime. Hasn't been seen since the day before that body turned up in the trash. Now it turns out he's missing from his job."

Madison nodded. "Good," she said halfheartedly.

"What?"

"Nothing."

"What?"

She sighed. "The guy got into a bar fight seven years ago and had the misfortune of winning. I just don't think that's remotely enough to link him to this."

"Prager used to work in a meat-cutting plant. They think he might still have the keys."

Madison shook her head. "I was just looking at the body with Spoons. He can't find any cut marks on the wounds. He's asking Sanchez to look for any kind of metal residue, but there's no way those cuts on Dawber are from a meat-cutting plant. The sharpest blade they could possibly have would leave very visible cut marks."

The lieutenant gave her a dubious look.

"And no," she continued, "it's not just because Fenton is such a dick."

He winced at her language, which annoyed her that much more; she knew he was capable of obscenity that would peel the paint off a battleship.

"Did they search his house?" she demanded.

"Well, yes. Fenton did," he replied calmly.

"And did he find anything?"

He smiled. "No, he didn't. He's thinking Prager might have a hideout somewhere, probably where he is now. Fenton has them running a trace on his bank accounts, see if they can find out where it is."

"A hideout?" she said sarcastically.

"Maddy girl," he said, letting her know the conversation was over. "Go call Ted Johnson."

"NOW WE'RE getting somewhere," Johnson said when she told him what she'd learned. "We checked up on the rest of the names on the other known associates lists, but nobody's home. There's another name on all their lists, another known associate. Guy named Carlos Washburn. Little bit older, bit more of a record than the others. Word is, he's the guy in charge of whatever it is they have. Goes by the name Carwash."

"Well, at least now maybe you know who the fight was with, if not what it was about."

"Yeah, that's a help, all right. Can you call Boone and give him an update?"

"Uh, sure."

He laughed.

"What?" she demanded.

"See ya," he said. Then he hung up.

She looked at the phone and frowned, then clicked down to Boone's number.

"Hey, Madison," he answered.

"Hey. Got another ID from the gas station shoot-out."

"Oh, yeah? Another member of 'Our Gang'?"

"Actually, no. Although we've learned a little more about those guys, too. Apparently their fearless leader is a guy named Carlos Washburn, goes by the name Carwash."

He laughed. "Sounds scary."

"Yeah. Anyway, this other ID is a guy named Frank McGee. Age forty-two. No known address. Record goes back twenty-five years, but nothing in the last fifteen."

"What sort of stuff?"

"Armed robbery. Aggravated assault."

"Hmm. So is this our first member of the opposing team?"

"That's what I'm thinking."

"What'd Ted say?"

"Same thing, basically. At least now we have an idea of who both teams were."

"I found out a little more on your pal Jimmy Dawber."

"Oh yeah?"

"Krulich, the kid's old boss, is away at a fishing tournament. Should be back in a couple of days. Dawber used to be a guide for Krulich, but the day after the DUI, the one that cost him his license and got him in the system, Fish and Game pulled his boat over after receiving complaints. Apparently, he was pretty lit up. Lost his boating license, too; that cost him his job. Krulich kept him on at first, but it's not a big operation."

"Thanks. Apparently Fenton likes one of the neighbors on Bucknell Street for the Dawber case. Found a print on one of the trash bags. Guy lives up the block."

"You don't sound convinced."

"I'm not, really. Guy got busted in a bar fight seven years

ago. That and a set of fingerprints. And the fact that the guy hasn't been home."

"I used to know Fenton."

"Yeah?"

"He's a dick."

She laughed, and after a moment he joined in.

"Yeah, he sure is," she agreed.

The laughter faded and they were quiet.

"All right," Boone said, almost reluctantly. "Well, you stay in touch. Call me if you find out anything else, and I'll do the same."

"You bet."

"All right. See you around."

"Hey, Boone?"

"Yeah?"

"Thanks for looking into Dawber for me."

"You got it. Still want me to let you know when Krulich gets home?"

"Sure . . . I guess. If it's not too much trouble."

He laughed. "It'll be my pleasure."

THE DATABASE search came back negative on the mysterious mummy. It had seemed like a solid profile, and the most likely explanation was that it was a legitimate nonmatch—that whoever it was simply was not in the database. But with all the oddities surrounding the body, especially the yellow fluid, it wasn't hard to imagine the DNA being somehow corrupted.

Of course, in Madison's mind, it wasn't hard to imagine that maybe she had screwed something up. She sat at her desk, running through all the steps of the procedure, mentally double-checking each one.

"What's going on?"

She looked up to see Aidan standing next to her. "What do you mean?"

"You okay? You seem kind of preoccupied."

She smiled and sat back in her chair. "No, I'm okay. I ran the DNA on our little friend and I didn't get a match."

He laughed. "Are you sure the thing is even human?"

"Not entirely. But you know me, I'm also not sure I didn't screw something up."

"Hasn't happened yet."

"Maybe I'm due."

"Stop it. And if it makes you feel any better, that yellow fluid it still a mystery, too. I've been able to identify a couple of the compounds in it, but not much."

"What've you got?"

He shrugged. "It has a high level of mannitol."

"What's that?"

"It's a type of polyol, or a sugar alcohol."

"Hmm."

"Apart from that, all I can tell you for sure is that it's yellow and it stinks like hell."

"Stinks like hell, huh? That's your professional opinion?"

He cleared his throat loudly. "Substance exhibits a distinct and extreme malodorous quality," he quoted in a droning monotone, "capable of curling observers' nose hairs and producing a distinct watering of said observers' eyes."

She laughed. "Stunk like hell."

"Stunk like hell, yes." He smiled. "All right. Back to work, I guess. I'll keep you posted if I find anything more."

"Thanks, Aidan."

She was watching him leave and pondering her next step when her phone started to chime again.

It was Spoons. "Hey, kid, how you doing?"

"I'm okay. I thought I got a solid DNA profile on our John Doe, but it didn't hit anything on the database."

He laughed. "Not everybody's a felon, you know."

"You mean not everyone's been caught, right? Actually, I'm just wondering if those chemicals might have damaged the DNA."

"Looked like a solid profile, though, right?"

"Looked like."

"Guy's probably a fine, upstanding citizen on whatever fucking planet he came from. Anyway, I'm going to crack the son of a bitch open tomorrow at ten, if you want to come watch."

"Wouldn't miss it."

CHAPTER 10

THE AUTOPSY room had a surreal quality, and not just because of the otherworldly figure stretched out on the table.

Word about the case had somehow gotten around overnight, and instead of the usual attendance—Spoons and maybe one or two others—a dozen figures were crowded around the autopsy table. Madison knew who most of them were, had seen them arriving, but all she could see now was a crowd of bulky hazmat suits, harsh overhead lights reflecting off the visors on their hoods. The room was surprisingly quiet considering all the people in there. In the claustrophobic confines of her hazmat gear, Madison's breath was loud in her ears.

At the center of it all was the mystery man, stretched out on the table. He had a black plastic block wedged under his back, between his shoulder blades, forcing his chest upward and arching his back slightly.

Standing next to the table was Spoons. Beside him was Alvin Tate.

Velasquez was nowhere in sight.

Spoons fumbled a bit with his little recorder, but he managed to turn it on and place it on the counter like he always did.

Probably still sweaty and jittery in that suit, Madison thought. He'd been sweaty and jittery when he put it on. Now he was in a room full of his peers and his superiors, with all eyes on him. He cleared his throat loudly a few times, then mumbled the case number.

With a jarring lack of hesitation, he picked up the scalpel and slid the blade into the cadaver's chest just below the sternum. The scalpel moved smoothly down the abdomen, through the skin, muscle, and connective tissues. Spoons kept the blade moving, swerving around the puckered slit of a navel and stopping a few inches south of it.

At this point in most autopsies, there was very little blood, but here there was none at all, just a small amount of yellow fluid seeping out of the incision. Spoons quickly made two diagonal cuts across the chest, from the front of each shoulder down toward the sternum, joining the first cut.

He quietly narrated his actions for the recorder—this incision, that incision, describing the yellow liquid.

He slid a gloved finger into the hole where the three incisions joined and started pulling back the left upper flap. With the other hand, he slid the scalpel under the flap, slicing through the connections under the skin and muscle. He repeated the same procedure on the other two flaps. With the starkly bright lights and the absence of blood, the glistening rib cage was peculiarly pale.

His narration paused for a moment, along with his hands. "It's cold," he mumbled.

Spoons kept his eyes front, barely pausing before he hefted a pair of stainless-steel rib-cutting shears and started snapping ribs, working his way up one side of the rib cage and down the other. When he was finished, he stepped back and gave a quick nod. Tate stepped forward and started lifting away the front of the rib cage, but he seemed to be struggling with it, meeting with more than the usual resistance.

Madison was surprised; Tate was a strong guy.

The chest plate finally came up a few inches, pulling away from rest of the body. Spoons reached in with a scalpel, cutting away some remaining soft tissue. It finally came away with a jerk, as if suction had been released.

Tate lifted the chest plate up and off, revealing the yellowy pink, plastic-looking organs underneath. He placed the plate on an exam table behind him.

Spoons leaned forward, looking closely at the exposed chest cavity. He stared at it for a second, then straightened and looked around. His head was barely visible through the visor.

He reached out a hand and placed it flatly against the stomach, then up against the heart.

"Fucking thing is frozen solid," he declared.

A muffled buzz of murmuring voices filtered through the hazmat suits that filled the room.

Spoons seemed to shrug inside his suit. He tried to slice through the larynx and the esophagus, but it was hard going. He cut away some of the connecting tissues in the front, but he was having obvious difficulty. He stopped abruptly and straightened.

"Sorry, folks," he announced to the crowd, "but that's all for today. We're going to have to finish this thing tomorrow."

He motioned to Tate to close it up and as Tate inserted the chest plate back in place, Spoons disappeared through the double doors into the scrub room.

The hazmat suits began murmuring again.

Madison followed him, but by the time she reached the scrub room, he was gone. His hazmat suit was hanging on a hook, still swaying. She quickly stepped out of her suit and caught up with him in his office, where he was pulling on his rumpled windbreaker.

"What are you doing?"

"I gotta get some lunch."

"What?" It was barely eleven o'clock.

"I haven't had lunch," he stated matter-of-factly. "I gotta go."

"But . . ."

"You can come with me if you want, but I'm outta here."

She struggled to keep up with him, which was a first. His usual shuffle had been replaced by an ungainly but surprisingly fast waddle. He tapped the button on the elevator, but when it didn't immediately arrive, he kept going, heading to the stairway without breaking stride. As far as she knew, the fact that he was taking the stairs was another first.

She stepped out into the parking lot, momentarily blinded by the bright sunlight, and saw Spoons getting into his car. He gave the distinct impression that he would leave without her if she didn't keep up. She got into the car and he pulled away before she could even close her door.

He sped down Thirty-eighth Street, left onto Walnut for two blocks, then another left onto Fortieth, where he pulled over in a handicapped spot less than three blocks from the medical examiner's building.

He was out of the car and walking down the sidewalk before she had her door open.

"You're parking *here*?" she asked as she got out.

"Fuck it," he said over his shoulder.

Madison grimaced as he pulled open the door to Smokey Joe's Tavern. "Smokey Joe's?" she said to herself, dismayed. "Really?"

Smokey Joe's was the quintessential college bar, the college bar all other college bars aspired to imitate. But while it earned points for authenticity, it lost them in Madison's mind for being exactly the kind of place she hated. Images of loud, drunken frat boys filled her head, spilling their beers and flecking each other with spit as they screamed into each other's ears.

But the place was mercifully quiet when she got inside. Apart from the photos of past clientele that bedecked the walls, it was almost empty. Lunch was still an hour or so away, and apparently even frat boys had to go to some classes. Either that or they were sleeping off the previous night's festivities.

Spoons was sitting at the bar when she wandered up behind him, a double-shot glass already in front of him, empty but wet, waiting for a refill.

"What'll you have?" he asked without turning around.

"Coffee," she said as the bartender grabbed the empty shot glass.

Spoons turned and gave her a look. "Bullshit. What'll you have?"

So it was like that. "Okay, Bud Light."

She slid onto the stool next to Spoons. "So what's going on?"

The bartender put a beer in front of Madison and another double in front of Spoons. He drank half of it. "It's already been a fucked-up week. I'm sick of that freaky little gnome back there. Fucking thing's weirding me out."

"What did you see?" She sipped her beer.

He took another sip. "Thing's frozen inside. Ice cold and hard as a rock."

"Which is weird."

"No shit, it's weird. What's really weird is that the outside wasn't frozen."

"Well, it probably thawed out, right?"

"No, I mean it was never frozen. You know what happens when you freeze tissue, what happens to the cells?"

"Yeah, they rupture. From the expansion of the ice crystals."

"Exactly. The water in the cells expands, pops all the cell membranes. So, I was trying to figure out what made those two cuts, those holes in the hip and the shoulder. I put it under a microscope. Didn't learn anything about what did the cutting, but the cells there showed no damage at all—not just no damage like you'd get from a blade or something, but no damage like you'd get from freezing, either. I wasn't looking for freezing, but the fact that there was no damage at all, it stood out, you know?"

"So how did it get frozen on the inside?"

He drained the glass and turned to her. "Fucking exactly. And what does it have to do with those freaky wires in the thing's head, that's the other thing."

He put the glass down on the bar and put a few bills next to it. "Fuck it," he said, motioning for the bartender. "One more and then I'm going home."

She took a few sips of beer but neither of them spoke.

"Okay," she said finally, "I gotta get going."

Spoons didn't offer her a ride and she didn't want one. It was just a few blocks back to the medical examiner's building, and she needed to think. A brisk walk and some fresh air would help clear her mind.

By the time she got there, she at least had an idea.

She told Tate that Spoons had gone out for "lunch" and that he was probably gone for the day. He nodded knowingly. Madison engaged him with some small talk before asking him if she could take some more samples from the body.

After seeing it so crowded earlier, the autopsy room now

seemed quieter than ever. It was the first time Madison had ever seen the room without Spoons in it.

Tate wheeled the body in and lifted off the chest plate, releasing an invisible cloud of stench. Madison took out a high-speed saw and flicked it on. The high-pitched whine filled the quiet room, then deepened as she touched it to the frozen liver. She sliced away a small section and placed it in the specimen vial. As she capped the vial, she smiled up at Tate. "Thanks."

After Tate set her up with a microscope, she used a razor to shave off a thin sliver of tissue, sawing back and forth to get through the mass.

She put the sliver on a slide and placed it under the microscope, fiddling with the knobs until the image came into focus. "Son of a bitch," she whispered.

Ten minutes on the Internet helped confirm her suspicions.

As she hurried back to the bar, she gave Aidan a quick call.

"What's up?" he asked, and Madison found herself wondering what he meant by that.

"You find anything else on that fluid?" she asked.

He laughed. "In the last two hours, you mean? No. Why?"

"I think it's vitrification fluid."

"Vitrification fluid? You mean, like a cryoprotectant?"

"Exactly."

"Hmm. I don't know. The only cryoprotectants I know are ethylene glycols, like antifreeze, or glucose-based bioagents. This doesn't seem like either of those. I could look into it, I guess. Why?"

She was just walking up to Smokey Joe's. "You know what? I'll tell you about it later. Give me a call if you find anything else."

"I always do."

AN HOUR had passed since she had left the bar, but she knew Spoons was the kind of drinker who rarely meant it when he said, "One more and then I'm going home."

He was right where she'd left him, working on another double scotch.

With lunch under way, the place had filled up a little, and

the young jocks filing into the place made Spoons look even smaller and older perched on his stool. As she made her way toward the bar, she had to throw a few looks to keep the frat boys at bay.

One of them, a guy with a big, shaggy thatch of hair in front of his eyes, apparently missed the visual cues. He came on undeterred and she had to hold up a hand.

"Don't," she said sternly, stopping him in his tracks.

As she resumed her place on the stool next to Spoons, his head swiveled over to look at her. He looked back at his drink, shaking his head.

"I took a sample of the liver. I looked at it under the microscope, and guess what?"

Spoons looked at her sideways. "What?"

"No signs of freezing there, either."

Spoons laughed, tired, but not too tired to patronize her. "Sorry, sweetheart, the liver is the big, dark squishy thing on top of the stomach." He patted his midsection, "Or sometimes not so squishy, something I probably have in common with that little fuck."

She smiled sweetly. "I know that."

"Well, you did something wrong. That liver was definitely frozen."

"How do you know?"

"Well," he said slowly. "When I touched it with my hand, it was as cold as ice and hard as a rock."

"Yeah, I know. It was ice cold and hard as a rock when I took my sample. I had to cut it off with a high-speed saw."

"Well, there you go. It was frozen. And I don't know how." She shook her head adamantly. "Not frozen . . . *glassified*."

"Look, kid, I'm fucking beat. What the fuck are you talking about?"

She placed a small sheaf of papers on top of the bar. "Glassified. The body was *vitrified*. The yellow stuff is vitrification fluid. They infuse bodies with it, flush out as much of the blood as possible so that the water doesn't crystallize when they freeze it." She stopped herself. "No, not freeze it, when they cool it down to two hundred degrees below zero. When they *glassify* it."

Spoons was looking at her like she had two heads. "Who's 'they'?"

"The people who do this. They replace as much water as possible, so that when they thaw the body out and try to resuscitate it, the cells aren't all ruptured. Here's the thing: that body was cryonically preserved."

"What, you mean like Walt Disney?"

"No. I've been doing some reading and apparently that's an urban myth, but like Ted Williams. That's for real. Yes."

"Cryonically preserved . . ." Spoons thought for a moment before looking up. "What about those wires sticking out of its head? What's up with them?"

"Crack mikes."

"What?"

"Crack mikes." She leafed through the papers and pulled one out. "Even with the vitrification, they have to be extremely careful when they're cooling down the bodies. They implant tiny microphones into the heads of the patients, so that if the brain starts to crack, they can slow down the process."

" 'If the brain starts to crack . . . ' " He was giving her the "two heads" look again. "That's some crazy shit."

She shrugged. "Maybe, maybe not. I'll tell you, you read up on it, some of it starts to make sense."

"Jesus Christ," he said, suddenly sounding more sober. "So where does this take us?"

"Well, I need to talk to the lieutenant. There's only three places in the country that do this sort of thing." She shrugged. "Maybe one of them is missing a body."

CHAPTER 11

WHEN SHE went in to talk to the lieutenant, he had been standing behind his desk with his eyes closed, one hand holding the phone to his ear and the other hand wrapped around his forehead, massaging his temples with his thumb and forefinger.

Judging from his end of the conversation, he seemed to be enduring some kind of lecture about overtime costs. Madison sat quietly until he ended the call with a promise to rein in overtime and catch up on his paperwork.

When he put down the phone, he gave her a weary smile.

"What is it, Madison?"

"Well, it's about that Germantown Avenue body, the weird one."

"Wasn't Spoons doing the autopsy today?"

"Yes, but it turns out the body was, well, frozen in the middle. So Spoons has to let it thaw first."

The lieutenant's eyes widened. "Frozen?"

"Well, actually . . . technically no, not exactly frozen. Here's the thing . . ."

He listened intently as she told him about the attempted autopsy and what she had learned about cryonic preservation, glassification, vitrification, and crack mikes.

He sighed. "Well, that's quite a story, Maddy. So what do you plan to do next?"

His phone started ringing again and he sighed.

"Well," she began, "there are only three places in the country that do that sort of thing. I think we should send an investigator to question each one, see if they've had any break-ins, or if they have somehow misplaced a body."

The lieutenant smiled and let out a quiet snort that with a little more energy might have been a laugh. "Well that's definitely not going to happen. We don't have the time or resources for anything like that, especially not this week."

His eyes darted in the direction of the phone and his hand inched toward it.

"Well, they should at least call the places," she said, "see what information they can get on it."

He shook his head. "Maddy, we're swamped, you know that."

"It's just a couple phone calls."

His hand was on the handset.

"Maybe we could have the local police go talk to them," she offered.

He shook his head impatiently. "Tell you what, why don't you call them. See if you can find anything." He picked up the handset, letting her know they were just about done. "Let me know how it goes."

He picked up the phone and started defending his latest requisitions, swiveling his chair away from Madison, in case she hadn't glommed onto the fact that their conversation was over.

She returned to her desk and looked at the list of cryonics facilities.

This was not exactly how she had envisioned the next phase of the investigation.

The first place she called was Mizar Incorporated in New Mexico, the largest of the three facilities. Most of what she had learned about cryonics on the internet had been sponsored or underwritten by Mizar, often in conjunction with some prominent university.

Madison identified herself, explained the situation and asked her question. The woman on the other end listened patiently, and then said, "Absolutely not."

She seemed offended by the question, but she agreed to take down Madison's contact information.

The second call was a small, for-profit facility in New York State, the Pollan Institute. Again, Madison identified herself to the woman who answered the phone, explained the situation and asked her question.

This time, the woman paused for some time before saying, "Um . . . definitely not."

"Are you sure?" Madison pressed.

"Yes. Absolutely," she said, much more quickly. "That's totally ridiculous." From what Madison had read, it made a certain amount of sense for people in the field of cryonics to be a little defensive. With all the strange rumors and urban myths they had to deal with, it was understandable.

"Okay," she said. "Well, if you hear of anything like that, it's very important that you give me a call."

The woman took Madison's information and hung up.

The third call was to a place in northern Illinois called United Cryonics. This time a young guy answered.

As soon as she started her spiel, the young guy started laughing. "Sorry, I'm not even the regular receptionist, so I don't know anything about any of that. Hold on, before I forget, what's your name and telephone number?"

Madison told him.

"Well, actually, Ms. Cross, everybody's in a meeting, so could you maybe call back in like a half hour or so?"

"Sure, but let me just ask you this: the body we've found appears to have been cryonically preserved and we're wondering if there's any chance you could be missing anyone, if you've had any break-ins or anything."

"No." He laughed again. "I'm pretty sure there's nothing like that. They run a pretty tight operation here. Same thing with Mizar. Did you try Pollan?"

"Why do you ask?"

"No, nothing. They just . . . they've had their problems, that's all."

"Problems like what?"

"They had a guy there named Troy Purnell. I think he got fired about a year ago. He might know about some of that stuff."

"Like what? What kind of stuff?"

She heard voices in the background and he laughed nervously. "You know what, that meeting is over now, and they're all coming out. I should probably go."

"Just a couple of quick questions."

"I probably shouldn't have been talking about any of this."

"The vitrification fluid, what does it smell like?"

"Stuff smells like shit," he said in a hushed tone. "But seriously, I can't be talking to you, so, do you want to talk to someone else? 'Cause I gotta go."

"Well," she replied, "actually, I . . ."

But he had already hung up on her. He had done it so quietly, she had to look at her phone to make sure.

Walking into the lieutenant's office to tell him how the calls had gone, the first thing she saw was Melissa Rourke's black scuffed boots, her legs stretched out across the floor. She didn't look particularly busy at the moment, but she definitely looked like she had been. She was sitting in the lieutenant's armchair with her hands clasped behind her neck. Her freckles were almost obscured by ash and soot and her reddish curls were dusty and gray.

She smelled like a rained-out campfire.

The lieutenant was talking about the Oxford case, relaying his concerns about overtime.

Rourke's eyes swiveled over to look at Madison and blinked once in greeting.

"Hey, Rourke. How you doing?"

Rourke shook her head. "Fried."

Madison sniffed the air. "Smells more like oven-roasted."

Rourke smiled but she was obviously too tired to laugh. "Heard you been having an interesting week, too."

"One thing after another."

Madison told them she had called all three cryonics facilities and asked if they were missing any bodies.

Rourke chuckled. "You just called them and asked them?" she asked. "Did you ask if they were cheating on their taxes, too?"

"What do you mean?" Madison said defensively.

The lieutenant shifted uncomfortably.

"Nothing," Rourke said, shaking her head. "Actually, police work would be a lot easier if you could just call your suspects and ask them if they did it."

"Hey, *I* wanted to send someone to ask them in person," Madison protested. "I was told to just call them."

Rourke cocked an eyebrow and looked at the lieutenant.

He laughed awkwardly. "You both know there's no budget for that kind of thing, and so far, we don't even know for sure there was a crime. Abuse of corpse, maybe—and you're right, it is quite a corpse—but I can't be flying people all over the country for that, or even wasting my investigators' time when they have more important things to do."

Rourke shrugged, conceding the point.

The lieutenant looked at Madison. "So did you turn up anything?"

She shook her head. "No."

"Okay, well maybe if Spoons finds something more, we can talk about putting more resources into it. But until then, it's Spoons' problem, not ours."

IT TOOK six rings, but Spoons finally did answer.

"Hey, Spoons, it's Madison."

"Great."

"How you doing?"

"About how you'd probably think."

His words weren't slurred, but his voice seemed to be weaving back and forth. Several hours had passed since he'd started drinking. If he'd been maintaining his previous pace, he would have put away a lot of booze by now.

"Are you home?" she asked.

He laughed softly at the question. "Yeah, I'm home." He took a deep breath and she could hear ice cubes clinking as he took a sip.

"I called the cryonics places."

"Anybody missing any body?" He snickered.

"I don't know. They said they weren't."

He had a good laugh at that, then it turned into a cough.

"The lieutenant doesn't want to put anything into it until we have something that says a crime was committed."

"You know what, kid?" Clink. "Let's talk about it tomorrow."

* * *

AT FIVE minutes to five, the Crime Scene Unit was empty. The entire unit had been putting in extra hours on the Oxford case, and now that things had eased up a bit, they had all cleared out.

Madison might not have been working the Oxford case, but she had been working. She had finished the DNA profile on "the gnome" as Spoons called it, but it didn't match anything on any of the databases.

Ballistics had come back on the bullets from the gas station scene. Lots of information but nothing useful.

It had been a long day, and her own fatigue was just starting to hit her when her phone rang.

"Hello?"

"Hello," said a quiet voice that sounded vaguely familiar. "Is this Madison Cross?"

"Yes, who's this?"

"Did you call the Pollan Institute a couple hours ago?" It was the woman who had answered the phone there.

Madison grabbed a pen and a pad, started scribbling. "Yes, I did. Why?"

"You were asking if the institute was, um, missing any bodies, right?"

"Yes, I was. Why? Are they?"

"Not really . . ." The second thoughts were almost audible over the phone line.

Madison stayed quiet.

"Okay, here's the thing," the woman said quickly. "I've been here about a year and a half. There was a guy named Troy who used to work here, a technician. Anyway, about a year ago this rich guy comes in, wants some kind of custom contract."

"What do you mean, a custom contract?"

"He wants to get prepped, you know, the whole thing, vitrified, preserved, everything. But then, instead of getting stored here, he wants to be kept somewhere private, at his house or something. His estate. Apparently, he was really rich."

"So what happened?"

"Oh, the administrators said no, right off the bat. It didn't matter how much money this guy had, that's just not something they do here. I mean the storage is as important as anything else, you know?"

"Right . . . So what happened?"

"Basically, Dr. Pollan found out that Troy went ahead and did it anyway. Dr. Pollan's not here all that much anymore. He's getting pretty old, you know? Probably be here full time soon, if you know what I mean. Anyway, Troy must have set something up on the side with the rich guy, because when he, you know, passed, they brought him in here and Troy got him all prepped, only instead of getting him into a tank, he let them take the rich guy away."

"Who is 'them'?"

"I don't know. They fired Troy when they found out. Right there on the spot. He disappeared after that. I hope he got a lot of money for it."

"Where did they take the rich guy?"

"I don't know, wherever he made his arrangements. I think he was from Pennsylvania or something."

The woman on the phone paused and Madison scribbled furiously, trying to catch up.

"I gotta go," the woman whispered. "If I get caught calling you, I'll get fired like Troy, only I'm not getting paid on the side."

"Wait, wait, wait. The rich guy, what was his name?"

"MacClaren," she said quietly. "Robert MacClaren."

A SEARCH through the archives of the *Philadelphia Inquirer* brought up eighty-seven mentions of Robert MacClaren. Most of them were on the business page, a dozen were in society columns, and three or four in metropolitan. Two were in the obituaries.

Madison scanned a sampling of the business stories. They described an impressive real estate and financial empire, tracking the mergers and acquisitions as MacClaren's business had grown over the course of thirty years from a one-man operation into Claren Incorporated, a conglomerate worth many millions.

The society columns described MacClaren's participation

and support of charitable events for a number of pet causes, including a cancer fund and several local hospitals. Photos showed him with his wife, Ruth; they were a handsome couple in their early fifties to late sixties, usually in a tux and a gown.

MacClaren was stout but solid looking, robust, with a shock of thick white hair. In each of the pictures, Ruth Mac-Claren always looked comfortably elegant and Robert looked like his cummerbund was too tight.

It was hard to imagine the man in the pictures turning into the creature they had found curled up on that mattress.

As she clicked through a couple more pages, she saw a few mentions in the Metro section, and the two listings in the obituaries. The first obituary, dated seven years ago, was for Ruth, loving wife and mother, and a tireless volunteer.

The second obituary was for Robert MacClaren, businessman, philanthropist, fly-fishing enthusiast. Survived by his son, Toby. The service was private.

He'd been dead for just over a year.

"A YEAR?!" Spoons exclaimed when she told him. "Jesus."

"He was in the deep freeze, remember?" Madison reminded him.

"Still, that's pretty fucking impressive," he said begrudgingly, his words slurring more now. "Stunk like hell, but he looked pretty fresh inside."

"Yeah. The vitrification fluid stinks all right, but it seems like it might actually work."

He snorted dismissively. "Big difference between looking fresh and coming back from the fucking dead. They'll never be able to do that."

"They've come pretty close," she said.

He laughed. "What do you mean?"

"I read about it in med school. I forgot about it until I saw it online, but they've done organ transplants in animals, using the vitrification fluid. A rabbit liver, I think. They vitrified it, froze it, then thawed it out later and implanted it. Worked fine."

"You think they can do the same thing with whole people?"

"Not today, but maybe someday. And that's the point. Once you're frozen, you got nothing but time."

He grunted, conceding the point if not the argument. "Still fucking nuts. Anyway, you tell the lieutenant about this yet?"

"It's my next call."

"MADDY!" AUNT Ellie exclaimed when she answered the phone. "To what do we owe this surprise?" she said, her delight quickly turning to sarcasm.

"Hi, Aunt Ellie," Madison said sheepishly. It had been a while since she and Ellie had spent any time together. "I was just calling . . ."

"Just calling to see how I'm doing? To catch up? To chat? That's so sweet."

"I know, I know, I haven't seen you much lately. I'm sorry."

"Lately? No, *lately* you haven't seen me at all. In fact, you haven't even been calling me back."

"I'm sorry, but . . ."

"But that's why you're calling me now?"

"Well . . ."

"Well, actually, you're calling for Uncle David, right?"

Madison took a quiet breath.

"I'll get him for you in a second, but first, I want a lunch date."

"A date?"

"Lunch."

"A week from Friday?"

"I'll see you at one. Hold on."

She heard Aunt Ellie's palm covering the mouthpiece, and the muffled "David! Maddy's on the phone!" She came back on the phone and repeated, "See you a week from Friday."

A couple of seconds later, her uncle came on the phone. "Hey, Maddy girl."

"Hi, Lieuten—I mean, hi, Uncle Dave."

He laughed. "Tricky sometimes, isn't it?"

"Sometimes it is," she agreed.

"What's a week from Friday?"

"Lunch."

"Oh, good. You know, you really should keep in touch with your aunt Ellie. I see you all the time at work, but she hardly ever gets to see you."

"I know, Uncle Dave."

"So, what's up?"

"I just wanted to let you know, I think I have an ID on our John Doe."

"The mummy case? Really?"

"Pretty sure. None of the places I called were missing any bodies, but someone at one of them said that another one, the Pollan Institute, had a history of irregularities. Then I actually got a call back from someone at Pollan." She filled him in on what the woman had said.

He grunted when she was done. "Who's the rich guy?"

"Said his name was Robert MacClaren."

"Robert MacClaren . . . Name sounds familiar."

"Businessman, local. Built his little company into a big one. Had some charities and stuff."

"Claren Incorporated?"

"That's the guy."

"Any family?"

"A son named Toby. He lives in the city, over in Society Hill. That appears to be it."

"Those calls paid off. That's good police work, Maddy girl," he said, sounding a little indulgent. "I'm sure the family will be grateful to have the body back. You ran DNA from the body, right?"

"Yes. No matches, though. With the state of the body, I don't know for sure that the DNA isn't damaged somehow."

"Why don't you and Rourke go see the son tomorrow, tell him about the situation without getting into too much detail, without upsetting him. See if you can get a sample to compare it to."

"Right."

"Good work, Maddy."

CHAPTER 12

TOBY MACCLAREN lived in a massive old Society Hill brick house that looked like a row home from the outside. Until you noticed certain subtle differences.

The first were the window boxes and shutters. Then the marble steps in the front, with the treads worn smooth from a couple of centuries of use. When you looked left and right, you noticed that instead of window, door, window, door, like in South Philly, this block was window, window, window, door, window, window, stairway down to the servant's entrance.

Madison and Rourke had decided the night before to get there early, talk to the guy face-to-face before he left for work. The morning rush was already in high gear on the outskirts of the city, but it would be another forty minutes before most of that traffic made its way into the heart of town.

Rourke had grilled her on the drive over, asking her to repeat some of the stranger details.

By the time they got out of the car in front of Toby MacClaren's house, Rourke had a slight grimace etched across one side of her face, like she had a bad taste in the back of her throat.

"So what exactly are we doing here?" she asked, resting one foot on the cast-iron boot scraper embedded in the brick sidewalk.

Madison shrugged. "We're just telling the guy we may have recovered his father's body. We ask him if it had been preserved, if so, where, and if he knew anything about it being missing. And we'll see if he can give us a DNA sample, so we can confirm the identity."

Rourke nodded but she still looked dubious. "I'll follow your lead."

As Madison ascended the steps, the trappings of wealth became more evident. The heavy, double front door had a flawless coating of thick, glossy royal-blue paint. The knocker was a lion's head that looked as if, at any moment, it could turn into the ghost of Marley.

Rourke rapped the door with her knuckles.

The block had an air of old money, but Madison knew that it hadn't always been that way. Until it was gentrified in the late sixties the place had been a dump, struggling even to remain working class.

Still, when a horse-drawn carriage turned up the block, heading toward Independence Hall, it felt like a scene from long ago. The costumed driver was stony-faced, saving his charm for the tourists. If not for the cars parked on one side of the street or Society Hill Towers looming in the sky behind them, it could easily have been two hundred years earlier. As the hooves clicked through the next intersection, Madison reflected that one of the things she had missed out West was a sense of permanence.

A cab suddenly turned the corner way too fast, blaring its horn as it screeched to a halt behind the carriage. Madison jumped, jarred from her reverie, and before she could regain her composure, the door swung open.

Toby MacClaren looked more like his mother than his father. He was slim and handsome, with a long neck and an unlined face of indeterminate age. His blond hair was a little bit longer than Madison would have expected.

His smile was open and casual, revealing teeth that were even and white.

"Hello," he said, almost bemused. Everything about him said wealth without too much responsibility. He was wearing an expensive suit and no shoes, his tie draped loosely around his neck, untied.

Madison smiled back.

"Hi. My name is Madison Cross. This is Melissa Rourke. We're with the Philadelphia police."

His smile faltered for a moment, the way smiles usually did when you told people you were with the police. But when it came back, it was even wider.

"Really?" he said, as if he thought that was absolutely charming.

"We were hoping we could have a word with you."

He laughed.

"Really?" he said again. "Um . . . sure. Would you like to come in?" He stepped back and opened the door wider, grinning.

"Thank you." Madison stepped past him.

Rourke followed her, giving MacClaren a sidelong glance up and down and rolling her eyes slightly as she stepped past him.

They were standing in a two-story foyer with rich red walls, lots of dark wood, and a plush Persian rug over black-and-white marble tiles.

"So, what can I do for you?" MacClaren asked, glancing in a mirror over Madison's shoulder as he casually tossed one end of the tie over the other, then once again, effortlessly tucking it through to produce a perfect Windsor.

"We actually wanted to ask you a few questions about your father," Madison said.

He was leaning against the wall, pulling on a loafer, but at the mention of his father, he stopped. "My father?" he said, surprised. "My father's dead."

"We know," Madison replied. "And we're sorry for your loss. Could you tell us where your father is interred?"

His smiled flattened out, a thin, grim line across his face.

"My father was a great man," he said. "He worked hard all his life, and he aided many worthwhile causes."

Madison waited while he pulled on his second shoe.

"In answer to your question," he went on, "no. No, I don't know where my father is interred. Is that all you want to know?" He said it like a challenge, but his eyes were moist.

"I'm sorry to have to ask about this, Mr. MacClaren, but do you know if your father had any interest in cryonic preservation?"

MacClaren's shoulders slumped and he leaned back against the wall. "Yes," he said quietly. "He did." He looked up at Madison, his eyes full of pain. "What happened?"

Madison looked at Rourke for guidance, but Rourke stepped back and shook her head.

"We found a body," Madison said quietly. "It was partially frozen. Actually, it appeared to have been cryonically preserved."

"Is it . . . ?"

"We don't know."

Rourke stepped in again. "I know this is difficult, but we have to ask again . . . Do you know where your father's remains are kept?"

He looked down and shook his head.

Rourke looked confused. "Why is it that you don't know where your own father was . . . interred?"

Toby MacClaren assumed an indignant look, but he couldn't maintain it. His face sagged. "I know, it sounds terrible. And I was very hurt at first, but . . . my father was a very proud man. A very private man. And he liked to be in control. He knew I didn't approve of . . . all that . . . He didn't want to make me participate. And I think he didn't want me to see him in that state." He laughed bitterly. "My shrink says my dad knew that if I thought of him in some . . . tank or something, somewhere, *preserved*, that I'd never come to terms with the fact that he was actually dead." He laughed again. "Like it was okay for *him* not to come to terms with his own mortality, but *I* had to."

His eyes slowly drifted back down to the marble floor. "So someone found where he was . . . kept." He looked up. "Where was he?"

Rourke shook her head. "That, we don't know."

He looked back up. "Then . . . what is this about?"

"I'll tell you what, Mr. MacClaren," Madison cut in, afraid that Rourke was going to blurt out that they had found the body on a tattered mattress in a crack house in Kensington. "If you can give us something containing a sample of your father's DNA, we can run tests to verify our information, to see if we're even talking about your father before we start talking details."

MacClaren's eyes drifted off, staring blankly for a second, as if he'd forgotten he was not alone. He came back with a slight start and a confused look. "What?"

Rourke flicked a glance at Madison. "I beg your pardon?"

"What would have his DNA on it? It's been over a year."

"Anything that he used personally: laundry, toothbrush, hairbrush. Anything like that."

He nodded silently and left the room, returning a few moments later with a leather grooming kit.

"This was my father's," he said softly, handing it to Madison. "It hasn't been cleaned or anything."

As she took the kit, she noticed a round, angry red mark, about a half inch across, on the back of MacClaren's hand, just peeking out from his cuff. She glanced at it, but tried not to stare, focusing her attention on the contents of the grooming kit: nail clippers, shaving kit, travel toothbrush, scissors.

"No one else would have used it?" Rourke asked.

He shook his head.

"Thank you," Madison said. "We'll get this back to you as soon as we can, and we'll let you know when we find out anything."

As soon as they were back in the car, Rourke turned to Madison. "Did you notice the burn?"

"The what?"

"The burn. On the back of his hand."

"I saw a mark, yeah," she said as they pulled away from the curb. "Is that what it was? I guess it did look like a burn."

"A cigarette burn," Rourke said with a leer. "Don't let the white-bread act fool you."

"What do you mean?"

"I knew a guy once who used to have marks like that. Turned out he was into all this S and M stuff. Kinky as shit."

Madison smiled and gave her a skeptical look. "Too kinky even for you?"

Rourke laughed. "Just a little bit."

ROURKE GOT a call on the way back to headquarters, so Madison dropped her off at her car. When she got back to the crime lab, Madison saw her own message light was blinking and experienced a tiny, momentary pang of woe. By her calculation, roughly seven times out of ten it was bad news.

This time it was Sanchez in microscopy. Could have been a lot worse.

"Hey, Madison. Nothing urgent, but you should come down here when you get a chance. I have something interesting to show you."

Madison smiled to herself. The definition of "interesting" had changed somewhat over the previous couple of days.

She finished prepping the DNA sample from MacClaren's travel toothbrush and went down to see what Sanchez had for her.

When she walked into the microscopy lab, Sanchez was sitting on a stool in front of a digital microscope. On a video monitor next to her was an image that looked vaguely like a flagstone patio. But on closer look, it appeared more like a flagstone patio to which someone had taken a sledgehammer.

As Madison studied the image, Sanchez rose and stood behind her, looking over her shoulder—watching Madison, but also studying the image some more.

"Okay, what is it?" Madison asked.

"Tissue from the Dawber body. Spoons sent it over here, wanted me to check for trace residues or tool marks or anything. I didn't find anything like that, but I did find this." She gestured at the screen.

Madison squinted. "There's serious cell damage. Looks like all the cell membranes are broken."

"That's what it looks like to me, too," Sanchez replied. "But why?"

Madison shrugged. "What kind of weapon would do that?"

"I don't know," Sanchez said. "The breaks are all in different directions. Different sides of the cells."

"Looks pretty traumatic."

"I know. The cut looked really clean, but up close it's a mess."

"Did you tell Spoons?"

"Left him a message right before I called you." She made a face. "Now I get to call Fenton."

As they were laughing, Madison's phone went off. "All right," she said as she took out her phone. "Thanks for the heads up, Elena."

She stepped out into the hallway before answering. "Hello?"

"Hey, Madison." It was Rourke. "I'm down at Graduate Hospital. They have a DOA with a GSW. Someone parked him in a stolen car in the hospital parking lot. Lieutenant asked me to come down and dust the vehicle. Anyway, Tate and Velasquez are coming to pick up the body; Lieutenant said he thought you might want to have a look first."

"Why?"

"Name on the driver's license is Frank McGee."

ROURKE WAS waiting for her in the hallway outside the hospital's morgue. She looked pretty beat, but not too beat to be chatting with a young doctor in scrubs. When she saw Madison, she whispered something to the doctor and a moment later he left.

Madison smiled. "Did I interrupt something?"

"Just trying to make my mom happy," Rourke said with a wink. "A doctor and all." She stepped backward and shouldered open a heavy swinging door. "In here."

Frank McGee was lying on a gurney, fully clothed but with his shirt and jacket open. He looked like it had taken him a while to die. His face was still locked in a grimace, like death had not relieved his pain. His fists were tightly clenched and there was blood around his chin and around his mouth.

His close-cropped hair was graying and his face looked substantially older than forty-two, but it was very possible that he had aged considerably in the last few days.

"Have you looked at him?" Madison asked, pulling back the right side of the shirt to get a better look at the small black hole in his side. The skin around it was bruised and bloody. There was no exit wound.

Rourke shrugged. "Shirt's soaked with blood, but there's no hole in it."

"So he at least changed his shirt. Maybe the rest of it, too, huh?"

Rourke pulled the shirt up more. A bloody clump of gauze and tape was stuck to the inside. "Someone field dressed the wound. I guess they at least tried. Probably trying to avoid the hospital's reporting requirement, put off bringing him in until it was too late."

"Is this the only wound?"

"Looks like. Spoons'll tell us for sure."

"How did they find him?"

"Someone called. Anonymous tip. Said there was a guy in a car out back. He was alive when they got to him, but only just. Dead by the time they got him in here. Car'd been stolen a half hour earlier, three blocks away. Owner didn't even know it was missing. I had a quick look inside, but it looked clean except for the blood in the backseat. I threw some dust down, a little bit, but there's no prints on the doors or the wheel. It's been wiped."

Madison took out her cell phone and punched in a number.

"You calling Ted Johnson?" Rourke asked.

"What?" she asked, but as she did, someone answered on the other end.

"Madison?" said the voice on the phone.

"Hi, Matt," she said, turning slightly away from Rourke's confused look. "Hey. Just wanted to let you know we got another body."

"Jesus, they're dropping like flies. Who is it this time?"

"Another one of your gas station customers. Frank McGee. The older guy, the one whose blood we found next to pump number two."

"Think it was the wound from the gas station that killed him?"

Madison paused, aware of the jurisdictional issues involved. "Hard to say. It looks like there's just the one wound, but we won't know until the ME gets a look at him. No exit wound, so the slug's still in him."

"Hmm." He paused. "Okay, so it looks like Washburn's gang took one of the other team with them."

"Maybe."

"So when are they taking him to the ME?"

"Probably in the next hour or so."

"Is Ted there? What does he think about it?"

"Actually, I have to call him right now."

"Huh." He sounded surprised.

Madison realized she should have called Ted Johnson first.

"Okay," Boone continued. "Well, thanks for letting me know so soon. I got nothing new on the Jimmy Dawber thing, but I'll let you know as soon as I do."

"Thanks."

"No, thank you. I mean it."

As soon as he was gone, she started punching in Ted Johnson's number, but Rourke started in before the first ring.

"Who was that?" she demanded.

"The guy who's jurisdiction this probably occurred in."

She grunted, then hooked a thumb at the body on the gurney. "So, what's the story on this guy?"

Madison closed her phone and took a deep breath before launching into the story, starting with the gangbanger on the expressway. She told Rourke about the trip out to Lawson and everything else.

Rourke played with an earring thoughtfully. "So that was Boone you were talking to? I know Matt Boone. Friend of Ted Johnson's, right? He's cute."

Madison quickly flipped open her phone to call Ted Johnson.

"So why did you call Boone first?" Rourke asked, but by then Johnson had answered.

"Yo, Cross. What's up?" Johnson asked.

"Got ourselves a dead Frank McGee," she replied, ignoring Rourke's question.

"No shit?" Johnson replied. "Talk to me."

As she explained the situation, the door swung open and Tate and Velasquez rolled in an empty gurney.

"Hmm. You better call Boone," he told her. "Could turn out this is his case."

"Yeah, I did."

"You did, huh?" He laughed. "This could get tricky, jurisdiction-wise."

"I know it."

"Does Frank McGee still have a bullet in him?"

"Yeah, I think so. I didn't see an exit wound. Why?"

"If ballistics ties it to one of the shooters at the gas station, that could settle the jurisdiction issue."

"Right."

"So what's going on now?"

"The boys from the ME just showed up. We'll see what Spoons has to say."

"All right, so . . ." His voice crapped out for a second. "I got another call. I'll meet you over there, okay?"

ROURKE SAID she'd stay behind at the hospital and process the car, even though she could already tell it had been wiped down pretty good.

"Even smart guys fuck up," she said.

Madison drove along behind Tate and Velasquez, relieved that Rourke wasn't riding with her. She didn't want to be stuck in a car with her, answering questions about why she called Boone before she called Johnson.

She wanted a little time alone with that question first.

There was no doubt that Boone was attractive—that hint of swagger, his sense of humor, and the vague vulnerability behind his strong eyes. But she wondered if part of her interest was that it had been so long since she had met someone new, someone who wasn't in the Philly PD.

She pulled into the back entrance as Tate and Velasquez were getting out of the van. Johnson was already there, leaning against the wall next to the back door. He nodded his greeting to Tate and Velasquez and approached Madison's car as she got out.

"Busy week, huh?" he asked.

"So far."

WHEN THEY walked into the exam room, Spoons was already doing a preliminary exam. His gloved index finger was poking deep inside the hole in Frank McGee's chest. He shook his head and pulled it out, covered in blood. "Nah."

"What can you tell us, Frank?" Johnson asked.

"What can I tell you?" he said sarcastically. "I can tell you I'm busy as shit and I'm pretty sure this guy died of a bullet wound to the chest. What else do you want to know?"

"Come on, Spoons," Johnson cajoled.

He sighed. "Okay, here's something. The wound was pretty inflamed and showed some signs of healing. I can tell you already he'd been running around with that hole in his side for at least a day. That's about all I can give you."

Madison smiled sweetly. "It would be nice if we could get the bullet."

"You guys want the bullet, huh?" Spoons laughed. "No shit. Unfortunately, its deep in there somewhere. That's going to have to wait until I do some cutting."

"When's that going to be?" Johnson asked.

Spoons shook his head. "You know how fucking backed up I am? I'm gonna need a fucking ice cream truck or something, keep all these stiffs cold."

"Come on, Spoons," Madison pleaded. "We're not asking for anything else. Just get us the bullet."

He shook his head but slipped his finger back into the hole. "I don't think so. Thing's probably banging around inside a lung or something." He wiggled his finger around, looking off into space and biting his lip as he did so. ". . . Unless . . ." He pulled his finger out again and started massaging the flesh around the rib cage, feeling around toward the back.

"Let's see," he said with a grunt, rolling the body onto its side, revealing a purple-black oval-shaped bruise. He grinned. "Wait a second."

As Madison and Johnson looked on, he pulled out a plastic block and wedged it under one shoulder blade, keeping the body on its side. He picked up a scalpel with one hand and squeezed the flesh with the fingers of his other hand until he found the spot he was looking for.

He slid the scalpel in and drew a small semicircle. Blood welled up around the hole, and a fat droplet formed and slowly rolled down across Frank McGee's back. Sliding his finger into the body again, Spoons felt around for a second before coming out with a slightly flattened, blood-covered bullet.

"Who's the man, huh?" He grinned, holding it up between his thumb and forefinger before dropping it with a clink into a metal bowl.

"Thanks, Spoons."

Johnson smiled. "You the man, Sponholz."

"Now, if you'll excuse me, our dead citizens await."

CHAPTER 13

As MADISON and Johnson were getting into their cars, a Dodge Durango police vehicle with "Lawson Township" emblazoned across the side came bounding into the parking lot. It stopped with an audible screech, parking them in.

The window slid down and Matt Boone poked out his head. "Where y'all going?"

"Boonie!" Johnson yelled. "What the hell're you doing here?"

"Jesus, that was fast," Madison remarked.

Boone reached up and tapped the roof of his car. "What's the point of having woo-woo lights if you can't use 'em, right? I hear you got one of my stiffs." He grinned. "Gotta make sure you're not trying to pinch my case."

"You kidding?" Johnson protested. "You think my lieutenant wants to have another unsolved stiff up there on the board if he don't need to?"

There was a tightness around Johnson's mouth that belied his words. It seemed to Madison that if McGee had died from wounds sustained out in Lawson, the case was rightfully Boone's.

Johnson didn't seem like he was ready to let it go. He cocked his head combatively and opened his mouth, but Madison cut him off.

"Ballistics," she said, holding up the evidence bag with the bloody bullet. "We got the slug out of him."

"I was hoping you'd say that." Boone grinned and held up a larger evidence bag. "I brought my dead guy's thirty-eight."

Johnson smiled, but it still looked forced.

Boone's grin widened as he noticed Johnson's expression.

He glanced at Madison and arched an eyebrow, inviting her to have some fun at Johnson's expense. But she looked away before he could see her smile.

THEY TOOK three cars to the ballistics lab. A little excessive, Madison thought, but there was no telling where they'd each be headed next. Besides, she was glad to have some time alone to get used to Boone being there.

Johnson got there first. He parked between two empty spaces and Madison and Boone pulled in on either side of him.

"All right, Boonie," Johnson said, waiting for them as they got out. "Now, the guy we're seeing is a little weird."

"He's not weird," Madison scolded. "He's just kind of . . . stoic."

"Stoic?" Johnson laughed. "Catatonic is more like it. Just don't be freaked out, all right?"

"Shit, Ted," Boone replied. "You remember my dad. I grew up with catatonic."

Chuck Gerald opened the door to the lab and looked down at Madison, glancing over her shoulder at Johnson and Boone before coming back to rest on her once more.

"You again," he said flatly.

Before he could stop her, she held up her bag and launched into an explanation of how the jurisdiction of their case was riding on the ballistics on this bullet.

Gerald stared down at her, his face an odd combination of blankness and intensity.

When she finished, he remained quiet.

She fought the urge to keep talking.

Johnson and Boone were silent, too, standing behind her.

"Well, luckily we have absolutely nothing else to do today," Gerald said, his expression frozen.

In the City of Philadelphia, the ballistics lab was always busy. Madison knew he was being sarcastic, but his face betrayed nothing. She sometimes wondered if maybe one of his facial nerves had been nicked in the same attack that wounded his leg, but she was fairly sure that Gerald was aware of the effect his inscrutability had, and that he took concealed glee in using it to its utmost effect.

She smiled nervously, scanning his lips for the slightest quiver of a smile. There was none.

"Seriously, Chuck, we need this."

"I gather 'now' is already too late?" The burst of air that shot through his nose was the closest thing she'd ever seen to him actually laughing. "Okay," he said. "What have you got?"

She held up the bag holding the bloody slug from Frank McGee's body. "We need to see if this matches any of the others."

"Or this," Boone added, holding up the .38 he'd brought with him.

"All right," he said, turning. "Come on."

He maintained his military bearing even with the asymmetrical shuffle of his ruined left leg.

They followed him into the ballistics lab. He stepped into a small side room and stopped to put on gloves.

He opened the bag and dropped the bullet into a beaker. "Gotta clean it up first," he mumbled, filling the beaker with a couple of inches of water from a squirt bottle. The water in the beaker turned pink from the blood. Tiny bits and clots swirled around the slug.

He poured off the bloody water into a sink, refilled the beaker with fresh water, and poured it off again. Next he covered the bullet with an inch of bleach.

"Bleach," he said. "Disinfects it."

He looked up at Madison, ignoring Boone and Johnson. "Because you're not just handling a bullet from inside one person's body, you're handling a bullet from inside every body that body ever worked on, too."

He continued to stare at her, perhaps waiting for a reaction, but Madison had no idea what reaction that should be. She could hear Boone and Johnson fidgeting behind her, but she just stared back at Gerald.

When he finally issued that percussive, exhale-through-the-nose laugh, she smiled, figuring he had made a joke.

Gerald turned to the sink, but stopped short.

"Hmph. There's some kind of residue," he mumbled.

"What's that?" Madison asked, leaning closer. She could feel Johnson leaning closer behind her as well.

"On the top," Gerald elaborated. "Some kind of oily residue."

Several small beads of a clear liquid had risen to the surface of the water, spinning as the water beneath it slowly circled the beaker.

Using a pipette, Gerald sucked up the residue floating on the surface and squirted it into a different container.

He dumped out the bleach and held up the bullet. "Thirty-eight," he said, dropping it back into the bowl with a metallic click. He turned and carried the bowl out of the room.

Unlocking a gray metal locker under his desk, he took out a stack of tiny manila envelopes. He flicked through the envelopes, pulling out three of them. "Shouldn't take long. There's only three thirty-eight slugs in here."

Boone held up the evidence bag with the gun. "Plus this. Left at the scene."

Gerald sighed and took out a new manila envelope. He scribbled something across it, then slid the bullet inside. "Right."

He held out his hand and Boone handed him the gun.

They followed him once again through a heavy swinging door, and into a large room filled with rows of shelves, each packed with countless varieties of ammunition.

Gerald grabbed a box off one of the shelves without slowing a step. Loading a bullet into the gun as he walked, he led them to another door with a large darkened warning light above it.

They stepped through the door and into an even bigger room, this one with a firing range extending out fifty feet. Three overhead racks held torso-shaped paper targets at various distances. Off to the side was a large tank of water with a funnel apparatus attached to one end. Gerald flicked on the warning light as he walked up to the tank. He inserted the gun into the funnel apparatus and pulled the trigger.

Madison flinched, from the abruptness of the procedure as much as the sound. Behind the explosive report of the gunshot was a second noise, a brief sharp sound of turbulence.

Gerald opened the gun and took out the shell, then grabbed a pole that had been leaning against the wall. It was six feet long and at the end of it was an irregularly shaped hunk of what looked like old rubber cement. He poked it into the tank, jamming it down on top of the spent bullet. When he pulled the pole out, the bullet was stuck to the end of it.

Without a word, he slid the gun back into the evidence bag, handed it to Boone, and led them back out of the firing range.

They followed him into another small room, this one dominated by a large comparison microscope. A video monitor showed a split screen, two fields of gray and white. Attached to the microscope were two platforms, each with a fully positionable, articulated arm. At the end of each arm was another dirty-looking glob.

Plopping down onto the stool with a loud sigh, Gerald flicked through the stack of envelopes until he found the bullet they had taken out of Frank McGee. He shook the bullet into the palm of his hand and unceremoniously jammed it into one of the globs. He stuck the bullet he had just fired onto the glob on the other arm.

By manipulating various knobs and levers, he positioned the platforms so that each bullet was centered in one half of the split screen.

Next, he twisted a knob on the left arm, rotating that bullet until a series of five grooves came into view.

"Line up the rifling marks . . ." he said to himself, twisting the knob on the right and rotating that bullet until an almost identical series of five grooves appeared. He quickly lined up the two sides of the split screen so that the five grooves seemed to seamlessly begin on one bullet and end on the other.

When the images were precisely positioned, he turned a knob on the bottom of the microscope. The line between the two sides of the screen slowly wiped from right to left and then back, from left to right.

The three of them stared at the screen, rapt.

Initially, Madison had thought the bullets were definitely a match, but as she now watched, the differences became more and more noticeable. The bullet on the left had a series of three smaller grooves just above the five rifling marks. The bullet on the right had a single deep gouge running the length of the bullet, just below the five grooves.

He repeated the process with the rest of the .38 slugs, then announced, "The bullet from your victim does not match any of the others."

"SO WHAT'S next?" Boone asked when they got back outside. They were standing outside in the parking lot, next to their cars.

Johnson shrugged. "I already put the word out on the street, got guys looking into those other known associates, see if anything comes back. Nothing's turned up so far."

"What about Frank McGee's known associates?" Madison asked. "Maybe we could talk to some of them."

Johnson shook his head. "There wasn't much on there, right? I mean, all it really said was that he was known to have worked for Ralph Caprielli. It's not like we can just go talk to him."

"Why not?" Madison asked.

"Caprielli is big-time, Madison, a real gangster. You can't just go in there."

"Whoa, whoa, whoa," Boone cut in. "What do you mean we can't talk to him? We're the fucking police. We're investigating a homicide."

"Yeah," Johnson replied. "And we got nothing that makes him a suspect."

"So who said he's a suspect?" Boone countered. "It's one of his guys, he's going to want to know what happened to him."

Johnson frowned.

"Besides," Madison added. "What's the worst that could happen?"

"Jesus, Ted." Boone laughed. "Don't be such a fucking wuss."

Johnson glared at him for a second, then shook his head, resigned. "All right," he said. "All right, fuck it. Come on, Boone." He turned to Madison. "You wait here."

"Yeah, right," she scoffed.

"I'm serious, Madison," he said. "This dude's heavy-duty."

Madison rolled her eyes. "That's bullshit. Like Chief Boone said, 'We're the police.'"

"No," Johnson corrected her. "*We're* the police. *You're* a civilian."

She cocked her head at him. "Oh, please," she said dismissively. "We just want to ask a few questions. Come on, let's go."

"Cross, I'm serious."

Boone laughed. "She's got a point, Ted."

"Fuck you, Boone."

Boone responded with a big, friendly grin that Madison quickly mimicked.

Johnson's frown deepened. "Whatever. Okay. We'll take my car."

Boone bobbed his eyebrows at Madison and called, "Shotgun."

CHAPTER 14

THE ADDRESS they had for Ralph Caprielli was a cinder-block factory in southwest Philadelphia. The walls were painted an ugly green and the same color paint coated the ground level windows.

In the middle of the block, a driveway punched through the wall. The entrance was sealed with a solid metal gate, but a strip of sunlight was visible over the top of it. Next to the gate was a sturdy-looking metal door.

Two security cameras looked down from the second floor.

Johnson parked twenty feet up the block and turned to Madison, looking her in the eye. "This shit's for real, Cross. These guys are cold-blooded killers. So you stay quiet, okay? Don't say a word."

"Come on, Ted," Boone said with a snort. "Laying it on a little thick there, don't you think?"

"Fuck you, Boone. This ain't Lawson. You need to take this shit seriously, too."

Johnson redirected his glare toward Madison. "Stay back, stay out of the way, and stay the fuck quiet."

Madison put up her hands. "Just like always."

They strode in silence down the street toward the entrance. On the wall next to the door was an intercom and a keypad. Johnson pressed a button on the pad before they had even caught up with him.

A gruff, staticky voice asked, "Who is it?"

Johnson held his ID over his head for the benefit of the security cameras. "Police. We need to talk to Ralph Caprielli."

"About what?"

"We just need to ask him a few questions."

The intercom was quiet for a moment. Johnson turned and gave them a look.

The intercom crackled. "Do you have a warrant?"

"We're just here to ask a couple questions."

"You don't have a warrant, you can fuck off."

Johnson pressed the button again.

After a second, the staticky voice came back. "What?"

"I know we've been unable to put together a strong enough case to get a conviction, but do you really think it would be that difficult to come up with enough warrants to ruin your week? . . . Frank McGee is dead. We just want to ask a few questions, see if we can find out who did it."

The intercom was quiet for a few more seconds, then the door buzzed.

They stepped through the door and into a long, wide brick corridor. Bright sunlight shone at the far end, and along the sides were random gaps in the wall, dark holes between the bricks. The rest of the wall seemed to be in perfect condition, and Madison's heart gave a little hiccup when it occurred to her that those holes might be gun slots, so any unwelcome visitor could be mowed down without a hope of reaching the sunlight at the other end.

Johnson walked without hesitation, purposefully marching down the tunnel. Boone stepped closer to Madison, squaring his shoulders protectively as they followed.

The tunnel opened out into a bright, sun-filled atrium. One wall was made entirely of glass, and the tableau visible on the other side of it seemed like another world. They looked out onto a wide courtyard with a fountain, a picnic area dotted with a few early daffodils, and in the far corner, a small, manicured stand of trees. It appeared to be completely encircled by the building, but the way it was landscaped with shrubs and evergreens, you could barely see that the building was there.

They turned with a start at the sound of a throat being cleared. A receptionist was looking up at them from behind a sleek, wooden partition. She smiled professionally. "Mr. Caprielli is in the residence. He'll be with you in one moment."

Before they could fully take in their surroundings, a door

off to the side opened and two immense thugs in ill-fitting sport coats stepped out.

One stepped forward and reached out with his hands like he was going to pat Johnson down.

Johnson gave him a look and said, "Don't."

The thug looked at his buddy, who shrugged. "All right," he said. "This way."

They followed the thug in charge down a series of long hallways. The second thug followed ten paces back.

The place had a claustrophobic feeling, like it was sealed tight. The air had a canned smell to it and there was a strange hush, an absence of ambient sound. At the end of the third hallway was a doorway and a keypad with a red LED. The head thug pressed in five numbers with great deliberation and the light turned from red to green.

Again they stepped into a glass-enclosed room, but this one had a decidedly residential feel to it. To the left was a grand entrance and vestibule, and to the right was an opening into a luxuriously furnished living room decorated in deep hunter greens and burgundies. Through a large window you could see the courtyard. A pair of black SUVs were parked under a cherry tree.

The two goons led them into the hall and stopped next to a sofa and a love seat.

"Sit down," one of them said.

They didn't.

"Suit yourself," he said with a shrug, and they walked away, disappearing through a different doorway.

As they waited, a pair of small fluffy dogs walked up to them, one white, one black. Their little tails wagged in unison.

"Well, hello," Madison cooed, sitting on the sofa as she reached down to ruffle the dogs' ears. They both reared up onto their hind legs, a pair of front paws on each of her knees. "Oh, you like that, don't you," she said as the black one tried to lick her face.

As she looked up, she saw that Boone was shaking his head with a smile. Johnson was rolling his eyes at her. They were both still standing.

"What?" she asked defensively.

Johnson gave her a look of admonishment.

Madison stood up with an exasperated sigh. "I was just petting the dogs," she mumbled. As she stood, she brushed her hands against each other, trying to rid them of the black and white dog hairs clinging to them.

Meanwhile, the dogs were looking up at her, waiting for more attention.

"Yikes," she said, as the clump of dog hair finally drifted to the floor. Watching it, she noticed how much hair was also clinging to her pant legs.

"Oh no," she said, futilely brushing at her pants, then turning to see that the sofa was covered as well. "Oh no," she said again.

Then she heard a short, high-pitched whistle and a voice saying, "Nanook! Kimba!"

The dogs instantly darted across the room, parking at the feet of a short but solid-looking man with reddish hair and hard eyes. Ralph Caprielli.

He was probably about five-six, but the two men on either side of him made him appear shorter.

The one on his left was at least six foot five. He had dull eyes, a massive upper body, and hands that looked like they could palm a Volkswagen. His left hand was wrapped in a bandage.

The guy on Caprielli's right was even scarier. At maybe six-two, 220, he was nowhere near the size of his comrade, but he had an aura of quiet lethality.

Standing between his hired hands, Ralph Caprielli was easily overlooked at first. But he was where your attention finally rested. He had violently smoldering eyes, and his entire body seemed to crackle, like a stack of wood in the instant before it explodes into flame. It was obvious he did not like having police in his home or business or whatever the place was.

Madison scanned the faces in front of them. There was an innate hardness to them, and she couldn't shake the feeling that they were humans of a different type entirely. She wondered how many lives their hands had taken, and, just for a moment, thought that maybe Johnson was right—maybe she should have waited in the car.

Caprielli's right-hand man studied them with stony gray-blue eyes, staring intently, first at Johnson, for a good long time, then at Boone. He seemed to be making mental calculations, like an undertaker measuring for a casket.

As Madison watched, his eyes moved on to her, and she had to suppress a shudder as she looked away.

Boone stepped closer, as if to shield her from whatever came next.

"So what?" Caprielli said.

It took Madison a second to realize he was referring to Johnson's mention of Frank McGee outside.

Johnson smiled. "Come on, Mr. Caprielli. With all due respect, the guy did three years for you at Graterford. Don't you even care that someone killed him?"

"Streets aren't fucking safe these days," Caprielli said with a shrug. "Somebody should do something."

"We're working on it."

"Maybe you need to work a little harder."

"Your friend Mr. McGee was involved in a shoot-out with another gang."

"Oh?" he replied, a little too eagerly for his nonchalant façade, Madison thought. "What gang was that?"

Johnson shrugged. "You know anything about it?"

"What gang was it?" Caprielli said again.

"Was there anybody McGee had been having trouble with?" Johnson asked, ignoring Caprielli's question. He paused. "Anybody *you've* been having trouble with?"

Caprielli stared at him. The muscles in his temple throbbed visibly.

Johnson laughed, shaking his head. "You got nothing to say that could help us? Nothing for your old buddy Frank? . . . All right, then." He pulled a card out of his breast pocket and held it out. ". . . If you hear anything, you give me a call, okay?"

Caprielli didn't take the card. "I know where to find you."

THE RETURN trip through the building was shorter. None of them spoke until they were outside again.

"Well, that was educational," Johnson said sarcastically as the door closed behind him. "Well worth the risk to our lives."

Boone laughed. "What risk? Those assholes back there? Damn, Ted, you really are a wuss."

"That was Donny Craig in there."

Boone scoffed. "Who? The big dumb guy?"

"No, not the big dumb guy. The other guy. The guy who was staring at you, thinking about all the different ways he could kill you. The guy with at least ten bodies behind him. Ten we know about. Donny Craig's specialty is killing big, mean motherfuckers in ways that make other big, mean motherfuckers not want to fuck with his boss. Never been able to pin a thing on him."

Boone rolled his eyes, refusing to be impressed.

"We did learn a little," Madison said as they got in the car.

"Like what?" Johnson shot back.

"When you mentioned that it was a fight with another gang, he didn't say, 'A gang?' like he was surprised. He said, 'What gang?' He knew it was a gang, but he didn't know who."

"So what you're saying," Johnson scoffed, "is that he knows he's in a gang war but doesn't know who the other gang is?"

Boone shrugged. "That ain't necessarily so crazy. Maybe these other guys are just trying to take him out. Sneak up on him. That shit happens."

Johnson's cell phone sounded. "Whatever," he said as he took out his phone. "Yeah?" he said, answering it. "A briefing?" He looked over at Boone and Madison, then looked down. "No, it's fine. I'll be there."

He pulled up behind their cars in the parking lot. "All right," he said, putting his phone away. "I got to go down to the Roundhouse. Some kind of briefing. I'll call you later."

He sped off and left Madison and Boone in silence.

Boone was smiling at her. He seemed to be trying to come up with something to say.

"There's something you might not know about the town of Lawson," he finally declared.

"And what's that?"

"There's no Thai food for about fifteen miles around. And no *good* Thai for probably twenty-five."

"Ouch."

"I know." He shook his head dramatically. "It's a hardship."

"How do you manage?"

"I take advantage whenever I get a chance to stock up."

"I see."

"Care to join me?"

It was half past three and suddenly she was starving. "Why not?"

CHAPTER 15

MADISON DROVE and they burned through small talk on the way. Walking from the car, they traded department gossip and details of the case. By the time they were waiting for a table, they were discussing the parallels between their lives and the reasons—or lack of them—for returning to where they had come from.

"At least you had a reason," Madison said as the waiter brought their spring rolls and chicken satay. "When people ask you why you went back. Taking over the family business after your father died."

"Yeah, I guess." He laughed. "It must be a good answer, too, because honestly, nobody really asks the question. It might not have occurred to *me* that I might come back, but people up there, I don't think it occurred to them that I wouldn't."

He tore off a strip of chicken and dipped it in sauce. "Why *did* you come back?" he asked, before popping it in his mouth.

"You lose points for asking, you know that, right?"

"Why?"

"'Cause I don't like answering it, that's why."

He smiled and kept chewing. "You don't have to talk about it if you don't want."

"No, that's okay. You've already lost the points, and it won't be much of an answer anyway."

He laughed and sipped his water.

She laughed, too, ruefully. "To be honest, I still don't know."

"Then I want my points back."

She held up a hand. "Here's the thing. I came up with a

grand scheme to get the hell away from here. I worked hard for a long time, but by the time I got out, I'd been working at it so hard and for so long, I didn't realize that what I was working for wasn't what I wanted anymore. That's part of it."

"What's the rest?"

She narrowed her eyes.

"Hey, if my points are already on the table . . ."

"I had a lot of bad stuff happen when I was a kid." She could feel her eyes moistening.

Boone leaned forward, concern evident on his face. "Hey, it's okay. I know something about what happened. You don't have to talk about any of that."

She bowed her head and took a couple of deep breaths.

"How do you know about it?" she said, looking up when she had regained enough control.

He laughed. "I asked around."

"I see." She was a little annoyed, but she found herself smiling. She felt comfortable talking to him. She wanted to tell him. "So, you know what happened to my mom. She was killed, or whatever. And . . . and about my dad, right?"

He nodded.

She looked away, out the window. "There was a lot of stuff I wanted to get away from, but my uncle Dave, that's who raised me—he's my lieutenant now, God help me—and my aunt Ellie . . . they were great. I got away as much as you ever can I guess, but it turned out I missed the other stuff a lot more than I thought."

They were quiet for a second.

"So it wasn't the cheesesteaks."

She laughed. "I'd be lying if I said that wasn't a factor."

He laughed, too, but his eyes were pinned on hers.

"I like you, Madison Cross," he said.

Madison smiled and looked away, but when she brought her gaze back to his, he was still watching her eyes.

"Stop it," she said. She knew she was blushing.

"It's okay," he said with a grin. "I can wait."

She leaned forward, about to tell him he'd be waiting a long time, but her cell phone went off.

It was Ted Johnson.

"Where are you?" he asked.

"Thai place on Lancaster."

"Where's Boone?"

"Across the table."

"You guys doing lunch? Ain't that sweet."

"Shut up, Johnson. What is it?"

He laughed, but only briefly. "Well, I was just briefed by a guy named Larry Metzger," he said. ". . . From the Organized Crime Task Force."

"And how was that?" she asked, still looking at Boone.

"They've been investigating Caprielli for a long time."

"And?"

"They went ape shit when I told them we'd been there."

"So?"

"They said what we're dealing with is a gang war."

"Well, duh!"

"They're taking over the case."

BOONE SLAMMED the dashboard with the side of his fist. "It's fucking bullshit!" he said. It was the third time he'd said it and at least the sixth time he'd hit the dashboard. Madison was vaguely concerned that if he hit it any harder, the airbag might deploy.

"I know," she said calmly. "I agree with you."

He had erupted instantaneously when she reported what Ted Johnson had said. She'd had to lay down two twenties and hustle him out before the owner threw them out.

Now they were driving back to the Roundhouse, Boone still frothing about jurisdiction while Madison tried to calm him down.

The worst part was that Boone was probably right. Technically, he probably didn't have enough evidence to prove that the fatal wound was delivered in Lawson, but circumstantially, it sure did look that way.

Johnson seemed ambivalent about whose case it was. He probably wouldn't have minded if it had ended up in Boone's jurisdiction; one less unsolved case on his board, right? Now that Organized Crime was involved, however, they would try to use this case to help out their other cases. The fact that the crime had probably happened outside of Philadelphia was beside the point. It might be kind of sneaky, but she knew enough about police work to know that's how it often went.

Of course, that didn't help Boone.

She could see why it bothered him—she respected him that much more because of it. A lot of cops in his position would be relieved to be rid of the case. Most of them probably would have given it up to the state police from day one. But not Boone.

Johnson was waiting for them back at the parking lot, leaning against the back of Boone's cruiser. As he squinted in the sunlight, he seemed amused, trying not to smile.

"Fuck you, Ted," Boone said, jumping out of the car before it had even stopped.

"Not my doing, Boonie."

"It's bullshit and you know it. I got a fucking battle scene in the middle of my town. I got blood evidence that ties the body to the scene."

"You're right," he said, letting a little laugh escape. "It *is* bullshit. I'm not trying to say it's right, but I am telling you this is how it's going to be."

"There's nothing he can do?" Madison asked. "That blood evidence is pretty compelling."

Johnson smiled grimly. "Compelling to you maybe. What's compelling to Larry Metzger is that he's had this asshole on his radar for like seven years. And now he's got a fresh body he might be able to pin on him."

Boone rolled his eyes. "So fucking what?"

Johnson shrugged. "The other thing is, and no offense, Boonie, but these guys think since they got the resources and whatnot, they stand a much better chance of solving the case than the one-man police department of Bumblefuck, Pennsylvania. Maybe even crack it before anyone else gets killed."

Boone's face reddened and his chest heaved as he stared back at Johnson. Madison wanted to put a hand on his shoulder to calm him down, but she was afraid that might just set him off.

"Yeah, I know how it works," he said sharply. "And I've

seen plenty of bad guys walk for ratting out bigger bad guys. Well, maybe I don't want my murderer taking a walk because he's ready to give up your crack wholesaler."

"It's not like they don't want your help," Johnson added. "They asked me to bring you down there, see if we can help each other out."

"They asked you to bring me down, huh?" He opened his car door, shaking his head. "Well, fuck that. You know what? You tell them, they want to talk to me, they can come up to Lawson. And don't think I'm not going to talk to our DA about this."

He paused as he got in his car and looked up at Madison, just for an instant. "Thanks for lunch."

Then he slammed the door and sped off.

They both winced as he bounced out of the parking lot and onto the street.

"Well, that went well," Madison said.

"He's an excitable boy."

Madison shrugged. "He's pissed. I can understand it, too. His case just got pulled out from under him. A murder was committed in his town, and he wants to find out who did it."

"Psh," Johnson scoffed.

"What?"

"Well, sure, it's fucked up, but face it, he's looking for a pissing contest. Mostly, though? He's bored as shit out there, and Metzger and his guys are moving in on the most exciting thing that's probably ever happened in the little town of Lawson."

Madison thought it was probably a combination of all those things. "So with Organized Crime taking over, how do I fit in?"

"You?" He looked down at her. "I don't know, Cross. Same as always, I guess." He shrugged. "We need something from C.S.U., I guess we'll call you."

Madison thought about chopped-up Jimmy Dawber and the shriveled little gnome, more interesting cases by far. But Boone had made this case interesting, and she was a little disappointed to see him go.

As she turned to leave, she heard her cell phone going off,

then she thought it was Johnson's, then she realized it was both of them. Her eyes met his as she answered it.

"Newbie!" Parker said loudly in her ear. "Whatcha doing?"

"I'm sure you're about to tell me."

"Looks like we got another good one. Corner of Third and Dauphin."

"I'll be there in ten minutes."

As she put away her cell phone, Johnson did the same.

"Dauphin Street?" she asked.

He shook his head. "New lead on Oxford."

"Busy week."

CHAPTER 16

PARKER LOOKED down on the figure tied to the wooden chair and shook his head. "I don't know if it's a full moon or what, but these knuckleheads are going crazy."

"I already checked," replied Lynch, the uniform who had discovered the scene. "Full moon's not 'til next week."

"Can't wait," Madison said with a grim smile.

They were standing in the kitchen of a run-down North Philly row house. Most of the linoleum had been peeled off the floor. The sink looked like someone had been building fires in it. A big, black stain had spread out across the ceiling above.

From the nail holes and splintering around the doors and windows, it looked like the place had been boarded up at least twice, but the boards had been removed, or at least some of them had.

The place had been abandoned but not by everybody. The crackheads and junkies apparently still found it useful.

And the rats.

One of the rats hadn't even run away when they came in, not right away. He'd been nibbling on the victim's toes and he stopped to look at them, but instead of bolting he turned back for more toe.

Lynch stomped his foot loudly, but the rat just flinched and turned to show its bloody teeth.

"Fucking thing," Lynch said, laughing nervously. He rested a hand on his holster and stomped again, this time feinting a lunge. The rat shrieked and took a step away, then shrieked again and disappeared.

"How'd you find him?" Parker asked.

"Anonymous call. Some community-minded crackhead, I guess. Came in to get a buzz, found this."

"Yeah, that would be a bit of a buzz kill," Parker said with a snort.

"Any ID on him?" Madison asked.

"I didn't want to check until after you guys were done," he said, making it plain that he didn't want to check at all.

Parker looked over at Madison. "Shall we have at it?"

Madison took out the camera and Parker pulled on a pair of exam gloves. She slowly circled the body on the chair, taking pictures, making a special effort to capture the ring of shoe prints that circled the body. Parker circled as well, keeping behind her so as to stay out of the shots.

The body looked Latino and was definitely male, a fact that was particularly evident because the victim's pants were down around his ankles. His scrotum had been stretched out and stapled to the wooden chair.

His hands and legs were tied to the arms of the chair with phone wire. One of his hands looked untouched. The other had been touched, and not in a nice way. Three of the fingernails had been torn out, and two of those fingers looked like they'd been broken, probably during the removal.

A single droplet of blood had run down his wrist below where the phone wire cut into the flesh. It was dried.

He had some of the same tattoos as the other bodies that had turned up that week.

With a gloved hand, Parker touched the skin on the arm, gave it a little wiggle. "The wounds are clotted. He's cold, but still stiff. I'd say probably about a day or so. Little more, maybe."

The face had been beaten to an even, puffy red pulp. One eye was either closed or missing. One ear had a half-inch tear in it, through the skin and the cartilage.

His T-shirt was dirty, a mixture of black, brown, and gray scuffs visible on what little of it was not soaked in blood. The left side of his chest had a black circle with a dark red hole in the middle of it.

Madison took a close-up of the hole. "Bullet hole. I guess he told them what they wanted to know."

Parker nodded. "Looks like. Still had plenty more finger-nails left."

"And that," she said, indicating the scrotum affixed to the chair. "That must have hurt."

"Yeah, I'll bet it did," Parker replied. "But that looks like prep work to me. I'll bet it was nothing compared to what was coming next, and I'll bet the guy with the questions whispered all sorts of plans into this poor bastard's ear."

Madison continued taking pictures.

"Jesus Christ," she said breathlessly as she moved around to the back.

Parker came around to take a look.

"What the fuck is that?" he asked.

Madison clicked a series of pictures of the back of the corpse's head.

The head was shaved, and the skin behind the left ear was a bright, angry red. The skin was bumpy and inflamed, covered with large, pus-filled lesions, some of which were leaking fluid.

Lynch made a strangled, gurgling sound as he stepped around to see what they were looking at.

"Do you think it's infectious?" Madison asked.

Lynch took a step back.

"I don't know what the hell it is," Parker said, "but I don't want those pussies in the hazmat suits taking over my crime scene."

It appeared as if they had a treasure trove of forensic evidence, but none of it told them much of anything. They found the bloody pliers in the sink, next to a short length of pipe that had probably been used to pummel the victim's face. But neither had any fingerprints, and they pretty much knew whose blood was on them.

The torn-out fingernails had been discarded on the floor. Blood was spattered in various directions, probably from the blows to the victim's face. Parker lifted half a dozen blood samples from around the room, just to be sure.

All the evidence seemed to be connected to the victim, but they already had him. The only direct evidence of the killer was the shoe prints circling the body.

"Strange-looking shoe prints," Madison said, crouching just outside the circle.

Parker crouched down next to her and laughed grimly. "Guy bagged his shoes." He looked around him. "Place is clean. No prints or nothing. I lifted some blood, if you can run DNA, but I'm pretty sure it's all from our vic. Whoever did this, the guy's a pro."

He stood up. "Okay, we're done here. Let's get him out of here. See what Spoons can tell us. Kid looks like another one of Ted Johnson's gangbangers. We should probably give him a call, too."

She stood up next to him. "I don't think it's technically his case anymore."

"What do you mean?"

"Organized Crime Task Force. They said it looks like a gang thing, took over the case."

"Well, call Ted anyway."

SHE CALLED Ted Johnson first. "Looks like you might have another one," she told him.

"Another what?"

"Another body."

"Why you say that?"

"We don't have a positive ID but we got another body with a lot of the same tats as Castillo and Alvarez."

"Jesus." He laughed grimly. "Can't be that many of them left."

"Yeah, and this one's a mess."

"How so?"

"Apparently the killer was looking for some information. Let's just say, he got it."

"Ouch."

"Got some kind of freaky skin condition on his head, too."

"Been a freaky week. Anyway, that's Metzger's case now."

"Just thought you'd like to know."

"Thanks, Cross. You should call Metzger, though. Sound of it, I'm glad it's his case."

* * *

"METZGER," A gruff voice answered on the second ring.

Madison introduced herself and explained why she was calling, why they thought this body was related to Castillo and Alvarez. There was a moment of silence on the other end.

"Okay," he said, sounding almost annoyed. "Well, call me when you get some kind of ID."

Then he hung up.

Madison gave her phone a dirty look and slipped it into her pocket. She checked her watch.

It was already past five. She had planned on staying with the body until Tate and Velasquez got there, but it was getting late. She had just made up her mind to leave when her phone rang.

It was the lieutenant. She thought nothing of it at first, but she started getting nervous when he asked her how she was doing and then waited for her to answer. Uncle Dave had never been one for extraneous phone conversations, even when he wasn't on the clock. When Madison was in Seattle, the vast majority of their phone conversations had consisted of "So, how are you, Maddy girl?" soon followed by, "Well, hold on and I'll get your aunt Ellie."

"What is it, Uncle Dave?" she asked, worried.

"Nothing, nothing," he said dismissively. "Just calling to see how you're doing, that's all."

"What's wrong?"

"Nothing." He laughed nervously.

"Is it Aunt Ellie?"

"No, it's not Aunt Ellie." He sighed. "Okay. I need you to help Rourke conduct a comprehensive forensic search of the Prager house." He paused. "Fenton requested it."

"He's coming up with nothing, isn't he?"

"It's not looking good. Turns out Prager's mother had been in a car crash. He's been by her side pretty much ever since. Prager called in to work to tell them, but the kid who answered the phone at work was caught getting high, got fired before he could pass along the message. Prager says he must have put his hand on the trash bag as he was getting out of his car when he came home to change his clothes that night."

"And the trash bag shows no sign of stress around his fingerprints, which suggests Prager is telling the truth."

"Right."

"Does Fenton have this poor bastard in custody?"

Lieutenant Cross took a deep breath. "Yes."

Madison growled. "Fenton is such a schmuck."

The lieutenant sighed. "Just talk to Rourke and do the search, okay? Get it over with as soon as possible."

"You got it, boss."

BACK AT the Roundhouse, Rourke was on the phone. She was talking about a shoe sale and she seemed engrossed.

When she caught sight of Madison, she slowly turned her chair around so she was facing away from her.

Must be a hell of a shoe sale, Madison thought.

Madison occupied herself by pulling dog hairs off her sweater, but it was a futile effort. She took it off and stashed it under her desk.

A few minutes later, Rourke was showing no signs of slowing down. Madison was getting anxious; she didn't want to be spending her entire night searching Prager's house. But she couldn't get started without Rourke. With a sigh, she started scanning the fingerprints from the Dauphin Street kid. She had planned on taking the prints at the ME's but after the lieutenant called, she had gone ahead and taken them at the scene.

The prints from the damaged fingers seemed to be slightly less oblong than the others, probably from swelling. Madison shook her head at the thought of it.

She finished scanning the prints and started the database search, then went into the DNA lab and started prepping the blood samples Parker had lifted at the Dauphin Street scene.

When she was done, Rourke was still on the phone.

Madison couldn't tell if this was the same phone call or a different one; Rourke was talking about something that had happened at a party. Madison hovered for a moment, then cleared her throat, loudly.

"Hold on a second," Rourke said, cupping the phone with her hand and looking over at Madison. "What's up, Cross?"

"Lieutenant said he wanted me to help you search the Prager house. For Fenton."

"Yeah, that's right."

Madison looked at her watch. "Well, I don't want to be doing it all night."

"All night?"

"He said Fenton wanted it done soon."

"Right, well Fenton can kiss my ass *soon*. If he wanted to wrap this thing up *soon*, he should have looked into arresting the right guy, no? As far as this bullshit search goes, how does tomorrow sound?"

"Okay."

"I got a busy day, so we'll need an early start. I left a message for Fenton. We're meeting at Prager's house at seven. Is that okay?"

Madison winced. "I guess so."

"I'll see you then." Rourke nodded and waved her off, resuming her phone conversation.

Madison backed away, quietly scanning the C.S.U. for signs of the lieutenant. She was satisfied that any shit from Fenton about the delay could be directed toward Rourke, but she didn't want to have to get into it with her uncle.

The computer behind her dinged, signaling that the fingerprints hit a match—in fact, all ten of them. Madison confirmed visually, then checked the ID.

Ramon Perez. She sighed, wondering how many of these guys were going to be dead before this thing was over.

She called Larry Metzger back and told him they'd IDed the body—one Ramon Perez—and that he was a known associate of both Castillo and Alvarez.

She paused, giving him time to thank her.

Instead, he said, "I knew it," in a tone of such self-satisfaction it was obvious he wasn't just taking credit, he believed he'd made the connection himself.

Madison didn't know how to reply.

"Let me know immediately if you find anything else," Metzger said. He hung up before she could say anything.

"Asshole," she muttered.

She tried to call Ted Johnson, but he didn't answer, so she left him a message. She left a message for Spoons, too, giving him a name to put to the body. Looking around once more for the lieutenant, she quietly packed up her desk for the night and slipped out.

The plan had been to stop by the ME to hear what Spoons thought of the Dauphin Street body. The skin on the back of Perez's head was unlike anything she had ever seen, and any other week they would have pulled an all-nighter to figure out what the deal was. But not this week.

When she called again, she found out Spoons was already gone for the day.

A plan took shape in her mind . . . General Tso's chicken . . . pajamas . . . stupid TV.

She smiled.

Then her phone chimed, and her smile faltered.

She looked at the number . . . It was Chief Boone's cell phone. She didn't answer it right away. It was nice to hear from him, and part of her was even mildly excited about it, but she wasn't in the mood to hear more ranting, however justified it might be. And mentally, she was already lying on the sofa in her pj's eating take-out.

With a sigh, she opened her phone and put it to her ear. "Hello?"

"Okay," Boone said. "So usually I try to hide the whole 'me being an asshole' thing until I know someone a little better."

She laughed wearily. "I guess that makes me special, then, huh?"

"I'm sorry. I'm not usually like that."

"It's okay. I'd be pissed, too."

"You sound beat."

"We just picked up another one. Ramon Perez, another one of Carlos Washburn's ill-fated crew. He was a mess, too. Tortured."

"Nice. Well, I'll let you go. I got a line on George Krulich. The guy who fixes my car is supposed to be showing him a boat tomorrow. If you want to come up tomorrow, I'll take you to see him."

She was just a few blocks from home, but the mental effort it would take to make that scheduling commitment threatened to sap the last little bit of energy she needed to get there.

"How about I call you in the morning?"

"Come on, you've been waiting to see this guy. Tomorrow's your chance. The shad are running, so you might not be able to see him again for a while."

"I don't know, Matt. I've got so much work to do. I don't know if I have time to drive all the way out there."

"Come on, it's barely an hour."

"Yeah, the way you drive. I don't have woo-woo lights on my car."

"I'll tell you what. I'll buy you lunch. We actually do have some decent food out here. What do you like?"

"Pad Thai."

"Ha, ha. No dice. But there's a place called Gret's out here. It's great. You'll love it."

"What time is your guy meeting Krulich?"

"Eleven o'clock."

"Okay, I don't know about lunch, but I'll see if I can rearrange some stuff, make it out there by eleven."

"I'll look forward to it."

CHAPTER 17

AS IT turned out, Fenton was apparently unable to attend his own party. He had a previous engagement at a management training seminar. He sent his regrets.

The six of them assembled in front of Arnold Prager's house. Rourke was the only crime scene investigator there. She was pale and quiet, wearing big, dark shades. When Madison asked her how she was doing, she said, "Late night."

A guy named Phil Isaacs was coordinating things for Fenton. Isaacs was a decent cop who had the extreme misfortune of sitting at the desk next to Fenton. They weren't partners, but they ended up working a lot of cases together.

Isaacs brought doughnuts and coffee, and the group stood in front of the house for a minute, eating and drinking, wisps of steam rising from their cups in the early morning chill.

Everyone but Isaacs agreed Fenton's absence was bullshit, but it made it a lot easier to bitch freely about what an asshole he was. There were a lot of comments about Fenton skipping out, but it was clear that nobody would have preferred it any other way. Not even Isaacs.

When the doughnuts were done, they bagged their shoes and went inside.

There wasn't much to search. The house was sparsely decorated and barely furnished. The first floor had worn, green shag carpet throughout and brown paneling in four-foot sections that alternated between buckling in and buckling out. There was a black vinyl sofa and matching recliner in the living room. In the dining room, a round fake wood table was surrounded by four chairs, one of which didn't match.

Upstairs, the carpet was maroon and there was no paneling.

The front bedroom was empty except for a dusty exercise bike. The back bedroom had a bed, an end table, a chest of drawers with a TV on it, and a hamper.

The hamper had a single change of clothes in it. Everything in the drawers was neatly folded. Arnold Prager may have been a lonely man, but at least he was tidy.

Rourke worked alone in the bathroom.

Madison worked with Eddie Amato, spraying luminol over every square inch of Arnold Prager's basement. By the time she was finished, even though the basement was filled with its chemical scent, the luminol had failed to produce the slightest indication of any blood.

"So how'd you get stuck doing this, Eddie?" she asked. "Who'd you piss off?"

He laughed. "Who'd I piss off? My wife I guess. I'm doing this for the overtime."

Sixty minutes and a bottle and a half more of luminol later, the entire group assembled once more in front of the house. They had found absolutely nothing of any consequence, but they lifted some prints and collected some fibers anyway, just to prove they had been there.

Rourke presented a bag of sweepings from the bathroom floor. Isaacs logged it in and sealed the front door with crime scene tape, even though everyone knew it wasn't a crime scene.

MADISON HAD plenty of time before she had to leave for Lawson, and she really wanted to see what Spoons thought about Ramon Perez's strange scalp condition.

She stopped in at the ME and found Spoons bent over a microscope.

"Did you look at Perez yet?" she asked as she burst through the door. "Is this a crazy week, or what?"

"The week is crazy as shit," he said, looking up at her, distracted. "But what the hell are you talking about?"

"Ramon Perez. The guy from yesterday, from Dauphin Street?"

"Haven't seen it yet. You know how fucking backed up I

am?" He went back to his microscope. "Why, another good one?"

Madison started backpedaling as soon as she knew Spoons hadn't seen Perez's body. It was eight thirty already, but if she could get out of there quickly, she might actually make it to Lawson in time after all. "I'll just say, this week will go down as one of the craziest ever. And I'm just glad I got to be a part of it. I'll call you later about Dauphin."

"Huh. Well, meantime, come take a look at this."

"Actually, Spoons, I'm kind of in a hurry here."

"Fuck that. If you were in a hurry, you wouldn't have stopped in. Come on. Get over here and take a look at this."

"What is it?"

"Something Sanchez found. I sent her a sample from the Dawber kid, see if we could pick up any residue."

"Yeah, she showed me this. The damage to the cell membranes. I don't get it, the damage is all in different directions."

"But she showed it to you, right?"

She nodded and he switched the slides.

"Okay, now look at this. First look at this one."

She looked through the microscope and saw a pale, rust-colored field of cells. They were irregularly shaped, but orderly. "Looks fine. What is it?"

"Well, hold on," he said, switching the slide. "Now look at this."

She looked in the microscope again and adjusted the controls slightly. When the image came into focus, it looked similar to what Sanchez had shown her, with random cell damage in all directions, except there were also very defined cut marks, ridges and furrows from whatever had done the slicing. "This looks kind of like what Sanchez showed me, except for the cut marks. Is this from Dawber?"

"Nope."

"So you duplicated the effect?" she said, her voice speeding up. "How?"

"I took that first slide from a steak before I cooked it and ate it last night."

"Okay . . . and the second slide?"

He smiled. "Same piece of meat. I put a bit in the freezer last night and thawed it this morning."

"What!?" Her head darted back to the microscope. "So that's what damaged the cells, of course . . ." She looked back up at him. "But the cut marks, they're plain as day."

Spoons's face fell. "I know. That's been keeping me up. I can't figure it out. And I sliced that fucking sample with a diamond-tipped scalpel, sharpest thing I could think of. So now we're looking for some kind of implement that's sharper than a diamond scalpel. And it doesn't leave any residue. I don't know what the fuck it is."

Madison looked off, thinking. "And was the cutting done before or after the body was frozen?" she asked herself out loud.

"I don't know, kid. Like I said, the shit's been keeping me up at night."

"Look, I got to go, but before I do, can we take a quick look at the Dauphin Street body?"

He sighed and shuffled over to the wall of drawers where they kept the bodies. "I thought you were in a hurry," he chided her as he pulled one drawer open.

"Tortured and beaten, then shot through the heart," Madison explained as he unzipped the bag. "The crazy part is the back of his head."

Spoons had found that much on his own. "Yeah . . ." he said as he inspected it up close. "That's a mess all right."

As he quickly examined the rest of the body, Madison told him about the circumstances in which they had found it.

"And you already got an ID?" he asked.

She nodded. "Ramon Perez. Known associate of both Castillo and Alvarez."

Spoons grunted as he examined the fingers, the face, and the nail holes in the scrotum. He ended up back at the scalp. "Curioser and curioser."

"What do you think it is?"

He shrugged. "I don't know. Looks like some kind of infection. A lot of inflammation. I'll try to get a better look at it this afternoon. Maybe get it under a microscope." He shrugged and slid the drawer closed. "Like I don't got enough fucking work."

"Thanks. I just wanted to see what you thought about it."

"Oh no, thank *you*," he said sarcastically.

"So what's the next step on the Dawber case, about finding the tool?"

He shook his head wearily. "I got no clue. I been researching that shit, too. Reading up on all the different high-end implements, all the different kinds of cut marks made by all the different tools and blades, and they all have one thing in common. You know what that is?"

"No, what?"

"They all leave a fucking mark, that's what." He laughed ruefully. "I mean cut me a break."

Her eyes shot over at him. "What did you say?"

"I said they all leave a fucking mark. That's what's so confusing."

"No, after that."

"What? Nothing. I said cut me a break, that's all."

Her eyes widened. "Spoons, that's it! It's got to be."

"What?"

"No residue, no cut marks. We've been looking for a cut— we should be looking for a break."

"What are you talking about?"

"The slides show that the body was frozen, but there's no sign it had been cut—because it hadn't been cut. It broke. It shattered."

Spoons laughed. "You're full of shit. A human body ain't going to shatter, just because it's frozen."

"If it's cold enough, it might."

"Yeah, well . . . what do you mean?"

"I mean if it was cold enough, it could shatter. No residue, no tool marks."

Spoons shook his head again. "No way. It would have to be really fucking cold, like, like . . ."

She put a hand on his chest to stop him. "Like liquid nitrogen cold."

*   *   *

"SO LET me get this straight," the lieutenant said, his eyes closed as he sat behind his desk considering what he was hearing. "The guy who we *know* was frozen wasn't actually frozen, he was *glassified*, which basically means he was frozen, but without the water in him. The guy we *thought* had been hacked to pieces actually *had* been frozen, and you think that because the body shows no cut marks or any other sign of whatever was used to cut him up, that he was actually frozen, then shattered?"

Madison felt her cheeks warming. "Basically, yeah . . . But it's not just that," she added quickly. "The cuts that are there, or the breaks or whatever, they go right through all the different kinds of tissue, all the same way. That's one of the things that struck me from the beginning, the way the kid's head was sheared through. It wasn't like his head was cut off, like through the neck; the head was cut in half, and it was a clean line, through skin, muscle, bone, everything, with no sawing, no tearing. I really don't think there is any tool that can do that."

"But a body doesn't just shatter, just because it's frozen."

"If it's cold enough it does. If it's in liquid nitrogen."

"But surely that would have left some kind of mark."

"It probably did, a little bit," she replied, "and we would have seen it if we had found it before it thawed."

He thought for a moment. "So you think this is related to MacClaren?"

"Hell of a coincidence."

He thought about it for a moment. "Okay, well, you better call Fenton, tell him about this."

Madison's face twisted. "Right," she said, unenthusiastically.

"It's his case," he reminded her.

"Well, it didn't seem like it was his case when we were searching his prime suspect's house this morning."

"What do you mean?"

"He wasn't there."

"What do you mean?"

"He wasn't there. He never showed up."

"You're serious?" He was incredulous. "Jesus, that is nervy."

"That's what I'm telling you. The guy's a useless piece of—"

"Madison," he said, cutting her off. "You're not telling me anything I don't already know. But it doesn't matter. It's his case. You need to tell him what you've found."

FENTON WAS at his desk, on the phone. He looked up when Madison walked over, but didn't acknowledge her. His desk was clear except for a cup of coffee, a bagel, and a *Daily News* folded to a quarter-finished Sudoku puzzle.

He seemed to be making a show of not hurrying to finish his call. When he saw her, his voice grew noticeably louder, and Madison got the distinct impression it was for her benefit.

It had sounded at first like he was talking to a friend, with Fenton laughing expansively and speaking familiarly, but as she listened, she could tell he was talking to some kind of salesperson, something about drapes or upholstery. He ended the call saying he would call the person back tomorrow and they could talk about it some more. Madison hoped the commission would be worth it, because whoever was on the other end was earning their money.

Fenton put down his phone, then turned and fixed Madison with a condescending look. "And what can I do for you now, Ms. Cross?"

He made it sound as if he had been doing a lot for her already and Madison struggled not to show her annoyance.

"We have some more information on the Jimmy Dawber case. I thought you might want to know."

"Okay." He sat back and waited.

"Spoons couldn't find any sign of tool marks on the cuts, so he asked Sanchez to see if she could find any residues, but that came back negative, too."

"Well, Ms. Cross, then they'll have to keep looking. Any implement leaves traces—cut marks and residues—isn't that what you people are always telling us? They're just going to have to try harder."

Madison took a calming breath. "One thing they did find was damage on a cellular level . . ."

"See?" he said with a smug smile. "There you go, they did find something."

She shook her head and explained how the cell damage indicated freezing.

"Huh." He looked vaguely thoughtful for a moment, so she paused to let the information sink in.

"Since there's no sign of cutting, it occurred to me that the body might not have been cut at all," she continued. "It might have shattered."

His eyes narrowed. "Shattered? Bodies don't just shatter."

"They do if they're cold enough. We had another body come in this week, turns out it had been cryonically preserved. When Spoons opened it up, it was still rock hard inside."

"And it had this same kind of cell damage?"

"Well, actually, no. The bodies that are cryonically preserved are treated so there won't be that kind of damage, but . . ."

"So wait a minute, one guy is rock hard, but has no cell damage because it was treated with something or other, the other guy is totally *not* frozen, but has this cell damage. They sound totally different to me."

"Except that in order to get the body hard enough to shatter, you'd need to freeze it in liquid nitrogen, like they do in cryonics."

He shook his head. "Seems like a bit of a stretch to me. I think you're coming up with all this crazy stuff because your buddies can't find what I need them to find. No, Ms. Cross, we've got prints that say Arnold Prager is our suspect, and once we figure out what he used or where he did this, I'm sure it will all fall into place."

"Prager's place was clean."

"Nobody's place is clean, Ms. Cross, isn't that how it is? Maybe you people just need to start looking a little harder, hmm?"

She was at a loss for words.

"Now, if you'll excuse me, I'm kind of busy."

Yes, she wanted to say, *those Sudoku puzzles aren't going to solve themselves.* Instead, she just turned around and left.

CHAPTER 18

MADISON WAS still fuming when she got back to her desk.

She sat quietly for a second, trying to calm down. On an impulse she picked up the phone and called Toby Mac-Claren's cell phone.

"Hello?" he answered, a hint of suspicion in his voice at the unfamiliar number.

"Hi, Mr. MacClaren, this is Madison Cross, from the Crime Scene Unit. We spoke yesterday morning about your father?"

"Yes, Ms. Cross. Have you learned anything?"

As soon as he said it, she realized that she had forgotten to check the results of the profile. She reached over and wiggled her mouse, sputtering for a second as the screen slowly came to life.

"Uh . . . Well, maybe . . ."

The profiles matched. The mummified body they had found was Toby MacClaren's father.

"And?"

She quickly regained her composure. "Actually, I just wanted to check to see when you'd be available to meet in person."

"For something like this? I can be available whenever."

"Okay, can you hold for one second?" Madison covered the mouthpiece with her hand as Rourke walked by. She still looked rough, still had an annoyed expression on her face from having her morning wasted searching the Prager house.

"Rourke!" Madison called over to her in a loud whisper. "I need a favor."

"Like I told you, got a busy day," Rourke said, giving her a very doubtful look, but stopping to listen.

Madison held up the phone. "I got Toby MacClaren on the phone. I need you to come with me to tell him the DNA from the mummy matches his father."

Rourke raised an eyebrow. "It does?"

"Yes. I have to tell him in person. Can you come with me?" Her shoulders sagged and the dubious expression deepened.

"Come on," Madison cajoled. "It'll only take a minute."

"I guess. But we're not breaking it to him gently."

"Thanks!" Madison took her hand off the phone. "Sorry about that, Mr. MacClaren. Where are you right now?"

"I work in the Public Ledger Building, on Chestnut. There's a Starbucks across the street."

"Okay, we'll see you there in ten minutes."

THE PUBLIC Ledger Building was only a few blocks away from police headquarters, but MacClaren was already there waiting for them, sitting at a table with three small coffees.

He stood when they walked in, smiling warmly.

Rourke responded with a brief, grudging smile. She had been quiet on the short drive over.

"Thank you for meeting with us, Mr. MacClaren," Madison said.

"Please. Anything I can do. And call me Toby."

"Thank you, Toby."

As they sat, he slid one of the coffees toward each of them.

Rourke nodded wordlessly and took an eager sip of her coffee.

"Thanks, that's very thoughtful," Madison said, "but you really didn't have to." She found herself smiling involuntarily. She had the distinct impression she was being charmed, but at least he was good at it.

"It's my pleasure," he replied, smiling back again. "So are you really a cop?"

Madison tried not to smile back. "Rourke is. I'm actually a technician."

"So you don't carry a gun and arrest people?"

Madison shook her head.

"Oh," MacClaren said, disappointed, as if he had quite liked the idea.

Rourke seemed immune to the charm, but not the coffee. She took another long sip.

"We ran the profile on the sample you gave us," Madison told him. "It does match the DNA from the body we found."

"I see." MacClaren nodded slowly, a vaguely confused look on his face, like he understood what she was saying, but maybe not all the implications. "So, what does that mean?"

"It means it is your father."

"Oh," he said quietly.

They gave him a moment.

"I didn't like the whole cryonics idea in the first place," he said quietly. "I knew no good would come of it, but . . . this?" He shook his head. "My father was a great man. Some of his ideas might have been a little . . . odd, but he didn't deserve this."

"I'm sorry, Mr. MacClaren," Madison said in a hushed tone.

"Do . . . do we have any idea . . . how this happened?"

Madison shook her head. "Not really. We're working on some leads."

"Did your father have any enemies?" Rourke asked.

He smiled wistfully. "You don't achieve what my father achieved without making some enemies, but . . . well, he's *dead*."

Rourke nodded.

"Right," Madison said. "Well, I guess we need to find some things out. First we need to find out where your father had been . . . interred. Can you tell me who was the executor of your father's will?"

"It was his lawyer. Don Rabinowitz."

Madison jotted that down.

"But he died six months ago, too."

She looked up abruptly.

MacClaren gave her a wan smile. "Surely, it should be on file somewhere, though, right?"

Rourke cleared her throat, reminding Madison that she'd said all this would only take a minute.

Madison continued. "Who was overseeing your father's situation?"

"Oh, I don't know about that. I know he set up a trust, the MacClaren Trust, something like that. It didn't really involve me. That should be in the will, too."

"Okay, one last question. Does the name Jimmy Dawber mean anything to you?"

Rourke shot her a look, but Madison ignored her.

Toby stared at her, thinking, before slowly starting to shake his head. "Doesn't ring a bell."

Madison paused, trying to think up any other questions, but Rourke stood up.

"Thank you for your help, Mr. MacClaren. Let us know if you think of anything else that might be helpful."

MacClaren stood as well. "Thank you," he said, turning to Madison. "Let me know if you need anything else."

By the time Madison got to her feet, Rourke was headed for the door.

"JIMMY DAWBER?" Rourke asked as they got in the car. "What's that about?"

Madison explained about the differences and similarities between the bodies of Jimmy Dawber and Robert MacClaren. Rourke half listened at first, but quickly made it plain that she was sorry she asked.

"So does Fenton know you're looking into this?"

"Actually, I was just asking to see how it might affect the MacClaren case."

Rourke laughed. "You're poaching Fenton's case. He's going to be pissed."

"I'm not poaching anything," Madison insisted.

"Hey, it's cool with me. God knows *he's* not going to crack it. Just be careful about pissing him off. Or do you figure you've pissed off enough of the current brass, you need to start pissing off the next generation of district commanders?"

They were just pulling into the parking lot at the Round-house when Madison's cell phone chimed. When she saw it was Boone's phone number, she smiled but didn't pick up.

"Aren't you going to get that?" Rourke asked.

"Thanks for coming with me," Madison said as she pulled over by the entrance.

"Aren't you going to park?"

"I have some errands to run."

Rourke eyed the still-ringing phone sitting between the car seats and she smiled. "Tell him I said, 'Hi,'" she teased as she got out. "Whoever he is."

The phone had stopped ringing by the time she got to it. She called him right back.

"Madison," he said.

"You just called me?"

"You coming out here?"

She laughed. "Yes, Matt, I'm coming out there. You miss me that much?"

"Hey, I'm just planning my day, that's all. Krulich is supposed to be meeting this guy in an hour and a half. What time are you coming out?"

"I'm leaving right now."

"I'll meet you at the office."

THE DRIVE to Lawson seemed quicker, quieter, and even prettier this time.

The boundary between late winter and early spring had swept north past Lawson since Madison's first visit. Alongside the highway, the buds were swelling on the trees. As she approached the town itself, she saw brave plantings of yellow and purple pansies and bright flashes of crocuses and daffodils bursting through the moist ground.

When she entered the town limits, Madison slowed, trying to remember the way to the police station. She paused at a stop sign and was refamiliarizing herself with her surroundings when she heard the hoarse, staccato bleat of a police horn and she looked up to see police lights in her rearview mirror.

She watched with a smile as Boone stepped out of the cruiser and walked slowly up to her window. He had on a big pair of mirrored aviator sunglasses and a mean scowl.

"You know why I pulled you over, ma'am?" he asked.

"I'm thinking it's because you really don't have enough to do out here."

"I'm afraid you're in a heap a trouble ma'am."

He stared at her, stoically, and she stared back, trying to keep a straight face. He seemed determined to maintain it until she took out a lipstick, and, using the twin mirrors resting on the bridge of his nose, began to apply it.

"Ma'am," he said gruffly, "what are you doing?"

"Just a sec," she said, smacking her lips together to even the coat out. "I'm almost done."

When she was finished, she smoothed out her eyebrows, but it wasn't until she started checking her hair that he realized she was using his mirrored shades to touch herself up.

"Hey, stop that," he protested, breaking character. "You're already in a heap of trouble, remember?"

"There really is nothing to do out here, is there?"

He slid the shades into his shirt pocket. "It's not so bad. Get to pull over the occasional pretty girl. Has its moments."

"Well, if you're not going to charge me with anything, I guess I'll be on my way."

"All right, all right." He grinned. "Why don't you follow me to the station, we'll take the cruiser out to see Krulich."

"Don't leave me stranded at any red lights," she said as he stepped back toward the cruiser.

"Don't worry," he shouted back. "Lawson's only got one, and I have it on good authority that the town's only cop doesn't carry a ticket book."

He trotted back to the cruiser and maneuvered around her.

She pulled out behind him and followed as he drove slowly toward the center of town, his lights still blazing. The handful of civilians she saw on the street watched them pass by, plainly wondering what she had done to justify the escort. Madison sank low in her seat, waving at the most obvious gawkers.

When they got to the police station, Boone pulled over and got out, directing Madison into the parking lot and then opening his passenger door for her to get in.

"You're an odd bird, Chief Boone," she told him as she got in the car.

"Don't make me put my tough guy shades back on," he replied as he got in next to her.

"Do you think we could turn off the lights?"

He turned to her, sincerely taken aback. "Seriously?"

She nodded.

"The lights are the best part of the job," he said, but he reached over and flicked a switch on the dash. "Man, I remember my dad letting me turn on the lights on his old cruiser when I was a kid." He smiled. "I still get a kick out of them. Your dad ever let you work the lights?"

She shook her head. "I don't think so. He'd already made detective by the time I would have remembered, but I don't think so."

"Hope you don't mind me asking, and it's not like I'm not happy to be doing this, but why are you still coming out to talk to Krulich? What I heard, it's Fenton's case and he already has a suspect. So what's this about?"

"Fenton's an idiot."

"Well, yeah, but that's not news. Still his case, though, right?"

She told him about the pointless search of Prager's house, about why it was irrelevant that Prager had worked at a meat-cutting plant, and how there was no stress on the plastic around his prints on the trash bag, meaning the plastic had been touched, but not grabbed or lifted.

"But I heard the guy had a violent past. A felony assault or something."

"He got into one bar fight. Seven years ago."

"Anything else?"

"Nothing else that makes him a suspect." She told him about Prager calling out from work and how he had been at the hospital, then she told him about how Dawber had been frozen, and how it was looking more and more like he hadn't been cut to pieces, but had somehow been smashed. She told him about the MacClaren body and how it had been vitrified and cryonically preserved. How in some ways it seemed to have been frozen and some ways it hadn't. She didn't mention the smell or the appearance or the strange wires in its head, but she did say she was starting to think they were somehow related.

He scratched his neck.

"Well, it's undeniable that Fenton's an asshole, but I gotta say I'm probably with him on this one."

"What do you mean?!"

"Well, come on, this one seems frozen in this way, that one seems frozen in the other way. It's like they're complete opposites."

"No, it's just that one of them was prepared. Vitrified. The other one wasn't. It's still a hell of a coincidence that they were both frozen."

"I guess," he said, sounding unconvinced. "What else is going on?" he asked, trying to change the subject.

She told him about Ramon Perez, his torture, and the bizarre rash of skin lesions on his head.

"Jesus, you guys *are* having quite a week down there. Any news on that big arson fire?"

"Oxford? Yeah. They found all sorts of drug-making equipment. Looks like somebody robbed a drug factory, set the fire to hide the fact, and it spread next door."

He shook his head. "Nice."

"Yeah."

That killed the conversation for a moment, then she asked if he'd heard anything about Dale, the guy from the gas station.

"No, not really."

"He must have been really scared."

"Yeah, I guess so, but he was probably teetering already, you know? He'd been doing pretty well just lately, but he definitely had a history."

He pressed lightly on the brakes and steered the cruiser into a small gravel parking lot with half a dozen boats on trailers and a couple of pickup trucks. At the far corner of the lot was a small wooden shack with a soda machine in front.

As they pulled up, a red-faced man with a white beard and no mustache stepped out of the shack, locked the door, and unlocked the driver's side door of one of the trucks.

Boone grunted.

"What is it?" Madison asked.

"That's him. That's Artie Axelrod, the guy who is supposed to be meeting with Krulich." He pulled up next to the guy, who paused halfway inside his truck and then got back out.

"Hey, Matt," he said, leaning in the car window.

"Hey, Artie. What's up? Where's Krulich?"

"He just called from a rest stop, running late. Said he'll be here in an hour."

"You serious? Goddamn." He turned to Madison and smiled apologetically. "Sorry."

She shrugged. "What are you going to do, right?"

Boone turned back to Artie. "So are you still meeting him?"

"Sure. He's going to be here at noon."

"All right, we'll be back in a hour, okay?" He turned to Madison for confirmation.

She could feel the day slipping away from her, but she had already come all the way out there. She nodded.

"All right," Artie said, climbing back into his truck. "I'll talk to you then, I guess."

Boone pulled the cruiser in a tight circle and out of the parking lot. "You hungry?"

She looked at her watch. It was eleven o'clock and the doughnut she'd eaten four hours earlier was long since gone. She suddenly realized she was starving. "Yeah, I guess I could eat."

He drove about a half a mile and pulled into another gravel parking lot, this time next to a corner deli with painted windows and a big, old-fashioned, red Coca-Cola sign. The bottom half of the sign said GRET'S in rusty green block letters.

"We might not have any decent Thai food, but a Gret's hot roast pork sandwich can make you forget about a lot of problems. Give it a try?"

"Sounds good." As they stepped out of the cruiser they were hit with a delicious waft of slow-roasting pork and Madison's stomach rumbled to life.

It was just after eleven, but Gret's was already doing a brisk business. Half a dozen people were lined up to order and half a dozen others were sitting at tables, waiting. The woman behind the counter shouted out, "Hey there, Chief."

As Boone shouted back, "Hey, Arlene," everybody else in the place looked over and said, "Hi, Chief."

No one said anything to Madison, but as they acknowledged the police chief, they looked her over thoroughly. Some
kept on staring, and Madison got the distinct impression that
she was with some sort of local celebrity.

Within a couple of minutes, they were at the front of the
line, a handful of people now standing behind them.

"How about a couple of Gretwiches and a couple of
Cokes," Boone ordered.

He looked over at Madison and smiled self-consciously.

Their order came up before anyone else's, but nobody
seemed to mind. Arlene insisted the sandwiches were on the
house, but Boone insisted on paying for them and eventually
she relented.

"Gretwiches?" Madison asked as they walked up to the car.

"I know, I know. It's a terrible name. We've tried to get her
to call them something else, but she's adamant. Insists you order them by name, too. But it's worth it." He held up the bag.
"These things are awesome."

"We eating in the car?"

He shook his head and got in the car. "I got us a table."

"Where?"

"Not far. Just up the road."

Madison sat back and watched the scenery as they drove.
They turned up a tight little lane that ascended sharply and
then gradually dropped off. The terrain was getting pretty
rough and Madison wasn't even sure they were still on a road.
Boone's Lawson Township Police SUV bounced and listed
but pushed ahead.

"Where the hell are we going?"

They stopped abruptly next to a small stand of high grass.

"This is just about it."

"Here?" She laughed.

He got out and came around to her side, opening the door.
"Almost. Come on."

He helped her out and she let him, clutching his arm.

"Next time, remind me to wear boots," she said as she
stepped down into the tall grass.

The soil was spongy underfoot. Boone held the bag up
high with one hand, and helped Madison through the grass

with the other. A couple of steps away, he guided her up a jumble of river rocks and onto a large boulder.

They walked out onto a wide outcropping of rock that jutted out over a ninety-degree bend in the river. Stands of evergreens lined the banks, extending a hundred yards in either direction. Above the trees, the rolling hills seemed to be shrouded in a pale green mist, the first hint of the thick green coat of foliage that would soon follow. A sprinkling of yellowy-green tree blossoms floated past on the gentle current of the river, resting lightly on the surface.

It was one of the most beautiful places Madison had ever seen.

Boone kept his arm under hers, as if he knew the vista before them could physically knock her over.

"Wow," she whispered.

"Something, ain't it?"

"It's breathtaking."

"Here," he said, leading her to a fractured bump on top of the outcropping that formed a sort of stone sofa. "Sit here."

He unpacked their lunch and handed her a sandwich and a soda with an exaggerated bow before sitting down next to her.

"Thank you," she said graciously.

She could feel the warmth of the sandwich through the foil, and as she unwrapped it, she was rewarded with a whiff of the same enticing aroma that had filled the sandwich shop. Her stomach grumbled loudly once again and she quickly took a bite before it could elaborate.

The pork was moist and salty, heavy on the pepper and absolutely delicious. She closed her eyes and chewed, savoring the flavor. As she took another bite, she looked over and saw that Boone's sandwich was half gone. His eyes were closed, too, but when her head turned, he opened them and smiled at her.

"Not bad, huh?" he said, taking a long swig of his Coke.

She shook her head, finishing the mouthful of sandwich before answering. "No, it's excellent. Worth the trip just for this."

He took another bite and grunted with pleasure, shaking his head. One more bite and it was gone. He balled up the foil and put it in the bag, then drained his Coke and dropped that in, too.

Madison prided herself on being a good eater, but she still had half of her sandwich left. She took a big bite, then another one.

While she finished up, Boone leaned back on the rock and stretched out his legs. He closed his eyes and let the sun warm his face.

Madison noticed with a wry grin that his arm had somehow ended up behind her.

"So is this where you used to take girls?" she asked as she took another bite.

He laughed without opening his eyes. "No, I didn't. But now that you mention it, I wish I'd thought of it. My granddad used to take me fishing here when I was a kid. I don't know if we ever actually caught anything, but we used to love to come here, just sit and talk. He was great."

She put the remainder of her sandwich in her mouth.

His smile changed, turning wistful. "This is probably my favorite place in the world." He raised his head and opened his eyes, shielding them from the sun with his hand as he looked over at her. "Sometimes I think maybe this is why I came back up here. This place right here, you know?"

Madison took a sip of her soda and wiped her mouth with a napkin. "It is pretty special."

He watched her and then sat up, leaning closer. "You missed a bit," he murmured.

As he raised his hand to gently brush her cheek, she wondered in the back of her mind if there was really anything there at all. But as her eyes closed, she realized she didn't care. His fingers felt like a warm breeze, barely touching her as they caressed her cheek and lingered.

When she opened her eyes, his face, with its small half smile and twinkling eyes, was only a few inches away.

She felt her lips part and she was just starting to lean forward when a raspy voice shouted, "Hey, Chief Boone!"

They both jerked their heads back to look for the source of the voice. At first, they couldn't see anybody, but then they heard a splash and they both whipped their heads around to see an older man in a canoe, paddling his way toward them across the river. He had on a fly-fishing vest and a hat covered with lures.

"Chief Boone!" he called again.

Madison leaned in and gave Boone a quick peck on the cheek. The smile he gave her in return was filled with both frustration and longing.

"You're very popular," she said facetiously.

"It's a burden," he agreed, before turning back to the fisherman. "Hi, Mr. Eldridge. What can I do for you?"

"Oh, fine, fine," he replied incongruously. "I was just wondering if you found out what happened over at Dale's gas station. My wife's still pretty upset about it, says she doesn't know if the town's safe anymore with this kind of thing going on."

By this point, he was right in front of them. He pushed the tip of his oar against the rock to keep the canoe from clanging against it.

"Well, we're working on it, Mr. Eldridge. You tell Mrs. Eldridge she doesn't have anything to worry about."

"You know, I saw them, those crazy idiots, doing ninety miles an hour down Timber Road."

"You did, huh?" he replied indulgently. "You saw them going *up* Timber Road, toward Dale's filling station, right?"

"Well, I saw that, too, later on. But I'm talking about before that, a half hour earlier. I was coming up the road and I saw them going *down* Timber Road, in that silver car they left at Dale's station. They turned onto that little side road there next to the creek, that little access road with the old lodge."

"Well, Jesus, Mr. Eldridge, why didn't you tell me?"

Eldridge rolled his eyes. "Well, that's what I'm doing now, isn't it, Chief Boone? Geez, no need to get snippy."

He pushed off from the rock, muttering to himself and shaking his head as he rowed downstream.

Boone looked at his watch and then at Madison. "That's the first I've heard about those guys having gone down that road. We still got a little time before Krulich is supposed to show up. You want to go take a quick look-see?"

Madison smiled. She wondered if men in other professions were so easily distracted by their work.

"Sure," she said.

CHAPTER 19

FIVE MINUTES later, they were back in the cruiser, bouncing back onto the main road. They drove in awkward silence. Madison looked out the window, sheepishly avoiding eye contact.

Timber Road was just a few minutes away. They slowed to a stop across from a small gap in the trees that lined the road. A sign said, PRIVATE DRIVE. KEEP OUT.

As they bounced up the steep, rutted access road, Boone leaned forward, looking around him out the windshield. The road leveled off and curved around a thick stand of trees before ending in front of a substantial wood-and-stone lodge.

It had only two levels, but the ceilings must have been fourteen feet. Each corner was anchored by a massive pile of river stone, and in between was more stone, rough-hewn wood, and lots of windows. On the south side of the roof was a satellite TV dish.

"Damn," Boone said, impressed. They got out of the cruiser and approached the house, looking around them.

"Wait . . ." Madison said, grabbing Boone's sleeve and holding him back.

"What?"

She pointed at a pair of tire tracks in the mud right where he was about to step. On either side of the tracks was a jumble of shoe prints.

Boone grunted.

"Your victim at the gas station, he have any mud on his shoes?" she asked.

He shrugged.

"We should take imprints, see if they match any of the

shoes. Same with the tire tracks, see if the treads match up with the car at the station."

They stepped around the tire tracks and headed up the front steps, onto the wide, wraparound porch.

Boone cupped his hand around his eyes and looked through the glass of the front door. Madison peeked through the window, but it was dark inside.

Boone looked at his watch. "If we want to meet Krulich, we need to get going."

She turned and started down the steps. "I have supplies back in my car. How far away are we from the station?"

He shrugged. "Maybe five minutes."

"We should cast these prints. You don't want to lose them."

"How long does that take?"

"Takes about thirty minutes for the stuff to harden, but it'll only take five or ten minutes to get it mixed and in there. We could pour it now and pick it up later."

He shook his head. "By the time we do all that, we might miss Krulich altogether. I mean, I don't think he's going anywhere, but he does seem to be hard to get hold of."

"Yeah, okay," she said, starting back to the cruiser, then veering off away from it. "Wait a second. What's that?"

"What?" he asked, following her over toward the trees.

"Look at this," she said urgently, pointing at a splintered gouge in a pine tree. It was about six inches across and had a narrow furrow in the middle about an inch wide. A long rivulet of clear sap extended down almost to the ground. It was already getting crusty at the bottom and around the edges, but the sap still seemed to be oozing out at the top. "That's from a gun."

"Well, yeah, but so what?"

"So what? Aren't we looking into a major shooting? Don't you think it just might be related?"

He laughed. "I guess it could be. But around here, people like their guns and they like shooting. A tree with a bullet hole ain't exactly news."

She gave him a dubious look but he just shrugged. Turning back to the tree, she stared at it for another second, then said, "Hold on, though. Look at that groove there. You follow that line, looks like the bullet came from up on the porch there, right?"

He shrugged a begrudging assent.

"And look; there's sap all over it, still dripping down, but it's getting crusty around the edges. I'm no expert on trees, but I know it takes at least a few days to dry like that, and it's probably not going to keep running much more than a week."

He shook his head. "I don't know about all that." He looked at his watch again. "But I do know that if we don't get going, we're going to miss our meeting with Krulich."

"Right." She bit her lip, thinking. "Okay, let's get going, then. But we should come back and get the tracks, do a proper search of the area."

ARTIE AXELROD'S parking lot looked exactly the way they had left it, except for the large chrome-and-yellow Hummer parked diagonally across three spaces.

Boone grumbled at the sight of it.

Artie emerged from the little shack just as they were getting out of the car. He was followed by a large man in a cowboy hat and cowboy boots.

Boone walked up to them and Artie gave him a quick, discreet nod.

"George Krulich?" Boone asked.

"Yeah." Krulich looked Boone up and down, pausing slightly to look at his badge. "Why?" he asked, without a trace of deference.

"You're a hard man to get in touch with."

"Not if you've got a lot of money and you want to catch some fish. Otherwise I'm a very busy man, too, so you're welcome to talk to me between here and that kick-ass Hummer over there, but then I've got to get going."

Krulich started walking and Boone cocked an eyebrow at Madison, inviting her to jump in.

"I wanted to talk to you about Jimmy Dawber," Madison said.

Krulich stopped and rolled his eyes. "What's that dope done now?"

"When was the last time you saw him?"

"Hell, I don't know. About a year ago, I guess. Dumb ass used to be one of my best guides. I was going to set him up with his own boat, 'til he lost his license."

"His license?"

"Poor dumb bastard. Got a DUI, lost his driver's license. So what does he do? Next night he gets drunk again, goes out on his boat, loses his boating license. I mean, come on. I tried to make room for him, tried to find work for him. But if he can't drive, can't guide a boat, there's only so much for him to do."

"Did you fire him?"

"I would have. I'd have had to. But he got another job. One of my clients actually. What did he do this time?"

"Do you know of anybody who might have wanted to harm him?"

"Harm him?" He laughed and shook his head, then stopped. "Wait, is he okay?"

"Jimmy Dawber is dead."

He scowled. "That's a damn shame. What happened?"

"We're still trying to figure that out. Do you remember the name of the client who hired him?"

"Yeah. Some rich guy. Guy named Robert MacClaren."

"SO, WHEN are you going to tell Fenton?" Boone asked, watching as Madison mixed water into a plastic bag filled with powdered plaster mixture.

She shook the bag vigorously for close to a minute before answering. "I don't know."

Boone grinned. "Got yourself into a bit of a pickle, didn't you? It's one thing poaching the dumb bastard's case when you're off on some goose chase and he's never even going to know about it." He laughed. "You went and found yourself a genuine lead."

She poured the plaster mixture out of the bag, gently splashing it against the back of a plastic spoon and slowly filling several of the shoe prints. She had already arranged numbered cards next to each of the impressions and carefully photographed them.

As she moved on to the next small grouping, she sighed and started pouring again. "If he had just done his job a little bit, I wouldn't have been put in this position."

"Yeah, but then you wouldn't have been able to spend so much time in our fair burg."

She raised an eyebrow and he laughed.

"Well, you got to admit, the sandwiches are good."

"The Gretwiches, you mean."

She finished pouring the last imprint and straightened, standing next to him and surveying her work: close to twenty shoe prints and sections of the two long tire tracks.

"What now?" he asked.

"When the plaster sets up a bit, I'll mark the back of each piece, so we'll know what was where. We can start taking them up in a half hour or so."

"Thanks," he said as she leaned backward, stretching out her back.

"Thanks for Krulich," she replied, taking out her cell phone.

"So what are you going to do next?"

"I don't know. Maybe talk to the lieutenant."

"Your uncle?"

"Yeah."

"So how do you think these guys fit together, anyhow? Dawber and MacClaren?"

"I have no idea. I'm sure the whole freezing thing is involved, and I imagine it has more to do with MacClaren than Dawber, but other than that, I don't know. But I'm sure Fenton will get to the bottom of it."

He laughed. "Well, look on the bright side. You might be making yourself a sworn enemy who's highly connected in the department, but at least you won't have to pretend to be civil with him."

"Just what I always wanted," she said with relish. "A nemesis."

They both chuckled.

"Seriously, though," he told her. "If you want, I could call in the lead about Dawber and MacClaren. Your name wouldn't have to come up."

She seriously considered it for a moment, then shook her head vigorously. "No, thanks. It's just going to come out anyway. I appreciate the offer, but I don't want to get caught in a lie, or have you get caught."

She didn't say it, but the fact of the matter was that she was proud to have tracked down this lead. She was going to catch some shit for it, but she was looking forward to sticking it to Fenton.

She smiled as she considered the deft way she was handling her career track.

"You love this shit, don't you?" Boone asked.

She laughed self-consciously, wondering just how accurately he'd been reading her face. "I wouldn't exactly call it love."

WHEN THE casts were dry, Madison carefully lifted each one out and marked it, then gently wrapped them in newspaper and placed them in the backseat of Boone's car.

"Once I get these back to Philly, I can get them cleaned up and we'll see if they match the shoes and the tires we have."

"Back in Philly? This is my jurisdiction." He said it with exaggerated bravado.

"Yeah? You want to keep these?" A mild trace of annoyance had crept into her voice, contingent on just how serious he was being.

"No, of course not," he said with a grin. "But I am thinking that if we can get an eyeball comparison with the tread on that Maxima, maybe we can get a warrant to look inside that lodge."

"An eyeball comparison?"

"Call it . . . preliminary."

She started to explain to him just how many reasons why that was not a good idea, but ten minutes later, they were at the Lawson Township Police Impound Lot, which was in the police station parking lot, in the space next to the one marked "Police Chief."

Boone poured a small cup of white latex paint on the asphalt, then backed up over it.

Madison shook her head, but dutifully took a picture of it.

"This will never hold up in court," she told him as she followed him into the police station.

Boone stopped at Gloria's desk. "Gloria, I need you to do me a favor."

He gently took her by the elbow and led her over to a large topographical map on the wall. "I need you to go over to the township building," he said, tracing Timber Road on the map until he found the access road. "I need you to see if you can find out who owns this land, here." He poked the map with his forefinger. "There's a big lodge on it, set back from Timber Road a ways."

She looked dubious.

"Don't worry," he assured her. "I'll be in here typing."

The doubtful expression remained on her face, but she turned and left anyway.

"Now, remember, this is just to get us inside the place," he reminded Madison as he started typing. "I'll just be sure to slip in the word 'preliminary' as much as possible."

Boone was still typing when Gloria called five minutes later. He seemed surprised she was calling so soon and from the other end it sounded like Gloria was annoyed that she was wasting her time over such scant information while Boone was stumbling around on her computer.

"Okay, well, thanks," he said sheepishly.

"What did she say?" Madison asked when he hung up.

"Not much. The property is listed as owned by a holding company, Bartlett Property Company. They have a post office box in Harrisburg, but there wasn't much information other than that. She said the address is 301 Timber Road, but that Carl, the mailman, said he'd never delivered any mail there."

She took out her cell phone and clicked on a number in her address book.

"Who you calling?"

"Friend of mine in Economic Crimes. See if we can find out who owns this place." She turned away from him as a voice answered on the other end.

"Economic Crimes."

"Hey, Ben, it's Madison Cross from the C.S.U."

"Hey, Madison. Long time no see. Apart from on the news Sunday night, that is."

She sighed. "Jesus, you saw that? I was only on for like two seconds."

He laughed. "Naw, I'm messing with you. I didn't see it. I heard about it, though."

Ben Moyers considered himself a bit of a cut up. Compared to the rest of the guys in Economic Crimes, he was.

"That's hilarious," she said. "I need a favor."

"Yeah," he said, "I could tell by the way you called and everything."

"Sorry, I just . . ."

"Madison, I'm messing with you. What do you need?"

"I'm trying to find out who owns a property in Lawson, Northampton County."

"Okay," he said slowly.

"The place is at 301 Timber Road in Lawson."

"All right," he said. "I'll do a little digging and get back to you as soon as I find out anything."

"What did he say?" Boone asked.

She shrugged. "Said he'll look into it and get back to me. Maybe we should wait until we find out who owns the place."

"Don't worry," Boone said with a wry smile. "This'll be fine. Judge Wilbur knows me."

"Oh, good," Madison said in mock relief.

Boone laughed.

"What?" she asked.

"I didn't say he liked me."

CHAPTER 20

JUDGE EUGENE Wilbur lived in a large white clapboard house surrounded by half an acre of lawn that was too lush and too green for that time of the year not to be chemically enhanced.

His hedges looked like they were sculpted out of stone and the topiary that flanked his front door looked like it was made of plastic. The grass along the front path had apparently been edged using a T square.

Boone cleared his throat before he rang the bell, then shuffled his feet, looking down at them to make sure he was standing just right. Madison gave him a reassuring smile. The entire time she'd been in Lawson, she'd gotten the impression that Boone might as well have been emperor of the town. Now she found his nervousness endearing.

The door opened and a massively obese man dressed in seersucker stepped halfway through. He looked wordlessly at Boone for a moment, then turned to Madison and extended his hand.

"Judge Eugene Wilbur," he said.

"Madison Cross," she said, shaking his hand.

He turned back to Boone and said, "Come on in, Chief," before turning back through the door and disappearing inside.

They followed him in, through the living room and into a den. The foyer and the living room were decorated in a frilly style that Madison immediately recognized as "wife of the judge." There was an abundance of lace and floral patterns and the window treatments all had a minimum of six parts, with nets and valances and swags and oddly folded pieces of material that Madison couldn't identify.

The den was different. Everything in the room was brown. The floors, paneling, desk, and bookcase all seemed to be of the same dark wood. The blinds were wood, too, half a shade lighter. The chair and the lampshade were brown leather.

Sitting behind his desk, Judge Wilbur seemed ethereally pale in the midst of all that darkness.

"All right, Boone," Wilbur said with a slight wheeze. "What do you want?"

Boone handed him the written request for the search warrant.

"I need a warrant to search an old fishing lodge at 301 Timber Road. It's up that access road a ways."

"Who lives there?"

"I don't know, sir."

Wilbur looked up. "Well, who owns it?"

"Bartlett Property Company. That's all we know. They have a post office box in Harrisburg listed as the address. But I have good reason to believe there is a connection to the shoot-out at Dale Hibbert's gas station last week," Boone told him.

Wilbur put on a pair of reading glasses and skimmed the warrant. "Reason to believe?"

"I have an eyewitness that says he saw the Maxima they left behind at the gas station. Says he saw it driving up that access road a half hour before the shooting started. Only thing up there is that lodge."

Wilbur was waiting for more.

"We've got tire prints that tie the two scenes together."

"A preliminary match," Madison explained, for accuracy's sake.

The judge looked at her, his eyes narrowing slightly.

"And there is at least one suspicious-looking bullet hole in a tree out front," she added.

Wilbur put down the paper and started laughing, an annoyingly high-pitched rasp. "You show me a tree around here that doesn't have a bullet in it, *that'd* be suspicious."

Madison felt the blood going to her cheeks.

Wilbur took off his glasses. "Who are you again, miss?"

"Madison Cross. I'm a technician with the Philadelphia Police Crime Scene Unit."

"Philadelphia, huh?" Wilbur looked dubious. "What is it you're hoping to find in there? What do you propose to be searching for?"

Boone looked at Madison.

"Well, more evidence to link it to the crime scene," she explained. "Ballistic evidence, a body, blood evidence . . . any of that would help."

Wilbur snorted. "I'm sure it would, Ms. Cross. How about some drugs or some kiddie porn? Maybe a falsified tax return?" He laughed, shaking his head. "I'll tell you what, you know what might make your job easier? Why don't I just give you warrants for all the houses in the township? I bet you could find all sorts of stuff."

Boone opened his mouth to counter, but Judge Wilbur silenced him with a hand.

"Young man, don't," he said curtly, picking up his pen. "I'll give you your warrant. I don't like people coming in and shooting up the town. But you go in, you see if there's any bodies in there, and you get the hell out. You don't mess up the place, you don't touch anything, you don't vacuum for fibers or dust for fingerprints. If you can give me more than what you've got here, I'll consider something more expansive, but with what you have now, I could get thrown off the bench for giving you this much." He looked Boone sternly in the eye. "And do *not* take more than I'm giving you."

"Yes, sir."

Then he turned to Madison. "We like to think the fishing is mighty good around here, young lady. But that doesn't extend to the law."

BOONE KNOCKED on the door a fourth time, and waited another full minute. They were standing on the porch of the lodge, search warrant in hand.

When the fourth full minute was up, Boone knocked one more time before punching out the lock with a sledgehammer. The door swung inward.

They stepped onto a lacquered stone floor that followed a high curved wall around to a high-ceilinged living area.

The wall was decorated with a large mirror and some paintings of ducks and geese in flight. The wall only extended halfway up to the vaulted ceiling, and perched on top of it was a random assemblage of taxidermy.

To the right was a carpeted living area with large windows looking out onto the woods. The place was furnished sparsely but expensively, with a leather sofa and recliner and a fully stocked entertainment center topped off by a massive television.

In the corner was a broom and a dust pan.

Beyond the living area was a wide wooden stairway leading to a second-floor loft. To the left was a small kitchen, little more than a galley, dominated by an oversized stainless-steel refrigerator.

The stove had a thick patina of grime and next to it was a microwave oven, stained brown and caked with grease and other residue. In the corner, a steel wastebasket was overflowing with trash, its hinged lid wedged open by the excess.

They exchanged a glance and a shrug and moved through the rest of the house. The rest of the first floor was occupied by a laundry/utility room with a towering, industrial-sized washer and dryer. In the corner was an impressive pile of laundry: soiled denim, flannel shirts, gray socks, and underwear.

A doorway in the corner opened onto a darkened stairway that descended into a basement.

This time, when they exchanged glances, Madison noticed that Boone's gun was in his hand. He gave her a reassuring smile and started down. He flicked a switch, lighting a single bulb at the bottom of the steps.

The basement had a concrete floor and cinder-block walls, a cavernous room with another door at the far end and some sort of large metal box in the corner.

Boone spun in a slow circle, covering the entire room with his gun, but it was empty. She followed a step behind him and they slowly crossed the room, toward the metal box.

Madison had always been vaguely afraid of basements, an unreasoning fear that now seemed to make perfect sense. As they drew closer to the box, her heart began pounding and she was filled with a sudden feeling of dread.

She noticed a thick electrical cord extending out from behind the box and plugged into the wall. The top of the box was separated from the rest of it by a white rubber gasket running all the way around it and a pair of hinges in the back.

Madison nudged Boone lightly in the ribs as she pointed at the cord. She detected a faint hum.

Boone looked up at her and she mouthed the word "freezer." Even as she said it, images flashed through her head of Jimmy Dawber, reassembled on the table, and Robert Mac-Claren, his shriveled, yellow body lying on a filthy mattress. She could feel the hairs stirring on the back of her neck.

Boone nodded and flashed a nervous smile. Crouching, he held the gun high with one hand so it was pointing down at the top of the box. With the other hand he reached out, his fingertips just under the edge of the lid.

He paused for a second and then in a startling motion that made Madison jump, he flipped open the lid and stepped off to the side, his gun aimed at the interior of the container.

As the lid started coming down again he caught it, already letting the hand with the gun drop to his side.

It was indeed a freezer.

A billow of cold air fell down around the sides of the freezer, the condensation visible as it hit the floor and then dissipated around their feet. Inside there must have been two hundred frozen dinners, stacked neatly, a different flavor comprising each stack.

Madison pointed to the hole in the middle of the arrangement and a box of Swanson Salisbury steak just visible at the bottom.

"Someone's partial to the Salisbury steak," she observed.

Boone laughed, the tension having momentarily dissipated. But when he closed the freezer and turned to the other door, his concentration returned.

In the instant before Boone opened the door, Madison caught a whiff of the stench, but as soon as the door was ajar, they were engulfed in it. A huge ball of it seemed to roll into the room, a cloud of flies borne along with it.

Boone winced and Madison put a hand over her mouth.

The door started to swing shut on its spring-loaded hinges, but Boone stopped it with his hip.

They stepped through the doorway, swatting away the flies as they entered a small room illuminated by daylight filtering in through weathered, wood-framed windows and a partially open door that led outside. It seemed to be some kind of a mudroom, roughly finished, with wooden shelves and a large cabinet along one wall and a sink against another.

Boone opened the cabinet. It was crammed full of fishing supplies, an orderly row of fishing rods and boxes with all sorts of lures and weights and bobbers and hooks. A fishing rod lay on the cement floor next to an open, full tackle box.

As they stood staring at their surroundings, the cloud of flies seemed to coalesce around the sink.

Three bloated fish lay inside it, brown liquid streaming out of their mouths and eyes. The flies were in a frenzy.

"Doesn't look like today's catch, does it?" Boone murmured.

Madison shook her head and stepped past him, through the doorway and outside. She exhaled loudly and took a deep breath of fresh air.

She was standing behind the house, in a shallow, level basin about thirty yards across that wrapped around the property, separating it from the hills that surrounded it on three sides. The ground was still papered with last fall's leaves. At the far end of the basin a path wandered up the hill between the trees.

She could hear Boone snort and spit behind her. "That's a heckuva fragrance," he said, briskly shaking his head. "What do you call that?"

"I don't know," she replied. "Chanel number six-six-six, maybe."

"Eau de toilette, right?"

"Something like that."

"Okay," he said, turning back inside. "Let's check out the rest of the place."

"Sure," she said, putting out a hand to stop him. "But let's go around and use the front door."

He laughed. "Good idea."

The terrain sloped gently upward as they walked around to the front. This time, as they went up the front steps and through the door, Madison noticed a few more details: the splintering on the inside of the doorjamb, the muddy foot prints on the carpet in the living room.

The tiny droplets of dried blood on the stone floor.

"Boone!" she called, terse but still quiet, pointing at the blood.

He followed her finger and nodded grimly. His gun was still out from before, but he raised it a few inches. They crept through the living room once again, this time heading upstairs to the loft.

At the top of the steps was a bathroom, then three large bedrooms. Two of the bedrooms appeared unused; the third was a mess.

The bed was unmade and a pile of laundry in the corner looked like a one-fourth scale replica of the pile they'd seen downstairs. A half-empty bag of chips was curled up at the side of the bed.

An entire wall of the room was taken up with a large, four-drawer dresser. Boone slid open one of drawers, revealing a tangle of identical, unpaired, dingy white socks. He looked at her and smirked, then opened the next drawer: BVD briefs.

The next drawer was filled with a narrow array of flannel shirts, none folded, and all extremely similar. The bottom drawer was all jeans.

Boone smirked again. "Gotta hand it to him. The guy's got a plan."

A closet was filled with sweaters, down vests, and folded fleece.

The bedside table had a clock, a lamp, and an extra-large pump bottle of Jergens hand lotion. Boone slid open the drawer to reveal a stack of magazines, an abstract jumble of nipples and pubic hair.

On the floor just under the bed were a handful of crumpled-up tissues.

Madison screwed up her face.

Boone snickered and closed the drawer.

Once they were confident they were alone in the house,

Madison got out her equipment and they returned to the blood spot on the floor outside the living room, standing on either side of it, arms folded, looking down at it.

"What do you think of that?" he asked. "Must have missed it when we came in."

Madison took a picture of the blood spot. "Could mean whoever brought in those fish came in the front door." She snapped another photo, this one closer, then she lay a six-inch ruler next to it and took a third picture. "Or it could be the piece that pulls this all together."

She put away the camera and looked at Boone.

"Aren't you going to take a sample?" he asked.

"I don't know. The judge said 'only if there's any bodies in there . . . ' "

He grinned. "Come on, it's like a tiny little piece of a body."

"Are you sure?"

"Absolutely."

She took out a bottle of distilled water. Pouring a small amount onto a bloodlift patch, she rubbed it over the blood spot until the cloth turned a faint, dirty shade of pink, then she placed it in one of the little vented plastic holders and sealed it in an envelope.

"Are we done?" he asked as she stood up.

She nodded.

"Well, it looks like something, right?" he said hopefully as they stepped out onto the porch.

"Could be."

He put some more police tape on the front door. "Maybe enough to get us a broader warrant?"

"Maybe."

He stepped in closer, grinning at her reluctance to commit to anything.

"Well . . ." she said, feeling suddenly nervous but thrilled at his closeness. "I should get these samples back to the lab. Get them started."

"Yup," he said softly, his nose inches from her hair. His lips were slightly parted and Madison's heart was pounding.

He was starting to lean in even closer when she leaned forward, gave him a quick peck on the cheek, and scurried down the steps to the far side of the car.

They drove quietly back to the station, a confused smile on Boone's face.

When they got back to the station, Madison quickly loaded her things into her car.

"So you'll call me, right?" he said, watching her.

"As soon as I know anything, you'll be the first person I call."

He said it again, more emphatically. "So you'll call me, right?"

She slammed her trunk closed and opened her car door. "Yes, Matt," she said, darting in close to give him another kiss, equally brief, but this one on the lips. "I'll call you."

Before he could react, she was in her car and on her way.

CHAPTER 21

DRIVING BACK to the crime lab, Madison knew her uncle would be annoyed that she was still pursuing the Dawber case, no matter how fruitfully. Instead of calling his cell phone, she left him a voice mail explaining the link between MacClaren and Dawber. Next, she called Spoons to see if he had learned anything.

"Heard you've been pissing people off again," he said in a mock chiding tone.

"Who are you talking about?"

"Heard you've been butting heads with Fenton," he said.

"He's such a dick."

"Yes, he is."

"Speaking of which, do you know Larry Metzger?"

He laughed again. "Organized Crime? Yeah, he can be a piece of work. Good cop from what I hear, though."

"Pain in the ass is what he is."

"So what are you calling about, anyway?"

"Just checking in on all these bodies you got there. Wondering if we've learned anything new."

"A little bit, maybe. I've been pretty bogged down with that Oxford Street thing. Let's see, nothing new on the Dawber kid, as far as cause of death goes." He laughed. "Except for the obvious, of course. I finished up MacClaren, too, after he thawed out. Looks like heart failure, just like on his death certificate, although who knows with all that other weird shit. All that freezing, vitrifiying, whatever the hell they do, the fucking mikes in his head, all that shit. Stinks like a motherfucker with that stuff they got in him."

He laughed wearily. "Anyway . . . Still trying to find out

what the fuck is up with that Perez kid's scalp. That's a mess. Looks like some kind of toxin, bunch of little cuts, all infected like shit. I don't know, maybe that was part of the torture program, but I think it would have taken a little while to get like that. A couple days at least. I sent a sample to Veste for analysis, and some to Sanchez for microscopy."

"Anything else?"

"Oh yeah. Found a little something on McGee, although I doubt it'll be any help."

"What's that?"

"Found some hairs on him. Inside the wound, actually. Stuck to it."

"What kind of hairs?"

"I don't know. Hairs. Black ones and white ones. Three to five inches long. I thought they were fibers at first, but I'm pretty sure they're hairs. I washed them pretty good, but I didn't get a chance to look closely at them. I sent them over to you a couple hours ago. Maybe you could ask Sanchez to ID them for you."

As soon as she got back to headquarters, Madison picked up the hairs at the evidence room, but before she could get them to Sanchez, the lieutenant poked his head out of his office, his face like stone. "Ms. Cross," he said sternly. "In my office, please." Then his head disappeared.

Her body sagged. It was just past three in the afternoon, but it had already been a long day. She was tired.

He was standing inside, holding the door, which threw her. Usually, when he called her into his office to chew her out, his tirade was preceded by a minute of him pretending to look for something on his desk or finish up some paperwork or some other pretense to make her sit and squirm while waiting for the coming lecture.

He nodded at the chair facing his desk, then he sat in his usual position.

"You were out in Lawson?" he asked.

"Yes, I . . ."

He held up a hand. "I appreciate your helping out there, but I need you to check in when you're out of the city. I need to know where you are, okay?"

She nodded.

"I got your message," he said flatly. "I assume you didn't call me on my cell phone because you didn't want to talk to me, you just wanted me to know about this connection between Dawber and MacClaren. And I assume you didn't want to talk to me because you thought I'd be annoyed that you were stepping on Fenton's toes, maybe I'd calm down a bit before we had a chance to speak."

She didn't say anything; in fact, she tried not to react at all. But she had the odd sensation that she was sinking into her chair.

"Actually, it was a smart move," he continued evenly. "I'm not as angry as I was, although, don't get me wrong, I am annoyed with the way you've gone about this."

He paused and let out a sigh. "First, I need to know where you're working. I'm a strong believer in giving my staff as much latitude as possible, but especially if you're working outside of our jurisdiction, I need to know about it. The second thing is, I know you might not be thinking about all this in terms of a career, and you think you can do whatever you like and piss off whoever you like, but you can't keep making enemies. Now . . . it pains me to be telling you this, because it sounds like you did some good police work. And I know Fenton is an insufferable little SOB. But you can't keep provoking him."

At the mention of Fenton's name, Madison sat forward. "So, what, I'm supposed to let him harass this Prager guy until he confesses to something he didn't do, just so I don't piss Fenton off?"

"Maddy, I'm not saying that . . ." he protested, backing away from the desk. But before he got a chance to tell her what he was really saying, they were interrupted by a terse knock at the door.

"Come on in," the lieutenant said.

The door shot open, and Fenton stomped into the room, cheeks red and eyes bulging.

"One of your . . ." he started, but he stopped when he saw Madison sitting there. "One of your *technicians*," he began again, sneering this time, "has been interfering with one of my cases, undermining my authority, and jeopardizing the outcome of my investigation."

"You call that an investigation?" Madison muttered.

"Madison, stop it," the lieutenant barked before turning to Fenton. "And which investigation is that?"

"You know what investigation! The Dawber case. The one you called and left the voice mail about."

Madison gave her uncle a sidelong look, but he refused to make eye contact.

"She's been poking around, asking questions, and fucking things up," Fenton continued. "And now she's come up with this nonsense that it's related to the MacClaren thing? Bullshit."

The lieutenant shrugged. "Sounds to me like she's turned up some good new leads for you, Detective. If I were you, I'd thank her and see where they go."

Fenton smiled patronizingly. "I have every intention of investigating those leads, Lieutenant, just as I had already planned to, *after* I was finished pursuing other more promising leads. The point is, you need to get your people under control, before they cause irreparable harm to my investigation."

Lieutenant Cross stood, hands on his hips, and looked down at Fenton from a six-inch height advantage. "You don't tell me what the point is, Detective, and you damn sure don't tell me how to run my unit, is that understood?"

Fenton recoiled at first when the lieutenant stood up, but his sneer had returned by the time he was finished.

"Oh, don't worry, Lieutenant," he said smugly. "I understand perfectly."

Fenton glared at Madison before turning on his heel and stomping off.

Madison watched him go, and when she turned back, the lieutenant was staring at her.

"Thanks," he said sarcastically, then he looked down at his work, letting her know she was dismissed.

There wasn't anything Madison could say, so she eased herself out of the chair and quietly slipped out of the office.

Entering the hallway, she was startled by Ted Johnson's loud voice. "Cross! There you are."

He was charging down the hallway, away from the crime lab. He grabbed her elbow without slowing down and pulled her along with him.

"Heard about your witness tying MacClaren and Dawber together. Nice work." He grinned. "Fenton's going to be pissed as shit, though. You know that, right?"

"He already is."

Johnson laughed. "Yeah, I didn't think that would take long."

"Where are we going?" she asked as they stopped in front of the elevators.

"OCTF briefing. Thought you might want to sit in."

"Right."

The elevator took them down to the third floor, and they hurried down a corridor to a large conference room.

At the front of the room, a guy in a suit was using a laser pointer to explain a PowerPoint slide being projected onto the wall.

Madison and Johnson tucked themselves into the back of the room, against the wall.

"Larry Metzger," Johnson said quietly.

Madison nodded. "Seems like a bit of a dick," she whispered back.

Johnson smiled. "A bit. Not too bad, though."

The chart being projected onto the wall showed twenty or so headshots, like a page out of a high school yearbook, except for the red lines connecting each picture to several others and the way the faces showed a distinct lack of that fresh, high-school-yearbook look.

Three quarters of the chart was taken up by a vaguely triangular mass of headshots, at the top of which was Ralph Caprielli, the guy in charge. There were three guys directly beneath him, one of whom Madison recognized as Frank McGee. His picture had a red X over it. Next to him was Donny Craig, giving the camera the same dead stare he'd given Madison at Caprielli's.

Madison recognized one of the pictures on the next row as the big guy with the bandaged hand who had also been at Caprielli's. The label underneath it said "Dennis O'Brien."

To the right was a smaller group of photos. At the top was a picture of a chubby-faced Hispanic kid who looked about fourteen compared to Caprielli's men. The caption said "Carlos 'Carwash' Washburn."

The second tier had four pictures: Luis Castillo, Hernan Alvarez, and Ramon Perez, each with an X over it, and Jorge Parga, who looked even younger than his dead comrades.

He looked scared, Madison thought, probably having just been arrested and photographed on his way to juvenile hall. It was an entirely appropriate expression for a picture surrounded by faces with red Xs on them.

Metzger was saying that neither Washburn nor Parga had been seen for several days. The presumption was that they were either dead or in hiding, maybe out of the city. He sounded like he was wrapping up after that, droning a few platitudes about doing the job right and not cutting corners, Sure enough, a couple of seconds later, he clicked off his laser pointer and flicked off the projector.

Immediately, everyone in the seats rose and started filing out of the room. Metzger caught Johnson's eye and cocked an eyebrow at Madison.

Johnson nodded and gently guided Madison toward the front of the room.

"Metzger wants to compare some notes with you," he told her.

Madison gave him a vaguely alarmed look.

"Don't worry, it's cool."

When they reached the front of the room, Metzger stopped packing up the projector and extended his hand to Madison.

"Larry Metzger," he said with a small, efficient smile.

"Madison Cross," she replied.

"We spoke on the phone, right? You've been doing some work on this Caprielli gang war."

"A bit, yeah. I helped Parker with the Castillo and Perez scenes. And I guess the Frank McGee scene, at the hospital."

"Some crazy stuff, huh?" he said, winding the cord for the projector. "Especially Perez, right? You know anything more about that?"

"I'll ask Spoons about it."

"I stopped in yesterday, but he didn't have squat. Hope you have better luck than I did. I heard you processed the scene out in Lawson, the gas station. I didn't see a report on it; why's that?"

"I wasn't really working in an official capacity. More of a favor to the Lawson Police Department. I filed reports with them."

He smiled condescendingly. "Yes, but this is *our* case."

"I don't know. It seems to me that two of those murders occurred in the jurisdiction of the Lawson Police Department."

"Look, Ms. Cross, I know the Lawson Police Department. I worked with Matt Boone's father on a case once or twice. He'd need a lot more than a favor from you to deal with a major crime like this."

"So," she said with growing impatience. "What can I do for you?"

"I know about you. I know you've pissed some people off and I know that you've done some good work. I don't care about that. I don't care if you piss people off. I kind of like it as long as I'm not one of the people you're pissing off. But I don't want you fucking up my case. Right now we're working on getting a wiretap on Caprielli, and I don't want you doing anything that could jeopardize it. Organized crime, these cases take a long time to set up. A lot of time and a lot of money. So don't fuck anything up, okay?"

"Anything else?"

"You find anything, you keep me in the loop."

"And you'll do the same?"

He smiled once more. "No."

CHAPTER 22

ELENA SANCHEZ looked up from her microscope with the same preemptively harried look she always had when she sensed her workload was about to put on some weight.

"I hope you're not asking for anything you need soon," she said, her back arching upright and her chin jutting out. ". . . Because I am totally backed up. Seriously, if you need it before the end of next week, you might as well ask the lieutenant to send it out."

Madison meekly held up the bag with the hairs Spoons had sent her.

Sanchez seemed to deflate.

"Madison! I'm serious," she protested, but with a growl, she took the bag and held it up to examine it. "What is it, anyway?"

"Some kind of hairs. Spoons found them on Frank McGee, in his wound."

"Psh!" Sanchez snapped her fingers. "That's dog hair. It'll take me a while to get it under the microscope, but I'm sure that's what it is."

Madison was taken aback. "You can't possibly know that just from looking."

Sanchez snickered. "Nah. Rourke found some of them on McGee's clothes, but she also found some in the car where they found him. She didn't think it was much of a clue. I don't know what breed it is or anything."

"Dog hair, huh?"

Sanchez studied the hairs in the bag again. "Yeah, if it's the same hair, and it looks like it is."

Just for a second, it looked like a dead end, then Madison

remembered Nanook and Kimba, Caprielli's little dogs. The ones whose hair now covered her sweater.

"If I got you another one for comparison, could you tell me if they are consistent?"

"Yeah, I guess so. Why?"

"Caprielli's got two little dogs, a black one and a white one. This might tie Frank McGee to Caprielli's place."

She dashed back to her desk and grabbed the sweater she had stashed there the day before. Using tweezers, she plucked a dozen or so dog hairs off of the sweater and put them in small evidence bags. A minute later, she was back at the microscopy lab.

"Here you go," she said, holding up the bags.

Sanchez looked at her dubiously. "Where'd you get these?"

"From my sweater. I was wearing it at Caprielli's. His little dogs were jumping up all over me."

"And you think they're the same dogs."

"Yes."

"All right. But like I said, I'm totally backed up, so it's going to have to wait. I can try to get to that, maybe tomorrow, but even that's pushing it. And I can tell you if the hairs are consistent, but if you need to know for sure if they're the same pooches, you're going to have to do DNA."

"DNA?"

Sanchez laughed. "Yeah, DNA. It's your little specialty, remember?"

"Not if it's not human."

"Why not? It's not like you got to check it against CODIS or anything. You just need to check the two sets against each other, right?"

Madison's face fell. "No, it doesn't work like that. You need different enzymes, different primers. The markers are all different. Yes, it's the same basic procedure, but everything else is different." She turned and started walking away, a preoccupied frown on her face.

"Hey, Madison!" Sanchez called after her. "You want me to do this or not?"

"What? Oh, yeah. I guess so."

Madison separated out a couple of white hairs and a couple

of black hairs from each of the samples. She bagged them separately, labeled them, and handed them to Sanchez.

Walking back to her desk, she considered her options.

The first thing she did was call Rourke and ask her what she knew about the hairs.

"Yeah," she replied distractedly. "He had some hairs on his pants, but they came from the car he was in. I found some on the backseat as well. I sent them to Sanchez for analysis. She said they looked like dog hair. Why?"

"Well, Spoons found some of those hairs in McGee's wound under the field dressing."

"And?"

"Well, that suggests he was exposed to the hairs after he was shot but before that dressing was applied."

"Madison, what are you getting at?"

"Did you ask the owner of the car if they owned a white dog, or a black dog, or if one had been in the car?"

There was a pause. "No, I didn't."

That was an oversight and they both knew it, but Madison didn't want to push it.

"How 'bout I call the car owner and call you back," Rourke offered.

"Thanks."

APART FROM the issue of which species the hairs belonged to, none of the hairs had a root ball, meaning that, the enzyme issue aside, a regular nuclear DNA profile would be impossible anyway. It would have to be a mitochondrial DNA profile.

Madison knew a little bit about canine mitochondrial DNA, and knew it had been ruled admissible in court. She had done some reading and had even met Joy Halverson, the woman who practically pioneered the field, when Joy was in Philadelphia testifying in a murder trial. But this was the first time Madison had encountered it firsthand.

Halverson's company, QuestGen, was the primary source of such canine profiles, but QuestGen was all the way out in California and Madison wanted to get this done fast. In the last year or two, some of the private paternity testing labs had started offering the mitochondrial DNA testing, but Madison knew they were just going to send it off to another lab. She didn't have that kind of time.

As she sat at her desk, drumming her fingers and wondering what to do next, she remembered meeting a veterinary geneticist named Charlene Wong at a conference a few months earlier. On a hunch, she picked up the phone and called the University of Pennsylvania's School of Veterinary Medicine.

She asked for Charlene Wong, and they put her on hold.

Three transfers later, Charlene came on the line.

"Hi, Charlene, this is Madison Cross. I don't know if you remember me, but we had lunch between sessions at the genetics conference at Johns Hopkins this past fall."

"Oh sure. Madison, yeah, I think you had just joined the Philly Crime Scene Unit, right?"

"Yeah, that's right."

"How are you? You still with the police department? I seem to remember you being a little ambivalent at the time."

Madison laughed. "Still here, still a little ambivalent."

"I hear you . . . So what's up?"

"I need a favor, but I don't know if you can help me or not. Maybe you can point me in the right direction."

"What is it?"

Madison explained about the two pairs of dog hair samples and how she needed mitochondrial DNA profiles to see if they were consistent.

"Oh, there's lots of places that can do that these days. You can just search it online, or if you like I can give you a couple of names."

"The thing is, I'm pretty sure they all send the samples out. That's going to take two weeks at least. I kind of need it sooner than that."

"And you just need to know if they match, right?"

"That's it."

She laughed. "Yeah, I can probably help you."

"Charlene, that's great. I really appreciate it."

"No problem. I always wanted to have someone in the police department owing me a favor. Look, I'll be here for another hour or so, if you want to bring it by. I'll see what I can do for you. I could probably get you results the middle of next week."

Madison's heart sank. "Next week?"

"Maybe. Maybe closer to the end."

"Oh."

"Is that a problem?"

"I was hoping to have it sooner."

"Sooner?" She sounded slightly annoyed. "Sorry. Even that's pushing it. You're probably spoiled with your human DNA. We don't have kits or automation. Even apart from the extraction, you got a couple hours for the quanitation, a few more for the PCR amplification, a couple hours to evaluate PCR—that's a full day right there. Then there's the purifying and sequencing reactions, that's three hours; another three for sequencing on the capillary instrument. That's two full days right there, not including data analysis, and not including any of my other work. And there's the weekend."

"No. No, that's great," she said weakly. "I appreciate your help, really. Thanks."

Now Charlene sighed. "Not much help, huh?"

"No, it might be."

"Look, like I said, I'll be here for another hour. And I'll be back on Monday. If you decide to get those profiles done, give me a yell and bring them by. I'll be happy to run them as quickly as I can, okay?"

Madison thanked her again and said she'd probably be calling her soon.

It was just a matter of a few days, but when she got off the phone, Madison felt like the wind had gone out of her sails. She was about to put her head on her desk when Rourke called back.

"No dog," she said when Madison answered. "I had to listen to the owner bitching about that, too. 'What kind of nut job steals someone's car and takes it joyriding with a dog?'" She laughed wearily. "Lady seemed more annoyed about the dog hair than the blood."

"Maybe she's allergic."

"Yeah, maybe so . . . Look, sorry I missed that."

"Rourke . . ." Madison cut her off. "How many of mine have you picked up?"

"Yeah, but still . . ."
"Don't sweat it."

MADISON FOUND Larry Metzger on the first floor, lecturing a pair of uniforms. He saw Madison from the corner of his eye, but did not acknowledge her in any way.

She waited a few seconds before loudly clearing her throat and saying, "Excuse me."

Metzger gave her a glance, but took his time finishing up. When he finally did, he turned to her with an annoyed look on his face. "Yes, Ms. Cross?"

"I think I might have something that can tie Frank McGee to Ralph Caprielli."

He shook his head impatiently. "We've already tied McGee to Caprielli. They have a long history together. We've been documenting it for years."

"No, I mean physically tied. Physical evidence."

"What are you talking about?"

She told him about the dog hairs from Frank McGee and the ones on her sweater, from Caprielli's.

"And are they a match?" he asked.

"Visually, they appear to be. I gave them to Sanchez in microscopy, but she's pretty backed up. I have someone who can run a DNA profile."

"On the dog."

"Yes."

"Dog DNA."

"Mitochondrial dog DNA. Yes, sir."

"And is that recognized? Is it admissible?"

"It's still fairly new, sir, but there's ample precedent. Unfortunately, it's going to take several days to—"

"Several days?"

"Yes, that's right."

He grunted. "But you gave samples to Sanchez, too, right?"

"Yes, sir. But she's pretty backed up, too."

"Okay, good. Is that it?"

"Yes, sir."

Metzger nodded and walked away without another word.

CHAPTER 23

SANCHEZ CALLED at quarter to five. "So what, now you and Metzger are buddies?"

Madison smiled. "What are you talking about?"

"Metzger, from Organized Crime. He called about ten minutes ago. I was getting ready to go. He tells me I have to drop everything else and compare those hair samples you gave me."

"He did? Huh. Well, I did tell him they might be enough to get a warrant on Caprielli."

"You did, huh? Well, I did the comparison and they're consistent, all right. I already called Metzger."

"Thanks, Sanchez."

"Psh. Thank Metzger."

MADISON REWARDED herself with a cup of coffee and a candy bar. Before she had finished it, Johnson called.

"Yo, Madison. Well, it looks like you've got a new number-one fan."

"What are you talking about?"

"Metzger. He's impressed, in his own little way. He says even just with the match Sanchez got on those hairs, he's going to get a search warrant for Caprielli's place."

"Really?"

As she spoke, another call came in. She looked at the display and saw that it was Metzger. "Speak of the devil, he's calling in on my other line. I got to take this. I'll call you later."

She cleared her throat and assembled her professional

phone voice before switching over, slightly nervous about accepting the anticipated praise.

"Madison Cross," she said, annoyed at the sing-song tone that had somehow crept into her voice.

"Cross," he said brusquely. "It's Larry Metzger. We have a warrant to search Ralph Caprielli's building. We're leaving in about five minutes. If you want to come, you can."

"Sure," she said. "That would be . . ." But he was already gone.

Four minutes later she met them in the parking lot.

Ted Johnson was there, along with three guys in OCTF windbreakers she had never met before.

Metzger didn't acknowledge her when she first walked up, but a couple of seconds later he looked in her direction and said, "Here she is," as if he had been waiting.

Madison turned around and saw that he was talking about Rourke, who was hurrying up, pulling on her jacket and sucking on a cigarette.

"Okay," Metzger said to the entire group. "We couldn't get a wiretap on this guy but we have been able to get a search warrant. Physical evidence—dog hair, actually—puts Frank McGee inside Caprielli's living quarters between the time he was shot and the time he died."

Johnson gave Madison a wink.

"What we're looking for," Metzger continued, "is any more physical evidence that would implicate Ralph Caprielli, or anyone else there, in the murder of Frank McGee, or in the negligent homicide that was perpetrated by whoever dressed his fatal injuries and deferred getting him medical treatment until it was too late."

He put his hand to his mouth and looked down at his feet, as if pondering his next words carefully.

"The events surrounding Frank McGee's homicide are our primary goals in searching Caprielli's place. But there are some other things we are interested in. As you might know, Caprielli and his associates have been under investigation for some time on a number of grounds: extortion, money laundering, drugs, prostitution, et cetera. Anything that might be relevant to any of these other areas of interest is fair game.

"Furthermore," he went on, "Caprielli's gang seems to have been involved in a struggle with an upstart rival gang, led by Carlos Washburn. In the wake of some kind of shoot-out at a gas station in Lawson, in Northampton County of all places, several members of this Washburn gang have turned up dead over the course of the last five days: Castillo, Alvarez, and Ramon Perez, who was brutally tortured before his death. Anything that may relate to any of these areas of interest is also fair game."

Metzger paused and looked around him. "Any questions?"

One of Metzger's men raised a hand. "Are we searching a business or a home?"

"The warrant is to search the living quarters only. Apparently, the building houses both, so we need to be careful." He looked at Madison, then turned to Johnson. "You've been inside, how would you describe it?"

"Front part of the building, right inside the door, there's a business area, reception, maybe a couple of offices," Johnson explained. "Past that, there's a residential area. That's where the dogs were, the ones Ms. Cross here used to tie all this together, get you guys your warrant. The entire building surrounds a kind of courtyard–slash–parking area."

"Thank you, Detective Johnson. Anybody else?"

They all shook their heads.

"Okay. Let's go."

METZGER AND the three OCTF guys took Metzger's black Caprice. Johnson and Madison rode with Rourke in her Bronco, taking advantage of the ride over to compare Metzger impersonations and complain that they were just starting the search at a quarter after five on a Friday evening.

"Got to admit though," Rourke said with begrudging respect, "Metzger does get shit done."

When they got out at Caprielli's, Metzger seemed to be eyeing them suspiciously, as if he was somehow aware of their antics on the way over. He gave them a sour look, then he pulled out the search warrant and scanned it one more time before pressing the button on the keypad next to the door.

This time, instead of a voice over an intercom, the door opened, revealing a painfully thin balding man with a weasely face.

"Is Ralph Caprielli here?" Metzger asked.

"No, he's not."

"Philadelphia Police." He held up the warrant. "We have a warrant to search the premises."

"Yes, we know," said the man, taking his time reading the warrant. "I'm his lawyer."

Metzger waited respectfully until the lawyer was finished reading.

"Okay," said the lawyer. "This seems to be in order. The living quarters are accessible from the courtyard. You can drive in through the gate over there." He pointed at the large metal gate set in the wall down the block. "I do not want to see you searching through parts of the building that are not living quarters, and since you're looking for physical evidence relating to the death of Frank McGee, you will not be searching files, computers, etc. And I'll warn you in advance, there are surveillance cameras throughout, so you would be wise not to get too creative with your mandate."

Metzger didn't reply; he simply turned back to his car and motioned for the others to do the same.

They backed down the street and turned in through the now-open gate.

From inside the courtyard, the idyllic illusion was less complete. The flowers and plantings were still nice, but there was an unavoidable sensation of being surrounded by a brick wall, no matter how well concealed.

The entrance to the living quarters was covered by a small sub-roof, like a porch. Inside the heavy, beveled-glass door was a small vestibule with terra-cotta tile floor. Beyond that was the living room.

With a warrant and half a dozen colleagues, Madison didn't feel quite as vulnerable this time. The absence of homicidal goons helped, too.

As they entered the living room, Nanook and Kimba, the two little dogs, were standing in the middle of the room, looking curiously up at them and slowly wagging their tails.

Madison reached down and patted them each on the head. When she stopped, they both jumped up on the white sofa and curled up, watching through sleepy eyes.

They paired up in teams: Madison with Johnson, Rourke with the best looking of the OCTF guys, and the remaining two OCTF guys together. Metzger was content to run the show, helping in the search, but mostly looking over everyone else's shoulders.

"This is the guy you said is now my number-one fan?" Madison asked as they sifted through a wastebasket in a utility room off the commercial-sized kitchen.

Johnson laughed. "Yeah, why? How many fans you think you got? Seriously, though, I hear this Caprielli guy has been up Metzger's nose for a few years now. Metzger's been trying to get him on taxes, RICO, you name it. So far nothing. I think he had big hopes for today."

They finished with the utility room and came out into the kitchen. Through a small window, they could see the setting sun angling across the courtyard, bouncing brightly off the gleaming yellow forsythias that obscured the wall on the other side.

Madison paused, thinking of the other ways she could have been spending a pleasant Friday evening in the spring. As she looked out the window, Rourke emerged into the courtyard, blowing cigarette smoke into the wind and warming her face in the sun.

Johnson turned to Madison and said, "Break time."

Rourke was just finishing her cigarette when they got outside, but she was content to hang out and let it burn down to the filter. She was leaning against a bench next to the porch.

"Bit of a waste of time so far, huh?" Johnson said as they walked up to her.

Madison plopped herself down onto the bench.

Rourke smiled. "Let's just say I've accomplished more in the last two minutes than the rest of the time I've been here." She sucked down the last tar-soaked morsel of her cigarette and flicked the butt into the bushes. "Still a good snag, though, Madison, putting the dog hair together."

"All right, come on," Metzger said, walking up behind

them, clapping his hands. "We're not here to bask in the ambience of Mr. Caprielli's lovely backyard."

Metzger was getting snappy; clearly, he expected they would have found something by then.

They all turned and headed back inside, positioning themselves so their rolling eyes would be out of Metzger's sight.

Madison pushed open the heavy entrance door, but halfway through the vestibule, she stopped.

"Actually," she said, looking down, "I think we might have something here."

"Don't fuck with him," Johnson mumbled. "He is not in the mood."

"No, seriously," she said, kneeling down, studying the terra-cotta tiles. "This looks like blood."

In the orange sunlight filtering through the glass door, a faint, reddish brown smudge was visible running across three of the tiles. The same substance had also collected on the grout between them.

Johnson and Rourke were crouched down beside her now, and Metzger stood over them, arms folded, looking down. "What is it?"

Rourke ignored him. "Madison, can you do a Kastle-Meyer test?"

Metzger watched as Madison opened her kit and took out a handful of small bottles and specimen vial. "What is it?" he asked. "What is she doing?"

"It might be blood," Rourke told him. "We can tell you in a minute."

Kneeling next to the stain, Madison opened the vial and removed the swab from inside. Using a dropper, she placed a few drops of distilled water on the swab, and rubbed the edge of the stain until the swab turned brown. Next, she added a few droplets of phenolphthalein to the swab, followed by a few drops of hydrogen peroxide.

The tip of the swab immediately turned pink.

Madison looked up at Metzger. "It's blood."

He looked at Rourke for confirmation and she nodded.

He nodded back, his head tilting barely two degrees up and back. "Maybe the day will turn out not to be a total waste."

They wrapped up the search shortly thereafter. Metzger confiscated a stained chef's knife, but everyone knew that was just for show. The only thing of any possible consequence was the blood Madison had found.

"You can do DNA on this, right?" Metzger asked as they prepared to leave.

"Absolutely," Madison replied.

"When?"

"I could get it to you tomorrow morning." *Saturday* morning, she thought.

"Let me know as soon as it's done." He got into his car before she could reply and drove away while her mouth was still open.

"Your number-one fan," Johnson said sarcastically, walking up next to her.

"Yeah," she replied. "It's that warm and fuzzy feeling that makes it all worthwhile."

MADISON WAS still annoyed at Metzger when she got back to the lab, but the way she saw it, coming through for Metzger might help counteract some of the political problems she was facing from pissing off Fenton. It bothered her that she was even thinking that way, but she figured it made sense. Besides, at least Metzger was a competent asshole who had achieved rank on merit, as opposed to an incompetent asshole who was only related to rank, like Fenton.

She got started prepping the blood sample as soon as she got back to the lab, but it was only after the thermocycler was running that she checked her computer and saw that she had scored a hit on the database.

Scrolling down, she saw that the ID was Jimmy Dawber of Bartlett, Pennsylvania. For a moment, she was confused as to what sample she had been running, but then she remembered—it was the sample from the lodge in Lawson.

She double-checked to make sure she was looking at the right search result, then checked to make sure she had input the right profile. She double-checked, then triple-checked everything. Then she sat for a while, staring at the screen.

Bartlett and Lawson were not far apart geographically, but that was all the two scenes seemed to have in common. A much bigger connection, Madison knew, was that she was processing evidence from both of them. The more likely explanation was that she had fucked it up, that she had somehow mixed up the two samples, or worse, had tainted one with the other.

She closed her eyes and sighed. She knew in the back of her mind that she probably had too many balls in the air. She had gotten cocky, taken on too much, and screwed it up. She admitted to herself that she was having a hard time keeping the cases straight conceptually; it was no huge leap to think that she had gotten them mixed up from an evidentiary standpoint.

"Shit," she muttered as she thumbed in Boone's number.

"Howdy, Mizz Cross," he answered in a nasally twang, like Goober from *The Andy Griffith Show*.

Madison laughed despite herself. "Hi, Matt."

"Ooh, don't you sound perky."

"I think I fucked up the DNA. The blood from the lodge."

"What do you mean?" He didn't sound so much like Goober anymore.

She sighed. "The DNA analysis, it came back all screwed up."

"How do you mean?"

"I think it got tainted somehow, or mislabeled. It came back as a match for Jimmy Dawber."

"Dawber?"

"Yeah, I know. I'm really sorry. I'll run it again, or maybe try to get a fresh sample. I don't know."

"Hmm. Can you fax it to me?"

"I guess. I don't see what good it'll do you. Don't you want to wait until I run it again?"

"Well, you can send me that, too, but meanwhile, why don't you send me what you have."

"Well . . . okay, sure."

"Thanks. And don't sweat it, okay?"

"All right. I'll fax this now, and I'll call you in the morning."

"Great. Now go get some sleep."

At the sound of the word "sleep," Madison suddenly felt utterly exhausted. She had been thinking about getting started on the second run of the Lawson sample, the one she had screwed up, but she was so tired she didn't want to mess it up again. Still, she was determined to wait until the Caprielli sample was finished in the capillary array so that she could start the database search before she left for the night.

At least that would be ready in the morning.

CHAPTER 24

IN THE back of her mind as Madison went to sleep that night was the tiniest of hopes that maybe she *hadn't* botched the DNA analysis, that maybe the sample *was* a match for Jimmy Dawber. As she slept, her subconscious explored dozens of different scenarios that could explain that coincidence, all of them different except that in all of them, she would be vindicated.

She woke at 7:00, and it wasn't until she was showered and dressed and headed for the door that she remembered it was Saturday morning. Metzger was waiting for those results, she told herself, that's why she was going in. And she needed to retest the samples from the lodge. The fact that she didn't seem to have a life outside of work had nothing to do with it.

As she drove in, she tried to remember the vindication scenarios from the previous night, but they all seemed ridiculously far-fetched.

Ben Moyers called on her cell as she was driving in and said he was having a hard time getting through the shell corporations and holding companies to find out who actually owned the property the lodge was sitting on. He said he had brought in a friend from the Treasury Department, Stan Creighton, and they had penetrated a few layers.

"Anything illegal?" Madison had asked.

"Nothing yet," he replied. "But anything that needs to be hidden this well can't be on the up and up."

"Well, thanks, Ben," she told him. "And thanks for working on it on a Saturday."

"Saturday? Oh, yeah, it is, isn't it?"

Ben's call was only faintly encouraging, but enough for Madison's purposes. By the time she got to work she was feeling guardedly optimistic.

Until she got to her desk. When her computer screen lit up, she saw that the Caprielli sample had gotten a hit on the database, too.

Jimmy fucking Dawber. "Shit!" she said out loud.

Jimmy Dawber had been smashed into tiny pieces, she reasoned, and while those pieces appeared to be accounted for, it was entirely possible that a few of them could have gotten around.

But that was bullshit and she knew it.

She'd fucked it up again. She looked at her watch, thinking she could run the sample once more, at the same time she was running the Lawson sample again.

Then her cell phone went off, and the display said it was Lieutenant Larry Metzger.

"Shit!" she said again, louder.

She stared at the phone as it rang again and again.

She knew she had to answer it.

"Madison Cross," she said brightly.

"Hello, Ms. Cross," Metzger said with a forced pleasantness. "I was just checking on the status of the DNA analysis from the Caprielli search yesterday. Have you had a chance to finish the analysis?"

"Actually, I was just about to call you, sir."

"Excellent, and what do we have?"

"Well, we have a bit of a problem."

"A problem?"

"Yes, I'd like to run the sample again."

"Well . . . What happened?"

"I'm not sure, sir. The result could be correct, but it's possible the sample was somehow tainted." She didn't want to even mention the possibility that the entire sample had gone missing, or that Dawber's DNA had turned up in another unrelated case as well.

"Tainted?"

"Possibly. With DNA from another case."

He made a strangled, gurgling noise that grew fainter, as if he had lowered the phone. After a few moments he came back on the line. "What was the result?"

"It came up as a match for Jimmy Dawber, sir. He was a victim in a different case, sir."

"Dawber? That's the dismemberment case, right?"

"Yes, sir."

"Jesus Christ! So there's bits of this kid all over the place down there? Is that it?!"

Madison's mind raced through all the interactions she'd had with Jimmy Dawber's remains.

"No," she said evenly. "No, sir, that's not it at all."

"Well, this is a goddamn mess! What are you going to do about it?"

"As I said, I'll run the analysis again, sir."

"And if it comes back wrong again?"

"I didn't say it was wrong. I said it was *possible* there was a problem. It's also possible the result is correct. In fact, it probably is," she added defensively.

Metzger breathed heavily into the phone for a moment. "I have a meeting with the FBI in D.C., but I'll be back at five o'clock. I expect an accurate result by the time I get back."

Then he hung up.

She immediately punched in Boone's number, to tell him that she'd gotten another bad result, and that she was even more convinced what she had given him was wrong.

He answered the phone practically singing.

"Hey, Boone. Well, I'm glad one of us is happy. What are you so up about?"

"We're going back in."

"What do you mean?"

"We're going back inside that lodge. I got us another warrant."

"Based on what?"

He laughed. "Based on the DNA results."

"Matt! You didn't! I told you those results were probably wrong. You used them anyway?"

"Well, I told him they were preliminary results, but it turns out Wilbur's nephew was friends with Dawber's brother or something. Something like that. Worked out for the best, right?"

She made a guttural sound in her throat. "No, it's not all right! Jesus, Matt, I didn't think you were going to use those."

"Come on, don't you think you're overreacting?"

She told him about the Caprielli search, and how that sample came up matching Jimmy Dawber as well.

"Oh."

"Yeah, 'oh.' I'm screwed."

"No, you're not. It'll be okay. Look, it's not like this is trial evidence . . . you got the result, I used it to get a warrant—we don't find anything, it doesn't matter anyway. We do find something, it probably won't matter if there was a lab error in the warrant request. Besides, the result's probably right."

"What do you mean, 'If *we* find anything'?"

He laughed again, nervously. "Well . . . I need you to come out and help me."

She laughed, too, but it was tired and exasperated. "Matt, I don't know if I can. I mean, I probably couldn't anyway, but now with all this, today is going to be a mess."

In the back of her mind, she wondered if maybe she had screwed everything up because she was slightly distracted.

"Come on, Maddy, I need you." It threw her when he called her Maddy. She usually only let Uncle Dave and Aunt Ellie call her that, but she didn't correct him. "We could pick up some Gretwiches," he sang seductively.

She sighed, finding it hard to resist him. The idea of getting out of town, even if just for a few hours, felt suddenly very appealing. And it *was* Saturday. She was still annoyed that he had used her faulty result to get a warrant, but she wanted to see him.

She looked at her watch. Metzger wasn't going to be back until five o'clock. That left her plenty of time to get the thermocycler started, get up to Lawson for a couple of hours, and get back in time to run the capillary array and compare the samples.

"All right," she said, surprised to hear herself saying it.

"All right?"

"All right."

"Sweet."

* * *

FIGHTING THE urge to hurry, she moved very deliberately as she once again prepared a portion of the Caprielli sample for the thermocycler. It was highly unlikely that any error had occurred during this part of the procedure, but she was determined that if it had, it wasn't going to happen again.

She turned on the thermocycler and shot out the door.

Seventy minutes later she was parking in one of the visitors' spaces outside the Lawson Police Department.

Gloria was sitting at her desk, typing. She looked up when Madison walked in, but before she could say anything, Boone came out from his office in the back.

"Hello, Ms. Cross," he said loudly, hurrying past Gloria's desk.

"Hello, Chief Boone."

He turned to Gloria. "You remember Ms. Cross, don't you, Gloria?"

"Of course I do," she said warmly. "Nice to see you again, Ms. Cross."

"Nice to see you, too, and call me Madison."

Boone leaned over the reception desk. "Gloria, can you do me a favor and check the fax machine in my office? I think there's some paper or something stuck in there, and I can't get it out."

"Certainly, Chief." She smiled sweetly and ambled back to the office.

Boone watched her go and as soon as she disappeared through the door, he pulled Madison to him and kissed her. She was taken by surprise, but without thinking, she responded, with a long, wet kiss.

His hand felt inconceivably strong against the small of her back, supporting her as she bent slightly backward.

He stepped back, just as Gloria emerged from the office.

"It seems to be working fine, now," she said as she walked back toward them.

"I've been looking forward to that," he mumbled.

Madison was still breathing hard. Gloria looked back and forth between her and Matt, who was grinning stupidly.

"Right," Gloria said, her eyes narrowing as a sly smile spread across her face. "Well, you let me know if the fax machine starts acting up again."

"Thanks," Boone told her. Then he turned to Madison. "Well, it's nice to see you, Ms. Cross. Thanks for coming out to help us."

She laughed. "My pleasure, Chief Boone."

Boone checked to make sure the warrant was in his shirt pocket. "Okay, let's go. So have you told Fenton yet that his vic's DNA is popping up all over the place?"

She shuddered and shook her head.

"Ugh, no. The last thing I want is to hear him going on about how I made a mistake. I can just imagine."

"Well, I can't believe he'd be in much of a position to criticize. Didn't he have half the department searching some guy's house near where Dawber was found? Didn't he practically have some neighbor sitting on death row even though there was nothing tying them to it?"

"Well, to be fair, the trash bag had the guy's prints on it. But it was pretty obvious early on that it wasn't him. Fenton wouldn't let it go, like he just didn't want that easy answer to not be the one. Anyway, I'm going to make damn sure I actually made a mistake before I fess up to it with him."

They drove past Dale's gas station, still encircled with crime scene tape.

"So whatever happened to Dale, the gas station guy?"

Boone shrugged. "He's up in the hills somewhere. Pain in the ass, too. Next closest gas station is ten miles away. Costs a nickel more, too. A couple people said they'd seen him, up on the hiking trails. Guy named Greg Howtzer said he ran across him at a campsite; Dale told him he'd seen something terrible at the gas station, something he wouldn't talk about. Greg came right to me and I got out there less than a half hour later, but Dale was already gone. All he left were some smoldering ashes and some fish bones. That's about it. He must have seen some shit, all right, because the guy is spooked."

A few minutes later, they turned onto the access road and pulled up in front of the lodge.

It looked exactly as it had before, inside and out.

Madison unpacked her supplies in the small kitchen area and headed upstairs to the bedroom.

Kneeling beside the bed, she shook open an evidence envelope and scooped up one of the crumpled tissues.

"Taking some 'tissue' samples, eh?" Boone said, walking up behind her. "Looks like exciting work."

"Just how I imagined it." She wrinkled up her face as she scooped up a second tissue.

"Hey, just keep telling yourself, maybe the guy had a bad cold or something."

"I'm just hoping I can get good samples off them."

"Yeah, I wouldn't worry about that. They look like they'll give you all the DNA you could need."

They worked separately and wordlessly after that, exchanging awkward smiles when they crossed paths.

Madison closed the curtains and used up two small bottles of luminol, spraying over much of the floors and walls, but the only reaction she got was on the stone floor, where she had originally found the other blood.

The pattern of the reaction was unusual: an irregular sprinkling of speckle marks with swaths of floor that were devoid of spots and then streaks in between where the spots were densely spaced. The spots were small, some small enough to suggest an impact with great force.

Looking more closely, she saw that the particles were irregularly shaped as well; some were round, others oddly triangular, but none showed the teardrop-shaped distortion most typical in blood spatter patterns. And even taking into account the effort that had been made to clean it up, the pattern of dots was strangely unlike any spatter marks she had ever seen.

There was no sign of blood on the walls, only on the floors. That in itself was odd in such close proximity to a high-velocity impact spatter. She thought at first it might be a void pattern, as if something had blocked the spatter, but the entire wall was clean and the spattering on the floor went right up to the wall.

Before moving on with the search, she took photos of the area while the luminol was still luminescent, then she blotted up several samples of the blood for DNA analysis later. She was painstakingly careful to follow procedure.

They searched the place for another hour, but found absolutely nothing. Madison reminded herself that the Caprielli search had been fruitless, too, until she found the bloodstain outside, but that reminded her of the possibly botched DNA analysis and all her anxieties came back.

When they were done with the search, Boone loaded the equipment into the back of the cruiser while Madison packed the blood samples away.

She felt anxious and yet apprehensive about getting back to the city, getting the samples processed, and finding out for sure that she had either botched the previous analysis or been correct. Whether she was vindicated or not, she had a lot of work ahead of her, especially if she had to start trying to figure out how these bizarre cases could be related.

They were both quiet driving back to the station, both lost in thought. As they approached Lawson's main intersection, Boone looked over and said, "It's nice to see you, Maddy."

She smiled. "It's nice to see you, too, Matt."

The light turned yellow and Boone slowed to a stop and came in for a kiss.

She kissed him back, then pushed him away, laughing at the sad-puppy expression on his face.

"I am *not* going to make out with the chief of police in a police car in the middle of town in the middle of the afternoon," she told him. "You must be nuts."

He gave her a sly look. "I guess I am at that."

"The light's green," she told him.

"How 'bout lunch?" he asked. "Ready for another Gretwich?"

She looked at her watch and thought about it. It was half past one, so she had some time before she had to get back, but with so much going on, she knew she shouldn't. "I'll have to take a rain check. I didn't really have time to come out here in the first place. I hate to think about what's waiting on my desk. Metzger is supposed to be back at five and I need to have everything ready, either to defend my results if they seem to be right, or get ready for the consequences if I botched them like I think I did."

"I'm starting to really dislike this Metzger guy. First he poaches the McGee case. Now he's coming between me and my girl."

She raised an eyebrow. "I beg your pardon?"

"Okay, okay. Sorry. Maybe that's pushing it."

"Maybe just a bit, yeah."

"But he did poach the McGee case."

Madison didn't say anything at first, but it was undeniable. "I know. It's messed up."

"I'd like to see the look on his face when I take it back from him," he said with hollow-sounding bravado.

She smiled.

"Hey, I know," he said, like he just had a thought. "How about we just *split* a Gretwich?"

"I'd like to," she said quietly. "But I shouldn't."

He looked disappointed but he smiled anyway. "Well, I'm glad you came out."

He put his hand on her thigh.

She let him keep it there, feeling the warmth of his skin. She even put her hand on top of his.

They were approaching the road leading to their picnic place, and Madison eyed it with longing, nostalgic already for the time they had spent there.

As they got closer, she snatched her hand away from his and put it in her handbag.

"Crackers!" she said.

"What?" he asked, bewildered by her outburst.

"Crackers," she said, pulling out a small package of peanut butter crackers. "I've got time for that, a quick picnic. I'll split them with you."

He grinned. "I love those things."

He swerved off to the side of the road, pulling into the same little lane they had taken to their first picnic. They bounced up the hill, a little faster than the last time, and stopped in the same small stand of high grass.

He opened her door and bowed as she got out. She tucked the crackers into the back pocket of her jeans and as she took his hand, he led her through the tall grass. This time, though, when they reached the boulder, instead of helping her up into the river rocks, he stopped and pulled her in tight.

His lips crushed hers and she crushed his right back. His hands roamed and she let them, her hands busy roaming as well. She felt like she was stumbling down a steep incline, like her hands and feet were keeping her upright but gravity was impelling her forward.

She pulled at his shirt, tugging it out of his pants. He started unbuttoning it but she yanked it up over his head. He pulled back to let her, grinning and cupping her face in his hands, kissing her again and again.

When she put her hand on his shoulder she felt a piece of fabric stuck to the skin. She looked around to see what it was.

"A nicotine patch?" she asked, surprised and disappointed. He looked down sheepishly. "I'm trying to quit."

She held his face and looked him in the eye. "You'd better." Then she kissed him again.

His hands were in her hair, then they drifted away, one of them sliding down her back, squeezing her ass.

His other hand slid up her ribs, then he grabbed the bottom of her shirt and lifted it off her in one motion. She held up her arms, a gesture that felt like outrageous abandon. The stone felt rough against her back, and with the warm sun and the cool breeze on her skin, she felt like part of it all, another element of nature.

Her bra was gone. The breeze caressed her nipples, then his thumbs did the same. She tugged off his belt, gasping at the urgency of his erection.

As his pants slid down his thighs, she whispered, "Do you have protection?"

He caught his pants before they fell completely and he tugged his wallet free, sliding a condom out with his thumb.

"So," she said with a wry smile as he frantically tore it open, "you're the kind of guy who carries a condom, huh?"

"Actually, I got two," he grinned, breathing hard. "But I bought them yesterday morning."

She swatted him playfully and he pulled her in for a kiss.

Then he was inside her, and she wondered if maybe it had been as long for him as it had been for her.

He was taking his time, at first, holding back. He was going slow and she was melting. For the briefest instant, in the back of her mind, she thought that if he didn't get on with it, she was going to be late getting Metzger his results.

Then he did get on with it, and she stopped thinking altogether.

CHAPTER 25

AS SHE drove back to Philadelphia, Madison's mind was all over the place. Her thoughts alternated between her relationship with Matt Boone, panic that she was going to be late getting results for Larry Metzger, and a frantic consideration of all the different scenarios that could spin out of all the different possible results for the evidence she had with her and the samples she was running again.

The peanut butter crackers were pretty well smashed, but she was hungry. As she poured the crumbs into her mouth, bit by bit, she considered the different scenarios that might help Boone claim jurisdiction on the Frank McGee murder. Everyone assumed McGee had been shot at the gas station; Metzger was being obtuse just so he could retain jurisdiction.

Complicating matters was the unnerving feeling that she had somehow put her clothes back on wrong, and the fact that she couldn't stop smiling nonetheless.

Her life had been the Crime Scene Unit since returning to Philadelphia. She'd been working hard and there hadn't been much time for a relationship. And even if there had been, it seemed like the only people she'd met since coming home had been cops and corpses.

Well, he's definitely not a corpse, she thought with a smile.

The thoughts were still whirling through Madison's head when she got back to the crime lab.

She had plenty of time before Metzger got back, but she still had some work to do.

The Caprielli sample was finished in the thermocycler. She said a little prayer as she put it in the capillary array, but she didn't know what result she was praying for. Just that whatever it was, it turned out to be right.

Once the capillary array was running, she pulled on a pair of exam gloves and opened up the envelopes with the tissues from the bedroom at the lodge.

Each tissue went into a separate bowl of distilled water to soak. When they were finished steeping, she pipetted a small amount of liquid out of each bowl and squirted it into a microtube along with some enzyme solution, then they went into the thermocycler.

She heard a knock on the door and opened it to see Ted Johnson standing in the doorway.

"Cross! There you are!" he said. "Where you been, girl?"

"Hey, Ted. What's going on?"

Johnson stepped into the small room and closed the door behind him, standing with his back against it. "Fucking Metzger and his OCTF assholes, that's what. He's being a total dick. And by the way, he ain't your number-one fan anymore."

"Yeah, I kind of gathered that. What's going on?"

"Guy's been getting up my fucking nose, calling me all day, asking me did I do this, did I do that. Motherfucker's got jurisdiction over the case, not over me. I didn't bust my ass to get to homicide detective so I could take shit from that pussy."

Madison smiled to herself. Ted Johnson was not someone who took kindly to being dissed.

"Yeah, don't laugh, there, Cross. I heard he's been on the phone, talking shit about you, too. He's saying you screwed up the DNA analysis on the results from Caprielli's place."

She shrugged. "Well, he might be right. I kind of told him that was a possibility. The cases seem to be otherwise totally unrelated. I had to consider the possibility that the sample was switched or tainted."

"Wait, wait, wait. Isn't Dawber the case you was asking Boone about when we were out there in Lawson?"

"Yeah. Dawber's from out near there."

"Metzger said he ain't even going to look into all that. Said it was 'not a valid area to explore.' You ask me, that's a connection right there. You got all these gangster types from around here going out in the sticks like that, then a guy from out there shows up in pieces around here? Doesn't seem like much of a stretch to me."

The way he said it, it was starting to seem possible that the two cases might actually be related.

"Look," he continued. "How confident are you that you got the sample right?"

She took a deep breath. "You know what? If the results weren't so strange, I would have sworn there was no chance I'd screwed it up. But there's more."

"More what?"

She told him about the result she got from the bloodstain they'd found in the lodge.

"Hmm," he grunted. "You know what, though? It doesn't even matter. These guys are just being dicks, they're trying to shoehorn everything to try to fit their needs. They don't give a shit about anything else, they're just trying to push their RICO case or whatever. Shit, maybe it was Jimmy Dawber's blood after all, right? Might not have anything to do with OCTF. Could be just a good old-fashioned homicide."

"Four of them."

"Whatever." He shook his head and picked up the phone, started punching in a number. "Fuck it."

"Who are you calling?"

He held up a finger while he listened to the phone ringing.

"Yes, hello," he said. "This is Detective Johnson from the Philadelphia Police calling for Mr. Caprielli."

He listened for a moment, then laughed. "Now, sir, there's no need to be like that. Just tell Mr. Caprielli I'd like to talk to him for one moment about getting Lieutenant Metzger off his back. Yes, I'll hold."

Madison shook her head. "Damn, Ted, you are cheeky."

He wiggled his eyebrows at her, then brought his attention back to the phone.

"Yes. Okay, I'll be there in ten minutes." He put away his phone and looked over at her. "I'm going to go talk to Ralph Caprielli. You coming?"

* * *

THIS TIME, Caprielli's door buzzed before they even got to it. They walked unaccompanied down the entry hallway and into the atrium. The receptionist was back on duty, and she waved them to the seats.

"Mr. Caprielli will be with you in one moment."

Johnson got to his feet when Caprielli arrived, towering over him but not intimidating him in the least.

"Okay, Detective, what's this about?"

Johnson shrugged. "I know Metzger's been a pain in your ass, and frankly he's been a pain in mine, too. I'm in homicide, and I have a few of those I'm trying to solve. He's in Organized Crime and we all know he's had his eye on you. That's fine as far as I'm concerned, probably an appropriate allocation of resources, if you know what I mean. Unless it gets in the way of my homicide, that is. So I have a quick question for you, might help me with my case, and might get Metzger to stop trying to make it part of whatever the fuck it is that you guys are up to."

"What's your question?" he said impatiently.

"Do you know a guy named Jimmy Dawber?"

He snorted and smiled. "Jimmy Dawber? Yeah, I know a guy named Jimmy Dawber. Why?"

"How do you know him?"

"I've known Jimmy Dawber for years. He used to be my fishing guide. Best damn guide in Bucks County until he lost his license."

"Has he ever been here?"

"Here in this building?"

"Yes."

"Yeah, I think so. Yeah, sure, he's been here a couple times. Why? What's this about? Is he in trouble again?"

Johnson smiled but didn't answer him. "Thanks for your cooperation, Mr. Caprielli."

"SO WHAT does that mean?" Madison asked when they got back into Johnson's car.

Johnson shrugged. "What does it mean? Doesn't mean a whole lot, really. But it means that there's a good chance you didn't fuck up that blood sample, and that's something. That blood could have been old, you know? But Caprielli's boys were still mixing it up with the Carwash gang, so we're not necessarily rid of our friend Metzger as we try to solve all these goddamn murders." He grinned. "But I'll tell you one thing it does mean. He's going to be pissed off like a motherfucker when I tell him the Dawber connection is for real. And I tell you what else, I was talking to your boyfriend, Boonie . . ."

"Don't," she said, trying to sound stern enough to divert attention from the color she could feel on her cheeks.

He laughed. "Yeah, all right. Anyway, he's still working on establishing his jurisdiction over the McGee case. He didn't think it was funny having Metzger steal his case like that, especially when everybody knows that shit went down out in Lawson." He shook his head and laughed again. "Boonie gets something in his head like that, he usually figures out a way to make it happen, and I hope he does, too, 'cause if he figures out a way to tie McGee to that shoot-out at the gas station, Metzger's going to go absolutely *ballistic*."

Johnson was laughing hard, having a good old time imagining that scene. But something about what he said set Madison's mind going, picturing a different scene.

In her mind, she was picturing the crime scene at Dale's gas station, all the different bullets they'd found, and the bloodstains on the ground. She'd been over the crime scene a hundred times in her head and she knew that with so much going on, there were bound to be dozens of unexplainable loose ends, but she had the sudden, unmistakable feeling that one of those loose ends was lying in plain sight, waiting for her to find it and tie it up.

She pictured the bloodstain that she'd sampled and ID'd as having come from Frank McGee—the one that marked Frank McGee's fatal injury, she knew. If they'd had the murder weapon, they could have tied the injury to the scene, and together with the bloodstain it would have been a no-brainer. But that gun still hadn't turned up.

Her eyes were closed as she tried to force the answer to come into focus. She could feel her forehead wrinkling into a tight knot.

"Damn, Cross. You okay?"

She held up a hand and shushed him, so his words didn't chase away the answer that was so tantalizingly close.

She could see the shells lying on the pavement . . . the slugs she'd pulled out of the car . . . the motor oil that spilled down the display.

Her eyes shot open. "Motor oil!" she exclaimed, loud enough that she felt the car swerve.

"Motor oil?" Johnson asked. "What the hell are you talking about, woman?"

"Motor oil, Ted," she repeated, with a raucous laugh. She got out her phone and called Chuck Gerald. She had his cell phone number, but she tried him at the ballistics lab first.

He answered on the second ring, and she thought for a second how sad it was that he was always working. Then she remembered how she was spending her Saturday.

"Chuck. Hi, it's Madison Cross."

"Hello."

"Hey, when we brought that bullet over, the one from Frank McGee, remember when you washed it? There was that residue floating on the top?"

"Yes."

"Do you still have that?"

"No. We throw everything out after twenty-four hours."

Madison felt her heart plummeting, until she realized that statement was ridiculous. "Chuck, don't fuck with me."

"Of course we have it. I sent a tiny bit down for analysis. I think Aidan Veste is doing it."

She smiled. "Thanks, Chuck."

"What's going on?" Johnson asked as she clicked down to Aidan's cell phone number and pressed call.

Aidan answered with an exaggeratedly annoyed tone. "What is it now, Madison?"

"Hi, Aidan. What're you up to?"

"Beautiful Saturday afternoon in spring, what else would I be doing? I was taking a break from analyzing accelerants from the Oxford Street fire so I could analyze your strange, smelly yellow fluid, which is looking more and more like some sort of cryoprotectant, but I had to take a break from that because I had a hunch you'd be needing an analysis on the residue from that bullet that Chuck Gerald sent over."

"You really do care," she said jokingly.

He laughed but didn't say anything.

"Did you find anything?" she asked.

"Seems to be about eighty-five percent saturated hydrocarbons, with most of the rest made up of detergents, some graphite, other stuff."

"So it's motor oil?"

"Very good." He seemed impressed she knew what that was. She didn't tell him she had known the answer ahead of time.

"Beautiful. Can you send me a copy of that analysis?"

"I already did."

"Thanks, Aidan."

"Bye, Madison."

She ended the call and immediately started punching in Boone's number.

"What the fuck is going on here?" Johnson demanded. "What are you talking about?"

"Remember in Lawson . . ." she started to answer, but Boone answered his phone. "Matt, it's Madison."

"Hey, babe," he started, but she cut him off.

"I'm here with Ted Johnson," she said.

"Hey, Boonie!" Johnson yelled.

"Oh," Boone said, sounding disappointed. "Tell him I said hi."

She ignored him. "Remember when we brought that bullet from Frank McGee over to ballistics? There was that oily residue that came off the bullet when Chuck Gerald washed it?"

"Vaguely, yeah. Why? What's up?"

"It was motor oil," she said proudly. "That's what."

"Motor oil," he repeated. "Okay."

"Don't you get it?"

"No."

"Me, neither," Johnson added, loudly, so he could be heard over the phone.

"Motor oil," she went on. "Remember at the crime scene,

one of the bullets we traced but didn't recover was the one that went right through that motor oil display, leaving oil all over the place? We knew which way it went, but there was no slug left behind, was there?"

". . . No."

"And it wasn't left behind because it was lodged in Frank McGee's back."

"So . . . what about the motor oil?"

"The bullet was coated in oil from when it passed through the display, through the can of oil. When Chuck Gerald washed the bullet in the ballistics lab, the oil came off."

"So, you think you can prove it's the same oil?"

"I would think so. Just need to test it against what's in that can, make sure it's the same kind of motor oil. That would put Frank McGee's murder at your little gas station there, Chief Boone. And I think it would be pretty hard to argue that was not in the jurisdiction of the Lawson Township Police Department."

Boone let out a short, incredulous laugh. "You're awesome, Madison. I mean it. I owe you."

"Buy me a Gretwich," she told him.

"You got it," he said. "You just need to get yourself back out here to collect."

CHAPTER 26

As she plopped down at her desk back at the C.S.U., Madison felt pretty good.

The retest on the blood they'd found at Ralph Caprielli's matched Jimmy Dawber again. That didn't prove anything about whether the sample somehow got tainted, but at least she could now be reasonably sure she hadn't screwed up the test itself.

Of course, while this might get her off the hook, it wasn't going to make Metzger any happier.

She leaned back in her chair for a moment and closed her eyes, pondering the fact that in her entire academic career, she had only really butted heads with at most two or three other people. She wondered what it was about police work that brought out the contrarian in her. Probably the people she was working with, she thought.

When she opened her eyes, she saw that the lieutenant was standing in front of her desk, his knuckles poised to rap on it. He was wearing a blue sweater and brown cords in deference to the weekend.

"Haven't seen you much this week, Ms. Cross," he said, smiling thinly.

"Been a busy week."

"Busy weekend, too. Could you step into my office for a minute?"

"Sure," she replied, wondering which infraction she was going to hear about.

The lieutenant waited at the door and closed it behind her before crossing around to his desk and sitting down.

"How's the Oxford investigation going?" she asked brightly.

He shook his head. "It's a lot of work. Seemed like a sure bet the meth factory was the target. Starting to look now like maybe the druggies were the innocent bystanders, or innocent of this, at least."

She leaned forward. "What do you mean?"

"I mean, now it looks like the fourteen-year-old girl who lived next door broke up with her boyfriend; he came back and torched her house in a fit of jealousy. The chemicals in the drug lab didn't take much coaxing to go up, and when they did, it looked like that was what started the blaze."

"What about the shooting? Weren't there people shot execution style?"

"That's what we thought. Turns out it was only one of them, and now it's looking more like he left his gun on his night table. The heat from the blaze caused the bullet in the chamber to go off. Shot him in the head."

"Wow."

"Yeah. The DA's got the kid in custody. Fifteen years old. Wants to try him as an adult."

"Six dead . . ."

"Yup. Six dead."

They were quiet for a second, then he leaned forward over his desk. "So what have you been doing with yourself this week?"

"Lots of stuff," she replied, wondering where this was going. "The MacClaren case, the Jimmy Dawber case, the whole Caprielli thing."

"And how's that all going?"

She had the distinct impression that he was leading her somewhere. "Well, actually, I think we're making some progress. There seem to be some surprising overlaps."

He raised his eyebrows, waiting for more.

"As you know, Dawber worked for MacClaren. And it's looking like Dawber had been in the deep freeze, too, although he didn't have any prep work."

"And you've been spending a lot of time out in Lawson."

She nodded but didn't comment. "The weird thing is, now Dawber's DNA seems to be popping up all over the place."

"Right." He looked down at his desk. "I heard about that.

I'm wondering if you're stretched a little too thin, maybe taking on too much. Maybe helping out in Lawson a little too much." He held up a hand before she could protest. "I'm just saying that it doesn't take much more than the tiniest bit of carelessness or sloppiness to undo a lot of good police work."

"You mean you think I botched the Caprielli DNA samples?"

"According to Metzger you pretty much said so yourself."

"Well, I thought so, at first. Especially when I analyzed a sample of blood from a lodge out in Lawson that was also connected to the gas station shoot-out. It came back as Dawber, too."

"What do you think now?"

"I don't know. I just finished the retest on the sample from Caprielli's and it's Jimmy Dawber again. Plus, now it turns out Ralph Caprielli knew Jimmy Dawber. He was his fishing guide."

"Really? How do we know that?"

"Caprielli said so. Ted Johnson asked him."

He grunted, processing that bit of information. "Does Metzger know about it?"

"The retest or the Caprielli/Dawber connection?"

"Both."

She shook her head. "I just found out myself. We just talked to Caprielli a little while ago, and I just finished the retest before I came in here."

"Right. Well, you should talk to Metzger. He's the lead on this, he should know about it."

She winced. "I don't even know how long he's going to be the lead."

"What do you mean?"

She told him about how the motor oil on the bullet they took out of Frank McGee put that murder in Lawson's jurisdiction.

Lieutenant Cross laughed ruefully. "You know, Metzger's got a lot of juice, and he was pretty impressed by that thing with the dog hair. I was thinking how nice it was that your work was starting to have some political benefit for you . . . Between

the DNA results, right or wrong, and now this, I don't know
how he's going to react."

Just as he said it, his cell phone rang. He looked at the display and held it up for her to see. "I guess I'm about to find
out." The display said it was Larry Metzger.

"He was going to call me when he got back. Can you . . .
tell him about the retest?" She smiled meekly. "Save him a
call?"

He frowned at her, but relented. "Okay. Close the door on
your way out."

She felt guilty but she was relieved not to be telling Metzger
about the results. As she closed the door behind her, she could
hear him answer the phone, "Hello, Larry. What can I do for
you?"

THE POLITICAL and jurisdictional ramifications of Caprielli's relationship with Dawber had been running through
Madison's head since the results in doubt had first come back.
It occurred to her that she hadn't really considered how it affected the actual investigations.

Boone was probably making a move to exercise his jurisdiction over the McGee murder at that very moment, since it now
seemed that two of the homicides had taken place in his town.
Johnson might even be doing the same, arguing that if it's not
OCTF, then he should be lead detective, since he had initially
picked up the Castillo case, the first one to turn up. Fenton was
probably in the fray, too, now, arguing that he should be lead.
Since his cousin was the deputy commissioner and all.

After she took the latest batch of Lawson samples out of
the thermocycler and loaded them into the capillary array,
Madison Googled Caprielli's name and found a handful of
hits on local newspaper sites, mostly stories about investigations that never seemed to go anywhere. Metzger's name figured prominently in several of the stories, mouthing
tightlipped but optimistic platitudes about the prospects of the
investigation.

After a few articles, she felt like she had read the same
piece over and over.

A search of Jimmy or James Dawber turned up a few obscure sports stories about a James Dawber in the north of England.

She sat back, her eyes scanning the results of her latest search while her mind wandered off.

If Caprielli was connected to Jimmy Dawber and Jimmy Dawber was connected to Robert MacClaren, could there be a connection between Caprielli and MacClaren?

She went back and punched up MacClaren again, scrolling through the pages of stories listed. Most of the stories were from the *Philadelphia Inquirer*. She had already read many of them, but as she skimmed through several more, one thing she noticed was that most were written by a staff writer named Sam Schuller.

She called the *Inquirer* and learned that Schuller had retired earlier that year. The woman who answered said they were not supposed to give out information other than that, but she did say Schuller had started his own public relations consultancy.

A search of "Sam Schuller Public Relations" gave her a link to his website, complete with a photo, e-mail address, and phone number. The website looked kind of old school, as did the photo, but it also had a certain polish to it.

Madison called the number listed and it was answered by an older woman with a quavery voice who asked her to hold.

A few moments later, a man's voice came on the line.

"Sam Schuller Public Relations," he said cheerily.

The picture on the website looked like a professional headshot of a white-haired, Waspy-looking guy in a suit. Madison had a hard time putting that face on the nasally voice with the thick Philadelphia accent that was coming from the phone.

Madison identified herself and Schuller asked what he could do for her.

"I've been reading some of your old stories in the *Inquirer* and I was hoping to ask you a few questions about Robert MacClaren."

He started laughing. "Oh, Jesus," he said, "I thought you were calling about one of my clients. Thought I was going to have to start earning my money."

She waited while he laughed a little more.

"Robert MacClaren, huh? Where are you, the Round-house?"

"Yes."

"I'll tell you what. I'm just heading out. There's a place called Zen Garden, right over on Sixth. Can you meet me there in, say, twenty minutes?"

"Great."

"I'll be sitting at a booth in the front."

"It's okay, I've got your photo here from your website."

He laughed. "That photo is very flattering and not very recent. I'll be sitting at a booth in the front."

Zen Garden looked new and it looked clean, but it did not look like a garden. The decor was industrial, with concrete floors, steel tables, and halogen lights hanging from metal conduit cable.

The ventilation system was noisy but effective, and what little aroma Madison could actually detect smelled pretty good.

Sitting at the booth closest to the front door, Sam Schuller looked more like his photo than he let on, a little more wrinkled around the eyes and around the collar, but definitely the same guy.

"Madison Cross," she said as she sat down across from him.

"Sam Schuller," he said, lifting his butt a tiny bit off the seat. He looked around the restaurant. "Guy that owns this place is a client. Don't look like much of a garden, does it?"

Madison smiled. "It's nice."

"I told him: the name or the decor, but not both. But does he listen? Whatever. So, Robert MacClaren, huh?"

"Yes. I need some background on him. You used to write about him quite a lot."

"Yeah, I did. He first became newsworthy when I was just starting. I covered him throughout my entire career at the *Inquirer*."

"You worked the business beat your entire career?"

"Our career paths had some interesting parallels." He smiled. "I started out working the crime beat."

"Crime?"

"Robert MacClaren did not start out as the successful businessman and patron of the arts and charities he was in his later years."

"Really?"

"When I started out at the paper, MacClaren was little more than a street punk. A smart one, a hungry one, but still a punk. He had a few guys under him, a little crew he'd put together. I used to do ride-alongs with the cops in the early days; MacClaren used to get pulled in all the time. But he worked his little operation into a big operation, got a lot better at it. He stopped getting caught, the cops stopped looking his way. I think his criminal empire was a victim of its own success . . . He had no choice but to go legit.

He stopped, and scratched under his chin. "Right around then I got moved from the crime beat to the business page. All of a sudden it's 'Robert MacClaren, up-and-coming entrepreneur.' I didn't think it was the same guy at first, but sure enough, there he was. Within a couple of years he had started his transformation into 'Robert MacClaren, pillar of the community.' He gets himself a classy young wife, gets involved in all these charities. Soon, he's getting more coverage on the society page than anywhere else."

"You know anything about how he died?"

He shrugged. "The death itself was nothing out of the ordinary, from what I hear."

She smiled. "What then?"

He lowered his voice and leaned forward. "There were a lot of rumors about what happened after he died, about how they buried him."

"Like what?"

"I don't know. People said he did a Walt Disney thing, frozen in a big tank, something like that. I pitched it as a story but the paper wasn't interested. Maybe by then he had too many powerful, upstanding friends."

"Do you know where he was supposed to be buried?"

"No." He shook his head. "That was a secret, which in and of itself was no surprise. MacClaren had his charities and stuff, but he was still pretty reclusive. He still had a lot of enemies, from the old days and afterward. You don't get to where he was without pissing some people off."

"Enough of an enemy to kill him?"

"Well, let's just say there were more than a few people who were sorry to hear he was dead because it meant they'd lost the chance to help him get that way."

"So, if MacClaren went legit, what happened to the criminal enterprise? Did he just give it up? Did it just fade away?"

"No. He gave up the day-to-day, but I think he kept a hand in it. From what little I've heard, it's probably doing better now than it ever was. No, he put his son in charge of it."

"Toby MacClaren?"

Schuller started laughing so hard that people on the other side of the bar looked over at them.

"Good Lord, no," he said, wiping his eyes. "Toby Mac-Claren is the straightest arrow I've ever met in my life. No, Toby has worked at Claren Incorporated almost his whole life. Robert made sure he got his MBA, set him up with a very cushy situation at Claren, kept him completely separated from the other side of the business. No, I'm talking about his other son. Toby's illegitimate half brother, Ralph."

"Ralph?"

"Yeah. Ralph Caprielli."

CHAPTER 27

STANDING IN front of the restaurant with her cell phone in her hand, Madison knew she had to call somebody, but she didn't know who. Things were spinning out of control, but instead of everything flying off in different directions, they were coalescing into a single, fucked-up mega case, and she felt like she was right in the middle of it.

Part of her wanted to call Boone. A completely different part of her wanted to call the lieutenant. But she figured as far as the case was concerned, she should be calling Ted Johnson.

"Where are you?" she asked when he answered his cell phone.

"I'm at my desk, eating a hoagie. Why?"

"I'll be in the parking lot in about two minutes. I need you to meet me there."

"Why?"

"I have to go talk to someone and I want you to come with me. I'll tell you more in the car."

Johnson was still eating his sandwich in the parking lot when she arrived. As she pulled up next to him, he threw the remainder in the trash can and wiped his mouth with a napkin.

"This better be good," he said as he got in the car.

"Caprielli is MacClaren's son."

For a moment, all Johnson could do was blink his eyes. "Damn. That is good . . . How do you know?"

"Guy named Sam Schuller, reporter. Used to write about MacClaren for the *Inquirer*. I had read a bunch of his stories online. Figured I should probably talk to him." She laughed. "I wasn't expecting that."

"Who'd you tell?"

"Just you, so far."

"So how do you figure all this adds up?"

"I don't know. I've been thinking about it, trying to tie it all together. We've got Frank McGee, who worked for Caprielli, Jimmy Dawber, who was an old friend, and Robert Mac-Claren, or his remains, who was his father. On the other hand, we've got Castillo, Alvarez, and Perez." She pursed her lips, thinking. "Maybe Metzger's right, it is some kind of gang war. Maybe Carlos Washburn's guys made a move on Caprielli, tried to hit him where it hurts, family and friends. Caprielli responds with overwhelming force, takes out the other gang. Something like that?"

Johnson had been slowly nodding while she outlined the scenario. "Yeah, that's what I'm coming up with, too. Doesn't explain the whole Lawson connection, though."

"Sure it does, if that's where Dawber was, or even Mac-Claren."

"Yeah." He looked off, thinking. ". . . So where the fuck were they keeping that body?"

"I don't know. Maybe Caprielli knows. Or we'll see if we can find out through the executor of the will, something like that. There has to be some kind of trail."

Johnson looked out the car window. "So, where are we going?"

"We're going to ask Toby MacClaren why he didn't tell us he had a half brother."

"And what am I doing?"

"I don't know. I guess follow my lead and look like a cop."

She pulled up onto the sidewalk in front of Toby Mac-Claren's house. It seemed to have lost some of its Old World charm.

MacClaren answered after the second ring. He seemed to have lost some of his Old World charm, too. He looked at Madison with that "everything is fabulous" smile, but it faltered when he saw that Ted Johnson was with her instead of Rourke.

"Hello, Ms. Cross. What can I do for you?" he said, more or less ignoring Johnson. He looked tired and the ring finger on his left hand was in a little splint.

"I'm sorry to bother you, Mr. MacClaren."

Johnson stepped forward and introduced himself, but Mac-Claren all but ignored him.

"Would you like to come in?" he said to Madison.

"Thank you."

The foyer seemed smaller with Johnson standing in it. Toby MacClaren seemed smaller, too.

"What happened to your finger?" Johnson asked loudly.

"It's nothing," he replied. "What can I do for you, Ms. Cross? Have you found anything out about what happened to my father's body? I must admit, I expected to hear something sooner than this."

"Actually, we're here to talk about your brother."

A nervous smile flickered across his face. "My brother?"

"Yes. Ralph Caprielli. The brother you didn't mention before."

"What about him?"

"Why didn't you tell us about him, Mr. MacClaren?"

"Well . . . you didn't ask."

"We asked about your father. The fact that you have a half brother is a pretty big thing to be holding back."

Toby MacClaren folded his arms, looking more confident, more at ease. "Surely there's someone in your family that you're not particularly proud of."

"You mean to tell me you don't think it odd that you've never mentioned him?"

"Look, Ms. Cross, I'm not particularly proud of my half brother. I hardly ever see him. Besides, there didn't seem to be any kind of connection to him." A look of alarm crept into his eyes. "Why, do you think there might be?"

Johnson stepped forward. "Did you know someone named Jimmy Dawber, Mr. MacClaren?"

Toby MacClaren looked up at him. "Jimmy Dawber? I don't know. The name sounds vaguely familiar, I guess. Why?"

"Do you know a Frank McGee?"

He rolled his eyes. "Frank McGee works for Ralph. Why? What's going on?"

"We're not sure, Mr. MacClaren. What we do know is that

a rival gang appears to be making a move against your brother. Do you know someone named Carlos Washburn? Goes by the name Carwash?"

That nervous smile showed up again, just for a moment. "Sorry, I tend not to hang out with people named 'Carwash.'"

Johnson smiled patronizingly. "Well, he's the leader of the gang that might be going after your brother. We believe they killed a friend of your brother's, Jimmy Dawber. We think they also stole your father's body, from wherever it was. And we know that they killed Frank McGee in a shoot-out."

"Is my brother in danger?"

Johnson smiled grimly. "Your brother's always in danger."

"But we think you might be, too," Madison added quietly.

"Me?" he said, surprised.

"Your brother's people seem to have the upper hand, here, Mr. MacClaren," Johnson explained. "Washburn's gang started out small, and they've been mostly wiped out by now, brutally so. One of them was even tortured. As far as we can tell, all that's left of them is Washburn himself and maybe one other guy."

"Okay." His face was a confused mixture of relief and alarm. "But why would they come after me? I have almost nothing to do with my brother or his . . . business."

"The thing is," Madison explained, "these guys have already demonstrated that they're willing to hit Ralph where it will hurt him, personally. Not necessarily where it will do the most damage."

"So?"

"So, actually, it's conceivable they could try to get at him through you."

"Through me?" He laughed again, a carefree laugh that trailed off in his throat. "You're serious, aren't you?"

He shook his head. "You guys don't understand. My brother and I have virtually nothing to do with each other. We never see each other. Hardly anybody even knows we are brothers."

"How many people knew where your father's body was?"

His face sank as he considered that. "What am I supposed to do?"

"Is there anything else you're not telling us?" Johnson asked.

MacClaren thought for a second, then shook his head.

"We could look into posting a squad car near here, or asking someone to keep an eye on you."

He smiled again, a small measure of his former bravado creeping back in. "I doubt that's necessary. I really do."

Johnson nodded slowly. "Okay," he said, holding out a business card. "If you think of anything you might have overlooked, you let us know right away."

MacClaren took the card and looked at it as he stepped toward the door. "All right. Thanks." He slipped it into his pocket.

Madison stopped at the door. "And Mr. MacClaren? Be careful."

THE LIEUTENANT sat back in his chair, listening without expression as Madison and Johnson told him what they had found. He had been just leaving when they came in to see him.

When they were finished, he closed his eyes slowly and exhaled loudly.

"Right," he said, reaching out and picking up his phone. He punched in a number and said, "If you two will excuse me."

Madison left first and as Johnson closed the door behind them, the lieutenant said, "Larry! David Cross here. We need to talk about some new developments in some of these cases coming through here . . . No, I'm talking about some *newer* developments . . ."

It had been a long day, especially with the trip out to Lawson. Madison was beat and she wanted to go home, but she was determined to stay until she got the DNA samples from the tissues loaded into the capillary array. She wanted to have the results waiting first thing in the morning. She knew she'd be stopping in at some point, but she didn't want to spend her whole Sunday here, so she was trying to get as much of it done as possible.

As she was packing up to go home, the lieutenant came out of his office.

"Eight a.m. tomorrow," he announced.

"What's that?"

"Meeting with Fenton and Metzger's team, try to straighten out this mess, see whose case this is."

Madison's shoulders slumped. "Sunday morning?"

"'Fraid so," he said with a smile. "But don't worry, we'll get you out in time for ten o'clock mass."

CHAPTER 28

TED JOHNSON knocked on the door to the DNA lab at ten minutes to eight, looking somehow even sharper than usual.

"You almost ready?" he asked.

"Do you ever just wear sweats?" she asked.

"I got to at least look like I'm planning on going to church later. I'll phone my regrets in an hour or so. Come on, let's go."

Madison looked at her watch. "We have a few minutes, right?"

Johnson looked at his. "I guess. Although I'd rather get there a few minutes early than a few minutes late."

"Well, I'd rather poke needles in my eyes than exchange fake pleasantries with Larry Metzger while waiting for the meeting to begin. Besides, I'm just finishing these."

"Whatcha working on?"

"I'm just checking the results on some samples we got from the lodge out in Lawson."

Johnson looked at his watch again. "Well, how long is that going to take?"

The computer chimed and she smiled. "About that long."

She clicked her mouse and frowned. "Shit."

She clicked again. "Shit!"

Again. "Shit."

And again. *"Shit!"*

Johnson was shaking with laughter. "Not the result you were hoping for?"

"It's Jimmy fucking Dawber. All of them."

"You think they're right?"

She put her hands over her face. "I don't know. It seems to

be. I mean, I was careful with the Caprielli sample, but I was *really* careful with these."

He shrugged. "It's probably right then." He looked at his watch one more time. "Now we need to go."

THEY MET in the same conference room where Metzger had delivered his briefing.

Metzger and two of his men sat on one side of the table. The lieutenant, Madison, and Johnson sat on the other side.

Vince Fenton sat by himself at one end.

Metzger's chart was already projected on the wall. Someone had placed a pitcher of water and a stack of cups in the middle of the table.

They all sat in silence for a few moments, waiting for someone to speak.

Metzger and Lieutenant Cross exchanged raised eyebrows, each offering to let the other start.

"Look, it's Sunday morning and I've got shit to do," Fenton blurted impatiently. "Is someone going to tell me what the fuck is going on?"

"All right," Lieutenant Cross began. He smiled grimly. "A lot of bodies this week. The Oxford fire, all this other stuff. It's been keeping a lot of us busy. I know we've all been working very hard. I haven't been in the middle of this, but let me just see if I have things straight, make sure we're all on the same page, then we can go from there."

He looked around the table, and with no objections, he began to outline the situation.

He began with Castillo, who they had found on the side of the Schuylkill Expressway, and Alvarez, both of whom appeared to have been gunned down at the shoot-out at Dale Hibbert's gas station in Lawson. Next he talked about Frank McGee, who also appeared to have died from bullet wounds he had suffered at the gas station, a characterization that elicited squirms from Metzger, but no objections.

"At that point," he said, "the Organized Crime Task Force came on board, as it appeared that Carlos Washburn's gang was making a move against Ralph Caprielli's gang. This view was reinforced when another member of Washburn's crew, Ramon Perez, was found tortured and executed."

He took a deep breath before describing the circumstances surrounding the discovery of Jimmy Dawber's body, and then Dawber's connections to Caprielli, both social and evidentiary.

Fenton frowned, slowly leaning forward.

Madison almost laughed out loud at the range of expressions crossing his face. Surprise. Confusion. Annoyance. And, most satisfying, fear and insecurity, realizing perhaps that if he had been doing his job better he would have already known about all this.

Lieutenant Cross pursed his lips, thinking, then looked down at Madison and Johnson. "Am I forgetting anything?" he asked.

"Robert MacClaren," Madison whispered.

"Right, right. In the midst of all this, we find the, the . . . What was it, Ms. Cross?"

She cleared her throat. "The cryonically preserved remains of Robert MacClaren."

"Right," he said. "So MacClaren's remains turn up, which was a story unto itself. Anyway, it turns out, not only was MacClaren Jimmy Dawber's boss at one point, but MacClaren was also Ralph Caprielli's father."

Metzger betrayed no reaction, presumably having been told about this the night before, but his underlings were stunned. They looked to him for guidance, but he ignored them, staring straight ahead, refusing to acknowledge this bombshell that he had failed to uncover.

Lieutenant Cross looked down at them, sympathetically. "Yeah, can you believe it? Anyway, that's where we are . . . Started out, what . . ." He paused to count in his head. "Five separate killings, plus another count of something else, maybe abuse of corpse, but definitely something. So now we need to figure out, not just how these are all connected and what's behind all this, but who is going to take the lead on the investigation."

Metzger smacked his lips. "Well, it seems pretty obvious that this is, at its heart, a turf battle. Washburn made a move against Caprielli, Caprielli retaliated."

"That explains the bangers and McGee," Lieutenant Cross conceded, "but what about Dawber? What about MacClaren?"

"Soft targets," Metzger replied. "They're going after him where they can get in easy and hurt him personally. Where was MacClaren's body being kept before it turned up?"

The lieutenant looked at Johnson, who looked at Madison.

"We still don't know," she said. "It turned up in some drug house. Toby MacClaren says he didn't know where the body had been kept. Apparently he didn't agree with the whole cryonic preservation thing in the first place."

"I'm with him; shit creeps me out," muttered one of Metzger's guys, eliciting snickers from the other one.

"Anyway," Madison continued, "he says his father knew he wasn't into it, didn't want him to have to deal with it."

Fenton rolled his eyes. "That's very sweet, but I don't see how it has anything to do with my homicide. You guys got gangbangers killing each other on the streets, fine. OCTF wants it, they can have it. My guy got chopped up and left in a trash can; it's a homicide, and it's my case. He's got nothing to do with this other stuff."

Now Madison rolled her eyes. "Except for the fact that he was friends with Caprielli, he worked for MacClaren, and his DNA was all over the lodge in Lawson where Washburn's crew stopped before the shoot-out at the gas station. Not to mention at Ralph Caprielli's home. Apart from that, though, you're right, no connection at all."

"I thought those DNA results were suspect," Metzger interjected.

Johnson gave Madison a nod and a nudge.

"The retests came back the same," Madison said with a shrug. "Jimmy Dawber. And that's not all." She explained about the lodge in Lawson, how the DNA from the blood and the tissues came back as Jimmy Dawber's, too.

Metzger laughed disdainfully. "Well, then that's remarkable. This guy's DNA is turning up more places than Wilt Chamberlain's." He waited while his lackeys laughed before continuing. "But regardless, I think it's disingenuous for anyone to argue that this would not fall under the purview of the Organized Crime Task Force. All these connections to those other cases only underscore the fact that this is a big, interconnected web. By definition it's Organized Crime's jurisdiction."

Madison snorted. "Well, if we're talking jurisdiction here, we should probably include the police chief of Lawson Township in the discussion, since at least two and probably more of these crimes occurred in his jurisdiction."

"That's pure conjecture," Metzger said dismissively.

"Bullshit it is," Madison snapped back. "I processed the crime scene. Have you even been out there?"

Metzger gave her a withering look that made it plain he was not about to reply.

"Apart from Hernan Alvarez, who died on the spot, we've got physical evidence that ties Frank McGee to that scene as well. The bullet we took out of him had motor oil on it, which it picked up passing through a display at the gas station in Lawson."

"Whatever," Metzger snapped. "I'll tell you what. If Lawson wants jurisdiction on McGee so bad, they can have it, *if* they promise full cooperation with OCTF."

"Well, that's very generous of you," Madison said sarcastically.

The lieutenant shot her a glare. "Look, look, look," he said, holding up his hands. "We all need to settle down. That's a good start, Larry. We can go ahead and transfer jurisdiction on Frank McGee out to Lawson, assuming he will agree to work in conjunction with our investigations. But we still need to hash out who's taking the lead on the remaining cases, and how they fit together into one single investigation."

While the lieutenant spoke, Metzger's third guy walked silently into the room and straight to his boss, handing him a note.

As Metzger read the note, Johnson's cell phone started ringing, then Lieutenant Cross's went off. Metzger folded the note and slipped it into the inside pocket of his jacket. Then he stood up.

"We're going to have to finish this later," he said. "They just found Carlos Washburn's body."

* * *

ST. PETER'S Church was about a dozen blocks away from
the Roundhouse, a straight line down Sixth Street, past Independence Hall, then two blocks down Pine.

Lieutenant Cross got them there in about three minutes, the
tires on his car humming a light, vibrato tone that was something less than a screech as he turned hard from Sixth Street
onto Pine. He parked on the uneven brick sidewalk.

Metzger and his men were close behind. They were all out
of their cars before Fenton's Caprice pulled up behind them.

It was a crisp, bright Sunday morning, and the streets were
relatively empty, but the sidewalks around St. Peter's were
packed. A throng of would-be churchgoers gathered behind
the police tape, speculating about what the police had found in
their churchyard.

"I'm afraid the nine o'clock services have been cancelled,"
Parker said with a laugh, emerging from behind the brick wall
that surrounded the churchyard.

"You're the CSI?" Madison said with a laugh.

"Must be your lucky day, huh?" he replied.

The lieutenant didn't break stride. "What do we have here,
Parker?"

Parker fell into step beside him. "Pretty sure it's Carlos
Washburn."

"You got a story yet?"

"Couple of holes in him, whole lot of dents and dings."

Parker led them down a row of headstones, some broken,
many crooked, and all worn thin by age. He turned and looked
past Madison and Johnson to make sure Metzger and Fenton
weren't within earshot.

"So what's with the parade?" he asked quietly, indicating
Fenton and the OCTF bringing up the rear.

"We were in the middle of a little parley about jurisdiction
when the call came in," the lieutenant replied.

Parker indicated with his arm and turned down another
row. "A parley?"

"You know OCTF had a hard-on for Caprielli, right?" Johnson asked, not waiting for an answer. "Thought they could use
this thing with Carlos Washburn to get at him. Then it turns out
that Fenton's case, the Dawber kid, is tied to Caprielli, too."

"Dawber was also tied to the frozen mummy guy we found at that crack house on Oxford," Madison added.

Parker stopped and looked at her, surprised. "No shit? You mean MacClaren?"

Metzger and his men caught up with them.

"Right." She smiled. "And get this: MacClaren? Turns out he was Caprielli's dad."

"Son of a bitch." Parker chuckled and started walking again. "I *bet* you were having a parley."

"Of course, probably half the murders took place out in Lawson," Madison added. "So a lot of this is ending up outside Philly PD's jurisdiction, anyway."

She expected Metzger to butt in at that point, but he was just listening and trying to keep up.

Parker gave her a strange look, then he looked away and pointed toward a cardboard-thin gravestone, leaning at a perilous angle. "I'm pretty sure this murder happened right here."

A pair of sneakers poked out from behind the gravestone, attached to a pair of legs clad in baggy denim and a tentlike 76ers jacket. The kid's head was misshapen and next to it lay a brick, both of them covered with blood.

Metzger walked up close to get a look at the face. "Fuck!" he spat, stomping his foot at the sight. His men stood back, out of his way.

Fenton hung back, too, looking both bored and confused.

Parker let everybody get a look before continuing. "I was thinking maybe he tried to mug someone who was packing, something like that. But the scene looks like someone snuck up on him. Then I checked and the guy actually had a wallet on him. Twelve hundred in cash and a driver's license that said Carlos Washburn."

"How do you make it?" the lieutenant asked.

Parker laughed. "I don't know exactly. He's got a couple slugs in him, small by the looks of them. I think he took a couple in the back, turned around, took another one in the face, kept coming. After that it looks like he took a brick to the head a couple of times. I'm not sure what finally did it."

"Could have been exhaustion by the sounds of it," Johnson cracked.

"Yeah, it was definitely not a work of surgical precision. But the guy is dead."

"This is not a good thing for the case," Metzger said as if to himself.

Everyone looked at him, waiting for him to elaborate.

"Caprielli has successfully taken out Washburn and his whole crew. Caprielli won. There's no one left."

"There's still Parga," one of his guys offered helpfully.

Metzger waved him off. "He's nothing. And he's disappeared anyway. Johnson, you guys turn up anything on him?"

Johnson shook his head. "Probably either skipped town or he's about to turn up like this guy. I know he's got people in Baltimore, but I know some people down there, too, and there's no sign of him."

"That's it, then. If Parga turns up, maybe we can slap together some kind of case. Otherwise, it's going to be tricky."

Metzger was backing away from the case, and Madison liked it. It would be a relief not to have to deal with him, and it would help Boone's efforts to assert his jurisdiction. So she was somewhat surprised to hear herself saying, "We might have an eyewitness to the shooting in Lawson. Someone close enough to the scene to ID Caprielli's men, put them at the gas station."

Everybody else was surprised, too. Their heads whipped around to look at her.

"What are you talking about, Madison?" the lieutenant asked.

"The guy who owned the gas station. Dale Hibbert. According to the other witnesses, he was standing right there by the pumps when the shooting started. We think there's a good chance he saw the whole thing."

Metzger's face darkened. "Why didn't I know about that before?" he demanded.

"Because of your complete failure to liaise with the Lawson Police Department."

Metzger's men looked horrified, and even more so when Johnson let out a short, involuntary snort.

"Where is this guy?" the lieutenant asked.

"He disappeared just after the whole thing went down. The

police chief spoke to him briefly, but when he came back to interview him, the guy was gone. Boone thinks he got spooked, went underground. Says the guy's got mental issues and he's probably living in the woods around there."

"He's probably dead," Metzger spat.

Madison shook her head. "Some of the locals have seen him, up in the hills. Apparently he's a pretty skilled camper."

"Whatever," Metzger huffed, rolling his eyes. "As I said, we're willing to give Lawson jurisdiction on McGee, but we expect full cooperation. For now, we're going to take a back-seat on this, let you guys work the crime scene." He turned to Johnson. "You want to be primary on this thing for the moment, fine by me. Hash it out with Fenton." He glanced at Madison. "If it's okay with Lawson PD, of course."

At the sound of his name, Fenton straightened, but he stayed quiet and didn't come forward, perhaps thinking that this was starting to sound a lot like work.

"I'm going to let you guys get to work here," Metzger continued. "Just make sure I get a copy of the crime scene report first thing. And if your mysterious camper turns up," he said, with an exaggerated smile for Madison, "please keep me informed."

With that, he nodded to his men and as a unit they turned and marched back through the gravestones to the street.

"Dick," Madison muttered.

Madison and Johnson looked over at Fenton, but he still didn't say anything, so they turned back to the lieutenant and Parker.

"Johnson," the lieutenant said. "What's your take?"

"I'm still inclined to think Washburn was making a move on Caprielli, a gang war, turf war, whatever. Caprielli's got him outmanned and outgunned, Washburn goes after the family and friends. What do they call it, 'asymmetrical warfare,' right? Hit 'em where it hurts, but hit 'em where you *can* hit 'em." He shrugged, looking down at the battered corpse. "It ain't the smartest of plans, as I'm sure this mug would now agree, but I've seen his rap sheet; he hasn't shown that much brain power in the past."

Lieutenant Cross nodded slowly as Johnson spoke. "Okay, I

have to get going. Apparently I have some paperwork to do now that Lawson is taking over jurisdiction on the McGee case." He turned to Parker. "You and Madison can finish up here."

The he turned to Madison and smiled wryly. "Madison, walk with me."

She fell into step beside him as he headed back to his car.

"About all this work you've been doing out in Lawson these past few days."

Madison could feel her cheeks warming, wondering what was coming next, and if it was from the lieutenant or from Uncle Dave. "You asked me to help out there. There was a lot of police work."

He smiled without looking at her as they made their way down a row of gravestones. "And you've been doing good police work, Madison. And I know you're feeling left out of the Oxford case. And I understand if you resent that. But you can't just go off and do whatever. You've got to keep in touch more. I need to know what you're doing, okay? Not every little thing you do," he said, glancing at her. "But especially when you're working in another jurisdiction, I need to know about that. I need you to check in regularly."

"Okay. I'm sorry . . . Lieutenant."

He held up a hand to stop her.

"Just keep in touch, that's all I ask. Now get back there and help Parker with the crime scene."

Madison nodded expressionlessly, then watched the lieutenant walking away, wondering how much he knew about her and Boone.

When she returned to the crime scene, she noticed that Fenton had disappeared as well.

"Guess you're the primary," she said to Johnson.

He looked around and saw that Fenton was gone. "Must be my lucky day."

Parker gave him a clap on the shoulder. "Shame you had to waste it here."

"All right, Parker," Madison said, crouching next to the body. "What do we have so far?"

Parker rolled the body over. "Like I said, two in the back." He indicated two small bloody holes below the right shoulder blade. "Bam, and bam. Then one in the cheek, here. Looks to be pretty small caliber. No exit wounds."

Madison tugged at the shiny blue fabric of the jacket, revealing a pair of small holes an inch apart separated by a fold of cloth above the shoulder. "Looks like he just missed with another one."

Parker looked around. "Might be a couple more around, too. Guess we'll have to look."

"So how do you figure it?" Madison asked, as she stood up. "He's coming from that way, right?" She pointed toward the middle of the cemetery.

"Hey, what's this?" Johnson had wandered off about twenty feet. He was looking at something on the ground.

Madison and Parker went and saw what he was looking at, a lumpy ball the size of a grapefruit, bright green in spots but mostly brown.

Parker grinned. "That's monkey fruit," he said proudly. "Hedge apples, Osage oranges, whatever. They got a bunch of names. I seen them before out West, never around here, though."

Johnson looked suspicious.

"He's right. They are from out West," Madison confirmed. "Lewis and Clark brought them back from their expedition and planted them here."

Now they both looked at her suspiciously.

"No, I'm serious! A tour guide told me about it. I looked it up and it's true. Things are all over the place around here in the springtime, but just inside these walls."

Johnson looked over at Parker. "So what does that mean?"

Parker laughed. "Absolutely nothing."

Johnson kicked the big ugly fruit around a few times while Parker and Madison resumed their search.

Parker walked up between two rows of grave markers and stopped. "Got a bloody handprint here," he said, pointing at the top of one of the smaller headstones a few feet away. "So, it looks like he was down but not out at that point. Still coming forward."

"More likely trying to get away," Madison replied.

Parker nodded. "By that point, probably, yeah."

Madison walked past him. "You got the spatter here?"

"Yeah, there's low-velocity spatter patterns, here and here," he said, indicating two of the headstones that were spattered with large drops of blood.

He walked to another headstone a few steps farther that had a more even spatter stain with much smaller droplets of blood. "Higher-velocity impact stains back here. I figure this is the bullet in the cheek. Probably got the two in the back, turned around, gets one in the face. That's when he turns again, maybe stumbles, going that way. The attacker follows him with the brick."

"Not the most efficient method."

"So, Carlos Washburn didn't have a gun?" Johnson asked dubiously.

"In his pocket. I think he was reaching for it when the brick treatment finally took effect."

"Better late than never I guess, but shit, this guy's a gangbanger. You'd think he'd go for that, first thing."

"I don't know," Madison said. "The two in the back probably took him totally by surprise. Wouldn't surprise me if one of them shattered his scapula, made it hard to move his arm. Then he gets one in the face; he'd be in bad shape. Probably just trying to get away when the brick started hitting him."

Johnson walked up behind them and cleared his throat, apparently having tired of the monkey fruit. "All right. I'll let you guys work. Give me a call when you're done."

After Johnson left, they finished searching the cemetery, methodically walking up and down the rows of markers. Madison felt a strange awkwardness emanating from Parker. When they had finished a couple of rows, he came over to her, wincing as he bent backward to stretch out his back.

"Nothing so far?" he asked.

She shook her head.

"So what's with all this work you've been doing up in Lawson?"

She shrugged. "Just helping out a bit. They needed some crime scene help with that gas station. Everybody else was

busy working the Oxford case, so the lieutenant sent me up
there with Johnson."

"Why didn't he call the state police. They'd have helped."

"Well, according to the Lawson PD, they're always willing
to help, not always so willing to leave."

Parker laughed. "Yeah, I've heard that before."

They were quiet for a second, and just as Madison was
about to get back to work, Parker asked, "Is there something
going on between you and Boone?"

A shocked and nervous laugh started in her throat but
couldn't quite manage to climb out.

Parker smiled, almost bashfully. "I'm sorry," he mumbled.
"That was out of line."

"No," she said, "it's just that . . ." It was inappropriate, and
she didn't want to talk about it, but she didn't want to confirm
his suspicions by saying so. Fortunately, she found a way to
change the subject. "Gun!" she exclaimed, pointing with her
finger. "Found it!"

"What?!"

"There! The gun!" She stepped over a row of small grave
markers and crouched down, pointing at a small gun nestled
in a clump of rotted leaves.

Parker came over and crouched down next to her. "Aw.
Cute little thing, too. No wonder it didn't stop him."

"That is tiny," she agreed. "Maybe it *was* a mugging or
something. Victim was packing."

Parker shook his head. "He was already crawling away. I
don't see a mugging victim going after him with a brick."

"No, you're right. Not exactly a tool of professionals,
though. Or even gangbangers."

"I'm thinking he was meeting with someone, someone he
trusts enough to turn his back on. Or at least someone that
doesn't raise any suspicions. Looking at that gun, it could
have been a woman."

"I don't know, those blows with the brick don't seem well
aimed, but there was some force behind them."

Parker laughed. "Maybe a woman scorned, then."

"Yeah, that could be it."

They were quiet as they completed the search. They found one more slug, probably the one that had gone through Washburn's jacket, embedded in one of the sycamore trees near the cemetery's entrance. That was it.

Tate and Velasquez showed up to pick up the body for the ME.

"What is up with you guys?" Tate said in mock exasperation. "Do you really have to investigate every one of these you find? Can't you just leave a couple where they are? Pretend you didn't see them?"

"Seriously." Velasquez laughed, shaking his head. "Can't you just cover them with leaves, maybe save a couple for later? I don't know if we even have room for all these damn bodies. You should have heard Spoons going on about it."

Parker laughed. "You tell Spoons he might just have to move some of his Rolling Rocks out of the cooler."

Tate and Velasquez got a big laugh out of that. There was a rumor, apparently floating around for years, about Spoons stashing a case of beer in a cooler with one of the bodies.

Madison didn't believe it, though. She knew these days he was drinking scotch. "All right," she said. "We're done here, right?"

Parker looked around and nodded, "Yeah. I reckon we are." He nodded at Tate and Velasquez and they put the gurney on the ground next to the body, started getting it ready to go.

Turning to Madison next, he said, "Help me get this stuff packed up and we can get out of here."

They had just started packing up when Madison's cell phone chimed. She checked the number and turned her back to Parker before answering it.

"Hello, Chief," she said in a quiet, businesslike voice.

"Miss me?" Boone asked. Even over the phone, she could practically hear the big, dumb grin on his face. And she had the distinct feeling that somehow Parker could hear it as well.

"Look, Boone," she said, feeling self-conscious. "I'm kind of in the middle of something." She was walking away from Parker, toward the opposite end of the churchyard.

A gust of wind rattled the still-bare trees, sending their branches swaying against the blustery blue sky.

"No problem," he said. "I understand. Look, I was just calling to see if you could come on up . . ."

"No, Boone, I can't," she cut him off. "I'm busy as hell down here, and I can't just drop everything and drive on out there every time you call." She still wasn't totally convinced that she hadn't screwed up the Dawber samples, and if she had made a mistake, it was because she'd been so distracted by Boone. After the lieutenant's little talk, she felt even more self-conscious about it. "I wish I could, but I can't."

"Jesus. Sorry," he said, sounding annoyed. "I was just calling because we found Dale Hibbert. I know where he is and I thought maybe you'd want to come up when I question him."

She had walked about forty feet away, but she felt Parker's eyes on her back.

"Are you serious?" she asked, in a way that was more accusatory than colloquial.

"Yes, I'm fucking serious," he snapped. "No, actually I'm making shit up because I just can't bear to be without you."

"Sorry. I'm sorry, Boone. I'm just having a real shitty day."

"Yeah, well, now I am, too."

She let out a deep breath. "So you really have a lead on Hibbert?" The fact was, getting Dale's testimony would go a long way toward redeeming herself.

"That's what I said, isn't it?"

"What time would you need me there?"

"Hell, I don't know. If you're coming, I can wait a little bit, but not all fucking day."

She looked at her watch then at Parker, standing there all pissed off next to the equipment that he had packed up without her help.

"I'll be there in an hour."

"Bring some hiking boots."

CHAPTER 29

AS SHE drove out to Lawson, Madison was in a bit of a funk.

She felt bad for having snapped at Boone, bad that the lieutenant felt he had to have a talk with her; she even felt bad about Parker, somehow feeling guilty about his jealousy or whatever it was.

Mostly, though, she felt bad about the job. She had gotten herself embroiled in a turf war, made more adversaries in Metzger and Fenton. And in the back of her mind, she still wondered how she might have messed up to make Jimmy Dawber's DNA show up in all those samples.

By the time she reached Lawson she was filled with melancholy and self-doubt. The voices that frequently whispered in the back of her mind were loud and vociferous now, reciting all the ways that she was ill-suited and unqualified for this job. The idea of bagging it all and moving on was looking very appealing, but she had done that less than ten months earlier. At the thought of bailing on two careers in a single year, her depression worsened.

When she walked through the door of the Lawson Police headquarters, Boone was staring at the front door like he had been waiting for her.

She felt better just seeing him.

He had a slightly incredulous smile on his face. She could tell he was still a little bit annoyed at her. He was slowly shaking his head in exasperation, as if they had just gotten off the phone moments ago.

Madison smiled apologetically. "Sorry."

"All right," he said in a tone that was forgiving but not

entirely forgetful. "Some day I'll show you my bad side, too. But, *damn*, woman."

"I said I'm sorry. Day from hell." As she approached him for a hug, he wrapped her up in his arms and his lips.

Madison wanted to stay there; to hell with the rest of it, none of it mattered. As she felt his arms loosen, his lips start to pull away, she felt a deep sadness. Her eyes were moist.

Boone pulled his face back six inches and brushed back her hair. "How 'bout that?" he said softly. "I even miss you when you're cranky."

She laughed and grabbed his hand, kissing it before it could get too far away. "Hey, I got you your case back."

He looked at her quizzically. "What do you mean?"

"With the motor oil thing and everything else, Metzger backed off. Said he would let you have jurisdiction over the McGee case, as long as you promised cooperation with his case, but I think he knew he'd lost it anyway."

"Madison, that's great." He grinned. "Do you have files or anything?"

"It's Sunday, Matt. I'm sure the lieutenant will call you to-morrow about it."

"Sweet." He laughed. "Now let's go track down the wild gas station owner of Lawson."

"A SCIENCE teacher at the local high school was up in the hills collecting mushrooms for breakfast," Boone explained once they were in the cruiser. "Saw Dale slipping into a little lean-to twenty yards off the trail. Knew him from the gas station, heard he disappeared after the gunfight. Luckily the guy didn't approach him or anything, but he marked it on his map and called me as soon as he got home."

As they drove through the intersection at the center of town, Boone handed her a hiking map, with a big X on one of the trails.

"That's where we're headed?" she asked.

He nodded without looking over at her then made the next right. "First, I got to make a quick stop at home."

He pulled into a driveway a block and a half from the center of town, a little blue house with a wraparound porch. He left the keys in the car and ran up to the door. With a cursory look around to see if anyone was watching, he reached under the welcome mat and took out a spare key. He was in and out in ten seconds, and he slipped the key back under the mat before he got into the car.

"That's quite a security system," she teased as he backed out of the driveway.

He grinned. "You saw that, huh? It's all right. It's Lawson. Most people don't even use a key."

"Is that the official position of the Lawson Police Department?"

He put his hand on her knee. "There're no worries with Chief Boone on the job."

They drove quietly like that for a while. Madison mostly looked out the window. The scenery was beautiful. Watching it, she felt enveloped by a peaceful lethargy, content but emotionally drained.

They were driving along a narrow, windy road when Boone reached over and took back the map. He studied it briefly, and a few minutes later they pulled over next to a small gap in the woods by the side of the road and got out.

The trail meandered a bit at first, but after crossing a small creek bed it jagged sharply to the left and started steeply climbing the hill.

Five minutes later the path leveled off and Madison caught a glimpse of the road, five hundred feet below them. They were both breathing heavily by that point and sweating despite the chill in the air.

They followed the crest of the hill for a while, briefly stopping a few times to admire the view or check the map, then they turned onto a path that started down the other side of the hill. The incline wasn't very steep, but the terrain was rough.

Ten minutes into the hike, Boone turned to her and whispered, "We're getting close, so try to keep quiet."

The trail narrowed and when they got to where a small tree had fallen across it, Boone slowed. "Right around here," he mouthed, drawing a circle in the air with a down-pointed fin-

ger. He climbed up a small side trail and gave Madison a hand
up. They pushed through the brush that encroached from both
sides. Fifty yards later, Boone ducked down and pulled Madison with him.

"No shit," he whispered, stifling a nervous laugh. "He's
right over there."

They slowly rose and she looked in the direction he indicated. About twenty yards away, in a small clearing surrounded by thick brush, she could see a figure dressed in
camouflage moving about.

At that distance and in that environment, the camouflage
was actually quite effective. He seemed to be tending to a
small fire.

They crept toward him through the brush. Even with just
the early spring buds, the undergrowth was dense. Boone was
managing to move fairly quietly, but in Madison's ears her
own footsteps sounded like the tromping of an elephant.

At one point the movement up ahead seemed to stop and
Boone put out a hand, telling Madison to stop. She caught a
glimpse of Dale's face, looking upward, listening. He had on
a camouflage hat, with some kind of branches sticking out.

As effective as the camouflage was, Madison found it
amusing. But when she smiled over at Boone, she saw that he
had his gun in his hand.

Boone had said Dale wasn't violent, but he also said he
might be mentally unstable. For the first time, Madison wondered if the situation might be somewhat more dangerous than
she had imagined.

As they snuck closer, Boone drew lower on his haunches
and Madison did the same, creeping forward in a crouch.
When they were almost upon the little campsite, Boone
stopped them again.

Listening closely, they heard a sound, a fast, rhythmic
scrunch, scrunch, scrunch, fading into the distance.

Boone popped straight up. "Dale!" he yelled. "It's me.
Chief Boone. I just want to talk to you."

He looked around quickly and saw a camouflaged blur receding through the brush to their left.

"Shit!" he said. "Wait here."

Boone shot off through the brush after him. Madison leapt up and followed close behind.

Dale was a skilled outdoorsman, but they were both younger and in better shape. They were gaining on him.

At one point they lost sight of him. A few seconds later, as they were passing under a low branch of an elm tree, it exploded into a cloud of splinters.

Madison dropped to the ground.

"Goddammit, Dale, you knock that off!" Boone yelled. "I'm just out here to talk to you, but you do that again, you're under arrest!"

He held still and listened again: *scrunch, scrunch, scrunch.*

They set off running again, this time to the right. Once more they seemed to be gaining on him, and once more he disappeared.

Boone slowed a step, looking around, and Madison followed his lead. They had all but stopped when a camouflaged figure with a shotgun stepped out from behind a tree ten feet away.

"Turn around and get the fuck out of here!" he barked.

He was wiry and tall, with a long nose and a protruding Adam's apple that bobbed when he spoke. His eyes were wide and sweat was trickling down his temple.

Boone and Madison raised their hands.

Boone stepped forward. "We're out here 'cause we want to talk to you, Dale."

"Well, I'm out here 'cause I don't want to talk to you, dumb ass."

"No need to be like that."

"Yeah. There is, Chief, if you won't leave me the fuck alone."

"Dale, you need to come back to town and tell us what happened on Sunday. You can't just spend the rest of your days hiding out in the woods."

"Bullshit, I can't. Better than coming back and getting killed by those gangsters."

"Dale, those guys are long gone. You don't need to be concerned with them."

"Yeah?" The barrel of the gun lowered a couple of inches. "Where are they?"

"Hell, most of them are dead."

Madison winced as soon as he said it.

The gun jerked back up. "Right, and if I come back to town I'm liable to be next."

Boone rolled his eyes. "Dale, this is ridiculous. You worked hard to get that gas station. You going to just let it fall apart?"

"Better that than getting killed."

Nobody said anything for a few seconds, and Madison was wondering if they were at an impasse.

Boone looked over at Madison. Then he turned around and sprinted into the woods behind them.

He disappeared so quickly, Madison didn't have time to respond or even react. One second he was right there beside her, the next second he was gone. She just stood there with her hands in the air.

Dale was equally surprised, but as it dawned on him what had happened, he grew enraged.

"Boone!" he screamed. "Get back here, Boone!"

Madison was infuriated, too. She'd had guys dump her before, or not call her back. But nothing like this.

"Goddammit, Chief!" Dale yelled, stomping his foot. "I'm not fucking around, Chief Boone! . . . Chief Boone! You come back here and get your little girlfriend or I'm gonna shoot her where she stands."

They stood in silence for a moment: Madison with her hands raised, Dale holding a gun on her. Both waiting to hear a reply.

But there wasn't one.

Dale leaned against a tree and eyed Madison suspiciously. "So, who the hell are you, anyway?"

"Madison Cross," she said begrudgingly. "I'm with the Philadelphia Police Crime Scene Unit."

Dale snickered. "Sorry. I thought you were his girlfriend or something."

Madison felt her cheeks warming but she ignored his

comment. "You know you're going to have to tell us what you saw, right?"

He snickered again, but it sounded like more of an effort. "If you knew what I saw, you might think different."

He looked at her for a moment, and as he did his face fell, as if it was dawning on him that now he had a hostage. He adjusted his grip on the gun.

"So what the hell am I going to do with you?" he said, as if to himself.

Madison was about to tell him he was just going to let her go when over Dale's shoulder, she saw Boone creeping toward them through the bushes. She had to resist the urge to react to the sight.

"You know what?" he said. "It must be your lucky day, 'cause I'm not going to do a goddamn thing with you." He grinned proudly. "That's it. Now, you just turn around and start walking, back the way you come. You'll hit a trail before long. You go either way and you'll hit a road. Pretty lady like yourself, I'm sure you'll get a ride in no time."

Boone was slowly creeping closer, carefully pushing branches out of his way and easing them back into place.

"Before I go," she said slowly, "why don't you just tell me what you saw?"

"Hah! You'd like that, wouldn't you? But that sure as shit ain't going to happen. Not with those crazy bastards still out there. They're liable to show up at the station one day, put a bullet in my head. I'd never know it was coming."

"But by the sounds of it, if you don't come back soon, you won't even have a station to return to."

Dale spat. "Well, if I lose the station that's too bad. I'm likely to lose more than that if I get those crazy gangsters after me, with that . . . with all that . . . crazy stuff."

Boone was less than ten feet behind him now.

"What crazy stuff?" she asked.

"I'm not telling you anything!" he snapped. "So you can just forget about it."

"Okay, okay," Madison said. Boone was just a couple of feet behind him now, but Dale's shotgun was still pointed at Madison's chest. "You know, I'm all the way over here, and that gun is making me kind of nervous. Can you just maybe point it down a little, so I don't feel like I'm about to get my head blown off?"

Dale laughed. "Yeah, I guess." He slowly lowered the gun until it was pointing at the ground between them. "Don't try any shit though, 'cause I will blow your fucking . . ."

He stopped talking when the gun abruptly disappeared out of his hand. As he spun around, Boone hit him with a sharp jab in the face, just enough to stun him.

Dale's head snapped back, and by the time he shook it off, Boone had the barrel pointed straight at his nose.

"Goddamn, Boone," he said, feeling his nose. "You didn't have to do that!"

"That was a foolish stunt you pulled there, Dale," Boone told him. "I could lock you up for a long time for what you've already done, so if I were you I wouldn't try anything else. All we want to do is ask you some questions."

"Well, you shouldn't have bothered, 'cause I ain't gonna answer 'em. I don't want those crazy bastards coming after me. Besides, I didn't see nothing."

"Yeah? Well I bet those 'crazy bastards' have plenty of friends in prison. Maybe you could tell *them* you didn't see nothing."

Dale slowly raised his hands. "I didn't mean no harm, Chief. I'm just scared. I don't want those crazy freaks coming after me." He sounded like he was about to start crying. "I don't want to die!"

"No one's going to kill you, you idiot. No one's going to come after you."

"Yes, they will! I know it!" he wailed. "And if they don't kill me, I don't want to know what they plan on doing to me!"

Boone looked at Madison and shook his head. "What are you talking about?"

"Anal probes, abductions, all that stuff."

Boone shook his head in disbelief and disappointment. "So what are you saying, Dale? Little green men shot up your gas station?"

"No, dumb ass. The gangsters did the shooting," he said. "And the Martian wasn't green . . ."

"He was yellow," Madison cut in.

Dale turned and looked at her. "You saw it, too!"

"Yes," she said. "I saw it."

Boone looked at her like she was nuts, too.

"And you saw that it had those little, like, like . . ."

"Antennae?"

"Right, right, except . . ."

"Except they didn't point up," she said. "They pointed down, out of the bottom of its head."

Boone looked back and forth between them. "What the hell are you two talking about?"

"Robert MacClaren," she replied.

CHAPTER 30

THEY TOOK Dale back to the station and showed him some photos. He didn't want to look at them at first, but he came around when Boone described how much better it would be to see their pictures than to run into them face-to-face in prison. As it was, he still only picked out one of them, Frank McGee. The connection confirmed some suspicions, but didn't tell them anything new. Even though Dale eventually cooperated, Boone locked him up, saying he didn't want Dale disappearing again before he could decide what he wanted to do with him.

Then they headed back to the lodge for yet another look.

"What are we searching for this time?" Boone asked as they got out of the car.

"I don't know exactly," Madison replied, grabbing her camera from the car before climbing the front steps. "Last time we were looking for bullets and bodies. This time, we're looking for signs of Robert MacClaren. If he was here, there must be evidence. I can't imagine a man in his state would be traveling too light."

BOONE SLIT the police tape on the front door with his penknife and they stepped inside. As a gentle breeze swung the door partly closed, Madison stopped at the doorway and turned around, looking back at the trees behind them, at the tree with the slug in it.

If the person firing that shot had been standing on the porch, it stood to reason that whoever they had been aiming at might have returned fire.

There were no holes in the wood around the doorway, or in the door itself. The breeze kicked up again and as the door swung open, Madison turned to look inside. Boone was standing in the middle of the living area, looking around with his hands on his hips.

Madison lined up a trajectory from the slug in the tree through the front door.

Directly through the door was that incongruously wide curving wall. The wall was about eight feet high, and on top of it, the row of stuffed birds and woodland animals were arranged in a haphazard fashion. Hanging in the middle was a framed painting, tilted at such an angle that Madison immediately felt compelled to straighten it.

The painting depicted three ducks taking flight over a gently meandering creek with a blue sky and puffy white clouds overhead. It evoked a feeling of peace and tranquility, until she stepped closer and saw a half-inch hole in the middle of one of the ducks.

"What is it?" Boone asked, as she gently touched a finger to the hole.

She took a picture of the painting then lifted it off the wall, revealing a similar hole in the wall itself.

"Possibly a bullet hole," she said, taking a couple more pictures.

"Seriously?" he said, now looking over her shoulder.

"Looks like."

Radiating out from the hole was a slight ridge, about a foot and a half long, extending away from the front door along the curved surface of the wall, like the wall itself had buckled.

Madison poked her finger in the hole, then snatched it back violently. "Ow!" she exclaimed, sticking her finger in her mouth.

It was cold on her tongue.

"You okay?" Boone asked.

She nodded, looking at her finger, which was slightly red at the tip.

With the tip of her fingernail, she picked at the edge of the hole. A chunk of material came away and fell to the floor. She

frowned and picked at it again, pulling off another chunk of
material and holding it up to examine it.

Boone squinted at it. "What is it?"

"I think it's . . . foam."

She pulled a pen out of her pocket and poked it into the
hole, sliding it in sideways along the ridge. When she pulled
on it, the wall tore easily and a misshapen bullet fell out onto
the floor.

She picked it up between her thumb and forefinger, but
quickly bobbled it between both hands before letting it fall
once again to the floor.

Boone looked confused. "Hot?"

She shook her head. "Cold."

"Cold?"

Sliding the pen into the tear she had made, she pushed
down this time and pulled back once again. This time, a large
section of the wall came away entirely, revealing a triangular
patch of a shiny metal surface.

"What the fuck is that?" Boone asked, putting his hand out
to touch the metal.

"No, don't!" Madison cautioned, putting up a hand to stop
him.

He looked down at her, confused.

"It burns."

As they watched, condensation quickly started trickling
down the bare metal.

Peering closely at it, Madison let out a short, curious
laugh. "Huh," she said, watching a droplet roll down the metal
surface. "It looks almost blue."

"Huh," Boone said, unimpressed. "Yeah, a little bit."

She flashed him a quick frown, mildly annoyed at his incu-
riosity. Then she looked up, to the top of the wall.

Earlier, the taxidermy had appeared to be randomly clustered, but now she could see it was a formerly even arrangement
that had been pushed out of the way to form a gap in the middle.

Boone leaned back his head, following her gaze, then he
looked back down at her, bemused. "What now?"

"I don't know," she said distractedly. "But I thought this
place seemed bigger from the outside." She moved a heavy

glass lamp off a large end table next to the sofa and pulled the table over next to the wall. "Here, help me up," she said as she stepped up onto the table.

Boone put a foot on the table to steady it and rested a hand against the small of her back.

Frost was already forming on the exposed metal, and Madison was careful not to get too close as she grabbed the top of the wall and pulled herself up so her chin was level with the top of the wall.

The top of the wall was about a foot thick, then it dropped down a few inches to a horizontal surface of brushed steel, roughly six or seven feet across. In the middle of it was a round hatch with a wheel in the center, like on a submarine. Next to that, a metal plate was bolted in place and several lengths of heavy-duty electrical cable snaked up through it and over to the far wall. A stack of several small pipes extended up through the roof. Lying next to them were a pair of thick, long rubbery-looking gloves and a wide hook on a six-foot-long handle.

"Holy shit," she exclaimed quietly.

"What do you got?"

"Could be liquid nitrogen."

"Up there?" He climbed up on the table beside her. "What are you talking about?"

She didn't say anything and he just grunted, staring for a second before reaching out to test the hatch. It was closed, but the wheel hadn't been spun to seal it. Boone tried to open the hatch, but he didn't have the leverage.

"Look out a second," he mumbled, bracing himself with an elbow as he swung a leg over the top and clambered up. He had to hunch over to stand, even under the highest point of the peaked roof. He lifted the hatch and a cloud of white vapor billowed out onto the steel and rolled past Madison, dissipating as it fell to the floor below.

"What the hell is this?" he asked.

"The not-quite-final resting place of Robert MacClaren."

MADISON WAS on the phone most of the way back to Philadelphia. In fact, she'd been on it almost continuously since they discovered the nitrogen tank at the lodge. Boone had been on his phone, too. He called Gloria at home, then the county prosecutor, with whom he had apparently already discussed the case. Several others, too.

They were both so intent on their phone calls that they almost didn't say good-bye. But she gave him a warm smile and a nod as she got out of his car and into her own, the whole time explaining to the lieutenant what they had found.

The lieutenant listened dutifully as she spoke, asking a few brief questions. He still seemed uncomfortable with the cryonic preservation aspect of the case.

"Where are you now?" he asked.

"I'm driving back from Lawson."

"Lawson?" He let out a loud, angry sigh. "Madison, didn't we just talk about that? Didn't I *just* tell you I wanted you to check in? Especially when you're working outside the jurisdiction."

He sounded tired and she felt guilty.

"Sorry, Lieutenant."

"Right," he said curtly. "Well, when you get back, I want you to stop into my office. I have something I need you to do. Now call Ted Johnson, tell him what you told me."

He seemed relieved to be done talking and anxious to get off the phone.

She called Johnson, but he didn't pick up, so she left a message on his cell phone.

Then she called Ben Moyers on his cell.

"Hey, Madison," he answered sheepishly. "Sorry I haven't gotten back to you, but there's nothing to report."

"Ben!" she scolded. "It's Sunday, for God's sake. I'm not calling to bug you."

"Okay, well, I called Stan yesterday and he still had nothing. He had penetrated a couple more layers but it's just more of the same: this shell owned by that holding company, some of them pretty much owning each other. Pretty elaborate. I mean, we'll get through it, eventually, but whoever set this up really didn't want it to be easy. Stan's intrigued at this point. He said he'd be working on it some more today. I figure I'll give him a call this afternoon, just to check in."

"I appreciate all your work. And Stan's."

"Oh, don't worry about that. To be honest, I'm pretty intrigued, too. With this much hiding, I figure at some point we'll turn up something to justify all the looking."

"Well, I have another lead for you. Might make it a little easier."

He laughed. "Okay, let's hear it."

"Do you know Robert MacClaren?"

He laughed again. "Robert MacClaren, huh? Well, that would explain a lot."

"Why's that?"

"Before he died, he was a big-shot businessman, right? But before that he was a gangster."

"Yeah, I know all that."

"Well, somewhere along the way, he turned a boatload of dirty money into a boatload of clean money. We looked at him hard for a long time, never found a damn thing. This setup has the same level of sophistication. You think he was involved?"

"He set up a trust before he died. MacClaren Trust. I think the trust might own that house."

"A trust, huh?"

Madison paused. "It seems MacClaren had himself frozen when he died. Preserved."

"What, you mean cryonically?"

"Exactly."

"No shit?"

"No shit."

"So what's the connection to this house?"

"It's a long story, but I think he had himself stored there. At that lodge."

"Huh."

"I'm not sure, but there's definitely some kind of connection. I know it's been complicated trying to work your way up through all the layers to get at the actual owner of the place. Thought it might help to have some idea what you might actually be looking for."

"Yeah, it might at that. I'll get back to you if I learn anything."

Madison got off the phone with Moyers as she merged

onto the turnpike. He called back just as she was approaching the Roundhouse.

"Bingo," he said when she answered.

"What do you mean?"

"Bingo. Your MacClaren lead. I called Stan. He plugged that into the equation, everything started falling into place. He called me back almost immediately. MacClaren Trust owns Landholding Trust Incorporated, which owns Tricounty Investments, et cetera. Nestled a few layers down is Bartlett Property Company, and that's who owns the lodge."

"Really?"

"And one of the other subsidiaries of the main trust is a holding company that owns half a dozen properties in the city, including Toby MacClaren's house and Ralph Caprielli's place."

"Huh."

"Yeah. I'll get in touch if I learn anything else."

"That's great. Thanks, Ben."

"No problem."

She put down the phone and it rang almost immediately.

It was Aidan.

She took a deep breath before she picked up.

"You ready for this?" he said when she answered.

"Jesus," she said, "doesn't anyone ever take a day off anymore?"

He laughed. "Not this week. I'm hoping maybe next week people will stop killing each other, I can catch up on my downtime. In the meantime, apparently, I need to catch up on some other things. Why, where are you?"

For some reason she didn't want to say anything about Lawson. "I'm chasing down some leads. What's up?"

"I have some new info on one of your bodies."

"Which one?"

"Perez."

"What about him?"

"That crazy scalp condition. Spoons sent over some samples for testing and microscopy. He said the way the flesh was acting, there seemed to be some sort of toxic irritant. Well, I isolated a few of the compounds, and it's crazy stuff. If I didn't have a sample to compare to, I'd have had no idea whatsoever."

"So what is it?"

"It's that same stuff we got out of MacClaren. That stinky yellow vitrification fluid."

"Jesus. What the hell does that mean?"

"That's not all."

"That's enough," she told him.

"More than enough, you ask me. But Sanchez did some microscopy. She said the scalp was covered with tiny little holes, wounds or incisions. So she sees there's these little particles inside, something embedded in the hole. She pulls a couple of them out. Guess what they are?"

"I don't even want to know."

"Skin."

"Skin?"

"Skin."

"What are you talking about?"

"That's what she said. Each of those tiny little holes had a tiny bit of skin implanted in it."

"You mean like hair plugs? Like some kind of hair transplant?"

"That's what I was thinking. I know there's been work using vitrification in transplants, so that would also make sense, except that they weren't bits of scalp. And she said they weren't really implanted, just kind of stuck in there, all haphazard."

"So where the hell did it come from?"

"That I can't help you with."

She thought for a moment, then blurted out, "MacClaren's ass!"

Aidan laughed nervously. "Okay."

"No, Aidan . . . MacClaren's ass," she repeated slowly. "Or his shoulder, I guess. Get it?"

"Not really, no."

"At the gas station in Lawson, there was this paper sign. It was peppered with little tiny holes, but it had this void pattern in the middle, a round spot in the corner maybe a foot across, where there were no holes at all. I didn't really think about it at the time, but if Perez had MacClaren slung over his shoulder, when the bullet hit that frozen flesh, it would have sent out those little shards like a cloud of razor-sharp frozen skin darts. That's what perforated the sign at the gas station."

"And the back of Perez's head, where it got in the way."

"Exactly. Perez's head caused the void pattern."

"Makes sense, I guess. Much as anything does this week."

"Thanks, Aidan."

"You got it." He was quiet for a second. "Hey, Madison?"

"Yeah?"

"This case is all over the place. You be careful out there, 'chasing down leads,' okay?"

She said she'd call him later and they hung up.

Almost as soon as she put down the phone, it chimed again. Ted Johnson.

"You called?" he asked.

"Yeah. What, are you screening me?"

He laughed. "It's Sunday, girl! I got a life."

"You must be the only one."

He laughed again. "Where are you, anyway?"

"I'm at headquarters," she told him.

"Yeah? You see the lieutenant?"

"No. Why?"

He laughed. "I think he's annoyed at you about something."

"Yeah, I know. He said he wanted me to see him when I got back."

"I thought you were back already."

"I just pulled into the parking lot."

"Then you're not back yet."

"What do you mean?"

"Keep the engine running," he told her.

"What?"

She heard a knock on the passenger window and looked over to see Ted Johnson standing beside the car, one hand holding a cell phone, the other adjusting his jacket collar.

"I knew you didn't have a life," she said.

"Open up," he said. "We gotta go see someone."

She flicked up the locks. "Anyone interesting?"

He smiled. "Jorge Parga."

CHAPTER 31

"APPARENTLY, PARGA'S mom thought he was acting kind of strange," Johnson explained as Madison drove. "Jorge disappears for a few days. When he comes back, he's spooked. Skulking around. She waits until he falls asleep, calls Ramon Perez's mom, figuring they were up to something. Perez's mom tells Parga's mom what happened to Perez, the shit that'd been done to him. That's when she called the police. Couple of uniforms show up to take him in, he bolts. Fell three floors from the fire escape."

Madison winced. "Ouch."

"Yeah, he broke his leg pretty bad, but he'll be okay."

She told him about the source of Ramon Perez's scalp condition.

"No shit?" was all he could manage to say.

The medical staff was prepping Parga for surgery when Madison and Johnson walked in.

The nurse who seemed to be running the show said Parga was already on a lot of pain medication and in about two minutes he would be on his way to surgery.

It could have been the hospital gown or the tubes and wires or the mixture of fear and pain in his eyes, but Parga looked much younger than his comrades.

The others had been straddling the worlds of childhood and adulthood. Jorge Parga was just a kid.

He was picking at the edge of his sheet with his thumbnails. His left leg was lying in some kind of brace that seemed to be holding it in place. It was loosely draped in bloodstained gauze.

Just below the knee, something jagged was poking at the

gauze. It could have been some sort of apparatus, but Madison knew it was bone. Compound fracture.

Parga glanced up when they walked in.

"What the fuck're you looking at?" he said, his false bravado wholly unconvincing. His words were slurred with painkillers and his voice cracked like he was close to tears.

"We're here to ask you some questions," Johnson said, pulling a chair up next to the bed. Madison hung back by the door.

"Fuck you," he replied. He pushed his head back into the pillow, trying to get his eyes to line up as he glared at Johnson.

Johnson ignored him. "How did you guys come to be stealing that body out in Lawson?" he asked.

The kid's shoulders slumped. In addition to the pain and the fear, he looked absolutely exhausted. "Man, I already told da other guy."

"Well, now you're going to tell me."

"Carwash set th'shit up." His head was starting to loll and his words were running into each other.

"Did someone pay you?"

He tried to roll his eyes, but he was having trouble with it. "Some white dude, s'all . . . big in da . . . da mob."

Johnson turned and shot a look at Madison before turning back to the kid. "What were you supposed to do with the body?"

"Bring t'the guy," he mumbled. "But we was jumped. Bunch of fucking white guys."

The nurse showed up at Johnson's elbow, clearing her throat.

Johnson turned to Madison and raised his eyebrow, asking if she had anything else to ask.

"Why did the guy want the body?"

Parga tried to shrug. "Money," he mumbled. His eyes were half closed, drifting downward, then they opened wider for a second, a thoughtful expression on his face. "Wuz th'guy's dad," he said, then his eyelids sagged again, almost closed.

"It was his dad?" Johnson asked loudly.

Parga nodded, but his eyes were closed.

The nurse stepped forward, putting herself between Johnson

and Parga. "Okay," she said, sternly. "That's enough. He should be out of surgery in a couple of hours; if you'd like, you can chat some more when he wakes up."

As soon as they were out in the hallway, Madison turned to Johnson. "Who does that sound like?" she asked. "Big in the mob and MacClaren's his father?"

"Oh, it definitely sounds like Caprielli."

"So how do you think that figures?"

Johnson shrugged. "I don't know. Maybe he hired Carlos Washburn, then double-crossed him. Get the guy to do the job, then take him out."

"Are you going to arrest him?"

Johnson shook his head. "Not based on that. I don't know if it would be enough even if the kid wasn't doped up like that, but in the state he was in, that counts for nothing."

"What are we going to do?"

"What are *we* going to do?" He laughed. "I don't know what *we* are going to do. I'm thinking *I* might go talk to Ralph Caprielli, feel him out a little while I wait to talk to Parga some more." He smiled condescendingly. "I don't know what you're going to do, but I thought you were supposed to get back and see the lieutenant."

"Shit!" she said, momentarily panicked at the thought that she had blown him off.

Johnson laughed. "Yeah, you pissed him off somehow. I got a feeling he's got a chore for you. I think he's going to have you gather up all that physical evidence your boy Matt Boone now has jurisdiction over, take that shit out to bumbledyfuck." He laughed. "Maybe you and Boone can have a picnic or something."

For an instant, she thought he knew what had gone on at their last picnic, and before she could convince herself otherwise, her cheeks grew hot.

"Well, before you go wasting your time duplicating my efforts," she said acidly, "let me tell you what *I* was calling *you* about earlier."

He gave her a smug, dubious look, waiting for her to enlighten him.

She started with how Dale Hibbert had ID'd Frank McGee,

and how he saw Robert MacClaren's body being stuffed into the back of the car. Then she hit him with the discovery of the liquid nitrogen tank. She finished up with what Ben Moyers had found out about Robert MacClaren's trust owning not just the lodge in Bartlett but also a substantial real estate portfolio in the city, including Ralph Caprielli's building.

The smug expression fell away quickly, soon replaced by begrudging approval, surprise, then disbelief. She wasn't sure he even heard the part about what Ben Moyers had told her, because he was still reacting to the discovery of the nitrogen tank.

"So the body was in a tank? Right there in the house?" he said with a grimace.

"Seems like. Oh yeah," she added. "And the Perez kid, remember he had that rash thing on his head?"

"Bit more than a rash."

"Yeah, well now it turns out that what caused it was the same stuff they had pumped into MacClaren."

"The yellow stuff?"

"Yup."

"This is a crazy motherfucking case."

"Yes, it is. So what are *we* going to do now?"

He shook his head, as if to clear it. "I guess we go talk to Mr. Caprielli."

Madison held out her hand for him to go first.

"Seriously, though," he said as he passed her. "You can skip the picnic if it's going to piss you off, but the lieutenant was pissed about you not checking in. Don't say I didn't warn you if he asks you to bring that shit out to Lawson."

That did sound like just the kind of lesson-teaching punishment the lieutenant would dole out. She sighed. "I was just out there today."

ONCE AGAIN, when they rang the bell at Ralph Caprielli's place, the door buzzed open without a word. They walked down the long brick entryway, but instead of a receptionist, Ralph Caprielli himself was there to greet them.

"What the fuck do you want?" he asked brusquely.

"We know your father was Robert MacClaren."

Caprielli smiled but his eyes went black. "Yeah? Well, I know your mother was a two-dollar whore, so what?"

Johnson ignored the taunt. "We're looking into what happened to your father's body. Do you know about that?"

"Yeah, I know about it."

"Any ideas about how that could have happened? Who could have done it?"

Caprielli's face darkened further, his eyebrows furrowed and trembling. "Not yet," he hissed.

"Any idea what Frank McGee was doing out in Lawson when your father's body was stolen?"

"I don't know. Shame we can't ask him."

"Were you against your father's decision to undergo cryonic preservation?" Madison asked.

Caprielli let out a short, sharp bark of a laugh, but his eyes burned. "No, I was fucking delighted. Who wouldn't want his old man to be frozen like a fucking Popsicle?" As he looked at their faces, the fire in his eyes raged. "Wait a second . . . You think *I* did this? I ought to kill you now, just for thinking it."

Johnson stiffened, taking a step forward. "Are you threatening us, Mr. Caprielli?"

Caprielli ignored him. "I'll tell you what, though. You better find who did it, and you better find him fast, because if I find him first, I'm going to fucking kill him. And I'm going to take my fucking time."

Johnson and Caprielli stared at each other, the room silent except for the sound of the two men breathing heavily.

"You charging me with anything?" Caprielli asked.

Johnson was silent.

"Then get the fuck out of here."

MADISON HAD to resist the urge to run as they walked through the entryway and out toward the street.

Johnson seemed to be intentionally taking his time, making a show of walking slowly, showing Caprielli his back.

"What do you think?" she asked as the door closed behind them, trying to keep her voice even despite her nerves.

"What do I think? Guy's a fucking animal, needs to watch his mouth."

She got in the car and started it up. "He seemed pretty upset by the implication," she said when Johnson got in. "You think he did it?"

Johnson laughed. "Let me tell you about his type. These guys kill their own brothers, two hours later they're crying with the widow, paying for the funeral, all that shit. You can't judge a goddamn thing based on their human reactions, because they ain't human. They're sociopaths; they got no real feelings, so it's no big deal to fake it when they need to."

Madison knew he was probably right, but the fire in Caprielli's eyes had been pretty convincing.

Johnson looked over at her face, reading the doubt. "Think of it this way. Guy's been in this business all his life, probably killed a dozen people or more, been questioned about most of them. You know each time, he's denied any involvement. Probably with the exact same righteous indignation."

"Yeah, you're right. So what now?"

"Let's go talk to his little brother."

THE TRAFFIC was dense on Toby MacClaren's street, busy for a Sunday. The nice weather had brought out the sightseers and history buffs and the cars were slowly creeping from east to west, looking for parking spots within walking distance to Independence Hall and the Liberty Bell.

A FedEx truck was stopped, completely blocking the right lane halfway down the block. The driver was methodically stacking boxes onto a hand truck, blithely ignoring the mayhem behind him as two lanes impolitely merged into one.

Everything ground to a complete halt as a battered Hyundai and a massive SUV wedged simultaneously into the single lane, each refusing to give the other an inch. The horn blasts and middle fingers were quickly replaced by obscenities and threats of violence.

Madison and Johnson stopped to watch, but the FedEx driver didn't; he just kept loading his hand truck, just a few feet away from the escalating tension.

When the driver of the SUV opened his car door, Johnson pulled out his badge and took a step toward them, but the Hyundai driver pulled up onto the sidewalk and sped away, his arm raised out the window with one finger in the air.

The SUV driver stood there for a moment, sending a torrent of obscenities after him, but when a second car pulled onto the sidewalk and drove around him, he quickly got back in his vehicle and drove off.

Johnson put his badge away, shaking his head with a smile as they continued up the street. "Imagine paying a million bucks for a house and having to live with this shit."

As they got closer to Toby MacClaren's house, Madison could see a small, dark-haired woman in a domestic's uniform standing on the top step, bent over at the waist.

"Check that out," Madison said, giving Johnson a nudge in the ribs. "That's MacClaren's house."

He squinted at the addresses. "So it is. Damn, she looks pissed."

She was tapping loudly with a key on the glass part of the door and she seemed to be shouting into the mail slot.

Madison couldn't quite make out what she was saying.

"Sé que usted está en la casa!"

"My Spanish is terrible. What is she saying?" she asked.

" 'I know you're in there,' " he translated out of the corner of his mouth.

They had both stopped walking as they watched the angry little woman yell into the mail slot. There was no way to tell how long she had already been there, but as they watched, she straightened up and growled, stomping her feet, then stormed off, down the steps and up the street, muttering to herself in Spanish the whole way.

They turned to watch her go.

"What was that about?" Johnson wondered.

"Who knows?" Madison replied. "Come on."

They walked up the steps but before either of them could ring the bell, the netting in the narrow side window beside the door was tugged to one side and Toby MacClaren peeked out.

He was not expecting them, judging from the way his eyes

widened. He quickly regained his composure, though, and opened the door with a charming, if hastily assembled, smile.

"Ms. Cross!" he said, opening the door. He looked at Johnson and gave him a quick nod. "Detective." Then he turned his attention back to Madison. "What can I do for you?"

"We have some new information about your father," Johnson said. "Can we come in?"

"Sure, yes. Come on in."

He led them into the house, but only as far as the foyer.

"So, what's going on?" he asked. He had his arms folded, hiding his injured finger under his arm.

Johnson fixed him with a serious look. "We believe Ralph Caprielli may have been involved in the theft of your father's body."

"Involved?" He looked back and forth between the two of them, but focused on Madison. "I thought you guys said whoever did this was trying to hurt my brother."

"That's what we thought," Johnson said, drawing his attention back.

"But now you don't."

"We have some new information," Madison told him.

"I see."

"Any idea why Ralph would do something like that?" Johnson asked.

MacClaren shook his head. "I don't . . . I seriously doubt he would . . . I mean, Ralph was very much against the whole preservation thing in the first place. I wasn't crazy about the idea myself, but Ralph . . . he used to get furious. He said it was an abomination. Unholy." He looked down, thinking. "Maybe he was . . . I don't know, jealous or something. My father offered him a place in the company many times, but Ralph . . . well, he saw his career path lying in . . . in other directions."

"Can you think of any other reasons?" Madison asked quietly.

Toby thought for a second. "Can I ask . . . what makes you think Ralph was involved in this in the first place?"

"Testimony from a witness," Johnson replied. "An accomplice, actually."

"What does Ralph say about it? Did you ask him?"

"He denied it," Madison told him, making it plain she thought that meant nothing. "He made a pretty big production about what he would do to whoever was responsible for this, that kind of thing."

MacClaren looked thoughtful but then he slowly shook his head. "My brother is not the most upstanding citizen. I know that. But still, I have a hard time believing he would do something like that . . . I don't know." He shrugged. "Maybe he would." He looked up at them, a pained expression in his eyes. "You really think he was behind it, don't you?"

CHAPTER 32

MACCLAREN HADN'T added anything of substance, but as they drove back to the Roundhouse, Madison felt confident they were on the right track.

"So what now?" she asked as they got out of the car.

Johnson shrugged. "We might find out some more when Parga wakes up." He looked at his watch. "But if I'm going to be working later, I got to go put my feet up now."

"Yeah, no kidding. Looks like it could be a late night," she said with a yawn. "Maybe I'll go try to squeeze in a nap."

Johnson laughed.

"What?"

"Ain't you supposed to be meeting with the lieutenant?"

"Shit! I forgot."

"Don't worry. Parga's going to be out for a few more hours at least. He tells you to take that shit out to Lawson, you could be there and back with time to spare."

She growled. "I wasn't kidding when I said I was just up there this morning."

Johnson got out of the car, laughing.

Madison didn't like to think of it as sneaking, but she tried not to make too much noise as she made her way to her desk. Once she sat down, she suddenly felt exhausted. She closed her eyes for a moment, warming to the idea that maybe she should just go home and get some sleep. Maybe not even bother with Parga or the lieutenant or any of it. There'd be hell to pay in the morning, but at least she wouldn't have to deal with it now.

She sensed someone in front of her, and when she opened her eyes, she realized that option was no longer on the table.

The lieutenant was standing in front of her desk, arms

folded, looking down at her. "Been pretty busy, there, huh?"
he asked, his voice heavy with sarcasm. "I expected you back
a while ago."

Before she could answer, he continued. "It's just as well
you have some free time now, because I have something I
need you to do. Since Lawson has jurisdiction on the McGee
case, I need you to get together all the physical evidence and
files and bring them on out there."

"But . . ."

"But what?" he asked innocently.

"Well . . . I was just out there this morning."

He flashed an exaggerated grimace of pain. "I know." His
face hardened. "It's a shame you didn't tell me you were going out there ahead of time . . . Like I *asked* you to. Could
have saved yourself a trip."

IT WAS almost three o'clock on Sunday and Madison
couldn't believe she was on her way back out to Lawson. The
weekend was almost over, and all she had done was work. She
didn't mind the work part so much, but this was just a waste of
time, pure and simple.

She called Boone from the car and told him she was on her
way.

"Miss me that much, do you?"

She laughed wearily. "I missed you more until your pain-in-
the-ass jurisdiction got me another three hours on the highway.
My lieutenant 'asked' me to bring out the physical evidence for
the McGee case."

"Well . . . it's not that I won't be glad to see you, but . . .
why are you bringing it out on a Sunday?"

"No good reason. He's pissed that I haven't been checking
in like I'm supposed to. I think he's teaching me a lesson by
making me spend my Sunday driving out there and back."

He laughed. "Bet it makes you wish you had some woo-
woo lights, huh?"

She told him about Jorge Parga and how he had further im-
plicated Ralph Caprielli, how they were waiting for him to get
out of surgery to talk to him some more.

"You've been busy," he said.

"Big time. I was seriously considering sneaking home for a power nap when the lieutenant told me I was coming out here."

"You can nap at my place," he murmured suggestively.

"I don't think I have the energy for that kind of nap."

"Yeah, I thought so. Be nice to see you though."

"You, too, Matt. I'll be there in about a half hour."

She was just outside of Lawson when her cell phone rang. It was Ben Moyers.

"Hey, Ben."

"Madison. Just wanted to keep you up-to-date on the details as we find them out."

"Ben, I really appreciate this, but you really don't have to spend your whole weekend . . ."

"We got a look at MacClaren's will."

"Really? On a Sunday?"

"We have our ways." He laughed. "The thing's huge, but here's the highlights: Toby got close to a million dollars. Caprielli got fifty thousand. The rest went into an extremely elaborate trust structure."

"What kind of trust?"

"Well . . . it's a special kind of trust. It pays out some of the money to the heirs, but what it's really all about is taking care of the . . . well, taking care of Robert MacClaren."

"I'm not following you."

"MacClaren was being preserved, right? Which means there are some maintenance costs, but it also means he's hoping to come back someday. To be revived. Instead of giving away all his money, he sets up a trust. So his people get some, but the bulk of it is protected, so he has resources if he's ever revived or whatever."

Madison was thinking back to something Toby MacClaren had said about his father being in denial about his own death when something Moyers said grabbed her attention instead.

"Wait a second," she said. "Did you say Toby got a million but Ralph only got fifty grand?"

"That's what it says in the will."

"Hmm. Okay, thanks, Ben."

"No problem. As I said, it's interesting stuff."

She got off the phone thinking that the inequity in the bequeathals would surely be enough to incite jealousy in Ralph Caprielli, but it didn't seem like it would be enough to motivate him to steal his father's body. And she still didn't understand how that would ease his jealousy, anyway.

Maybe it was revenge against the old man. If Robert Mac-Claren really did believe that he would one day be revived, then stealing and thawing his body would be tantamount to murder. As the highway rolled under her tires, Madison rolled all the different parts of the case around in her brain.

Without really thinking about it, her hand took out her cell phone and dialed the last incoming call.

Ben Moyers answered on the second ring.

"Hey, Ben, it's Madison again."

He laughed. "If you're looking for something new, you're going to have to give me a little more time than that."

"Just a quick question this time."

"Okay, shoot."

"With the kind of trust Robert MacClaren set up, what happens if he is somehow rendered 'unrevivable'?"

"What do you mean?"

"Well, the whole thing is set up so his assets are available to him if he is ever brought back to life, right? In this case, his body was stolen and dumped, left to thaw out. What happens if it is undeniably impossible that he will ever be brought back?"

Moyers grunted, thinking about it. "Let me call Stan. I'll get back to you."

The more Madison thought about it, the more she was convinced she already knew the answer. When Ben Moyers called back a few minutes later, he confirmed that she was right.

"There is a dissolution provision."

"Which means?"

"It means that if Robert MacClaren's body is destroyed or damaged in such a way that he cannot possibly be revived, the trust is dissolved and the assets are distributed to the beneficiaries."

"And is Ralph Caprielli one of the beneficiaries?"

"Hold on a sec."

For a minute and a half that felt like much longer, Madison listened to the sound of the road, and her own loud breathing.

"Half," he told her when he came back on the phone. "Ralph Caprielli gets half of everything."

She tapped the brakes without thinking about it.

As she quickly thanked Moyers, her mouth felt suddenly dry. She dialed Johnson and told him what Moyers had said.

"Motive," he said.

"Exactly."

"All right, that should be enough to bring him in. Keep in touch."

She started to call Boone, but she was so close she figured she would just wait and talk to him in person.

BOONE WAS on the phone when Madison walked into the station with the evidence bags and files.

"She just walked in," he told whoever was on the other end. "I'll tell her."

Madison felt a vague sense of dread at the thought that she was being talked about.

"What's wrong?" she asked as he put down the phone.

"Nothing," he said, pulling on his jacket as he crossed the room and kissed her on the cheek. He took the evidence envelope from her and locked it in a locker. "Come on. We got to go."

"Where?"

"I'll tell you on the way." He stopped and looked down at the loafers on her feet. "You don't by any chance have those boots with you?"

"They're in the trunk. Why?"

He held open the door. "You're going to need them."

"What's going on?" she asked as she opened the trunk.

"That was Ted Johnson," he explained as she put on her boots still covered with damp mud from earlier in the day. "Using what you guys just put together, he got an arrest warrant for Ralph Caprielli. His receptionist or whatever told them he was out of town for the day, so on a hunch, Ted got Metzger to check for any credit card activity. Turns out Caprielli filled up at a gas station about thirty miles south of here. Ted asked if we could take a look, see if he's out at the lodge."

Madison's eyes widened as they got in his cruiser. "We're going to arrest him?"

Boone laughed. "Yeah, just you and me. I'll be the good cop, okay?" He laughed some more, and she could feel the color on her face. "No, we're just going to have a look. If he's there, we'll call for some backup."

"I didn't think you had any backup."

"There's always backup. I just never need it."

"Yeah, I forgot; you rescue those cats all by yourself."

He shot her a glare, and as Madison returned it, she saw the entrance to the access road leading to the lodge pass by on their left.

"You missed your turn," she said smugly.

He shook his head, slowing down and taking the next left, about forty yards down the road.

"Seriously," she said. "Where are we going?"

"This takes us up the hill above MacClaren's lodge. We can look down from there. No need to waltz up to the front door, just in case Caprielli is there. And in case he brought friends."

They drove almost vertically. Madison held tight to the strap hanging above her car door as they bounced up and down and heaved from side to side. The road leveled off for a bit before continuing on up, presumably to the top of the hill, but Boone pulled over into a small clearing.

"It's not far from here," he told her. "There's a creek bed running down the ridge behind the lodge. Should give us a good vantage point to look down on it. We should be able to see anything from up there."

They hiked through thirty yards of dense brush until they reached the creek bed. It was not dry; the spring rains were still draining at a decent rate and the creek bed was a creek, running almost straight down the hillside. The sides were eroded so that even though the creek itself was less than a foot deep, the walls of the creek bed were almost six feet high. With so much soil washed away, the creek itself ran over a ribbon of rocks and stones ranging from a few inches to several feet across.

Boone stepped down, halfway into the creek bed. He put out a hand to help her down and she felt herself bristling. She ignored his hand, stepping down unaided. When she reached the bottom, she stepped out onto the rocks in the middle of the stream and put out a hand as if to help him.

He rolled his eyes and nodded; point taken. Then he hopped across the rocks and up the other side of the creek bed, keeping his head down and sticking close to the side.

She climbed up beside him and they both peeked over the edge.

The lodge was surprisingly close, less than fifty yards away. There was absolutely no sign of people or activity. The windows were dark, the police tape looked undisturbed, and there was no sign that any cars had come through since they had left it. They looked at each other and shrugged.

Boone whispered, "Wait here," then climbed out of the creek bed and started down the hill toward the lodge. He had his gun out. Madison followed a few feet behind.

She wasn't particularly scared or even nervous, although part of her wished she had brought a gun, too.

When they reached the level clearing that surrounded the lodge, Boone circled warily closer to the building, moving almost laterally.

He motioned for Madison to stay back as he ascended the porch steps. She waited a ways off as he stood with his back to the wall beside the door and knocked hard, identifying himself as police.

After a second unanswered knock, he slit through the police tape on the door and entered.

A minute later he came back out and motioned to her that it was safe to come in.

They gave the place a quick walk-through and ended up back in the living room.

"There's no sign of him, right?" she said.

Boone shook his head.

"I'll call Ted," she said, taking out her phone.

Boone nodded, looking around the place.

"Ted," she said when he answered. "Yeah, there's no sign of Caprielli."

"Tell him the place looks pretty much how we left it," he added.

"Except that," she replied, pointing at the damaged wall where the metal had been exposed. It was covered now with a thick layer of white frost.

"Wow," he said. "That didn't take long." He tapped the ice with the barrel of his gun and it fell away in large sheets, smashing when it hit the floor.

Johnson told her Parga was out of surgery and in the recovery room, but Madison's attention was on the bare metal where the frost had fallen away. "Okay. Keep me posted," she told him.

Condensation was already dripping down the bare metal, and again it had that strange, faintly blue tint. She put down her cell phone and went over for a closer look, watching as it soaked into the yellow-and-white rag rug on the floor.

Boone came up and stood beside her. "Looking at that again?"

He reached out a finger to touch it and she slapped his hand away. *"Don't!"* she scolded.

"What?" he said, shaking his hand and laughing. "It's just condensation."

"Yes, it is," she said. "It's condensed *air*."

"Condensed air?" He scoffed.

"Yes, and it's tricky stuff, so don't mess around."

He could see she was serious. "Really?"

She nodded. She had heard operating-room stories about liquid air dripping off nitrogen lines and causing fires. "It's flammable."

Now he looked dubious. "You're telling me air is flammable?"

"Well, no, the air itself isn't, but when it's concentrated like that, it makes anything that's even a little bit flammable burn like rocket fuel."

He still looked dubious.

"Just trust me on this and be careful, okay?"

"All right," he said. "Let's get out of here."

CHAPTER 33

THE SUN was low as they climbed back up the hill toward the creek bed. A chilly breeze swept past them. Shadows were already settling around the lodge, but shafts of orange light from the setting sun broke through the trees as they crested the hill.

After their previous hike and without the adrenaline rush of what danger might lie ahead, the climb was more of a chore.

Boone climbed halfway down the creek bed and stretched out his hand for her to take.

"It's okay," she said, again trying to hide her annoyance. "I got it."

"Come on," he said. "Don't be silly."

He stretched his hand out even farther toward her and gave it a little shake. As he did so, his feet slid out from under him, and he slipped down into the creek.

Madison started to laugh at him, but then she heard him cry out in pain.

"Are you okay?" She slid down next to him.

"I think I'm stuck." His teeth were clenched.

In the shadows of the creek bed, she could see that one ankle was wedged between two large rocks in a little pool about a foot and a half deep. Wisps of dark red curled away from his leg, trailing downstream with the creek water. Even crouching down next to him, she couldn't quite see how his foot was stuck.

"Okay," she said calmly, "let's see what's going on here."

The icy water coursed around her ankles and soaked into her jeans, and she was starting to feel shivery from the cold.

She knelt down in the water anyway, feeling gingerly around his ankle.

By the time she had figured out which rock was pinning him and where, her hands were numb.

"Can you see what's got me?" he asked, his voice infused with a false calm.

"I think so." She rolled up her sleeves and reached as far as she could, but she couldn't quite get a grip on the rock she needed to move. By the time she reached far enough, she was half submerged.

He let out a nervous laugh. "Chilly, ain't it?"

"Sure is."

"Snowpack. Still melting."

"That's exactly what it feels like. Okay, here we go. I'm going to pull on this rock, and when it releases, you get your leg out of there, okay?"

"Got it."

She got down low in the water, pushing off with one leg as she pulled with all her might.

Boone cursed through his teeth and his leg moved a bit, but it didn't come out. The bleeding was getting worse.

"Sorry," she said.

"No, no, that's good," he said, breathing heavily. "You got it moving."

"Not enough."

"Here you go, see if you can find a thick stick, maybe you can pry the rocks apart."

"Okay."

She found a three-inch-thick branch and wedged it between the rocks, next to Boone's leg.

"Okay, you ready?" she said.

He looked at her and started laughing.

"What?"

He shook his head. "Nothing. Feel like a bit of a goober is all."

She smiled. "Okay, here we go."

She pulled back on the branch as hard as she could. She could hear the wood splintering, but the rocks moved and so did Boone.

"Got it, got it," he said, as soon as he was free.

She let go of the stick and the rock plopped back into place with a deep, gulping splash.

Boone grabbed the branch as it fell and leaned on it. With Madison's help, he one-legged his way to the other side of the creek.

His ankle was badly abraded on the inner side and had a deep gash on the outer side that was definitely going to need some stitches.

No longer immersed in the icy cold creek water, the leg was starting to swell now and the blood was running freely down his leg.

"Matt," she said. "That really doesn't look good."

"Yeah, that's a boo-boo all right." He winced as he took a step. "I'm pretty sure it's sprained. There's a medical center a couple of miles east. I'll be fine once I get there."

She started shivering in earnest as she helped him back to the cruiser.

"You're soaked from head to toe, aren't you?" he asked. "Jesus, you must be freezing." He pulled away from her and grabbed a tree for support. "Here," he said, shrugging his shoulders out of his jacket. "Put this on."

"Matt, don't be ridiculous."

"No, seriously. Put it on. Look, I'll be honest with you, my leg hurts like hell right now, but I am not cold. I'm really not."

Balancing on one leg, he held out his worn brown leather bomber. She relented after only a few moments. It felt heavy and thick and warm, and as soon as she put it on, she was glad she had.

"Thanks," she said as she guided him through the brush.

"We're quite a pair," he said with a laugh.

She got him into the cruiser and slowly drove it back down the hill. Boone was in obvious pain, but when they reached the road, he let out a small laugh and flicked on the police lights.

She gave him a look, but left them on until they got to the medical center, just a few minutes away.

They took Boone right away, and in no time he was sitting in a wheelchair, the intake nurse launching into a battery of questions.

Boone answered the first couple, then he held up a hand and turned to Madison.

"This is going to take a while," he told her. "You might as well get going. I can get a ride home. I'll give you a call later."

She was about to protest, but he was right; she really didn't have time to be waiting there for three or four hours, and that's how long it would probably take.

"Are you sure you're okay?" she asked, tousling his hair.

"Yeah. Thanks."

"Call me when you get out," she told him.

She gave him a kiss and walked out the door.

The plan was to shoot back to the police station, pick up her car, and head back to Philly. When she got back into the cruiser, she decided to call Ted Johnson, see if Ralph Caprielli had been found.

That's when she realized she didn't have her cell phone. That's also when she realized Boone had a pack of Marlboros and a lighter in his jacket.

Trying to quit, she thought. She wasn't completely sure which development was more troubling. She had feared for a moment that her phone had fallen into the creek. But then she clearly remembered putting it down inside the lodge, when she noticed the condensation on the tank.

Her phone was on the kitchen counter.

When she reached the road that lead to the hill above the lodge, she slowed down. But after what happened with Boone in the creek, she decided she'd be better off just taking the road directly to the lodge. If anyone was there, she could just turn around and come back later. If not, she would run in, get her phone, and get out.

Easing off the brake, she drove on and made the next turn, up the access road that led to the lodge. It looked different in the growing darkness, quiet and still. She killed the lights as she got close to the lodge and stopped at a safe distance to watch for a minute or two.

When she was satisfied no one was in there—and feeling increasingly anxious that if she waited there any longer, someone might come up behind her—she eased the cruiser up close to the house and got out. She left the engine running.

The cool air hit her wet clothes as soon as she got out of the car and she suppressed a shiver. The place was dark, but apart from that it looked exactly as they had left it.

She quietly opened the front door, then scurried quickly inside, dashing to the kitchen area. Even in the waning light she could easily see the phone sitting on the counter. She grabbed it and turned to leave, but when she heard the cold metal click of a gun being cocked she froze.

"What the fuck are you doing in here?" Ralph Caprielli's voice quietly asked.

He stepped out from the shadows, the gun held out in front of him. "You?" He smiled, surprised.

She didn't have the authority to arrest him even if she wanted to, and she didn't have to ask him any questions, even though she wanted to. All she needed to do, she told herself, was get out of there alive.

"What are you doing in here?" he asked again.

"Forgot my cell phone," she replied, holding it up. She caught a whiff of alcohol on his breath.

He snorted. "Fucking people, think you're above the law." He stepped closer with the gun. "You know, even if you got a warrant, you have to knock. You have to identify yourself." He smiled grimly. "Far as I know, you could have been an intruder. I would have been totally within my rights to blow your fucking head off. Still might."

She decided not to inform him that, since it was a crime scene, she had every right to be there. She didn't want to tempt him to test his theory.

"I'm just here to get my cell phone."

"So, what, are you spying on me?"

"Like I said, I just came for my phone." The place felt colder, and she wondered if, with the missing insulation, the liquid nitrogen tank was cooling the room down.

He shook his head, letting the gun lower a bit. "You people really think I could do something like that? Desecrate my own father, leave him in the fucking ghetto? You don't know shit, do you?"

She didn't respond.

He laughed bitterly. "You know what? Fuck it. Just get the

fuck out of here, okay? Out of my sight. But if I ever catch you in here again, I swear to God, *bang*!" His voice was gradually getting louder. "So go on. Get out! Get the fuck out of here! *Now*!"

She stepped quickly toward the door and out onto the porch, half expecting a volley of bullets to follow. Even so, she resisted the urge to run until she was halfway down the porch steps.

The way her hands were shaking when she got into the cruiser, she was glad she had left the engine running.

She pulled the car around in three tight, sharp turns, and then she shot down the hill. The road wasn't actually in such bad shape, but she was taking it pretty fast, bouncing around inside. Halfway down she slowed a bit, for fear of hitting a deer. She turned the heat on full blast.

It wasn't until she turned onto the main road that she saw the messages waiting for her on her cell phone.

The first one was from Ted Johnson.

"Madison! I just got out of Parga's room." He laughed nervously. "Seems he's changed his story a bit, or at least his pronunciation of it. Fucking kid." He laughed again. "Seems that the guy who hired them wasn't '*in* the mob big-time,' like he told us earlier . . . No, apparently what he meant to say is 'the guy is *into* the mob big-time.' So we're not looking for a kingpin, we're looking for a deadbeat. Fucking kid laughed in my face when I told him we thought he was talking about Ralph Caprielli. Anyway, call me."

The next message was Johnson, too. "Okay, here's what we got, and I quote: 'I don't know who it was, some skinny-assed white dude in a suit, into a guy named Smoky Walters for like a half a mill or something. Shit was starting to get rough an' shit.' I asked him what he meant and he said Walters was going to kill this guy. Anyway, it sounds like Caprielli ain't our guy. I'm still talking to the kid. I'll let you know if anything else comes up. Meanwhile, give me a call when you get this message."

So Ralph Caprielli was in the clear.

That changed things. She tried to remember what he had said in the first place, but Ralph Caprielli was definitely not some "skinny-assed white dude."

She called Ted, but he didn't pick up. She left him a message. Then she tried Boone, but she immediately got a message that he wouldn't answer and in case of an emergency dial 911. The hospital had probably made him stow it.

Her mind was racing, trying to reconcile this new information with everything else. When she looked around her, she realized she was sitting at the lone traffic light in the town of Lawson. She had no idea how long she had been sitting there, how many times the light had changed. There was no other traffic to impel her forward.

The light turned green again, and as she was rolling through the intersection, something occurred to her.

She abruptly pulled over to the side of the road and punched in Ben Moyers's cell phone number.

"Ben, thank God," she said when he answered. "I need you to do one more favor."

He let out a tired laugh. "Madison, it's Sunday night. I mean, I'm as much of an obsessive workaholic as the next guy, but . . . can't it wait until tomorrow?"

"I'm sorry, Ben. I really am. I just . . ."

He sighed. "What do you need?"

"Can you get me a credit check on Toby MacClaren?"

"Is that it?" He blew air through his mouth, a staticky gust over the phone. "Hold on a second."

Madison listened to his keyboard clicking in the background, warming her hands over the blower, watching in the rearview mirror as the traffic light cycled through its colors. The lights seemed to be getting brighter as the darkness settled in around her. It was on its third green when Moyers came back on the line.

"Okay . . . here we go," he mumbled. "You know the worst part is, I was already sitting here at my computer." He snorted with disgust.

"Okay," he said again. "Here we go . . . Wow, for a rich guy, Toby MacClaren seems to be broke."

"Really."

"He's got credit all over the place, and he's maxed out on all of it. Not keeping up on his payments. I can't tell you what his assets are like, but looking at his liabilities, and the way he's managing his debt, I'd say he was headed toward bank-ruptcy."

Moyers was quiet for a second as Madison considered what he had just told her.

"So . . ." he said eventually, "can I get back to my own work now?"

"What? Oh, yeah. Hey, thanks a lot, Ben. For all of this."

"No problem. I'll talk to you soon . . . But not too soon, okay?"

She sat for a while longer, thinking about Toby MacClaren. In her mind's eye, she was picturing him, remembering each time she had met him—the charming smiles, the pained eyes, the tears. She dissected every move, every facial expression, every aspect of Toby MacClaren, trying to figure out if he could destroy his own father.

Johnson had quoted Parga as saying things had gotten rough between the guy who had hired them and his debtors. She pictured the burn mark on the back of Toby MacClaren's hand, the one Rourke thought was some S and M thing. The finger in a splint.

She couldn't quite reconcile the person she had met with the suspicions she couldn't possibly avoid. She thought about what Johnson had said about sociopaths, about how they can fake the emotions because they don't really have any.

But that was Ralph he'd been talking about, a lifelong vio-lent criminal. This was Toby.

Same family, though. Same father.

Ralph still had a motive, having inherited only fifty thou-sand dollars of his father's vast wealth. Or had he? Schuller had said Ralph Caprielli had inherited his father's criminal empire. That in itself was probably worth millions.

And that brought her back to Toby.

She was staring in her mirror, the thoughts zipping through her head, staring at the traffic light: red, yellow, green, slowly over and over again.

As she stared, the intersection was suddenly illuminated, and Madison realized a pair of headlights was approaching from the side. It was the first car other than her own that she'd seen the entire time she'd been sitting there.

The car slowed almost to a stop, arriving at the intersection just as the light turned green. As it rolled on through, Madison caught a glimpse of the driver.

He looked just like Toby MacClaren, and he had a determined look on his face.

She blinked her eyes, wondering if she had actually seen him, or if she had been concentrating so hard on him that she had imagined his face. When she opened her eyes, the car was gone, replaced by the fading red glow from its receding taillights.

Without a second thought, she turned the car around to follow him. As she rounded the corner, she saw a pair of tiny red dots wending their way down the dark country roads.

Toward the MacClaren lodge.

She tried to follow without getting too close, but with all the twists and turns, she lost the taillights long before they reached the access road. As she approached, she thought she glimpsed a pair of taillights disappearing around a bend far past it, as if Toby had missed his turn. She slowed when she reached the turn, letting the car idle as she debated what to do. She tried Boone again, but his phone was still off.

She could think of countless reasons not to go up there, and the first two or three should have been enough to convince anyone in their right mind. But she knew that if Toby Mac-Claren had been willing to do what she suspected he had done in order to get his half of the inheritance, it wasn't hard to imagine him going even further for the other half. And Toby MacClaren surely knew that while a lawyer might get him off with a slap on the wrist, no lawyer in the world was going to protect him from his brother.

A faint band of royal blue on the horizon was all that was left of daylight, but Madison killed her headlights anyway. The moon slipped in and out of the clouds and Madison's foot matched it on the accelerator, creeping slightly faster when she could see where she was going, then slowing down again when it got dark.

A large cloud passed in front of the moon, plunging the woods into total darkness. Madison pressed her foot firmly onto the brake. Seconds crawled past as she waited for another glimpse of the trees, just enough to inch forward, but all she could see was her own dashboard lights, and their reflection on the inside of the car.

The cruiser's slight valve tap was loud in her ears and she realized she was holding her breath. She felt a momentary panic thinking the clouds might never break; she could be stuck in the darkness all night under a thick ceiling of clouds, surrounded by trees she couldn't see.

In the quiet and the darkness, the blinking and chiming of her cell phone made her jump. It seemed as loud and bright as the cruiser's lights and siren. She dove on it, in such a hurry to shut it off that she answered without looking to see who it was.

"Hello?" she answered in a whisper.

"Madison? Is that you?" It was Aidan.

"Hey," she whispered hoarsely.

"Are you okay?" He sounded concerned.

"I'm fine," she replied in a more normal voice. "What's up?"

"Where are you?"

"I'm up in Lawson. Why? What's up?"

"Lawson?" He didn't seem to like that.

"What is it, Aidan?"

"Did you talk to Ted Johnson?"

"I got a message from him earlier, yeah. Looks like Ralph Caprielli is off the hook."

"Yeah, maybe. I heard he might have headed out there."

"He is out here."

"What?"

"He's here. I spoke to him."

"You what?"

"Aidan, he didn't do it."

"Jesus, Madison. Just because he's off the hook for this, doesn't mean he's not a vicious killer."

She sighed and it came out loud on her phone.

"Madison, I'm serious."

"Aidan, it's fine. I'm actually more afraid *for* him than *of* him."

"What do you mean?"

"I think Toby is behind all this. And I think he's planning on taking Ralph out next."

"Why do you say that?"

"Because I think I saw Toby drive by a few minutes ago. I think he's looking for the lodge, looking for Ralph. I think he missed his turn, but he'll find it eventually. And I don't think Ralph suspects a thing."

"What exactly are you saying?" His voice was getting loud and high, alarmed and incredulous.

"I'm saying someone's got to tell him."

"Jesus Christ, Madison! Are you insane?"

In the back of her mind, she knew he was right, but she was also getting annoyed at his condescending tone. She sighed again, and this time it didn't bother her how loud it was over the phone. The moonlight flickered just for a second, but disappeared again before she could even ease up on the brake.

"I'm just going to give him a heads-up and leave," she told him. "It's up to him to protect himself."

"No, you're not!" Aidan was practically yelling now, and the part of Madison's mind that had been acknowledging his point was overwhelmed by irrational irritation.

She clenched her jaw and took a calming breath, but before she could compose a reply, the clouds broke and in a flood of moonlight that seemed as bright as day, she saw the road clearly in front of her, all the way up to the lodge, sixty yards ahead.

She eased her foot off the brake and crept forward through the illuminated trees. "Look, I have to go. I just need to give Caprielli a heads-up, then I'm out of there."

"Madison," Aidan said sternly, but she ended the call. He immediately called back, but she turned off the ringer.

The windows of the lodge were brightly illuminated, throwing rectangles of light on the ground around it, but there was no sign of any cars. Madison wondered if Ralph had left, but she had seen no cars there the first time.

She briefly wondered how he had gotten there.

The front door was open but the screen door was closed.

She tapped gently on the frame, then a little harder.

"Mr. Caprielli?" she called. "This is Madison Cross. I was here earlier, Mr. Caprielli. I need to talk to you."

There was still no answer.

She waited another minute or so, standing in the cone of yellow light coming down from the porch light. Then she opened the screen door and stepped inside.

"I'm coming inside, Mr. Caprielli," she said loudly, but there was still no reply.

"Hello?" she called as she walked through the entryway. The section of wall where the insulation had been torn away was once again covered in a thick layer of frost. The sight of it reminded her how cold she was, and she caught a glimpse of herself in a mirror, looking pale and cold and wet, lost inside a jacket five sizes too big.

She hugged the jacket around herself again, holding it tight for warmth.

"Hello?" she said again, louder. She was turning to head upstairs when she saw him, standing behind her. He had a gun pointed at her and his face was a mixture of amused exasperation and murderous rage.

"You are un-fucking-believable," he said. "Tenacious. Like one of those fucking ghetto dogs the police have to shoot because it won't let go of some kid's leg."

"I need to talk to you, Mr. Caprielli."

"I gave you a fucking chance. I told you to get the fuck out of here. And I also said next time would be different." He smiled coldly, but he did seem to see some humor in the situation. "This is 'next time.'"

"I need to talk to you, Mr. Caprielli. About your brother."

"Fuck you." He smiled again, enjoying it. "I don't want to talk to you about my fucking brother. I don't want to talk to you about my fucking father . . ."

"Look, you need to know, your brother is—"

"Right here," said Toby MacClaren, cutting her off as he stepped out from behind the curved wall that hid the nitrogen tank. He came from the direction of the basement steps, the back door.

"Toby! There you are," Ralph said, shaking his head condescendingly. "What the fuck, did you get lost?"

"No, the directions were fine." He smiled coldly. "What's she doing here?"

Caprielli smiled again, thumbing back the hammer of his gun. "Don't worry about her. She's just leaving. Although I haven't decided how."

Madison took a deep breath, preparing for one more try. "Mr. Caprielli, you don't need to talk to me about your brother, but you should talk to him. Ask him why he paid Carlos Washburn to steal your father's remains."

That made him pause.

". . . Or ask him how much money he owes Smoky Walters."

Toby MacClaren flinched at the mention of Smoky Walters, and Caprielli saw it.

Quickly regaining his composure, Toby rolled his eyes and shook his head. "Can't you people just leave us alone to grieve?"

But Ralph was staring straight at him. "Wait a second, Toby. Is this true? Smoky fucking Walters?" He seemed surprised and hurt, but even as he said it, the surprise was turning to anger.

"No," Toby said dismissively, a forced nonchalance failing to mask the nervousness in his voice.

Ralph crossed his arms, listening sternly, the rage in his eyes approaching a critical mass.

"It's like this," Toby began. "Ms. Cross over here," he said, pointing at Madison.

Ralph glanced from Toby to Madison, just for a second, and as he did, Toby fumbled with something behind his back. Before Ralph's eyes shifted back to look at him, Toby produced a gun and shot him.

CHAPTER 34

IT WAS a thunderous explosion, followed by another as Toby fired wildly a second time, his arm swinging from the recoil of the first shot.

The second shot ricocheted off the metal tank, knocking off more of the foam insulation and shattering the heavy glass lamp. The layer of frost that was covering the metal exploded into the air and settled to the ground like snow.

Ralph groaned on the floor, clutching the red blossom that was spreading on his shoulder.

Toby turned the gun on Madison and stepped toward Ralph, but he seemed afraid of getting too close.

"You bastard," Ralph gasped, grimacing up at Toby. "I'm your brother, for Christ's sake."

Toby smiled sadly down at him and shot him again. "Half brother," he said, shaking his head.

The concussion from the shot shook the remaining frost loose. It fell to the floor and shattered.

Ralph curled around his shredded abdomen, making wheezing and gurgling noises. Toby reached down and took Ralph's gun. He got some blood on the back of his hand and he wiped it on Ralph's sleeve.

"Let's see," he said as he straightened. "Who's next?" He looked over at Madison and said, "Oh, right!"

He walked toward her, his arm extended, the gun pointed at her chest. His face was blotchy and covered with a thin sheen of sweat. His arm was shaking, and for a fleeting moment, Madison worried that he was going to pull the trigger by accident.

As he approached, her eyes closed involuntarily, waiting for a bullet, but then she felt him patting her down.

When she opened her eyes, he was holding up Boone's cigarettes and shaking his head.

"Cigarettes?" he said disapprovingly. "Tsk, tsk, tsk. I'm very disappointed in you." He tucked the cigarettes back into the inside pocket and backed away from her with a smug grin.

When he had put ten feet between them, he seemed to relax, although he kept the gun pointed at her. "I don't want to hurt you, but there's not really much I can do about you, is there?"

She didn't say anything. She caught sight of herself once again in the mirror, looking even more pathetic than the last time, like a drowned rat. She looked like someone who was about to die. She didn't like to think of herself as vain, but somehow it bothered her that she was going to die looking like that.

"I feel bad about it. I really do," he said sincerely. "I actually quite liked you."

The way he referred to her in the past tense brought home to her how soon she might be dead. But the urgency imparted by that fact was tempered by a strange sense of calm.

She found herself staring once more at the exposed metal, at the condensation dripping down onto the floor now that the insulating layer of frost had been shaken free. The yellow-and-white rug was getting damp again, soaking up the barely blue liquid that was rapidly dripping onto it.

Off in the corner, Ralph groaned.

MacClaren was starting to look edgy, fidgeting with his gun and watching her with nervous eyes. It seemed to Madison that he really didn't want to kill her, and he was nervous because it was getting to be that time.

She was oddly unafraid. More than anything, she just felt cold. Watching the pale blue condensation trickling down the exposed metal made her feel even colder, but she couldn't take her eyes off it.

She was still staring at it when she heard herself say, "Do you mind if I smoke?"

"I actually do, but go ahead." He smiled condescendingly. "If not now, when? Right?"

Madison tapped a cigarette out of the pack, the way she had seen people do, and put it in her mouth.

Her lips had never even touched one before.

"I'm still having a hard time thinking of you as a smoker," he said.

Her numb fingers fumbled with Boone's disposable lighter and it took her a few tries to get it lit. The acrid smoke burned her throat, her chest. She wondered how anybody ever picked up the habit.

Toby was standing off to her right, about ten feet away from the yellow and white rug.

She took a small puff and let some of it into her lungs, trying to look elegant like in the movies, while at the same time struggling not to cough.

He gave her a funny look, amused but incredulous, vaguely suspicious.

Exhaling nonchalantly, she crossed over to an accent table with a vase on it.

MacClaren realized with a start that she was getting too close to him, and he backed away, sidestepping around, closer to the rug.

Madison grabbed the vase from off the table and tapped her ashes into it.

Now standing on the yellow-and-white rug, MacClaren let his gun hang lower, leaning slightly forward to watch her more closely.

She put the cigarette in her mouth and sucked on it, ignoring the burning in her lungs as the tip of the cigarette crackled and glowed, the burning ember growing to half an inch or more.

"Those things'll kill you," he said, as she started to cough.

"Tell me about it," she shot back hoarsely.

A flicker of realization passed through his eyes, but it was too late. As he started to raise his gun, she flicked the cigarette toward the faintly blue wet spot on the rug at his feet.

It was over in an instant.

One moment he was standing there, raising his gun, a slight tinge of alarm distorting his smug expression. Then there was a flash, a blindingly bright ball of fire that erupted in fury and then disappeared.

For a moment, Madison didn't feel cold.

Even with the taste of the cigarette still strong in her mouth and her nostrils, she could smell the stench of burnt plastic and hair and flesh.

The rug was gone. Most of the foam insulation was gone, too, or at least melted back to a thin layer of black molten plastic.

On the floor was a blackened circle six feet across, and in the middle of it was Toby MacClaren, or what was left of him.

He was standing perfectly still, blackened, with his skin in tatters, just like the bodies from Oxford Street. His clothes were mostly gone, only cinders left, and so was his hair.

The gun was still in his hand.

A strange clicking, gurgling noise seemed to be coming from his throat. His foot moved, as if to take a step, and he teetered for an instant. When he fell over, his arms made no move to break his fall.

He hit the floor with a heavy thud and a distant groan.

Black cinders from his clothes skittered across the floor.

Madison knelt next to him to administer first aid, but she didn't know where to begin. She tried to take the gun out of his hand, but it was still hot to the touch and it seemed to be fused to his fingers. His breathing was rapid, shallow, and raspy.

As she crossed the room to where Caprielli was lying, she took out her phone and called Boone. His phone was still turned off. As she knelt down, she thumbed in 911.

Caprielli was barely conscious, emitting a low, constant groaning sound that she could only hear when she was close to him.

She held his hand and squeezed it. "You're going to be okay, Mr. Caprielli," she told him, although she doubted his prognosis was much better than his brother's. He gave her a slight nod.

The emergency dispatcher answered and Madison said she needed an ambulance and police immediately, for gunshot wounds and third-degree burns. She gave them the address and told them the location as best she could.

Caprielli started to cough and she turned her attention back to him. She didn't know if he was going to have time for an ambulance.

He opened his mouth and muttered something in a faint raspy whisper.

"What's that?" she said, leaning closer. "I can't hear you." She gave his hand another squeeze.

With great effort, he opened his eyes partway to look at her with a vague expression of annoyance, but when he did, his eyes widened in terror.

She followed his gaze, turning, and saw Toby, up on one arm, pointing his gun at them. His blackened skin was coming off his body, revealing raw, red flesh below, like magma under a fractured crust of rock. His eyes were wide open now, an angry red against his blackened skin. It looked like his lids were gone.

His jaw wasn't moving, but his throat was making an unintelligible screeching noise. The screeching grew quickly louder, angrier, and more urgent, and the gun in his hand started to tremble.

Madison realized he was trying to make his fingers work. He was trying to pull the trigger.

The screeching got louder and louder.

Madison ducked down, but there was no place to hide. Her hand found the heavy glass base of the broken lamp. She picked it up and threw it as hard as she could. The glass made a loud thunk as it hit him squarely in the forehead, opening a deep gash and sprinkling more cinders onto the floor. The screeching stopped immediately and a small trickle of blood started down the middle of his face. He was still for a moment, except for his eyes, which slowly rolled up into his head. He swayed slightly and collapsed.

BEFORE TOBY MacClaren's body had fully come to a rest on the stone floor, the front door opened and Donny Craig stepped in. He had one arm wrapped around a bag of groceries and the other hand wrapped around a bottle of scotch.

He paused for the briefest fraction of a second, his face showing no reaction other than the flicker of his eyes as they darted from Madison to Caprielli to Toby MacClaren's ruined body. He let the groceries drop, and before they hit the floor

he had a nine millimeter in his hand, aimed at Madison, and
he was striding across the room toward her.

She looked around but there was nothing at hand except
more shards of the lamp, and that wasn't going to work this
time.

"Wait!" she cried, holding up her hands. "I'm trying to
help him. He needs a doctor."

Craig stopped a few feet away and cocked his gun, which
was still aimed at her. The bottle of scotch was still in his
other hand, the amber liquid sloshing around inside.

Caprielli opened his eyes once more and gave Craig a
quick nod. "It's all right," he rasped, holding up a hand for
Craig to help him up.

"We've got to get him to a hospital," Madison told him.

Craig put down the bottle and stared at her with granite
eyes. He looked away from her without saying a word and
turned to Caprielli, staring appraisingly for a moment before
he tucked the gun into his waistband and effortlessly scooped
him up. Caprielli groaned, looking small and insubstantial in
Craig's arms.

Craig started toward the door but stopped, looking down at
Toby. "What happened to him?"

"He shot Caprielli . . . He tried to kill us both." She knelt
down next to Toby but when she couldn't find any signs of
life, she looked back up at Craig. "I guess I killed him."

Craig smiled, a strange smile but not without compassion.
"I guess you did."

A FRENZY descended upon them as soon as they entered the
hospital, a blur of blue scrubs and white smocks, frantically
poking and stabbing and shouting. It reminded Madison of
sharks in a feeding frenzy. Then they disappeared through the
heavy double doors, taking Caprielli with them.

She had packed Caprielli's wounds with paper towels before
they left and kept pressure on them, directing Craig as he drove.
To her surprise, Caprielli was still alive when they got there.

The ride to the hospital had been almost silent except for
Caprielli's ragged, sucking breathing. Craig was obviously

uncomfortable driving a police cruiser with the lights flashing. For her part, Madison was uncomfortable with a homicidal sociopath in the driver's seat. Suddenly, now it was quiet once again, the waiting room suffused with a surreal calm.

The swinging doors had just about come to a stop when they banged open again, this time issuing forth a washed out–looking Boone, sitting in a wheelchair with a pair of crutches across his lap.

The orderly parked him just beyond the doors and Boone smiled when he saw Madison.

"I told you not to wait . . ." he started to say, but he stopped when he got a better look at her. His eyes shifted over toward Donny Craig, who looked back without expression.

"Matt," Madison said. She took a step toward him, but not fast enough; he sprang out of his wheelchair and closed the gap, hopping to her with both crutches in one hand.

"Jesus, are you okay?" he asked as they embraced.

As Boone squeezed her, his face buried in her hair, the question sunk in. A surge of emotions welled up inside her, a delayed reaction to everything she had just experienced. Her eyes started to water and she felt the beginnings of a tremble, but she clamped it down, clenching her jaw against it.

"What happened?" he asked quietly.

"It was Toby. He was behind everything."

"Where is he?"

"He's dead."

"How?"

"I'll tell you later."

CHAPTER 35

BOONE WANTED to stay there and wait with Madison, for official as well as unofficial reasons, but he had a fractured fibula and nine stitches. He was tired and in pain.

When four state troopers showed up, alerted by the hospital that they had a gunshot victim, Boone made sure they acknowledged his jurisdiction, then he let two of them drive him home.

Madison stayed behind with the other troopers. And with Donny Craig. She wasn't sure if the troopers knew *who* Craig was, but they seemed to have a pretty good idea *what* he was. They eyed him warily from across the small waiting room.

She felt a strange connection now with Craig, forged during their wordless drive to the hospital. He reminded her of a faithful dog; homicidal, maybe, but loyal beyond question. He would not be going anywhere until his master was out of danger.

One of the troopers questioned her about what happened at the lodge, writing down her answers as she told him. Craig watched, listening intently.

By the time the trooper closed his notebook and said, "Okay, that's all for now," Madison somehow had the feeling that Craig was now guarding her, too.

She took out her phone, remembering that she had turned the ringer off. She had missed eleven calls, one from Aidan followed by ten from her uncle.

She called Ted Johnson first and quickly told him what happened.

Then she called the lieutenant.

"Jesus, Maddy are you okay?" His voice was husky with emotion. "I spoke to Aidan. Where are you?"

"I'm fine, Uncle Dave," she told him. "I'm okay."

She told him she was at the hospital, waiting for Ralph Caprielli to get out of surgery. She told him Toby MacClaren had been behind the whole thing, for the money, and that he had shot Caprielli.

"Where's MacClaren now?" he asked.

She didn't want to answer, but she knew he was going to find out anyway. "I . . . I killed him."

"Jesus, Maddy," he said again, the concern cracking in his voice. "Are you okay?"

"He was going to shoot me."

"Are you okay, Maddy?"

"I'm fine," she told him, although as she did the emotions threatened once more to bubble over. Again, she clamped the lid on it, wondering in a detached way if she was headed toward post-traumatic shock. "I'll tell you more about it later."

"I'm coming out there," he stated.

"Don't, Uncle Dave. Seriously. I'll be heading back before long, anyway. I'm okay, really. But I might be late tomorrow."

"Don't come in tomorrow. You take the day off. You'll need the rest, okay?"

"Yes, Uncle Dave."

He paused for a moment. "You know Aunt Ellie's going to find out about this."

"We'll figure something out to tell her."

"You better start thinking now." He sighed, probably envisioning Aunt Ellie's reaction. "You're sure you're okay though?"

"I'm tired, that's all."

"Promise to take the day off tomorrow. Get some rest."

"Yeah, I might do that. Spend the day in bed."

"Good idea."

"Love you, Uncle Dave."

"Love you, too, Maddy girl."

It was barely ten o'clock, but it felt much later.

The other troopers had returned from bringing Boone home, and now they were chatting up a pair of nurses.

Craig was sitting in the corner of the room. He seemed to be staring at her, but he seemed to be staring at everything else, as well. Maddy felt oddly comforted by his presence.

They sat there wordlessly for almost an hour in those hard plastic chairs, but eventually, Madison had to close her eyes, just for a moment.

When she opened them, a flat blue glow was shining in through the windows and the chill that she'd felt since stepping in the creek had worked its way deep into her bones.

The troopers were nowhere in sight, but Craig was sitting in the same chair, the same watchful expression on his face.

She smelled a familiar yet out of place smell, and it took her a second to recognize it as Aidan's aftershave. Her head was resting on something firm yet soft, and when she looked up, she realized it was Aidan's shoulder.

He smiled down at her. "You hung up on me."

"What are you doing here?" she asked around a yawn that erupted without warning.

"I was worried about you," he said softly. "As it turns out, with good reason."

A nurse she didn't recognize was crouching in front of her. "Are you Madison Cross?" she asked gently.

She started to sit up, but her stiff and aching joints complained loudly. "Yes."

"Mr. Caprielli is awake. He wants to talk to you."

"Okay," she replied, slowly standing.

Aidan stood, too.

"When'd you get here?" she asked him, rubbing her face and yawning.

"A couple hours ago." He looked down at her. "Nice jacket."

She didn't say anything.

Craig's eyes were still on her. Madison gave him a little smile, but he just stared blankly back at her, watching as she and Aidan followed the nurse across the waiting room and down the hall.

"Been meaning to talk to you about the company you're keeping," Aidan said, tilting his head back toward the waiting room.

She smiled. "Who, Craig? Did you two get a chance to get to know each other?"

He laughed. "Buddies for life."

The nurse led them to a room on the second floor. One of the state troopers was sitting in a chair outside it, reading a magazine.

Aidan showed his ID. "I'm with her," he said dryly.

The trooper examined Aidan's ID, then his face. When he finally nodded, they walked past him and stepped through the door.

Caprielli was surrounded by hospital equipment and his skin was an ashy gray, but his eyes were sharp and wide open. He snorted and smiled when he saw them.

The nurse stopped just inside the door, then turned and left them alone.

"I didn't say nothing about anybody else," Caprielli said, lifting his arm an inch or two off the bed to point at Aidan.

Madison shrugged.

Caprielli shook his head wearily. "Whatever."

Madison sat in the chair next to the bed. Aidan remained standing in the corner, leaning against the wall.

"You're something, aren't you?" Caprielli said with a smile that wavered for a second, interrupted by some unseen pain. "I still don't know what the hell you did back there."

I killed a man, Madison thought.

"But," he continued, "whatever you did, you saved my life. I guess I owe you one."

"You owe me an explanation," she replied quietly.

His midsection shook as he quietly snorted. He winced again. "I don't usually talk to police without my lawyer. But I guess I got nothing to hide. What do you want to know?"

"What happened?"

"I'm hoping you could tell me."

"You go first. I saved your life, remember?"

"Oh yeah. Right."

"You can start with what happened to your father."

He thought for a few seconds, then shrugged. "Well . . . when my pop set up the whole cryonic thing, he wanted to keep it quiet. Mostly to protect the family name, I guess. The business name. Maybe he knew that with so much money at stake, there was a good chance someone would come knocking . . . Maybe he knew Toby better than I did." He shook his head. "But mostly, I think he was worried people would think it was nuts."

He smiled again. "He was right about that, too. *I* thought it was fucking nuts. Crazy bullshit. But you know what? My old man was a lot smarter than me, and if he thought there was something to it, who was I to argue. They say you can't take it with you, right? Well, if anyone could figure out a way, it would be my old man. And he deserved to take it with him, too, you know? Worked his ass off to get what he had."

He was quiet for a moment, looking away as his eyes grew moist. "What pisses me off about it most is that the old guy's never going to know if it would have worked." He lifted his arm against the mat of wires connected to it and wiped his eye with the back of a finger. "I tell you, I never believed in any of it, but in the back of my mind I thought there was a chance, not a big one, you know, but a chance someday I'd see him again."

Madison was silent for a moment, letting Caprielli stare out the window and compose himself. When he looked back at her, the hardness had returned to his eyes.

"What happened last Sunday at the lodge?" she asked him.

He shrugged. "Those greasy fucking spics stole my dad's body."

"How did you know?"

"Jimmy Dawber was taking care of the place, taking care of the tank. He was just coming back from a hike when he saw them. He called us, told us something was up. Luckily, Frank McGee and . . . well, luckily Frank was already on his way out there. He caught up with them in Lawson."

Madison nodded, thinking. "Why was *he* heading out there?" she asked, emphasizing the word "he" like she was playing along, even though she knew McGee hadn't been alone.

Caprielli gave a little shrug. "Bringing some supplies. Checking on things for me."

"Who killed Dawber?"

"I'd like to blame the spics," he said with a shrug, "but I don't think anybody killed him. Jimmy was a good kid. Dependable. Near as I can tell, he went to check on my dad. Fell in the tank."

"Then what happened?"

"Whoever found him fished him out of the tank, fucking dropped him." Caprielli shrugged again. "Let's say it was Frank McGee."

"So how did Dawber end up in South Philly?" Madison asked.

Caprielli snorted. "I imagine whoever dropped him must have been pretty spooked. They probably didn't know what to do, so maybe they bagged him up and brung him to someone who could tell them what to do. And that person would tell them to get rid of that fucking mess."

Madison was quiet for a second. Caprielli sighed and started to open his mouth, like he was about to end the interview.

"Okay," Madison blurted out quickly, "Who killed Alvarez, Castillo, Perez, and Washburn?"

Caprielli's eyes smoldered the way they had when Madison first met him. "I don't know who the fuck took out Washburn, but I'd like to thank him. I don't know what happened to the rest of them, either, but they got what was coming." His face creased into a cruel smile. "Especially Perez."

She didn't ask him how he knew about Perez, but it occurred to her that Craig was probably the guy who had actually done it. She wondered if she'd been riding in a car and sitting in a waiting room with someone who was capable of doing what had been done to Ramon Perez.

Caprielli winced again and closed his eyes for a moment. "Anyway," he said when he opened them, not quite completely. "We should do this again some time. But for now, you need to get the fuck out of here. And send Craig in here."

AN INSPECTOR from the state police showed up as they were leaving. He insisted that he was taking jurisdiction and Madison said he could take that up with Boone if he wanted to. The inspector handed Madison his card and she slipped it into her pocket without looking at it.

The sky was bright and the morning air was cold when they walked out into the hospital parking lot.

"You've been through a lot," Aidan told her as they walked up to his car, parked next to Boone's cruiser. "You should let me drive you home."

"No, I'm okay," she replied, smiling and suppressing a shiver as the breeze blew her hair. "Really."

He gave her a dubious look. "All right, well, at least let me follow you. It's too long a drive after all you've just been through."

"I'm fine," she told him, which was a lie. She was toast. But that was okay, because she wasn't driving all the way home. She took out the keys to the cruiser. "I have to make a stop, anyway."

He gave her an odd, awkward look as she unlocked the door.

She smiled. "I have to return the loaner."

She did follow him part of the way, just into the middle of town.

Morning sunlight flashed through the trees as she drove, and in Madison's mind, images from the past week flickered along with it: Oxford Street, Jimmy Dawber, Ramon Perez, Robert MacClaren, Toby MacClaren. The more she thought about it, the more amazed she was to still be functional, or at least to the extent that she was.

It was eight in the morning by then—Monday morning— and what passed for a rush hour in the town of Lawson was already under way. The school buses full of children seemed strangely incongruous after what she'd seen the previous evening.

As she pulled up behind Aidan at the traffic light in the middle of town, she had a hard time believing that just a few hours earlier she had been sitting there in the darkness, piecing it all together.

They drove on to the next block, and when she came to the stop sign at the church, she slowed to a stop, watching for a moment as Aidan's car rolled slowly through the intersection, then kept on going. She watched him driving away, feeling the slightest pang of regret. Then she turned right, up the hill to the little blue house with the wraparound porch.

As she got out of the cruiser and walked up to Boone's front door, she fought shivers that tried to overwhelm her. She couldn't tell if it was shock or just the early morning chill.

She let herself in with the key from under the welcome mat.

The curtains were drawn, but in the semidarkness she saw Boone hobbling toward her from the bedroom, wearing only a cast on his leg and a pair of boxers.

"I was hoping you'd come," he said.

She put her arm around him, her shoulder under his, and steered him back toward the bedroom.

He looked down at her. "Do you want to talk . . . ?"

Shushing him with a finger over his lips, she shook her head and led him back to bed. She put a pillow under his leg and made sure he was comfortable. Dropping his jacket onto the floor, she kicked off her boots and pulled off her socks. She didn't bother with her clothes.

She got into bed and wrapped herself around him, feeling the tug of sleep and the beginnings of warmth.

"Madison?" he said, his voice heavy and sleepy.

"Yes?"

"Your feet are cold."

She slipped them underneath him. "Not for long."